A Return to Hawthorne House

A Return to Hawthorne House

Kristi Ann Hunter

Oholiab Creations

Published by Oholiab Creations, LLC
110 Walter Way #1065
Stockbridge, GA 30281

ISBN 978-1-959589-01-3 (Trade Paperback)
ISBN 978-1-959589-04-4 (Cloth)

For more information and questions contact Kristi Hunter at KristiAnnHunter.com.

Cover Design by Angie Fisher of WTX Labs.

To the One who dares me to step out in faith
2 Thessalonians 1:11-12

To Jacob, who willingly walks unknown paths with me.

And to everyone who came alongside and offered support, assistance, and belief when mine was lacking.

Contents

ALWAYS A LADY

A Hawthorne House Novella

Chapter One

London, England 1811

"A lady never refuses a dance unless she wishes to cause a great scandal or make a definitive statement, Mother."

The words were merely a parroting of instructions Caroline, Duchess of Riverton had frequently imparted upon her eldest daughter Miranda, but their familiarity, and their truth, didn't knock Caroline from the trance she'd stumbled into. She continued to stare at the man's gloved hand as if it were a wriggling fish that had been plopped before her at the dining table. When was the last time she'd danced with a man other than her sons?

Probably fifteen years ago, at the last ball she'd attended with the duke before his unexpected passing.

"Mother." Miranda accompanied this whisper with a nudge of her elbow into Caroline's ribs, causing her to stumble half a step forward.

Instinctively, Caroline reached out to salvage her balance and jabbed her fingers right into the outstretched palm of the man who had asked her to dance. His hand closed gently but firmly around hers before he turned and repositioned the hold so he could escort her properly to the floor.

She blinked at the stark contrast of her white glove against his dark sleeve, then snapped her gaze up to look Lord Blackstone in the eye. Polite habits had her returning the earl's small smile while her wits gathered themselves back into some semblance of order.

Not until they'd reached the center of the dance floor did control of her tongue return. "You honor me with your attentions, my lord."

"The honor is mine, your grace." Lord Blackstone smiled as he grasped her fingers in one hand and placed the other across her back.

The music swelled as Caroline stared once more at their joined hands. Dash it all, this was a waltz! Not that she need worry about her reputation. She was a titled widow, after all, not some fresh-faced debutante. Nor was she concerned for her ability. She and the late duke had enjoyed waltzing long before it became at all socially acceptable, and she'd maintained those skills by circling many a ballroom with her adult sons.

Still, unease gripped her middle, threatening to spread from her throat to her toes.

Moments ago, before Lord Blackstone's appearance, Caroline had been guiding Miranda into the perfect position to catch the eye of Lord Rickford when he returned his previous dancing partner to her mother. Yet somehow it was Caroline swirling her way across the floor instead of her eligible daughter.

She tilted her head so she could see around Lord Blackstone's shoulder and searched for Miranda's face or a flash of her white velvet gown. Perhaps someone had asked her to dance after Caroline walked away?

No, there Miranda was, standing behind the row of hopeful young faces, beaming at her mother as if she'd orchestrated this entire business.

The whole reason they'd stayed in London for the winter had been to allow Miranda an opportunity to circulate more than she could during the regular busier Season when every eligible young man seemed to have two dozen women vying for his attention. Now the girl had given up positional advantage and aligned herself with the spinsters, chaperons, and mothers.

Hadn't two full Seasons in London taught her that a lady had to make herself available in order to find a match? She couldn't hope to just run into the perfect gentleman while wandering about her own home.

"I do believe Lady Miranda can suffer your absence for one dance." Lord Blackstone pressed against Caroline's side, forcing her to turn with the dance and lose view of her daughter.

The tips of Caroline's ears burned as she pulled her head back to an appropriate position. "Of course."

She allowed her face to settle into a polite smile as she sorted through possible topics of conversation. The way things were going, Miranda would enter her third Season without a serious prospect in sight. Rumors of a mother so unsociable as to dance an entire waltz without talking to her partner wouldn't help the situation any.

Fortunately, Caroline was a well-bred lady of London's aristocratic elite, and she was more than capable of providing amiable conversation while still devoting her true attention to the needs of her daughter.

"Are you in London for the entirety of the winter, my lord?" she asked while subtly searching through the dancing couples to see whom Lord Rickford had brought to the floor instead of Miranda.

Lord Blackstone glanced to the left before giving Caroline a returning smile. "My plans are not yet decided."

"Oh?" There was an art to portraying the appropriate amount of curiosity in a conversation. One wanted to show just enough that the other person believed the interest but not so much as to appear to be after an intrusive tidbit of potential underlying gossip. Caroline had perfected the balance over the years of navigating society on her own, acting as both duke and duchess until her son had been old enough to take on his inherited role.

Unfortunately, Lord Blackstone appeared to be cut from a different cloth than the rest of the aristocracy who'd learned the art of polite conversation from infancy because he merely lifted his eyebrows and said, "Oh."

Caroline ceased examining the other couples and considered her dancing partner. Just because he couldn't be bothered to behave as an appropriate gentleman didn't mean she had to abandon being a lady. A lifetime of small talk refused to come to her rescue, though. Giving him her full attention flooded her with the unfamiliar sensations she'd been trying to ignore. Her mind seemed capable only of considering the heat of his palm on her back and the press of his side against hers as they executed a turn.

Finally she managed to ask, "Have you business to complete in Town, then?"

"Of a personal nature, yes."

Caroline fought the desire to frown at yet another closed conversational door. It wasn't as if she and the earl were strangers. They were of a similar age and had therefore moved about in similar society for decades. They had even married within a year of each other. He was now a widower, though he'd worn the mantle for far less time than she'd borne the title of widow.

Conversation should not be this difficult, particularly since they both needed to be aware of every potential social misstep. When one had a daughter to marry off, every perceived flaw mattered, even the seemingly insignificant. Of course, Lord Blackstone was seeing to the marriage of his last while Caroline had yet to find a match for her first, but their positions were similar nonetheless.

She would give it one more try. "Have you tried the tarts they are bringing about? A most delicious confection."

"Yes, they are quite tasty."

Good heavens, was she going to have to resort to discussing the weather? The clothing of the couples around them? The very pattern of the dance around the floor?

She'd forgotten how tedious this could be and should probably convey a bit more sympathy for her daughter's complaints, but that would have to wait. Right now, Caroline had a far more pressing problem.

"The dresses are quite fine tonight. Winter weather does not always lend itself to the most fashionable of fabrics, but I do enjoy immersing myself in the colors of a ballroom. 'Tis so drab and grey outside."

There. She'd provided him multiple avenues from which to respond. All he had to do now was pick a topic.

"Hmmm."

A lady never resorted to futile violent outbursts, even when riddled with frustration, so Caroline resisted the urge to strike the man across his ear. She did, however, give in to the far more subtle desire to tighten her grip and crush his knuckles together.

The arm resting across her back stiffened in response. "Are you all right?"

"Of course. Why wouldn't I be?"

He glanced toward her feet. "Did you not just stumble?"

Caroline gave him a sweet smile. People were watching, after all. "Only in conversation, my lord."

It was his turn for a blush to redden his ears. "My apologies. I'm afraid I've become accustomed to merely being one of the circle during these events. Murmurs are usually all that is required of me."

Was he implying he didn't often dance? He was far too old for Miranda to consider, so Caroline had given little attention to his movements or sought out any bits of gossip about him. If his stepping out was an unusual as hers, this pairing would have many a tongue wagging before the violins stopped playing.

There was nothing she could do about it now, though. She must make the best of the moment and engage him in conversation while she had his full attention. "It would seem the night's fine weather has brought out every member of the *ton* still residing in London."

"Hmmm," Lord Blackstone murmured as he nodded in agreement, his gaze sliding over the other couples.

Treading upon a man's toes was forgivable when he deserved it this much, wasn't it?

There was no way for her to see what continued to pull her partner's gaze over her shoulder, but Caroline could easily view the numerous eyes turned upon her. Heads tilted toward companions, and lips moved in the quick, quiet motions of newly formed *ondits*.

How many of them were discussing the apparent discomfort of her tour about the floor?

"'Let those who are in favour with their stars, of public honour and proud titles boast.'"

Lord Blackstone's eyes widened. "I beg your pardon?"

"'Whilst I, whom fortune of such triumph bars, Unlook'd for joy in that I honour most.'"

His surprise slid into a confused frown. "What on earth are you talking about?"

"Do stop frowning." Caroline gave a light laugh, or at least the appearance of one. "People are looking."

Finally, his vast public experience was put to good use, and his expression smoothed into a more neutral appearance. "What has that to do with you spouting nonsense?"

"It isn't nonsense. It's Shakespeare."

"Is it now?"

She gave a slight nod. "One of the sonnets. Number twenty-five, I believe."

They turned about at the end of the designated dance area and began twirling their way down the other side. Lord Blackstone tilted his head, his dark eyes giving her far sharper consideration than they had just a few moments ago.

Despite his increased attention, the silence was stretching between them once more, and they were in close view of an entirely new set of curious people.

Caroline fought back a sigh as she continued. "'Great princes' favourites their fair leaves spread, but as the marigold at the—'"

"Do you commonly quote Shakespeare to your dancing partners?"

"As I don't commonly dance, no."

"I see." He cleared his throat and glanced about the room before dropping his gaze back to hers. "That might explain a few things, then. I had wondered."

The bizarreness of his statement almost caused Caroline to frown, but she persevered and maintained her smile. "Wondered about what, my lord?"

"Your daughter."

Gossip or not, she refused to pretend to approve of any maligning statement against her family. The false smile flattened, and her eyes narrowed as she asked in a low voice, "What about my daughter?"

He tilted his head with a curious look but gave no other indication that her change in mood bothered him. "Next year will be her third season, yes?"

"Yes."

He nodded. "While many find it more comfortable to think I've left the raising of my daughters to their aunt, the truth is I've been rather involved in all of their seasons."

"That is hardly a secret, my lord. Your engagement is well known and to your credit." It was the one thing Caroline did know about this man, and she couldn't fault him for it.

His elder two daughters had married well by the middle of their second seasons, and the youngest had recently completed her first year with enough success to expect to follow a similar pattern. Through it all, Lord Blackstone had been an active, visible participant, occasionally even sitting through afternoon visits and copious amounts of tea.

Caroline had to respect him as a father even if she detested him as a dancing partner.

"Then you will understand that I've the best of intentions when I tell you that reciting Shakespeare during a dance is, well, rather unusual. If Lady Miranda is performing such orations, it might explain her lack of… serious attention."

The sudden stiffness of Caroline's body caused Lord Blackstone to stumble through the next two steps.

"Miranda is the daughter of a duke. It is not she who must attract attention but her attention that must be gained." Though Caroline had frequently lectured Miranda on proper dance floor conversation, she would not stand for someone else to offer criticism. Especially not someone who couldn't be bothered to attempt polite conversation himself. "And any gentleman with whom she much resort to poetry recitation in order to maintain the appearance of conversation is not worthy of her consideration."

Instead of looking properly cowed by her criticism, Lord Blackstone grinned. "Is that what you were doing?"

"Utilizing Shakespeare to accommodate for your apparent conversational ineptitude? Yes. I was."

The grin grew to a full smile. "Such cutting sentiments, Your Grace. I'd no idea your tongue could cause such a wound."

"A lady is fully capable of protecting those in her care without calling for pistols at dawn."

Now a soft chuckle filled the space between them. Caroline did not care for the way it seemed to brush across her skin like a laundered blanket brought in fresh and warm from hanging in the sun.

"You think my advice a matter of dishonor, then?"

"I think your rudeness an insult."

"My rudeness?" His smile stayed as his eyebrows lifted in surprise. "For asking you to dance or—"

"For cornering me into a waltz and proceeding not to speak."

He winced. "I'm afraid I'd lost count of the pattern and didn't realize this was the next dance."

So he hadn't deliberately asked her to dance a waltz? While Caroline had been somewhat flattered under her earlier irritation, now she was nothing but confused. Her marriage had been a notorious love match, still talked about by many of the *ton*. Such a reputation had kept any unmarried gentleman from approaching her before, even though she'd been a widow now for longer than she'd been a wife.

If Lord Blackstone hadn't wanted to waltz with her in order to have a captive audience and test her acceptance of his attentions, what had he intended? "What dance did you resolve to ask for my participation?"

His gaze shifted again but this time it was more in avoidance of her than in search of something else. "I hadn't any intentions. It was an impulse of the moment, I'm afraid."

"I beg your pardon while I determine whether I am flattered or insulted."

"When given the choice, one should never choose to be insulted."

She nodded her acknowledgment even as she fought for a smile to cover the unexpected pain at his admission.

The last strains of the dance brought their swirling to an end. Thankfully they were not dancing sets at this gathering, and Caroline would soon be able to escape. That gave her the courage to ask, "If I may be so bold, what inspired your impulse?"

He gave her a courteous bow. "I couldn't begin to say."

Her thoughts tripped to a confused halt as she relied upon habit to rest her hand on his arm and allow herself to be escorted from the floor. Halfway back to where they'd left Miranda, Caroline's mental faculties reengaged as she spied Lord Rickford. He still stood at the edge of the dance floor, smiling down at the brunette he'd apparently waltzed with. They didn't seem to be having the least bit of difficulty finding conversation as they turned and moved toward the refreshment table.

As a woman and a mother, Caroline had a habit of perusing all the gowns when entering a social engagement, and she immediately recognized that pale yellow dress.

Lord Rickford had danced with Lady Cressida, a young lady who had still been making her way to the side of the floor from the previous dance when Caroline and Miranda had been waylaid by Lord Blackstone. Had Caroline not been distracted, Miranda might have caught the man's attention before Lady Cressida was even available.

And now Lord Rickford did not seem the least inclined to end his conversation with the youngest daughter of the Earl of Blackstone.

Calmly, Caroline lifted her hand from Lord Blackstone's arm. "I believe I am capable of seeing myself back to my daughter's side." She looked up at her bewildered waltz partner with a serene smile. "It would seem your chaperoning duties have moved to the lemonade."

A flare of red flushed above the white of his starched cravat, but before he could utter a word of defense, Caroline stepped into the crush of bystanders and waiting dancers, her head held high and regal like the duchess she was.

Lord Blackstone didn't know it yet, but he had just declared war, and Caroline had no intention of losing.

Chapter Two

William should probably feel at least a little remorse for interfering in the duchess's plans the way he had, but he didn't. He'd accomplished his main goal of securing Cressida a waltz with Lord Rickford, but he'd also surprisingly enjoyed his own dance with Duchess Caroline.

Of course, he wouldn't be repeating that pleasure any time soon. Her resentment toward him had been more than obvious.

Considering the glare she'd given him as they parted ways, resentment might be understating it.

Why was she so cross? It wasn't as if mothers of the ton didn't do worse to each other as they jockeyed about, moving their daughters into position like horses at Ascot hoping to gain the attentions of the most favorable men in the room. Besides, Lady Miranda had taken Lord Rickford's arm a mere three dances later, so no real harm had been done.

Of course, that dance hadn't been a waltz. Still, Lady Miranda had been out for two full years. If Lord Rickford had been intrigued enough to court her, it would have happened by now. Instead he'd started quietly visiting William's house on a regular basis at the end of last season, and Cressida had been twirling about the house ever since.

Hence William's remaining in London as the weather grew colder instead of relaxing in the calm, quiet bliss of his country estate. The sooner Cressida was settled, the sooner William wouldn't have to spend as much time in Town.

It wasn't that he hated London, but...well, he hated London. More to the point, he hated his life in London. He enjoyed his political duties, and one couldn't deny the convenience of every sort of shop imaginable, but so many other aspects of town life felt frivolous and pointless.

Instead of caring for his lands and tenants, he read reports from his stewards and managers. Instead of gathering with a small group of intimate friends, he participated with the rest of Society in a ridiculous play put on for the amusement of the other performers. What evenings he did spend at home were never quiet and contemplative unless he carefully found a position in the house that wouldn't be disturbed by the sounds of carriages and revelers on the street outside.

Before his daughters had come of age, he'd found a happy balance between fulfilling his duties in the House of Lords and enjoying the pleasures of his country home. Not that he begrudged his daughters their successful seasons or happy marriages, but he was on the cusp of being able to reclaim that balanced life of peace and purpose. He wasn't going to let a mother desperate to keep her daughter off the shelf endanger that.

Lady Miranda was the daughter of a duke, passably pretty, and appeared in excellent health. If she hadn't found a suitable match by now, she was either too selective or too flawed in some unapparent manner. She'd had more than enough time to gain the attention of Lord Rickford.

She hadn't. Cressida had. That was how the game was played.

William did regret that were he to ask the duchess to dance again—even if only for his own enjoyment—she would likely run the risk of social scandal and decline. Considering he rarely took a turn about the floor these days, such disappointment was puzzling. Fortunately—or perhaps unfortunately, given the way his mind was fixating on the duchess—William liked puzzles.

"Father?" Cressida pushed gently at his shoulder. "Where are you?"

He gazed down at her, smile at the ready. "I do believe this is called a ballroom. Did I overpay your schoolroom tutors?"

She shook her head with a soft, indulgent laugh. "I've spoken your name three times."

"Oh." And he thought he'd been getting so much better about staying in the moment. His goal for the evening had been achieved, and now he couldn't find enough mental stimulation to remember where he was. Social gatherings such as these were simply boring now. The first year he'd escorted Elizabeth about, he'd had to learn the game, discover the unspoken rules, and determine how he, as a titled father, could best step in to the role reserved for aunts and mothers. He wasn't about to leave the happiness of his children up to his sister, who'd married her own daughter off to a gentleman in Cornwall and saw her perhaps once a year now.

Yes, his niece was pleased with her choice, but William preferred his progeny be happy within an easy two-day journey of either London or his country seat. It was a simple matter of limiting which suitable gentlemen his girls were allowed to meet. They couldn't choose a man to whom they hadn't been introduced, and there'd been plenty of likable gentleman that fit his limited qualifications.

If Lord Rickford came up to snuff, it would be a successful three-out-of-three achievement.

"Father?" Cressida asked again, laughter clear in her voice.

William sighed and smiled down at her. "Yes, my dear?"

"Why don't you go home?"

It was still early by the ton's ridiculous standards, but William would be glad to quit the evening's festivities. "Are you feeling unwell?"

"Not at all. I am having a fine time. You, however, are clearly not. Aunt Mary can see me home easily enough if you send the carriage back for us."

William frowned. His sister could indeed see Cressida home, but he wasn't certain he should leave his sister as the evening's overseer.

Cressida must have sensed his thoughts because she laid a hand on his arm. "Lord Rickford intends to call upon me day after tomorrow. I shall spend the rest of the evening dancing for simple enjoyment or giggling with my friends in the corner."

Her rationale was entirely logical, and William gladly accepted her offered escape with one minor alteration. As the ballroom was still quite crowded, chances were the carriages would be mired in a similar crush outside. "I shall leave the carriage at your disposal and hail a hackney or walk."

"As you wish." She gave him one more grin before flitting away to join her friends.

He made his polite goodbyes and strode from the house. Outside, the carriages were indeed in a tangle. His driver probably couldn't extricate their carriage, even if he'd wanted to. It would be quite a mess at the end of the evening. The creaks of waiting carriages, shuffles of bored horses, and murmurs of servants and drivers was a welcome change from the music and chatter of the ballroom.

William took a deep breath and started making his way through the vehicles.

"Did you say walk?" An incredulous female voice cut through the shuffles and murmurs, pricking William's curiosity. He turned to investigate.

"It's not unbearably far. We are still in Mayfair, after all."

William grinned. That second voice wasn't quoting Shakespeare now, but it was still undeniably familiar.

"But it's night," the first, younger female said. Presumably Lady Miranda. "And we're in evening clothes. See? Slippers?"

A few more steps and the pair of women came into view, standing beside their carriage which had obviously had a mishap while attempting to leave the area. One side was caught on a stone planter, lifting two wheels off the ground. Had there been room to maneuver, it would have been a simple remedy, but as the situation stood, that carriage wasn't going anywhere for a few hours yet.

Duchess Caroline waved a hand at her daughter, who was jutting one slippered foot out from beneath the hem of her embroidered cream skirt. "Do put your foot away. A lady does not raise her skirts to display her ankles. Besides, you'd have trekked at least that distance back and forth across the ballroom had we stayed."

Lady Miranda stuck one finger in her mouth and bit her glove before pulling her hand free. Then she placed her bare hand upon her mother's forehead while removing the glove from her mouth with the other hand. "Are you feeling well?"

William covered his mouth to hold in the chuckle. Perhaps there wasn't anything necessarily wrong with Lady Miranda, but he would put money on her being far too much of a handful for most of the men in that ballroom to bother with.

The duchess batted her daughter's hand away. "Of course I am well. I simply desire the quiet peace of our own home for the remainder of the evening." Her skirts swirled as she spun away and strutted down the pavement. "Come along."

"Er, your grace?" the coachman called. His uncomfortable misery was obvious, and Lady Miranda appeared on the verge of laughter. Not the polite laughter he'd heard all evening, but a full guffaw of amusement at the expense of her mother.

Duchess Caroline turned back. In all the years William had known her, he'd never seen such an expression of haughty power on her face. Was that how she covered her unease? No wonder she had a reputation of unwavering confidence.

With a shaking finger, the coachman pointed away from the duchess. "Hawthorne House is that way."

With a huff, the woman returned to her daughter's side.

"If you please, Your Grace," the poor servant continued, "it will take but a moment to find a footman to stand with the horses so I can escort you home. Or we could borrow another carriage?"

"And have our predicament be this week's drawing room fodder? I think not. Given the slowness of the winter season, it will take far too long for something else to come along and replace this news."

William couldn't stop his chuckle from escaping. He stepped into the light of a nearby lantern as three heads turned his way. "Might I be of assistance?"

Duchess Caroline's eyes slid closed as if she were praying for relief from a particularly difficult penance. Lady Miranda gave him a wide smile. "I don't suppose your coach is on the edge of this crush, is it, Lord Blackstone?"

"I'm afraid not. We arrived soon after you." William smiled at the duchess, who still refused to look at him. "I do, however, know the way to Hawthorne House and would be happy to provide an escort."

The duchess's gaze snapped to his. "John can do it."

Voices drifted from the house's open front doors. It was impossible to tell if people were on the brink of leaving or simply gathering in the front hall, but the duchess glanced that way with apprehension.

In that moment William very much wanted to escort this woman through the streets of London. He wanted to spend more time with her, perhaps engage her in conversation when she didn't have to be so careful and guarded and concerned about what other people saw.

He cleared his throat. "You are, of course, free to stay here and wave people off in an awkward show of misplaced propriety."

"Propriety is never misplaced."

"All the more reason to leave the scene now." He had to acknowledge that her concern over people watching the two of them dance had been legitimate. There'd been more than a few whispers behind his back afterward. This was his chance to put right the precarious position he'd put her in earlier this evening. "The longer we wait, the more likely it is that someone else will make an early night of it and see you upon the road."

"If we leave now," Lady Miranda added, "we can reach the side road before any of these carriages make their way out."

William held back a grin. The daughter at least was still on his side. Or perhaps she simply enjoyed antagonizing her mother.

Duchess Caroline's response was an indulgent glare. "Now is when you choose to care what others think?"

"I always care. There are simply certain things I don't mind them thinking that you seem to find unacceptable."

Decades ago, it had been obvious how in love the Duke and Duchess of Riverton were. It would seem that love had carried to the children as well. Seeing such was a pleasant change from the cold formality he too often saw between aristocratic parents and their children.

After several moments of silent communication with her daughter, Duchess Caroline turned to William. "Very well. Your assistance is appreciated."

William offered her his arm. "Shall we walk, then?"

She stared at his arm until Lady Miranda nudged her heavily with her elbow. With a sigh, the duchess placed her fingers lightly upon William's coat sleeve, the pressure barely enough to dent the fabric.

Apparently holding an obvious grudge was permissible when there was no one else to witness it.

"Lovely," Lady Miranda said. "I shall walk two paces behind like the good little chaperon that I am."

William chuckled as Duchess Caroline stiffened. "You are hardly chaperon material."

"The rules are different for widows. I should think an innocent, unmarried daughter the perfect chaperon in this situation."

William bit his lip to hold in a laugh Duchess Caroline would certainly not appreciate. He'd had no idea Lady Miranda possessed such a quick wit or blunt charm. "Your logic is impeccable."

"You are both nonsensical," Duchess Caroline grumbled.

As soon as they were clear of the noise and lights of the ball, Lady Miranda started a conversation filled with outrageous observations about the houses they passed and the people who lived in them. The duchess was so involved with correcting and instructing her daughter that the pressure of her hand upon his arm became firmer as she relaxed.

Until tonight, William had always seen the duchess as the epitome of cold English ladylike perfection. While she was indeed every inch a lady, he could no longer consider her cold. There was passion and caring behind her admonishment of her daughter, as well as restrained amusement and indulgence.

William was utterly fascinated.

He added a few of his own observations, and though she was slightly more restrained in her responses to him, it was the most genuine conversation he'd had with a woman in years.

All too soon, they were in Grosvenor Square and approaching Hawthorne House. The door swung open as they climbed the steps, and William escorted both women all the way into the front hall. They'd managed to avoid being seen so far, and he didn't want their polite thank-yous and farewells on the front step to be the ruination of his rescue.

They were at least an hour earlier than most *ton* members would be expected home, and the hall was dark aside from a single candle on a table near the door. Long squares of moonlight pierced the windows and slashed across the floor, keeping the room from total darkness. Duchess Caroline's blond hair caught the fragments of light as she turned to face him.

"We've a curricle in the mews. One of my grooms can take you home."

William shook his head. "I live but a few streets over. If I walk, I shall be there before the horses could even be readied."

"Of course." She gripped her fingers together and glanced from him to the door before clearing her throat and straightening her already perfect posture. "You should have some refreshment first, then."

"Yes, tea," Lady Miranda agreed. "Or at the very least, lemonade." She hooked arms with the butler, inspiring a wide-eyed, stunned expression to cross features that were likely accustomed to presenting stoic impassivity. "Gibson and I will see to the preparations."

The young woman hauled the butler away, leaving William alone with the duchess in the front hall. He didn't know whether to laugh or shake his head. "It would seem," he said while giving in to the urge to do both, "that you and I were not the only matchmakers in the room tonight."

Even in the pale darkness, the sudden flush of her cheeks was visible.

He liked flustering her and couldn't resist the urge to push a little more. "Is this how you taught her to conduct a courtship?"

One corner of her mouth kicked up even as the blush covered more of her cheeks. "This is far more like a liaison."

William chuckled, amused even as a strange feeling crawled through his middle. How had he not noticed the graceful curve of her cheek when they'd been dancing? Or the charming way her head tilted when she peered up at him?

Suddenly the thought of his own house seemed lonely. It would be quiet and dark. Empty. Just like it would be every night after Cressida got married. Why hadn't he ever considered that lonely aspect of regaining his peace?

And why did he have an abrupt, undeniable urge to do something about it?

"Lord Blackstone," Duchess Caroline said, "I wish to—"

"Call me William."

She blinked up at him. "I beg your pardon?"

"William," he repeated, even as part of him was a confused as she appeared. "It's my name."

"I...I know, but—"

"May I call on you?" He hadn't consciously considered such an idea, but as soon as he uttered the words, they felt right.

"No one has called on me in a long time," she said in a stunned whisper.

"Then we'll be out of practice together."

She considered him for a long moment. "Do you wish to court me?"

Did he? "Yes, I believe I do."

Why should he spend the rest of his years in lonely solitude just because his daughters had gotten married? Tonight, Duchess Caroline had been more engaging and entertaining than any woman he'd conversed with in a long time. From the way they'd talked as he walked her home, he guessed she would say something similar. Didn't they owe it to themselves to see if there was more to that connection?

It may be impulsive, but it had been a long time since a decision felt so right.

Her smile was softer, more genuine than the ones she'd given him in the ballroom. "Why me?"

"Because for the first time in years, the idea of going home is less appealing than staying where I am."

One side of her smiled tilted up more. "Are you afraid of an empty home, then?"

He shook his head and stepped closer, reaching out to grasp her hand in both of his. "I think perhaps I'm more afraid that I might embrace an empty life."

"I suppose a man must be more than just a father."

"And are you more than just a mother?" He swallowed. "It's been a long time since I've considered what it's like to be a husband."

Their hushed tones wrapped around them, joining with the darkness to pull them closer and closer together. It was like their dance all over again, yet more consuming, more confusing. How long had it been since he'd stood in the dark with a woman? Since he'd allowed their hearts to slide into the same pounding rhythm?

Her gaze locked with his, and her breath whispered across his lips as she said, "I don't think I know how to be a wife anymore."

Despite the gravity of the moment, William couldn't help but grin at the prospect of getting to know more about the woman he'd glimpsed tonight. Nor could he resist the pull to softly brush his lips across her upturned mouth.

The fireworks of Vauxhall Gardens exploded within his chest as he whispered, "I think both of us could remember how."

"Thank you for helping me retrieve the lemonade," Lady Miranda's loud voice carried through the house before her stomping footsteps approached the hall.

William stepped back, shivering at the aching chill that raced across his skin as his hands fell back to his side. He missed the physical connection to the duchess, but her gaze was still joined with his, and her eyes held the same hesitant excitement that churned through his body.

He accepted the glass of lemonade and drank half of it down before returning it to the butler's tray. It was far too late to pursue any more conversation, so he said all the proper farewells and stepped to the door. Before walking into the night, he turned back and gave the duchess a wink. The catch of her breath sent a thrill through him he hadn't felt in years.

As he walked the short distance to his home, he couldn't help but notice that while the puzzle he'd been contemplating in his mind earlier in the night had gotten far more complicated, he just might finally have all the right pieces.

Chapter Three

A lady should always remember that reputation was what truly opened Society's doors, no matter her skills and abilities. With that in mind, Caroline resolved not to utter a word to anyone about her conversation with Lord Blackstone.

Not the ladies she met with to discuss the needs of the Foundling hospital.

Not the myriad of other mothers she drank tea with in drawing rooms.

Not her lady's maid.

Not her children.

Not even herself in the mirror since one never knew who might be listening in.

Such resolve did not, however, extend to her thoughts, and from the moment she awoke, mere hours after he'd seen her to her door, her mind refused to contemplate anything else. Over and over again, she mulled over the memory of their dance, their walk home, their moments in the darkened hall.

Their kiss.

In the years she'd been a widow, she had of course missed her husband's touch, but it had been his smile, his support, his care, and his fun she'd thought of most often. Still, it had been nice to be in a man's arms again.

Was he sincere in his intention to court her? Did she want him to be? It was no small feat to get four children happily married and settled, especially when the family carried such an expectation for love matches. She'd been one half of the most desperately, romantically in love couple London had seen in an age. If people saw her differently, would it harm her children's chances of making as genuine a match as she'd had with their father?

It certainly wouldn't help Miranda's situation to have her own mother find a husband before she did.

Not that Caroline was ready to marry Lord Blackstone. William. But that was the goal of a courtship, was it not?

She couldn't afford to contemplate it any more today. This morning she was receiving visitors with Miranda, and she needed to be the epitome of ladylike grace who gossip papers and mothers alike held up for all of London's gently bred misses to emulate.

It would be helpful, of course, if her own daughter would aspire to such an endeavor.

Caroline entered the drawing room, pleased to see Miranda already in attendance. Less pleasing was the book she held open before her. "Where is your embroidery? A lady always needs something to occupy herself between visitors."

Miranda looked up and blinked. "That's why I have a book."

Shaking her head, Caroline moved into the room and sat on a white brocade chair. "Books are far too engrossing. To be seen closing one as a guest arrives implies they are intruding upon your restful solitude. A gentleman should never be so rude as to interrupt a lady reading a good novel."

The look her daughter gave the book before shifting her glance to the door was as clear as if she'd spoken. If reading books would get Miranda out of at-home visits, she'd read every book in the library.

Caroline sighed. "Don't you want to get married, Miranda?"

"Of course," the younger woman said without hesitation. "I simply can't think of anyone who might be coming for a visit that would tempt me to reserve St. George's."

"As we attend Grosvenor Chapel, reserving St. George's would be unnecessary." Caroline fought to keep the smile from her face. Sometimes a mother's greatest pleasure was in exasperating her children. "What about Lord Rickford?"

"What about him?" Miranda crossed the room to place her book on a table next to a basket from which she extracted her current embroidery project.

Apparently intentional exasperation wasn't reserved for mothers.

"One day he will be the Marquess of Blatham. He would make a fine husband," Caroline said, trying to keep the conversation on track as Miranda returned to her seat on the white sofa.

"I suspect he will." Miranda stabbed her needle into the fabric with more force than finesse. "In a few months, I will ask Lady Cressida if that is true."

"He's made no public intentions known about Lady Cressida or anyone else." Agitation had Caroline rising to her feet in the guise of ensuring the curtains were properly framing the windows. "If you assume every good man is meant to marry someone else, you'll never win a husband."

"Is it a competition, then?"

Caroline narrowed her gaze at her daughter. Must the girl always twist Caroline's words about? "A lady must always know how she compares to her peers if she is to place herself at an advantage in society. That is good sense, not competition."

"Sounds like competition to me."

Before Caroline could offer a rebuttal, Gibson appeared in the doorway of the drawing room. "Lord Rickford is here, Your Grace."

"Show him in." Caroline grinned at Miranda. "And please have tea brought as well."

"You look rather triumphant for a woman who isn't engaged in competition." Miranda cast her gaze to the ceiling as she set her embroidery aside.

"It is hardly my fault that Lady Cressida's father has not learned that being at home the day after a ball creates the most opportunities." Caroline put a smile on her face and prepared to greet their guest. It was admirable of Lord Blackstone to be so involved in his daughters' lives instead of foisting them off on their aunt, but there was no getting around the fact that he thought like a man. He probably considered it wiser to rest the day after large, late-night gatherings and take callers after one was refreshed.

Foolish man. The best gossip was discussed the following day, and the women with open drawing rooms were the queens of deciding what news gained the most legs. As for suitors, well, far better to solidify a connection while they were still consumed with their infatuation from the evening before and hadn't yet filled that space with politics, sport, and cards at their club.

Was Lord Blackstone contemplating such things this morning, or was he still thinking of her?

She shook her head. Lord Rickford and Miranda needed all her attention.

The young man entered with a smile on his face and bowed to the ladies in greeting.

Caroline gracefully returned to her seat and gestured toward a chair for Lord Rickford. "Your timing is impeccable, my lord. Miranda and I were just about to have tea."

As she was speaking, a maid entered with a heavy-laden tray. This was a trick Caroline had yet to pass along to Miranda. There was much to adore about her eldest daughter, but Miranda was still struggling to maintain the broader ideals of being a lady. Finer skills, such as keeping a tray with hot water at the ready so a preferred visitor could be induced to stay because they had the good luck to arrive at the same time as the tea tray, were somewhat beyond Miranda's current needs.

Tea was poured, social pleasantries were made, and Caroline turned the conversation to coming social events. She'd been slow to firm up their social calendar, waiting until the last polite moment so she could discern who else would be in attendance at each event. They weren't wintering in London because they liked it, after all.

"Will you be spending the whole of winter in London, my lord?" Caroline gave a soft laugh. "This is our first time staying through the colder months. We don't want to miss out on any particularly enjoyable affairs."

Lord Rickford shifted his position in his chair. "I've business that will keep me in Town for a while, but my plans are not yet firmly settled. I've spent other winters here, though. Mrs. Chapman has a splendid gathering after the first decent snow every year, and of course there will be ice skating in Berkley Square."

It wasn't the best of openings, but Caroline had worked with less. "Ice skating." She turned to Miranda with an enthusiastic smile. "Doesn't that sound delightful?"

"Indeed," Miranda said before taking a bite of biscuit.

"It's been ages since I tied on skates. I fear we'd fall all over ourselves, but it sounds like such a wonderful excursion."

"It is." Lord Rickford took a sip of tea. "When it opens—"

Gibson appeared in the doorway once more, and Caroline frowned. She'd given explicit instructions that none of Miranda's other potential suitors—and certainly no eligible young ladies—were to be shown in for half an hour after Lord Rickford's arrival.

"Lord Blackstone is here to see you, your grace."

That, at least, explained the butler's actions. The earl would hardly be offering for Miranda's hand and certainly wasn't a young lady.

A strength-stealing breathlessness warred with a protective tension as Caroline watched the door. Last night he'd declared intentions of an amorous nature, but he'd also displayed a desire to thwart Caroline's attempts to garner Lord Rickford's attention for Miranda.

Which motive had brought him here this morning?

He appeared in the doorway, as neatly coiffed and turned out as any suitor. He even held a small bouquet of flowers that must have cost him dearly this time of year, unless he had his own hothouse.

And he was looking directly at her.

Once more, Caroline fell back upon years on ingrained habits and rose to greet him politely. Lord Rickford jumped to his feet, and Miranda rose as well, smirking as if to say, *Everyone else is standing so I will, too.*

Caroline would manage her impertinent child later.

Lord Blackstone extended the flowers. "For you, Duchess."

A tingling sensation rolled along Caroline's arm and settled in her middle as she accepted the bouquet. How many years had it been since a man brought her flowers?

"Ah, Rickford." Lord Blackstone stepped further into the room. "How's the tea?"

The swirl of excitement crumbled into ashes of dread. Caroline clutched the flowers closer to her chest.

"Excellent." Lord Rickford's smile was far wider and warmer than it had been moments before. "The chocolate biscuits are quite good as well."

"Might I join you, Duchess Caroline?"

"Allow me to pour," Miranda said before Caroline could come up with an excuse to rush him out. The tray was on the table in front of the seat Caroline had been occupying, so Miranda took the chair and set about pouring the tea.

She did not rise after she was finished, which meant the sofa was the only seating left for Caroline and Lord Blackstone.

Miranda did not need lessons in ladylike manipulation.

"Lord Rickford," Miranda said, addressing the gentleman directly for the first time since he'd arrived. "Have you an interest in the writings of William Blake?"

Caroline took a bite of biscuit to avoid groaning aloud. How had Miranda known?

"No particular interest for myself." Lord Rickford's relaxed demeanor remained as he answered. "My mother enjoys his work immensely, though. I came, well, that is, while I am here, I'm to borrow a book of his work for my mother."

Miranda sent Caroline a look of such false wide-eyed innocence that it was all Caroline could do not to laugh. "Truly? How convenient that one was left on the table in the front hall this morning."

It wasn't the least bit convenient. It had taken Caroline ages to find a book by that man after hearing Lord Rickford's mother discuss her love of his poetry at dinner two weeks ago.

Lord Rickford gave a sheepish shrug. "Well, yes, Her Grace sent word around this morning that it would be waiting for me."

Lord Blackstone turned to look at Caroline, eyebrows raised and a half smile on his lips.

Heat climbed up her neck, as tangible and constricting as a high-collared pelisse. She truly had to stop blushing in front of Lord Blackstone. What was it about this man that threw her confidence off kilter? Was it because she couldn't quite anticipate his next action, or was it something else?

Miranda set her teacup aside and rose to her feet. "Why don't I show you where we put it so you don't forget to take it with you?"

Lord Rickford glanced from Miranda to Caroline and Lord Blackstone, his confusion obvious. Clearly Caroline needed to remind Miranda that a lady always employed subtlety when attempting to direct the actions of others.

The young man's cup rattled in the saucer as he hastily set it aside and rose to his feet. "I would be delighted, of course." He bowed to Caroline. "Thank you for the tea, Your Grace."

"You're welcome," Caroline murmured as the younger people departed, leaving her and Lord Blackstone alone in the drawing room. At least Miranda was spending a moment of time with Lord Rickford. Perhaps they would have a conversation while they were in the hall together that would inspire some form of affection.

"Handily done." Lord Blackstone saluted her with a biscuit before breaking it in half and popping a portion of it into his smiling mouth.

"Why are you here?" Caroline would not insult them both by pretending she didn't know what he was talking about. Nor would she allow him to set her back on her heels by admitting anything aloud.

"I do believe I announced my intentions last night."

"To visit me?"

"To court you."

Miranda's bumbling of moments before proved Caroline could not entertain such an idea even if part of her was thrilled to consider it. She fought the streak of pleasure that tried to push her lips into a girlish smile and instead made a point of scoffing before taking a sip of tea. "We're both far too old for that."

Lord Blackstone held his hand in front of his face and gave a loud open-mouthed exhale into the palm. "I do believe I'm still breathing." He extended his hand toward her, stopping it mere inches away from her face. "Same appears to be true of you."

"We've far too many responsibilities, then."

"All the more reason to share the burden."

"My children are not a burden, my lord." Even if Caroline did want to swat her twenty-year-old daughter like an irrepressible toddler.

He grinned at her. "Then carrying them into a courtship shouldn't be a problem."

The implications of his statement nearly stole Caroline's breath away. She'd been on her own for so long, unable to trust that anyone—even those she considered friends—wouldn't see a moment of weakness as an inability to carry this family.

And she had carried this family.

Griffith had been but ten years old when he'd become the duke. A mere boy who still needed to attend school, make friends, and discover what it meant to be a man. In the midst of mourning a husband she'd loved with all her being, she'd had to become duke and duchess, mother and father, protector and comforter.

Looking at her family now, Caroline couldn't help but feel she'd conquered those challenges with aplomb. Griffith had taken over the dukedom and estates, her children were all of strong mind and character, and the family's reputation was as free of blemish as one could get.

If there were times she felt more than a little lonely, well, that was the price one paid for being human.

At least, that was what she'd always reasoned. She glanced at the man seated beside her on the sofa, proposing the idea that the part of her that cried into her pillow to relieve the pressure of it all didn't have to forge ahead alone anymore.

Fortunately, she'd had many years of practice at not letting that overly emotional side of her control her actions. A lady should think first and feel second if she wanted to maintain control of her life.

Lord Blackstone leaned toward her and murmured, "I'd give a great deal to know what you're thinking right now."

Caroline examined the earl as she took a sip of tea to buy herself a bit more time. "I am fortunate, then, that I am not in need of your charity and can therefore keep my thoughts to myself."

"You think my being here is charity?"

"I think your being here is foolish."

He set his cup down and turned his body until he was facing her. "Why would you say that?"

"I loved my husband."

She watched him carefully, but the man didn't wince, look away, or shrug off the reminder. Instead, he said, "I believe everyone in London is aware of that." He even laughed as he regarded the ceiling, a small smile indicating the memories he was considering were joyful ones. "I remember that time well. His buying an estate next to your father's so that he could court you without hindrance was all anyone could talk about for months."

Caroline dropped her gaze to her tea, remembering how she'd been both flattered and frustrated by his perseverance. His unshakable commitment to his goals, his family, and his faith were what had finally won her over. There'd been so much depth to their conversations, and they'd easily shifted from the serious to the nonsensical. Those memories were treasured and dear, but Caroline had long accepted that she would be adding no more pictures to that mental gallery.

She cleared her throat and gave her attention back to Lord Blackstone. "You understand, then, why I cannot allow you to pursue me."

"Are you still in such mourning for your husband, then?"

"I will always love John, but no. I would not say I am in mourning. I am, however, counting on my reputation to pave the way for my own children to find love matches."

"I see no reason why another love would hinder that."

"Do you claim to love me then?"

He opened his mouth, then snapped it shut and shook his head. "I will not insult either of us by pretending such, but I could see it happening. We are not strangers, Duchess."

Caroline winced at the reminder of what she'd become when she'd married John. If she were to marry an earl, she would be taking a step down the social ladder. How would such a move impact Miranda's chances of finding a match? "If we must have this conversation, you may call me Caroline, but I see no need to continue it."

Lord Blackstone stared silently into his tea for several moments before setting the cup aside with a nod. "I understand. Forgive me for intruding upon your day."

He rose and crossed to the door.

The slight rounding of his shoulders had Caroline wanting to call him back, to tell him she was flattered by his attentions, that his apology was unnecessary. But she had a feeling that if she gave this man any opening at all, he would wedge his foot into the door and insist upon finding a way in.

Caroline wasn't certain she could withstand a campaign from himself and her own emotions so she maintained her serene, confident silence.

At the door, he stopped and gave her another grin. "You should know that this doesn't mean I've given up."

Hope pressed through Caroline's chest before she could stop it. "It doesn't?"

He shook his head. "No. But I know when to retreat and formulate a new plan." His smile widened into a grin. "Besides, I should return home and prepare for tomorrow. Lord Rickford is coming to take Cressida for a ride. And I didn't even have to bribe him with a book."

Then he bowed his head and left before Caroline could give in to the childish urge to throw a biscuit at him.

Chapter Four

A lady should never let a cup of tea sit about growing cold. If she had such time to linger and daydream, she had time to add more productive pursuits to her plate.

Or so Caroline had always said.

Yet when Miranda entered the breakfast room the following morning, Caroline was staring into her third tepid cup of tea. Was there a way to dispose of it without her daughter noticing? Miranda would never let such an event pass without comment.

Fortunately, the staff at Hawthorne House was efficient and discreet and before Miranda was settled at the table, the cup of wasted tea and the useless teapot it had been poured from were whisked away and replaced with a fresh pot and two new cups.

Unfortunately, Miranda had grown up with two elder brothers and had learned to notice such covert attempts. She gave Caroline a smug look as the servants bustled about the room setting a full plate in front of her and delivering the freshly pressed paper to the table.

All too soon, Caroline and Miranda were alone. For the first time this winter, Caroline regretted sending her other children back to the country. Giving Miranda all her focus and attention had seemed such a good idea at the time, but today she would welcome the distraction her family could provide.

Miranda took a slow bite of eggs and an even slower drink of tea before nodding toward Caroline's cup. "Are you planning to drink that one?"

"Of course," Caroline said, reflexively reaching for the cup. "A lady never lets a cup of tea go to waste."

"Hmmm." Another bite. Another long drink. "And if I were to ask downstairs how many cups they'd washed this morning?"

"They'd wonder about your purposes, I'm sure." Caroline shifted in her chair and lifted the paper to disguise her nervous fidgeting. "I trust Cook completely and have no need to manage every aspect of work in the kitchens."

"Hmmm." More slow chewing. More long drinking.

Caroline lifted her cup and gulped half of it down, nearly burning her tongue in the process. It was time to encourage a new subject. Anything would be better than this speculative, uncomfortable silence.

"I've been considering other potential prospects you can add to your list. Lord Rickford is, of course, the most eligible gentleman making the rounds at the moment, but it wouldn't hurt to create as many opportunities as possible."

Miranda laughed. "Desperate to marry me off, are you? Perhaps I should throw it all in and dangle my dowry in front of a destitute lord."

Caroline's cup clashed against her saucer as she fumbled it to the table. "Whyever would you say that? I intend to find you a happy marriage with a man you love."

Miranda put her elbow on the table and propped her chin in her hand as she considered her mother. "One who deliberately asks me to dance?"

"Well, yes, of course." Where did Miranda come up with these questions? In their social world it was all but impossible for a man to court a woman without asking her to dance.

"A man who comes calling of his own volition?"

Ah, she was trying to convince Caroline that Lord Rickford wasn't interested. "Some men require a modicum of guidance to see potential opportunities they may otherwise miss. Men are not so accustomed to considering romantic endeavors as women are, you know."

"Hmmm." Miranda sat back in her chair, cup cradled uncouthly in both hands. Caroline let it pass since correcting her daughter's posture could be seen as an attempt to get out of this conversation, and Caroline would much rather discuss Lord Rickford's suitability than risk having the topic shift to her own wandering thoughts.

Miranda eyed Caroline over the rim of her cup. "I should absolutely find a man willing to come to my rescue."

"Do you intend to fall into some sort of scrape requiring a rescue?"

"No one ever intends such things, do they?" Miranda shrugged. "But it is impossible to predict when one's carriage might become...immobile, shall we say."

They weren't discussing Lord Rickford at all. Caroline pretended to look at the paper on the table. "A gentleman should come to the aid of any distressed lady, whether they are in love or not."

"How fortunate for us, then, that Lord Blackstone is a true gentleman." Miranda's grin was wide and mischievous and Caroline had to fight the urge to sigh. Why couldn't her daughter be subtle like other ton women who went about having entire conversations without actually stating whom they were discussing?

Now that it had been bluntly stated Caroline could hardly ignore it. "Yes. We are quite fortunate."

"He even went so far as to visit yesterday and ensure your, or rather our, welfare."

Caroline nodded, afraid of what might emerge if she tried to utter actual words. Miranda would never betray her confidences, never gossip about her, never trade her secrets for social power, but Caroline couldn't bring herself to confide in her daughter. It was her job to guide Miranda, to offer a ladylike example to aspire to, to be a safe place of wisdom.

Still, Miranda had been out in society for two years now. She was an adult who had seen and heard a great deal and never had any lack of opinions or thoughts on a subject. In truth, she'd probably discussed the details of far more courtships than Caroline had.

"I would be surprised," Miranda continued, "if a woman's head wasn't turned by such—"

"He kissed me," Caroline blurted out. Heat immediately suffused every inch of skin on her body.

It was Miranda's turn to fumble a teacup. She was far less successful, and the cup flipped sideways as she lowered it to the table, sending the remnants of tea rolling across the smooth wood surface. The commotion was enough to alert the waiting servants, and they rushed in to quickly see to the disarray.

Soon they were alone again, with fresh cups of tea before them once more. Miranda started giggling. Soon she was nearly doubled over in full, loud laughter.

Caroline resisted the urge to cast her eyes to the ceiling in exasperation and reached once again for the paper. "I do hope you aren't going on like that in public. A lady always laughs with refinement."

"Does a lady also kiss her escort in the darkened front hall?" More giggling. "I don't think I've learned that lesson yet."

"Nor will you." Caroline turned a page without having read a single story. "It is hardly becoming behavior for a young lady."

"But perfectly acceptable for a widow?"

Caroline set aside the paper. Why had she envisioned talking to Miranda about this as a good idea? "I have no idea how it happened, truly. It was a fleeting moment, and no, it is hardly acceptable." Only it was acceptable, wasn't it? At least, in a way it was. She wouldn't be ruined for it, wouldn't be ostracized, not unless she went about causing a public scene. She was a widow and well past the fresh face of her youth. Truly no one was much concerned with what she did in her own time unless it was decidedly scandalous.

She blinked as her mind wandered once more. Was she actually considering accepting William's proposal of courtship? She'd had good reason for declining it yesterday, but today those arguments were harder to remember.

"Mother? Mother!"

Miranda's voice caused Caroline to jump as her attention went to her once again laughing daughter.

"Do you want to know what I think?" Miranda asked.

"No, but that's never stopped you from telling me." Caroline sighed. "Truly, Miranda, a lady doesn't have to say—"

"Everything that comes into her head. Yes, yes, I know. But in this particular case I think it truly signifies."

"Very well." Caroline folded her hands in her lap. "What do you wish to say?"

"I think," Miranda said, making the word excruciatingly long, "that Lord Rickford is a terrible match for me."

As Caroline had been expecting something entirely different, she didn't have a ready response.

"However," Miranda continued, "I do believe Lord Blackstone might be absolutely perfect."

Chills covered Caroline's skin. "For you? Darling, he's much too old." Not to mention he'd already kissed Caroline.

Miranda's expression was horrified enough to be comical. "Goodness, no. For you, Mother. He'd be perfect for you." With a shudder and a truly unladylike gagging sound, Miranda pushed away from the table and fled the room, calling over her shoulder, "I'm going for a walk to think about anything other than the image you just put in my head."

It was going to take far more than a walk to clear Caroline's mind. She poured herself another cup of tea and settled in to watch it grow cold.

William glanced over the top of a book he'd read three times before as he turned the page. Across the drawing room, seated appropriately on opposite ends of the sofa, were Cressida and Lord Rickford. They'd returned from the ride half an hour ago, and Cressida had declared that the man simply couldn't leave before warming up with a cup of tea.

The tea still sat on the table in front of the sofa, long forgotten as the couple smiled and chatted and smiled some more. Cressida was probably going to need a cold compress for her cheeks tonight.

The young man would have be on his way soon. Though he obviously had a *tendre* for William's daughter, no official intentions had been announced. Until that happened, utmost propriety in appearance as well as actuality needed to be observed.

Still, it was nice to see them enjoying each other's company to such an extent.

Caroline certainly hadn't sought ways to prolong William's visit yesterday.

He frowned at his book. Was he a fool to chase this fledgling idea? Was it Caroline herself or simply the companionship of a second marriage that he wanted? Perhaps he needed to contemplate those ideas separately before moving forward. Yes, Caroline was the only woman who had inspired him to even imagine what sharing his space and life again would be like, but he hadn't consciously considered anyone else.

Was that because no one would do but Caroline, or because he'd been too occupied with his daughters?

William examined the last daughter in question once more. Her smile was wide, her cheeks still flushed with a hint of pink that could no longer be blamed on the brisk winter air outside. He'd been blessed to see such a look on his other daughters' faces when their husbands had been courting them, and he was grateful to see it again.

That was not the expression Caroline's face had worn.

Then again, she wasn't fresh from the schoolroom. Perhaps maturity and experience caused a different display of interest.

Although it was doubtful being essentially tossed from a woman's home could be construed as an indication of interest no matter how one formed the conditions.

With a sigh, William set his book aside and rose. Lord Rickford gave him a swift nod before rising and beginning his goodbyes. Cressida escorted him to the front hall in an excruciatingly slow walk that would make the snails in his country garden proud, but soon enough, the front door closed and his youngest daughter was floating through the drawing room once more.

"What are the plans for this evening?" William asked.

"Dinner and a card party. Shall we meet in the hall at six?"

William nodded and picked up the book he'd set aside just to give himself something to do as he attempted to nonchalantly ask, "Who is hosting this dinner?"

"Mrs. Crenshaw." Cressida gave him a slight smile. "Why?"

Was Caroline acquainted with Mrs. Crenshaw? Of course she was. The *ton* wasn't so large that everyone didn't have at least a passing knowledge of each other. Unfortunately that didn't mean everyone was always invited.

He attempted a casual shrug. "I'm merely considering who might be in attendance tonight." He cleared his throat. "I need to prepare my topics of conversation and such."

Cressida hooked her arm through his as they walked from the drawing room and up the stairs to the first floor. "I'm sure she's invited the ladies in her foundling charity as well as her daughter's friends, like me. Then, of course, she'd add whoever was needed to even out the numbers."

He'd heard Caroline mentioned in connection with some sort of hospital charity, but was it for foundlings? Was it the same one Mrs. Crenshaw was a part of? Cressida seemed to be expecting a reply, so William said, "Yes, yes. Makes sense."

Cressida laughed. "Did that help you at all?"

Not in the slightest. "Of course."

"Hmmm. Name one person that will be there tonight."

William opened his mouth.

"Aside from the Crenshaws."

He gave her a wry grin. Should he guess Caroline and see what Cressida said? No. Whether or not Caroline was there, he owed it to himself to consider the other widows or even spinsters who were in attendance. If Caroline were truly the only option for him, he would pursue her until she outright rejected him. If not…well, he would consider that when another appealing candidate crossed his path.

William stopped at Cressida's door and patted her hand. "You will be there. That is all I need to know."

She kissed his cheek and shook her head with an indulgent smile. "I do hope you find something more interesting to occupy your attention this evening than watching my conversations."

Before William could respond, she stepped into her room and closed the door. That was probably a good thing since he wasn't certain how he would have responded. It was possible this idea of remarrying would disappear as quickly as it had occurred to him. There was no reason to get his family in a dither over it. At least not yet.

If Caroline wasn't there tonight, she would certainly be at some other event he attended in the next few days. He would take his cue from her as to whether his attentions should continue or cease. It wasn't as if he *needed* to marry. His nephew was a fine young man and would do the earldom proud when the time came. The idea of having babies underfoot again was a little too daunting to contemplate anyway.

No, were he to marry, it would be strictly for solid, easy companionship.

Throughout the next few hours, no matter what he did, part of his mind was contemplating Caroline and marriage and life after his daughter was gone. He'd come to no conclusions.

And yet, as soon as he entered the Crenshaws' drawing room that evening, it was as if no one else was in attendance but Caroline. His gaze immediately found her on the other side of the room. He couldn't name a single person who stood between them, but he could have given a detailed account of the blue gown she was wearing.

Her eyes widened as their gazes met and held. How long they stood that way, he couldn't say, but it had likely been only seconds before her mouth pressed into a thin line and she returned to her conversation.

Not even a smile or a nod in his direction. Was that his answer, then? If so, it pained him far more than the crumbling of a three-day old infatuation should.

He made his way through the room, greeting acquaintances and talking with friends. Whenever he glanced Caroline's way he found she was keeping an eye on him. His increasing closeness didn't seem to make her happy.

Finally he made his way to where she was standing. Whether by luck or design, she was momentarily alone. "Might I have a word?"

"I shan't step out onto the terrace with you. No one would believe weather such as this is an enticement to anyone."

William sighed. He was looking to make his life easier and fighting a woman for her affections didn't fall into that category. "Have you seen the statue over here?"

She walked with him to an empty corner where a small Greek-looking statue was situated. "Is it authentic?"

"I haven't the slightest idea. Nor do I care. I wanted to speak to you."

Her soft sigh stabbed him through the chest but underscored his resolve.

"I'll not be calling on you again."

She blinked up at him. "I beg your pardon?"

"I am not a man who needs to chase a bride. I thought—I still think—that we would be capitally suited, but I've no desire to make you uncomfortable in your own home or in our shared society." An unexpected lump swelled in his throat, and William had to swallow before continuing. "I wanted to let you know you've no need to worry when I walk in a room."

She gave a stiff laugh. "I was hardly worried."

"You certainly weren't happy." William nodded his head at her and then the statue so anyone watching would assume they'd been discussing the art this whole time. "Enjoy your evening."

As he moved to talk to someone else, his head congratulated him on maintaining the simple freedom he was soon to gain, but his heart wasn't quite as sure.

Chapter Five

A lady never took risks with her reputation, and yet here Caroline was, wrapped in a dark cloak, head tipped down, carrying a basket like a common servant as she made her way down Lord Blackstone's street. Why was she doing this? If anyone discovered her it would be the talk of London before nightfall, even by people who weren't scheduled to be home for visitors. Gossip about the Duchess of Riverton walking to a man's house alone would be far too enticing to be limited by something as frivolous as manners.

Manners and propriety were the backbone of society. Without them relations would descend into utter chaos. It was why she'd raised all of her children to know the rules - both spoken and unspoken - and admonished them to follow them strictly.

Yet here she was, breaking at least four significant rules and who knew how many minor ones.

Of course she wouldn't have had to resort to such behavior if *that man* had followed the rules the night before. Yes, she'd been outwardly unenthusiastic about his attentions, but that didn't mean she hadn't secretly been thrilled by them. She'd even been in the process of reconsidering.

He hadn't known that, though. And she'd assumed he would do as men had done before—very well, as John had done before—and be politely resilient until her resolve wore thin and she lowered her guard.

But William wasn't John. He didn't act like John, didn't move in politics like John, didn't run his estates like John.

Didn't kiss like John.

There were so many obstacles in the way of she and William being a true couple that Caroline was more than a little hesitant. She was also curious. How many years had she crossed paths with him and never given it a thought? Yet, these past few days, she'd been able to think of little else. She felt pulled to him whenever she saw him, and last night there'd been a decided pang of loss after his announcement.

She wasn't ready to put a notice in the paper, but she owed William—and herself—a discussion at the very least. A real one that gave the idea of a relationship a chance.

Just as William wasn't the man who'd courted her decades before, Caroline was no longer the ingénue who'd been flattered by John's persistence. Life and maturity had turned her into a strong, capable woman who could open doors herself. Or at least keep them from closing. William had been the one to introduce the idea, after all. All she was doing now was shoving her foot in the doorway he intended to close.

Caroline frowned as the mental analogy descended into madness. Such nonsense did nothing but distract her from considering the true possibilities and ramifications. What she needed to do now was ensure that William knew she might possibly still be interested.

And she needed to do that away from the prying eyes of London in case it didn't go well.

Because his daughters were out in society, William held a surprising number of social events for a bachelor. Caroline had been to his home several times in the past five years, but she'd never been there for a call.

Not that this was a call, either. This was a...a...

She didn't know what it was. For the first time in years, she was following a plan that wasn't thought out, wasn't considered, was nothing more than a driving impulse she couldn't bring herself to deny.

The closer she got to his terrace house, the more holes she found in her unplanned plan. How was she to get inside? Dressed as a servant, she could hardly knock upon the front door. Entering through the kitchens would give the entire scullery a fit of the vapors and servants gossiped as much as their employers.

This was why a lady should always act according to her station. When one behaved properly, there was never any question of the next right step.

Still considering her options, she continued past William's house and turned the corner to walk up the alley behind the row of houses. As much as she would like to think she'd raised her eldest daughter to be the epitome of a proper lady, at this moment, she was rather glad she hadn't been entirely successful. Pondering how Miranda would face such a dilemma was the only thing keeping Caroline from slinking her way back home.

The shadowed alley was different than the sun-dappled street. Occasionally, people bustled past her or busied themselves in the back gardens. Doors opened and closed. People called out to one another.

But no one knocked.

Caroline lifted her head enough to consider the back of the houses. No one except perhaps a delivery boy had reason to knock on a back door. Most of the activity was servants going in and out as they went about various duties.

Was it possible that she could simply walk up to William's house and let herself in?

She counted down the row to make sure she approached the correct home, then crossed the tiny back garden to climb the steps to the small veranda.

What would she do if William wasn't home? Or if a servant was cleaning in whatever room lay beyond that door? Maybe the family never used this door, and it was going to be locked.

Oh bother, Caroline was not meant for life like this. Give her the open trickery of a *ton* ballroom any day. She should turn around, return home, and manipulate William into meeting her in a dark corner at their next social function like any proper lady would.

That she was even considering doing anything else was proof that man was addling her brain.

Caroline did not need an addled brain. She had one daughter approaching her third season and another set to come out the year after. Not to mention two sons that had yet to show serious intent on finding suitable matches. That was where her attention needed to be. If her name fell to scandal, it would damage their reputations as well. Yes, she was a widow, but she was also a mother.

Which meant she probably shouldn't skulk off into dark corners either.

She pressed a hand to her temple. She'd run a dukedom while her son finished school. She'd raised four fine children on her own. She'd wielded her societal position as duchess in a way that brought about more good than harm. And she'd done it all without so much as a single whisper about her drifting through a ballroom.

So why was she suddenly standing in a London alley, wracked with indecision? A lady never wallowed in indecision. She set her mind and forged ahead on her path, which was why Caroline intended to have a private word with William.

Squaring her shoulders and attempting to appear as if she was supposed to be doing it, she crossed the small terrace. The door latch lifted silently under her fingers, and in less time than she'd spent dithering in the lane, she found herself inside the earl's home.

Now to find the earl.

She hadn't seen William's study on those previous visits, so he was likely one of those men who preferred to work at the back of the house instead of the front. John had always said it was easier to concentrate when one didn't hear the clatter of wheels all day.

Caroline entered through a music room. Next she peeked into a drawing room and a dining room. Hopefully his study was only one floor up, because she would have to leave otherwise. Even she had to admit that a lady should alter her plans if they required rising to the floor on which a gentleman's bed chamber might be located.

Thankfully the stairs didn't creak, and soon she found herself standing before the earl's open study door. He was bent over a ledger, quill in hand, as he compared the book's contents to a letter on the desk beside it. Occasionally he made a small mark on the page.

She stood watching him for long moments, but then she must have made a noise, or he somehow felt the weight of her stare, because he looked up.

Their eyes met.

And Caroline stopped breathing.

A myriad of emotions rolled over his expression as he set down his quill and rose to his feet. Only when he took a step to round the desk did air rush back into her lungs and sense into her head.

Or what little sense had managed to follow her on this harebrained errand

"I don't know why I'm here," she said.

"I don't know that I care," he answered as he quickly crossed the room and placed a hand upon her elbow to guide her further inside. He nudged the door all but closed before moving to stand in front of her. "Unless there's been an emergency. Is everyone well?"

"Of course. If it had been an emergency, I'd have sent a footman, or rung at the front door, or, well, probably stopped at one of a dozen other homes between my house and here."

"That would have been more practical, yes."

Caroline nodded. She did like to be practical. And yet...

"I'm glad you're here."

She blinked up at him. Hadn't he said he'd given up on her? "You are?"

He nodded. "I can't say that I particularly liked what I had to tell you last night." He shifted his weight. "I'm afraid I'm getting ahead of myself again, though, assuming you've come because you wish me to change my mind."

"As I said, I'm not sure why I'm here." Caroline took a deep breath. "We need to have a conversation. A private one."

The tension slid from William's shoulders, and he chuckled. "I'd be happy to listen to your suit."

"I beg your pardon?"

His wide-eyed look was filled with such false innocence that he could have passed for a naughty little child. "You aren't here to ask for my hand?"

Caroline frowned. Could this man be predictable just once? "A lady does not do the asking. Whyever would you—"

Muffled voices rang through the house followed by the bang of a closing door and the distant shuffling of feet.

"It would appear Cressida is home." William cocked his head as the footsteps climbed the stairs and voices grew louder. "Perhaps you would like to ask her permission to court her father?"

"I'm not—" Caroline broke off and fought the urge to stomp her foot. Why did she seem to lose her composure around this man? "She cannot find me here."

"I'm afraid there isn't another exit."

Caroline's gaze darted about the room. "Then I will hide."

He waved his arm in a wide arc. "Be my guest."

The room was filled with bookshelves, tables, and chairs with thick, carved legs. The only furniture of substance was the desk, a large, hulking antique monstrosity with solid sides that reached nearly to the floor.

"Dear Lord, if you get me out of this, I will promise to never do anything so foolish again," she mumbled as she lowered to her knees and crawled beneath the desk.

If her daughter could see her now, Caroline would lose all credibility. Sneaking off to a man's house. Being forced to hide his under his desk to avoid his family. It was beyond unseemly.

William's legs came into into view, and he sat in his chair and slid it closer to the desk. Caroline couldn't come out now even if she'd been so inclined.

She opened her mouth to object, but a knock at the door kept her silent.

"Enter," William said, an obvious urge to laugh underlying his voice.

"I wanted to let you know we've returned." Cressida's voice grew louder as she entered the room and approached the desk.

"Did you enjoy yourself?"

"I always have a fine time shopping with Aunt Mary."

Scrapes, clinks, and shuffles echoed into the cavern beneath the desk. Caroline frowned at the wood over her head. Was William moving things about, or was Cressida fidgeting with her father's items?

Cressida's voice was barely audible over the other bits of noise cluttering Caroline's ears. "Father, have you ever considered getting remarried?"

Caroline gasped.

William coughed to cover the sound.

Caroline plastered her gloved hand over her face. What had she been thinking when she'd hidden under here? Being found in his study would be damaging enough, but to be discovered under the desk?

"I, er..." William cleared his throat and leaned back in his chair. "The idea did occur to me recently. Everything gets still when you're gone."

More dings and scrapes. Obviously Cressida was a fidgeter since William's hands were resting upon his knees.

"Have you considered anyone in particular?"

"Why? Did you have a suggestion in mind?"

The thudding of her heart had Caroline pressing her other hand to her chest. Logically, it couldn't be loud enough for anyone to hear, but it just might cause the room to vibrate.

Was Cressida going to suggest Caroline? Did Caroline want her to? What if Cressida mentioned someone else? What if William agreed with her?

Caroline let her forehead fall to her bent knees. Shouldn't she be hoping for just such an occurrence? That would solve her problem, after all. The fact that she was desperately hoping to hear her own name uttered was a rather telling emotion.

The clanking and scraping stopped and Cressida's voice became firmer as she said, "I thought you and the Duchess of Riverton were quite handsome dancing together." She sighed. "I had hoped she was even the reason you left early and had Aunt Mary see my home. But then you barely spoke to her last night. I believe she was hurt by that."

How much of a groan could Caroline indulge in before Cressida would notice?

"Do you?" The obvious smile was once more apparent in William's voice. "What makes you say that?

"She watched you."

"Watched me?"

"Father, I know you've spent years observing the men who've called on my sisters and me. You're always telling us what they are thinking and what their behavior means, and you are truly proficient at it. I believe that's why we've all made such wonderful matches."

Caroline considered the legs covered in light brown trousers. Would he be willing to share his knowledge? Perhaps that would help Miranda.

"You've not made a match yet, my dear."

"Not officially, no, but that's not what I want to discuss."

"It's not?" William asked.

"No. While you are, of course, a man and therefore understand men, I am a woman."

"And you understand women?"

"Likely more than you do."

"Of that, I have no doubt. Women are illogical, mysterious creatures."

Caroline gave in to the urge to punch his toe. He didn't even flinch while she had to tuck her throbbing hand back close to her chest.

"We are not illogical." Cressida sounded more amused than irritated.

"We shall roll on with mysterious, then."

Cressida gave a *hmph* of apparent agreement as she pressed on. "After your brief conversation with Her Grace last night, she watched you."

Caroline's mouth fell open. She'd done nothing of the sort. Oh, very well, she'd given him a glance or two, but she certainly hadn't stared. Someone aside from Cressida would have noticed.

"I do believe more than just you would notice if the duchess stared at a man all evening," William said.

Caroline looked up, as if she could somehow see William's face through the top of the desk.

"I didn't say she stared. I said she watched. She frequently glanced right at you before returning to whatever she'd been doing."

Well. That was true.

One of William's feet slid forward until it was lightly touching Caroline's hip. "Is that so? What do you think it means?"

Cressida clapped before gleefully stating, "I think she must be at least a little taken with you. You should consider courting her now, while there aren't as many prying eyes."

"You believe she would be amenable?"

"It wouldn't hurt to ask." There was a pause. "That is, if you are interested. I do so hate the idea of you being alone soon."

"A man is often alone at some point in the later portion of his life."

"But you've years to live yet."

"God willing."

"And if you live them alone, you'll become as dusty as an old statue."

"I do believe I hire sufficient staff to keep me clean in my lonely stagnation."

"You know what I mean, Father. 'Tis only your duties to family and country that make you leave this house."

"I've two other houses I can loiter about in if that makes you feel better."

In the moment of silence that followed, Caroline could only imagine the glare Cressida must have given her father before she said, "If you wait, you'll miss your chance. By middle of next Season, she'll be far too busy. And if the idea of marriage has appealed to her and you appear uninterested, she might look for someone else."

What a horrifying idea. If considering one man was causing her this much agony, how much worse would it be to consider all of them? Caroline shuddered at the thought.

"That is a point I shall have to consider." William nudged Caroline once more with his foot.

Caroline sat on it.

"Thank you," Cressida said. "I'm going to help the maid put away my purchases."

Soft foot falls preceded the click of a door latch, and then complete silence descended upon the room.

Finally William slid his chair back, a low chuckle shaking his entire body as he reached down an arm to assist Caroline from beneath the desk.

As she unfolded, aches and pains that reminded her she'd birthed four children and lived four decades nearly drove a groan from the depths of her soul. She clamped her teeth together to keep it in.

William stood, still holding her hand loosely in his own, a wide grin splitting his face. "Is it true, Caroline? Do you have a hint of affection for me?"

She wanted to be calm, to remain aloof, but the delighted gleam in his eyes wouldn't let her. "A hint," she admitted, unable to refrain from giving him a smile of her own.

"Does this mean you *will* allow me to court you?"

"It means..." Caroline trailed off into a deep sigh. What did it mean? She'd come here today to tell him that she hadn't liked their discussion, or rather the lack thereof, from the night before, but all her concerns were still valid. They'd settled nothing.

"What?" He tucked a strand of hair that had come loose from her bun behind her ear.

"It means that I…would be amenable to you asking me to dance again." Just considering such an action brought heat to her cheeks. "Perhaps you could come calling again as well. Maybe seek me out when we attend social functions."

His eyes grew serious as he cupped her cheek. "Does kissing you again fall on the list of acceptable behaviors?"

"The list is negotiable." Was that Caroline sounding so irrationally breathless?

"That sounds a lot like the beginning of a courtship."

"The nice thing about being a widow and a widower is that we've no need to officially label it as anything."

"Indeed." William leaned down and brushed his lips against hers. The sweep of his mouth was as slow as it was light, but there was nothing gentle about the way it shot sparks through Caroline's entire body.

He lifted his head, and they stared at each other for long moments.

Finally Caroline stepped back and set about fixing her cloak, which was already laying exactly as it should. "Well." She had to stop and clear her throat. "Now that we've settled that, do you perhaps have an idea for getting me out of here unseen? I'll not participate in anything that damages the reputations of my family, no matter what we decide to call it."

"You do remember that you were the one who chose to come here?"

Caroline gave him a sharp look. "You do know that if we are to consider marriage, the union will be a total partnership?"

He chuckled as he walked to the door. "Come along. I know the habits of my household well enough to get you back on the street unscathed."

Caroline gave a regal nod. "Thank you."

"And if I just happen to be walking toward Grosvenor Square right now, know it has nothing to do with my belief in your capabilities and everything to do with my duties as a gentleman."

"As long as we both understand," Caroline said, unable to stop herself from giving him a girlish grin.

It had been so long since she'd felt this light, this fun, this free. If this was an indication of what it would be like to actually allow Lord Blackstone to court her, there might not be any way she could say no.

Chapter Six

Over the past five years, William had attended every sort of social engagement, sat through innumerable afternoon calls, and endured countless inane conversations.

What he had never done was act as escorting chaperon. When going out to the shops or for rides and walks, he'd left that duty to his sister or his daughters' capable maids.

Yet here he was, on his way to a chocolate shop because his youngest daughter had contrived some ridiculous story about her maid needing to stay behind and repair a dress for that night's ball and it being too late to contact her aunt.

Cressida had always been a mischievous child, though she'd never been particularly circumspect at enacting the schemes she concocted. Most times the family simply played along with her obvious ploys because they were always harmless.

This time, William had welcomed the distraction. For the past four days, he'd been able to think of nothing except how to best court Caroline without giving the overt appearance of courting Caroline.

Aside from stealing glances at her across the church aisle during Sunday's service, he'd come up with nothing. If this were the regular season, events would be numerous and crowded enough that it would be a simple matter, but the smaller intimacy of the winter months meant any overtures he made, no matter how subtle, would be noticed.

"Tell me again why it is so important that you go out for a cup of chocolate right now instead of tomorrow or even in a couple of hours." William gave his daughter a considering look as the carriage rolled away from their house.

"Because," she said, drawing the word out into a long sigh as she plucked at her skirts. "Tomorrow Lord Rickford might not be there. And he certainly won't still be there in a few hours."

"I see." William relaxed into the rocking of the vehicle. In the time-honoured fashion of females, Cressida was not resting on the many indications Lord Rickford had given that he returned her affections and intended to do something about them. While William had to agree the younger man was moving far slower than the social norm, he didn't think Cressida needed to manipulate and create situations in which to promenade her charms before him.

Still, Lord Rickford might as well learn now that the woman he was drawn to was prone to indulging in terrible plots and plans.

They entered the chocolate shop, and Lord Rickford was indeed at a table. He was not, however, alone. Two cups sat before him. One was empty, but the other still had steam curling from the top. Lady Miranda and Caroline sat to his right, each with a single warm cup of chocolate in hand.

"Oh dear." Cressida's flat voice indicated genuine concern. Did she have reason to worry?

William turned back to the group at the table. While they were all chatting amiably, there was nothing to indicate a particular rapport between Lady Miranda and Lord Rickford. "Nothing to worry about." He took his daughter's elbow and guided her across the shop. "The table is large enough. We'll simply join them."

If he arranged the seating correctly, it would almost be as if he'd brought Caroline there himself.

"Might we join you?" William asked, even as he guided Cressida into the empty chair beside Lord Rickford. Lady Miranda's greeting was friendly and open while Lord Rickford's demeanor changed entirely, his smile both widening and softening as he stood to welcome Cressida to the table.

The table was round with six chairs. Leaving the one between him and his daughter empty might be unusual, but not so much that it would draw undue notice. He eased into the seat beside Caroline. She said nothing until he'd settled and ordered. Then, with a small smile, she simply said, "Good day."

Lord Rickford laughed. “The way my day is going, I may never leave this chocolate shop.” He smiled at Cressida. “I can’t complain, though, if I get to sit in comfort while the best of London stop by for conversation.”

Two more chocolates were brought to the table, and the young people engaged in their own conversation while William enjoyed the chance to talk somewhat privately with Caroline. They discussed current events in a way William had never done with a woman before. He supposed Caroline’s having to watch over the dukedom for so long had something to do with her wider interests, and he was fascinated by how pleasurable it was to hear her opinions and share his own.

By the time Cressida touched his shoulder and said it was time to leave, the image of him and Caroline sharing the paper during quiet mornings in the country had lodged itself in his mind and refused to dissipate. In fact, it was quickly becoming an idea he couldn’t imagine living without.

A lady always kept outward impressions in mind when she dressed, but it had been many years since Caroline had considered any specific person’s opinion. Over the past three weeks, she’d been reminded of the giddiness that accompanied selecting an ensemble with the intent of appealing to one particular gentleman. Despite the vague familiarity of the ritual, Caroline couldn’t help but notice how different this time around was.

For one thing, she didn’t have to worry about someone else winning his affection. While she had no doubt that other aristocratic widows would be delighted to trade places with her, William had all but declared himself. He wasn’t smiling at other women or seeking them out when he walked into a room.

Another difference was that this time, she didn’t feel as if everyone were watching. Oh, people took note whenever they danced together ,and more than one sly smile had been sent her way after they’d stood to the side of the room talking for longer than was proper. The truth was, though, that their union—if they were to make one—wouldn’t cause a dramatic ripple in society.

At least, that was what she told herself when she sat alone at night contemplating the wisdom of allowing this courtship—and yes, she at least had to admit that was what it was—to continue.

The children had been so young when John had died that she'd not had a chance to truly imagine him with her in London, guiding their daughter through a season. Now a dream she'd never even contemplated considering refused to leave her thoughts.

What would it be like to have William at her side as she watched over and guided her children? To not have to rely on secondhand accounts of what the gentlemen were discussing in the clubs? To go out in society as a couple instead of always throwing off the numbers?

The idea of companionship at home was rather nice as well. If Miranda and Cressida married soon, it would give Caroline and William nearly a year to spend on their own before Georgina entered society.

That was a rather large *if,* though.

Still, it was possible. And that possibility had her deliberating more and more about taking a chance and allowing her connection with William to take on a more official appearance.

They'd seen each other frequently over the past three weeks. Not just at dinners and parties but at the coffee shop, the museum, and even the park on one unseasonably warm day. To any onlooker, it might have been mere chance that they'd seen each other while out and about.

If she were to make obvious plans, though...

She frowned at the paper on the desk in front of her. Was she ready to make such a leap?

"Are you at that much of a loss on what to do with yourself?" Miranda asked from the doorway to Caroline's private library. It had once been a sitting room, but she'd become so accustomed to having a study that she'd converted it when Griffith took over the one downstairs.

Caroline folded her hands over the piece of paper as if her thoughts were going to appear on the blank surface and give her away. "What do you mean?"

"Do you miss the paperwork?" Miranda flopped into one of the chairs facing Caroline's writing desk. "You can't possibly have that much correspondence."

"I couldn't possibly write as many letters as you do each day." Caroline smoothed the paper against the desk. "And a lady does not collapse into a chair. She delicately floats into it."

Miranda grinned. "Perhaps you should demonstrate again."

"There's is no need. I've seen you accomplish the feat numerous times."

"Then perhaps the edict should be that a lady does not collapse into a chair unless no one can see her."

"I can see you."

"You're my mother. You are required to love me no matter how impish I become."

As Caroline couldn't refute the statement, she pushed on. "Did you come for a reason or simply to be exasperating?"

"I wondered if we had plans for the day."

Perhaps. If Caroline could get up the nerve to send the letter. "We could contemplate potential husbands for you." Or for Caroline.

"I don't see the need. I believe that subject is as settled as it can be for the winter. You've informed me Lord Rickford is the only acceptable gentleman about, and I am doing my best to see that he does not remain available much longer."

Caroline restrained her show of delight to a small smile and slight shifting of her feet. Caroline had been all but ready to give up on the man until he'd started appearing everywhere they'd gone. They encountered him on their outings almost as often as they crossed paths with William.

Most of Caroline's attention had been consumed by William, but she'd kept enough of an eye on her daughter to know that the conversations between her and Lord Rickford had been easy and constant. They'd both smiled nearly the whole time.

While the young man had made no formal overtures, it was good that Miranda was making an effort. Perhaps if he didn't see Miranda for an evening, he would be prompted to declare his intentions. "We should take in a show this evening."

Miranda lifted one blond brow. "From our box?" She grinned. "Just the two of us?"

"Er, well, no." It wasn't as if William needed prompting, after all. He'd been rather clear that he was following her lead on this. "We could ask if Lady Cressida would like to join us. The two of you seem to be quite friendly of late."

"Oh, yes, we've found a few topics of common interest."

"Then a relaxing evening for both of you might be just the thing."

"She won't want to leave her father at loose ends."

Caroline cleared her throat. "Of course not. We'll invite him along as well."

Miranda shook her head. "If that's what you need to tell yourself, Mother, by all means. I'd love to attend the theater with Lady Cressida tonight."

With the entire scheme, or rather plan, settled in Caroline's mind, she jotted off a note to Lady Cressida and rang the bell for a footman.

In six months, would they be making plans over the breakfast table instead of via messenger? Would they be discussing their children's prospects together? Would they be comparing calendars and discussing invitations?

When she was once again alone, the happy bubble in her chest burst out in a giddy squeal. She'd thought herself safely alone until Miranda's soft laugh echoed from the corridor beyond.

Caroline couldn't quite find it in herself to care.

Chapter Seven

William glanced around at the many familiar faces in the various other boxes around the theater. This was as close to a public declaration of intent as he and Caroline had come. Any rumors that the two of them were forming an attachment would carry enough weight to be seen as fact after tonight.

He turned to look at Caroline, her straight, thin nose, high cheekbones, and small, pointed chin creating a striking silhouette in the flickering candlelight. She was as unlike his late wife as a woman could be, so the inexplicable way he was drawn to her couldn't be an attempt to reclaim a memory or return to the past. Still, everything he learned about Caroline, every conversation, every touch, every quiet smile and stolen glance, tied another rope around his soul, binding his future to hers.

His prayer was that God was creating the same infatuation on her end because at this point, any rejection on her part would create a heartache far worse than any his younger years had dealt. This time around, he knew what he would be losing, knew what it was like to have a companion he liked, respected, and cared for, knew that women who could fill that position in his life were rare.

"The girls seem to be getting on," Caroline whispered from her seat beside him in the second row of chairs. Cressida and Lady Miranda were pressed up against the front wall of the box, heads tilted toward each other as they watched the play and discussed the activities of the other theater attendees.

He'd been concerned that Lord Rickford's attentions to Cressida would create a rift between the younger ladies, but either Caroline had ceased pursuing the viscount or Lady Miranda had refused to participate in the chase. Either way, William was glad that the competition for the young man's interest was no longer an issue in his courtship of Caroline.

William grinned at his companion. "It's almost like they're sisters."

A flush of bright pink tinged her cheeks as Caroline pressed her lips together and turned to fully face the stage.

A pleasant silence fell between them as they took in the entertainment and when, ten minutes later, William reached over to loosely hold her hand in his, Caroline didn't pull away.

Whenever there was a break in the on-stage performing, guests would arrive in the box. Some claimed to have business with William, while others crowed over how long it had been since they'd spoken to Caroline. The younger ones made a show of greeting Cressida and Lady Miranda.

No matter whom the visitors declared they were there to see, their gazes would flit speculatively between Caroline and William.

And Caroline didn't seem to mind.

It was as good as an advertisement in the paper. When his friends asked him about the relationship at the club tomorrow, he would be able to acknowledge that it did indeed exist. He would no longer have to brush aside the inquiries with vague statements of how life was always changing and no one knew what would come next.

Just thinking about it kept a smile on William's face for the remainder of the evening. There were, of course, still their families to consider, but he had to assume that even if Caroline hadn't contacted her other children about him, Miranda would have written to them. Her apparent approval was all William had to go by, but it was promising.

They'd come to the theater in William's carriage, and he couldn't help but compare seeing Caroline home this time to the evening he'd walked her home a few weeks ago. With his daughter at his side and a crowded London square behind them, he couldn't linger with Caroline in the shadows. The loss of such an opportunity was negligible when compared to the boon of knowing she was giving serious consideration to a life with him.

Once they were back in the carriage, Cressida gave William a wide grin. "Perhaps I should tell Aunt Mary to plan a double ceremony for next Season."

"I wasn't aware we were planning a single ceremony as of yet." If Lord Rickford and Caroline settled their intentions in the same day, William could only imagine how well he would sleep that night.

Cressida bit her lip and squealed as she wiggled in her seat. "On our ride today, he asked if I thought you amenable to a visit. He knows he must ask you, but he said since I would be the one actually marrying him, it was only right to talk to me about it first."

William couldn't deny that logic or the peace that flooded him at her revelation. Now it was simply a matter of time before his life was everything he wanted it to be. His final daughter would be getting married, and at last this constant consideration of Society's ups and downs would end. He could almost feel the freedom that would come with a life of easy, quiet companionship with Caroline.

"If you are both certain, why wait until the Season?"

Cressida sighed. "I want to marry Lord Rickford, but I would like my friends to be there." She blushed and giggled, reminding William what it was like to be caught up in the excitement of starting a life with someone. "It would also be nice to spend a few weeks of the Season with a loyal beau."

"Understandable." William gave his daughter's hand a squeeze. "I'm afraid you will be the only member of this family walking the aisle of St. George's during the coming Season, my dear."

Cressida deflated. "But tonight went so well."

"Should the duchess deign to become a countess, I will place a notice in the paper the following morning."

Only as he said the words did William realize just how much he meant them. Charming but calm, ladylike without being stodgy, settled and responsible without being solitary, Caroline was perfect for him. More than that, though, he respected her, enjoyed their conversations and, of course, their kisses, and cared whether or not she was happy and healthy.

A month ago, she'd been simply another face in the ballroom, and now he couldn't imagine not having her in his life.

When had his practical idea become an undeniable craving? Did he love her? Already?

He spent a great deal of the night staring at the ceiling, and the next day as he saw to his business, went to his club, and talked to his friends, the idea swirled about in his mind. By the time he shrugged into his jacket for the next night's dinner party, he had come to the conclusion that he was, indeed, in love with Caroline, Duchess of Riverton.

The pressure to get her to agree to his suit increased immensely.

Of course he couldn't tell her yet. Women took far longer to settle such ideas for themselves, and she'd been somewhat behind him in the first place.

One day soon, though, William would ask her to change her title, and when she agreed everything would be perfect.

Shards of icy winter air speared through Caroline's clothing on the short walk from her carriage, with its blankets and heated bricks, to the shelter behind Lady Blatham's front door. The hall beyond wasn't much warmer due to the frequent opening and closing of the door, but at least there was no wind.

Caroline suppressed the desire to shiver as she relinquished her cloak to a servant and moved forward to greet her hostess.

"I haven't had a chance to thank you for the loan of the book." Lady Blatham clasped her hands to her chest and sighed. "Such an enjoyable volume."

Caroline returned the curtsy and the smile. "You should keep it, then."

Lady Blatham's smile widened as she reached out to take Caroline's hands in her own. "Truly?"

"Of course." Caroline leaned in and whispered, "I've encountered your son so often this winter, it practically feels like we're family." The statement was a bold one, but Caroline wanted to know for certain if Lord Rickford had any intentions. Miranda had refused to confirm anything in any direction as she continued to lead Caroline about to various locations where to young viscount happened to be.

Since William was nearly always at those same locations, Caroline hadn't pressed too hard for details or complained, but after last night, well, she rather wanted the matter settled so she could consider other things. It would circumvent a great deal of unpleasant gossip if Miranda was married or at least affianced before her mother wed again.

Assuming, of course, that William intended to ask for her hand. Such assumptions were safe given his insistence upon a courtship and agreement to attend the theater with her. It had been something of a public declaration.

Lady Blatham gave a conspiratorial grin. "Are the rumors true, then?"

Years of practice kept Caroline's expression impassive. Was her hostess inquiring about Caroline's connection to William, or did Lord Rickford not discuss his prospects with his mother? "Rumors are always so plentiful that I couldn't begin to declare their truth."

"Of course." Lady Blatham laughed as if both women were in on the most delicious joke. She glanced toward the dining room, a thoughtful look on her face. "I'm certain whatever life holds for you, having a year of peace and quiet would be preferable to another hectic Season."

How was Caroline to respond to that? If Miranda didn't marry, Caroline could hardly expect a year of peace. Was Lady Blatham implying her son had serious intentions? In truth, despite her desire for it to be otherwise, part of Caroline had begun to assume he, Miranda, and even Lady Cressida were simply amusing themselves until their friends returned for the Season. They'd been companionable in public, yes, but he never came to the house. "I...that is..."

"Would you pardon me for a moment?"

As Caroline was a guest in this woman's home and had spent far too long in the receiving line as it was, she could hardly object, but still she nodded, and the other woman trotted off to the dining room.

At least Lord Rickford's somewhat strange behavior made a little more sense now.

Caroline and Miranda entered the drawing room. A group of young ladies soon drew Miranda's attention, and Caroline left her to chat while she worked her way through the room. Her target was, of course, the cluster of ladies and gentlemen near the window. William frequently glanced her way, marking her progress with a grin and sending a surge of happiness flowing through her.

When they were called in to dinner there was much joking and laughing as it was discovered that tradition had been tossed by the wayside and the place cards had been set about in a seeming haphazard order. Such a lark could only be done in the winter, but Caroline was pleased by it as she located her seat directly beside William's.

Miranda was, unfortunately, not as blessed. In fact, her placement was something of a puzzle. She was surrounded by gentlemen who were hardly unfortunate dinner partners—Lady Blatham would not invite anyone who couldn't carry a pleasant conversation—but they were also known to be on the hunt for a large dowry. Caroline had spent more than a little effort keeping Miranda away from them this winter.

As the daughter of a duke, Miranda had a more than respectable fortune awaiting her future husband. Such a purse should never be her daughter's most appealing trait, though.

Caroline frowned as she observed the room. Lady Cressida's position at Lord Rickford's right was rather telling. The man might have a serious interest, but it did not appear to be toward Miranda. The realization was not as disappointing as Caroline would have expected.

There was nothing to be done during dinner, so Caroline focused on enjoying herself with the company around her. When the ladies withdrew, however, she made a point of working her way into a private moment with Lady Blatham. Not wanting to give undue import to her true question, Caroline started with a discussion of winter fashions and moved to the possibility of the Thames freezing over again before saying, "Miranda's placement was rather unique tonight."

Lady Blatham stood a little taller and gave Caroline a knowing grin. "Your daughter has many charms, and I'm sure it will be years before anyone would even begin to think her on the shelf, but it would be a true shame for you to put off your own happiness because she has yet to settle down."

Caroline had been at a loss for words before. A woman didn't raise four children without encountering experiences that left one speechless. This was, however, the first time she could remember not being able to find something to say because there were too many words in her head. So many thoughts. Even more questions. She finally landed on repeating Lady Blatham. "My own happiness?"

"With Lord Blackstone." Lady Blatham leaned in. "I'm certain he's merely waiting for Lady Cressida and my son to make everything official before he asks you."

"That's"—Caroline swallowed—"quite an assumption."

"I can't thank you enough," the other woman continued as if Caroline hadn't spoken at all. "My son probably would have drug his feet for another year if he hadn't been able to spend so much time with Lady Cressida with you as a chaperon. It truly settled his heart and mind."

Well, at least Caroline was helping someone find a match.

"Moving the cards at dinner tonight was such a little thing, but I wanted to do my part to help."

Miranda may very well need some sort of assistance in finding a husband, but that was not the kind Caroline was willing to accept. "I hardly think Miranda's status will restrict me overmuch. I've another daughter, after all."

Lady Blatham frowned. "But I thought—" She cut her sentence short and gave an awkward laugh. "I suppose that's what happens when one listens to rumors. Lady Hullsman told me her husband had talked to Lord Blackstone at the club, and the other man talked on and on about how he was looking forward to building his new, quiet life in the country after his daughters were wed, and I simply assumed he was including Miranda in that sentiment."

Awkward silence fell between them. Caroline could only imagine what her expression was saying because Lady Blatham appeared more and more uncomfortable.

"I'm certain I heard wrong," she said as she inched away. "Perhaps you've decided to take Miranda with you. Her prospects in the country might be better." Another half a step. "Lord Mitchell and Mr. Dristan are good men, you know," she said, referring to the gentlemen who'd been seated on either side of Miranda. "Neither of them is mean or a spendthrift."

Caroline murmured a sound that was somewhere between a grunt and a scream, but it must have been enough for Lady Blatham to pretend it had been a response because she gave a small nod and went in search of other conversation.

How could Caroline have let herself get so distracted? She didn't believe William had orchestrated this evening's debacle of a dinner, but he likely wouldn't see anything wrong with it either. Of course he was looking forward to a quiet life and would assume Caroline intended to join him in it. That was what wives did.

No, she couldn't blame the man, even if she was disappointed. She could, however, blame herself. Miranda's future depended upon decisions made in the next few years. As her mother, that should be Caroline's one and only priority. From now on, she couldn't let anything—not even her own heart—keep her from remembering that.

Chapter Eight

It had been many years since William had walked into a social engagement and taken an immediate account of the women present, but he could no longer walk into a room and not look for Caroline. Even on the rare evening when he escorted Cressida to an event Caroline didn't plan to attend, he looked.

Earlier this week, though, Caroline had said the Longsford musicale was on their social calendar. So where was she? Not that she was late yet, but William missed her. He hadn't seen her since they'd dined with Lord and Lady Blatham, but that seemed far longer than two days ago. The conclusion of this courtship was settled in his heart and mind, and he was ready to make it happen.

Just imagining a life with Caroline made him smile. Sharing the paper over simple breakfasts. Discussing their days over quiet dinners. Walking or riding through the countryside, enjoying the view and visiting tenants.

People were still milling about drinking surprisingly delicious organdy and visiting with friends, but none of them were a regal blond with intelligent blue eyes.

"Are you intending to stand all night, or shall we take our seats?" Cressida nudged him in the side with her elbow. "Rickford is looking a little uncomfortable by himself."

William dropped his gaze from the people being herded into the music room by their host and smiled at his daughter. He had to get her settled before he could enjoy his visualized future.

"Of course." He offered Cressida his arm. "Where do you have us sitting? This is an excellent room, so I believe we'll be able to hear from anywhere."

"I agree." Cressida smiled and pulled him away from the cluster of instruments at one end of the room.

Normally his daughter liked to be early to musicales and chose to sit as close to this front as possible, so it was something of a surprise to see Lord Rickford situated in the middle of a nearly empty back row.

Cressida moved into the row and sat beside the young viscount, indicating that William should take the seat beside her. It left two chairs to his right, likely intended for Caroline and Lady Miranda. Where were they?

Just as the musicians were moving to the instruments and adjusting their music, the door opened, and two figures slipped silently into the room.

William couldn't help but smile as Caroline tried to sneak along the wall while still maintaining perfect ladylike poise and posture. Her eyes trailed down row after row. Whether she was looking for him or looking for empty chairs didn't matter since the only remaining seats were in this back row.

In moments, she stood two chairs away from him and his grin of welcome faded under the darkness of her frown. The obvious concern on Lady Miranda's face didn't give him any comfort.

"So good of you to join us," William tried to joke, hoping he could break her free from whatever displeasure had caused them to be late in the first place.

A red flush worked up Caroline's neck as she guided her daughter around to the other end of the back row.

Beyond Lord Rickford were two more empty chairs, but they would have to move past Lady Jean and her brother Lord Martin if Caroline intended to sit there.

Sure enough, the duchess made her apologies to the siblings just as the first notes floated through the room. Once she was seated with Miranda between her and Lord Rickford, she stared forward, lips pressed into a tight, thin line.

William barely heard the music even though he adjusted his body to face forward and give every appearance of paying attention. When the musicians paused to switch instruments, William nudged his daughter as he rose and went around behind the row. He gave his vacated chair a pat and Cressida nodded in return.

Fabric rustled, feet scuffed the floor, and chairs creaked as Cressida, Lord Rickford, and Miranda all shifted over one seat.

Caroline didn't move.

William went to the end of the row and gave the siblings an apologetic smile before moving to slide in front of them and make his way down the row of chairs. He should have climbed over his own family, but there was no going back now.

Lord Martin gave him a sour frown, but Lady Jean's eyes were wide with curious glee as she leaned back to make room.

When the musicians took a break, gossip about this moment would be served right alongside the refreshments, but William didn't care. Lord Rickford obviously cared for Cressida enough to put up with whatever nonsense was going on in this back row. It was time for William to put his own future on the same steady footing.

Since Caroline refused to move, William eased past her as well before lowering into Lady Miranda's recently vacated chair. He leaned toward Caroline and whispered, "Have I done something to vex you?"

"Yes. You're whispering at a musicale. It's rude."

"So is being late."

Her icy blue gaze speared past him to her daughter. "It would seem Miranda was incapable of walking down stairs without damaging her dress tonight." Her lips pressed into a line so tight her lips almost disappeared. "Twice."

Music swelled around them as William searched his mind. The last time he'd seen Caroline, it had been all soft smiles and coy glances. What had happened in the past two days to inspire such obvious distaste? "Why didn't you sit by me?"

She didn't acknowledge his whisper, so he gently bumped her shoulder.

"Do you mind?" The words slid out from gritted teeth.

"Not at all."

Finally she turned to look at him, but the ice in her glare almost made him wish she hadn't. "I am attempting to make a love match for my daughter. And listen to music. Please leave me alone to do so."

William glanced over his shoulder at the three younger people all making no pretense that they were watching this conversation and not the musicale. He turned back to Caroline. "Your daughter isn't interested in Lord Rickford."

Lady Miranda leaned around William to whisper, "That's true."

“Nor,” William added, trying to quiet his voice even more, “if Lord Rickford interested in her.”

Caroline pointedly stared straight forward. “I never said he was.”

“I don’t think he ever has been,” Lady Miranda chimed in. “I can ask him if you’d like.”

“Miranda.” Caroline’s voice was calm, but her head snapped around to stare down her daughter. William almost expected to see a spot of blood from the stab of the glare. “A lady never acts in such a forward manner.”

Miranda leaned further around William, all but climbing into his lap to whisper to her mother, “Does a lady toss away love in a fit of spite?”

“Of course not.”

“Good. Then you slip off with Lord Blackstone and sort out this ridiculous business and leave the rest of us to enjoy the music.”

“Excellent idea,” William said.

“Utter nonsense,” Caroline returned.

What was going on here? Five days ago, they’d gone for a walk in the park and ignored everyone as they discussed how pretty the trees would be in the spring. Then, of course, there’d been the theater. He’d finally been comfortable telling his friends at the club about the relationship after that. This morning, he’d been contemplating asking for her hand and tying up the whole business before the rest of the aristocrats started flooding back in to London.

But now Caroline thought him the worst sort of vermin.

He opened his mouth, ready to press her for an answer, but Lady Jean’s wide, attentive eyes met his over Caroline’s shoulder.

With a sigh, he settled back to wait for intermission.

As soon as the musicians set down their instruments, he turned to Caroline, “Your Grace, might you desire a glass of lemonade?”

“If retrieving one will relieve me of your presence, absolutely.”

This was bad. Caroline rarely administered such a blatant set down, and she almost never did so in public. William turned to Lady Miranda, but she was of no help. If anything, she appeared even more shocked than he was.

Lady Jean squeaked. She was nearly vibrating as she looked from Caroline and William to the crowd at the nearby refreshment table.

Caroline stood and turned her back to the other woman. She lifted a brow at William as if he was supposed to know what she wished him to do. A breath ago, he'd believed it was to climb back under the rock she seemed to think he'd been living under, but now she appeared to want something else.

He clambered to his feet and offered her his arm. "A turn about the room?"

She laid her hand lightly on his arm and slid from the row. William followed, confusion deepening by the second.

Instead of moving toward the groupings of people around the refreshment tables, she stepped into a window alcove a few feet from where they'd been sitting.

Lady Jean still watched them avidly, but from this distance she wouldn't be able to hear anything they said as long as they kept their voices down.

"Caroline, what—"

"I have a question."

William went silent with his mouth gaped open. The coldness in her tone made his stomach roll over. "Of course."

"If we had married," she began, and William's heart plummeted into his churning gut. If they *had* married? Did she no longer see it as a likely occurrence? Or even an optional one?

"What sort of life did you see us having?"

Hadn't they talked about that repeatedly over the past few weeks? They were both older with grown children. Yes, hers weren't married yet, but that was a simple matter. Wasn't she ready to be free of having to be constantly moving and aware of the nuances of everything she said and did? "A rather quiet one, I suppose."

"In the country?" She leaned in, sounding almost accusatory as she described his ideal future. "Just you and me? Away from all the hustle and bustle of the city? That was what you told your cronies, isn't it? That you couldn't wait to be able to turn down more invitations than you accepted from now on?"

Gracious, but people liked to talk. And Caroline apparently liked to listen. He did remember saying something about invitations yesterday, but he'd said something similar to Caroline. Hadn't he?

Besides, what was she angry about? That he'd confirmed to people he had affection for her? Wasn't that what all women wanted? His daughters always seemed relieved when the gentleman let it be known. William cleared his throat. "I'm not certain what part of that you want me to address."

"Shall I simply toss Miranda to the nearest fortune hunter to get her out of the way so we can sit about your country estate identifying birds and contemplating dead philosophers?"

William frowned. "I've never had much interest in philosophy."

"That is not the point, William."

"Right." He coughed. What was the point? Miranda, most likely. "I don't want Miranda to be unhappy, and I don't see her as an obstruction."

"So, you are prepared to continue living in London, then? To move Miranda and Georgina into your house and have the flowers pile up beside the invitations? To wade through soirées and dinners until two more futures are settled?"

A violent shudder accompanied a strong wince, and he couldn't stop either one. It wasn't the reaction she would like, but it was honest. Still, it would have been nice had he been able to express that truth differently.

He *did* want a quiet home, *did* want to be done with the courtships and the calls and the constant gadding about. But he also wanted Caroline.

Caroline's shoulders straightened until they nearly met in the back. "I see."

"Caroline." William sighed. There was nothing to say. He had no defense. The truth was he had considered more than once that Miranda might want to take up a position acting as hostess for her brother as other near spinsters had been known to do. She was going into her third season with nary a prospect in sight, after all.

Caroline's other daughter, Georgina, was already known and liked about Town. She'd likely be engaged within a month of her official debut.

William reached out to take Caroline's hand so she couldn't run away. "I do not see your daughters as a stumbling block to our life together."

"But you don't see them in it."

"Frankly, no. I don't."

She snatched her hand free. "Well. I shouldn't be surprised. You found it easy enough to push your own daughters out of the house quickly. Why should mine be any different?"

William frowned. "I would say I've pushed my girls less than any *ton* mother, including you, does."

"And yet, yours is the one with the eye of the most eligible man currently in London."

He hadn't deemed Caroline a woman capable of allowing emotion to overcome logic, but obviously he was wrong. Anything he said would not be in his favor, but the woman had already condemned him, so he might as well get in his words while he could. "Daughters aren't meant to stay home so no, I didn't imagine yours in my future. Yes, I prefer the country, but Parliament forces me into London enough that you would never lack for time to enjoy the benefits of the city."

"I will not condemn Miranda to a loveless marriage simply to suit your preferences."

William almost laughed. As if Miranda would ever lower herself to a match that she didn't want. That girl had her mother's backbone. "I believe you think too little of Miranda."

"I believe you are right."

William blinked. "I...what?"

"I have been thinking too little about her. I should be thinking of nothing *but* her until she has found the beginnings of a bright and beautiful life. That I was even considering my own future before hers was settled is preposterous, and I will not make such a mistake again."

If William didn't say something now, he would lose Caroline, but he was stunned into silence by her declaration. What could he possibly say to combat such a sentiment?

Without another word, she huffed off, taking Miranda and leaving the musicale entirely.

The chill of loss that seeped into his bones made the ice of her last glare seem almost warm.

He rejoined his daughter, managing an unconcerned smile for curious on-lookers, but for all the attention he gave the rest of the room, the musicians could have been replaced with a stampeding herd of horses and he'd never know it.

He was too busy feeling his heart fall apart.

Chapter Nine

"Mother?"

Caroline clenched her teeth at the timidity of her daughter's voice as she sidled into Caroline's private parlor the next morning. As if she needed to be coddled because one wrong word could break the fragile strings holding her together.

It was reminiscent of those days and weeks after John had died. Everyone constantly asking if she was hungry, if she'd managed to sleep, if she needed to move to one of the other houses, if she wouldn't rather hire a manager and a team of solicitors to oversee the care of the estates and the training of Griffith.

At least that concern had been understandable. She'd been married to her great love. They had a family. Their future had been set. She'd spent many nights over the next year broken and crying into her pillow. Her maid had been sworn to secrecy and tasked with seeking out every known remedy for disguising her emotionally ravaged appearance.

This was not the same.

Yes, she had taken an extra pillow to bed with her last night so she could curl into it and muffle her sobs, but she was allowed one night of heartbreak.

Now it was morning. It was time to renew her attention on what mattered and work to create the order and structure that would ensure life went as planned and didn't surprise her again.

"Have a seat, Miranda."

Her daughter stepped farther into the room and looked about. "Where?"

"In the chair, of course."

"The one with the half-eaten breakfast tray?"

Caroline frowned. She'd forgotten the tray she'd had them bring up earlier. It had gotten in her way about an hour ago, and she'd moved it to the chair instead of ringing for someone to come collect it. "Of course not. Use the other one."

"Ah, you meant the one holding the household ledgers."

Those had been in the center of the desk, and she hadn't wanted to take the time to store them in the credenza where they normally lived.

"If you're going to be obtuse about it, forget sitting and come around and see what I've got."

Caroline shuffled through the papers strewn about the desk surface and found the latest copy of what she'd been working on since she'd risen with the first hint of sun.

Miranda examined the paper as she leaned her hip against the desk. Golden eyebrows drew tight ,and green eyes far too much like John's finally looked at her in confusion. The paper crinkled accusingly as Miranda waved it at her mother. "What is this?"

"What does it look like?"

"A list of targets."

"It is a list of prospects." Caroline snatched the paper and smoothed it atop the desk. "Obviously staying in Town this winter hasn't been successful, but we've still time before the next London Season starts. We need to be strategic in how we spend it."

"Or." Miranda drew the word out for far too long as she began stacking the papers. "You could spend that time arranging your own affairs."

"You are my affair. And Georgina. Trent and Griffith, too, though they require somewhat less of my attention, of course." Caroline rescued three of the more important note pages from Miranda's cleaning efforts. "I've done you a disservice, but my priorities are now properly realigned."

"Meaning you intend expand your efforts to get me married," Miranda said flatly.

"You need not sound like I've sentenced you to the scullery like that tale about the little cinder girl."

Miranda focused on aligning the papers into a perfectly straight stack. "I remember Father, you know."

"I would imagine so since you weren't that young when he died." Georgina, on the other hand...That poor girl always received an extra dose of sympathy from Caroline. She'd been so little when John passed that everything she knew about him was likely from someone else's stories. "What has that to do with your marriage prospects?"

"I remember watching you and Father."

"Then you know marriage can be a wonderful thing." Caroline held up the papers she'd rescued. "We need to take this list and look through the invitations we've received for country house parties. We can make some logical guesses as to who might be in attendance. I've grouped them by geographical region since they are most likely to attend parties within a day or two's ride from home."

"My point"—Miranda grabbed the final papers and added them to the stack—"is that I am the product of a love match."

"Of that I am well aware." Caroline had been one half of that infamous love match, after all. She was well aware of how much happier she'd been than most of her friends. "That is why I want the same for you."

"That requires me to be in love."

"Yes."

"I'm not."

"Which is why you need to socialize more. Meet more people."

Miranda stabbed a finger at the list of names on the stack's top paper. "I've met all these people."

"Very few people fall in love at their first meeting. You must get to know someone, encounter them in different environments, see them in different ways. Love can grow, you know."

"The most I feel toward any of them is a vague friendliness."

"I felt the same about your father at first."

Miranda moved to the sofa across the room from Caroline's desk and fell into it. "Fortunately for my existence, he felt differently."

Caroline frowned, torn between following her daughter and reorganizing her notes across the desk. "What do you mean?"

"He loved you. He pursued you." Miranda waited until Caroline met her gaze. "None of those men are pursuing me. No one is rearranging their schedule to see me. No one is filling their social calendar with every event I might possibly attend. No one is dragging their daughter about as an excuse to spend time with me."

Miranda was referencing William with the subtlety of a horse race through Hyde Park, but that didn't mean Caroline had to respond. "If the man is old enough to have a daughter out in society, I don't think you need to consider him. You want a man young enough to start a family with and form a future."

With a growl of frustration, Miranda rose to pace the room.

"A lady never allows her emotions to drive her to fidgeting."

"Yes, yes, I know. She maintains an outward appearance of calm no matter her inner turmoil so that she has the opportunity to control the situation." Miranda jammed her fists onto her hips. "I do listen. I just don't always obey."

Caroline's only response was to quietly lift her eyebrow.

Miranda braced her hands on the back of the sofa and stared down her mother. In that moment she wasn't a young girl anymore, trotting into the study to show Caroline her latest watercolor. She was a woman, fully grown.

"Would you have ended your courtship with Lord Blackstone last night if I was married?"

That was not the question Caroline had been expecting, and her knees suddenly gave out, sending her slamming inelegantly into her desk chair.

She swallowed. She'd made it a point to never lie to her children, at least not completely and not blatantly, but this time she didn't want to honor that commitment. In this case, she could not give Miranda a clear affirmative answer.

Even though she still had a duty to Georgina, there was plenty of time to create a plan, to structure routines, to make adjustments. It was Miranda's unattached state and lack of interest in changing that state that concerned Caroline.

Miranda shook her head. "You would toss away your happiness simply because I've yet to find a man who fits into mine?"

"I've already had my happiness, Miranda. First with John and now with the children he gave me."

Miranda stared at Caroline until the urge to move was almost too much for Caroline to control. Then Miranda gave a stiff nod and moved toward the door. "Very well."

"What are you going to do?"

"Write a few letters to people currently in the country?" Miranda grinned over her shoulder. "That is the plan, is it not?"

Somehow Caroline couldn't quite shake the idea that her daughter's seeming acquiescence was only going to make things more difficult.

The house was silent.

Not the silence of a house at rest, waiting while everyone followed their own pursuits for the afternoon, but an empty silence. The kind that swelled during the weeks before a house's abandonment. Not even the servants had reason to bustle about in the upstairs rooms. With only William and Cressida in residence, there was only so much to clean or fuss over.

Twenty minutes ago, Cressida had departed for a ride with Lord Rickford.

Ten minutes ago, William had collapsed into a chair, the weight of his silent future pressing him into the cushions and filling his ears with air even as his lungs emptied of it.

A few months ago, he'd been looking forward to the day when Cressida would marry and peace would descend, but now...Now it wasn't peace that awaited him. Now all he could see were the places in his life Caroline could fit so well into but would never occupy.

He'd mourned his wife, spent a year turning toward where she should be, speaking to the space she'd once taken. This was different.

Countless friends and family had suggested he remarry and give his girls a new mother, as if a wife was a role to be filled like that of housekeeper or cook. Others had said he was still young enough to father children and should take the opportunity to find a wife that might give him a son and heir.

He could not be more thankful that he'd ignored every last piece of that advice, because anyone he'd married would have been little more than a companion to walk through the rest of life with.

Caroline would be a partner.

He wasn't the same person he would be had Rebecca lived, and he wouldn't waste time speculating how he would be different if he'd made one of a thousand other possible decisions along the way. Who he was now couldn't imagine growing old with anyone other than Caroline.

He couldn't imagine doing much of anything without Caroline.

It had been three days since the musicale. Three days of examining every moment of their unusual courtship. Three days of picking over every part of that conversation.

Three days of realizing just how much he'd gotten wrong and everything that could have been right.

Nowhere in that last discussion had she said she didn't love him, didn't care for him, didn't want a life with him. She'd said she couldn't abandon Miranda.

And she should never have felt like he expected her to.

William jerked the bell cord as he left the room. The servants would be able to follow the heavy tread of his determined steps and find him as he made his way to the front hall.

Moments later, he was shrugging into his coat and walking toward Grosvenor Square.

She wanted to move Miranda and Georgina into his home? He'd have the maids air the rooms tonight. She wanted to throw a few balls and have a drawing room reeking of cut flowers and rose water? He'd buy the first bouquet himself. She wanted him to escort them about town and watch over them like he'd done his own? He would order a fresh set of evening clothes.

Would he despise every moment? Probably not, but a great deal of them would be nothing short of torture. What was two or three years of occasional agony compared to a lifetime of constant pain, though? He could do everything she'd asked for because he loved her. Love for his daughters had gotten him through the process three times. Love for Caroline could get him through two more.

Except she wouldn't see him.

Only the butler of a duke could get away with closing the door in an earl's face, but there William stood, nose inches away from the heavy wood panel keeping him from Caroline's domain.

His walk home was slow, and with each step, he pondered his options. Some he tossed aside, others he held until he'd built a sturdy base of resolved intentions. With two unwed daughters, she'd be spending a lot of time in London. So would William. He had friends and contacts that could get him into any social gathering she attended, and eventually her daughters would either marry or take up the life of a spinster.

Either way, William could wait it out. She was worth it.

Cressida was in the drawing room when he returned home. He'd entirely forgotten her in his rush to see to Caroline. Heat and shame flooded him. Was this what Caroline felt? This was but a moment of distraction, and William was nearly weak in the knees from the weight of the guilt over what could have happened to Cressida's reputation. Yes, everything was all but official, but she was still at this moment unwed.

How much worse would it be for Caroline to feel this way?

"Is something wrong?" Cressida asked as she rushed to meet him in the hall.

William shook his head. "I tried to see Caroline."

Her features immediately slid from concern to sympathy. "It didn't go well?"

"No. She won't even see me. All those weeks of encountering her everywhere on accident, and now I can't even see her on purpose."

Cressida bit her lip. "It wasn't entirely accidental."

William had suspected as much, but since he'd never determined how Cressida could manage such a feat, he'd decided he must be wrong. "Can you make it happen again?"

"If I did," she said slowly, "what would you do?"

What would he do? Tell her he loved her? Tell her he was wrong? Tell her he would wait? All of those things? "I would make this right."

She studied him a long while before giving a sharp nod. "Then I suppose I need to send a message to Miranda."

William shook his head as she retreated to the drawing room. He should have suspected who Cressida's partner in manipulation had been. If this worked, it would mean Miranda still thought he was a good match for her mother.

Maybe it wasn't quite time to give up hope.

Chapter Ten

A lady should strive never to be so early that the later guests might mistake her for the gathering's hostess, but if Miranda did not come down soon, they were in great danger of arriving so late as to not be greeted by their hostess at all.

Part of Caroline—a significant part, if she were honest—wanted to grab the excuse and stay in for the night, but she could not. Just because she'd all but given up on the idea of Miranda finding a match this winter didn't mean they could stay away from society altogether. Too many people knew of the tense conversation at the musicale a week ago, and she needed talk of her and William to become nothing more than an uninteresting piece of minutiae to be mentioned in passing from time to time.

If he was in attendance, and given that it was a ball that was rather likely, she would smile and be friendly, wish him and Cressida well, and move on through the evening. The gossips would get nothing from her.

Now all she needed was for Miranda to cooperate with the concept and come downstairs.

"Shouldn't we have left by now?" asked a young man with a wide smile and a flop of elegantly messy blond hair.

Her younger son, Trent, had arrived at the town house late the previous evening. He was always a welcome surprise but this time a confusing one as well. When Miranda had mentioned the ball, he had immediately declared an intention to act as escort, something he normally avoided as often as possible.

Caroline frowned up the stairs. "Your sister has not yet come down."

"We should leave without her, then."

She gave the charming scamp a wry glance. "You remember the reason we remained in London, do you not?"

"To marry one of the unattached women of my family off into beloved wedded bliss, yes, yes, I know."

She did not have time for her son's antics this evening. "I'm going up to see what is keeping your sister."

"Wouldn't leaving her teach a better lesson?" He leaned on the newel post and gave Caroline a mischievous grin. "We wouldn't want to be rudely late after all."

"She's not going to just stumble out of her room and attract a beau. She needs to leave the house to accomplish that."

"One evening at home won't hurt her." Trent shrugged. "You could spend the time catching up with friends, socializing freely without having to watch over anyone else."

Caroline narrowed her gaze at her son's innocent expression. Was it too innocent? Even as a mother, she couldn't always tell with Trent. She liked to pretend he couldn't fool her, but the truth was half the time she was guessing and counting on intuition and the Lord's guidance to help her get it right.

This time she said nothing. If Trent knew about William, she didn't want to hear his opinion. If he didn't know anything, that last thing she wanted to do was explain it to him. She didn't want to think or talk about William.

Even if her decision to walk away from him had hurt her in ways she hadn't thought possible anymore. It was a mother's job to sacrifice for her family, and she was a mother before she was a woman now.

"I'm going to hurry her along," Caroline said as she all but stomped up the stairs.

She was already lifting the latch on Miranda's door as she gave a sharp knock. The door opened, but instead of finding Miranda at the dressing table fussing over a particular curl, she found her wrapped in a dressing gown and curled into a chair by the fire. Her hair was smoothed into a long braid and a book lay open in her lap. A cup of tea and a plate of food sat on the table beside her.

Caroline rushed across the room. The younger woman had been the picture of health this afternoon, but stomach ailments and fevers could come on quite suddenly. "Are you unwell?"

Miranda smiled up at Caroline, eyes bright and cheeks a healthy pink. "Oh, don't you look lovely."

"Thank you," Caroline said reflexively, then frowned at her daughter. "Why aren't you ready?"

"I'm staying in. Trent can escort you."

As if this were Caroline's social season and not Miranda's. "If you need a rest, we can of course plan one into the schedule, but we stayed in just last night. It is important that we present a united front to any rumors at tonight's ball."

"Or," Miranda said, dragging the word out in that uncouth way she'd developed of late. They really must have a talk about this new habit. "You could give them something to truly talk about."

"I beg your pardon?"

Miranda's face scrunched up. "I'd rather you beg Lord Blackstone's pardon. He is the one who needs to forgive you, after all."

"Forgive me?" Caroline hated the way her voice nearly screeched the question, but there was no containing her outrage. "I do not need to ask that man to forgive me for taking care of my family."

"Of course not." Miranda turned the page in her book. "You should probably ask him to forgive you for being pigheaded about it, though."

"Miranda Hawthorne, did you just call your mother pigheaded?"

"No one ever said there was anything wrong with your hearing."

Caroline snapped her mouth shut, afraid anything she said would come out a sputter.

"You should be leaving," Miranda said. "Soon you will be far later than a lady should reasonably be."

"Miranda, a lady never changes her plans without informing her intended companions for the evening. It is rude for you to make this decision without consulting me." Caroline didn't know what to say about William, so she would ignore her daughter's statements on the subject. That was how a lady got out of an unwanted discussion, after all. Instead, she would focus on Miranda.

"I will take that under advisement." Miranda turned another page.

Was she actually reading a book while they had this discussion, or was she using it as a prop to demonstrate her disinterest? When Caroline had taught her such a tactic, she had not meant to have it used against herself.

"Miranda, you cannot throw away this opportunity. We cannot stay London every winter, you know. It would begin to look desperate."

Miranda looked up from the open book and regarded Caroline. "Are you implying that I am currently tossing away my chances of finding a suitable man to care about me and create a family with me and see me into my doting years with comfort and companionship?"

There was a trick happening here. Caroline knew it. But despite the question being something of a trap, she couldn't not answer it. Nor could she answer in any way but the affirmative because Miranda would take any permission Caroline gave her to shirk society and become a hopeless spinster. With a sigh, Caroline said, "Yes, I am."

"Good," Miranda said with a grin, shocking Caroline down to her toes.

"Good?"

"Yes." Miranda lowered her eyes back to her book. "I do aspire to be a lady, Mother, and as everything you do is the epitome of ladylike behavior, I can only assume such self-destruction is an esteemed quality."

Oh, no, she was not twisting this around. "The situations are not the same. You need me, Miranda."

"Of course I do. I should think I will always need you. Just as I need Griffith and Trent and even Georgina, though please, for the love of all our sanity, don't tell her I said that." Miranda closed the book and set it aside. "That is what family, or at least our family, is about. We are an entwined mess of love and annoyance, and I wouldn't have it any other way. I do intend to marry, despite what you think, but I am not willing to settle for anything less than a man who loves and annoys me more than my family. He's out there somewhere, and I will find him. One day all of us will. But, Mother, you are far too young to while away your days in the dower house. You've given us so much of yourself, but we're grown. Even Georgina is practically an adult."

Caroline swallowed. "I don't think I'll tell her you said that, either."

"Wise woman that you are. No wonder I admire you so. Which is why I will not sit by and let you make a mistake like this." She grinned, looking as mischievous as her brother. "Instead I shall sit by while you go and make it right."

"Trent is not here because of a frivolous urge to get a new pair of boots and meet with friends, is he?"

"You did tell me to write to people in the country."

Just because her children were conspiring against her did not make them correct. Caroline had lived her life already, had her love, created her family. It had been cut short, yes, and that was the price one paid sometimes.

She had to attend tonight's gathering without Miranda, but that had no bearing on her decision about William. It would be the first step in showing her family how pleasant her life would be after they married. "Very well. I shall leave you to your book."

Miranda gave a small wave. "Tell Lord Blackstone I said hello."

Trent was waiting by the door in his hat and coat when Caroline returned to the front hall. She glared at him as she pulled her cloak on, as they descended the steps, and as the carriage rolled away from the house.

"Is this ability to walk and glare something you are teaching Miranda, or does it simply come with age?"

"I don't know what inspired this coercion, but it will come back to haunt you."

Trent shrugged. "I've nothing but respect for Lord Blackstone, but I do believe I am past the need of having a new father figure." He tilted his head with a smile. "Older brother does well enough on that front."

"Griffith is a wonderful duke and leader of this family. You should be proud of him."

"Oh, I am," Trent said. "I'm also proud of the mother who made him that way." He leaned forward and placed his elbows on his knees. "And that mother should be able to claim a life of her own."

Caroline shook her head. "I can't have people speculating about Miranda because I remarry."

"So it's about being better than others?"

Caroline frowned. "What?"

"This decision is about appearing to be better than others." He shrugged. "You want us to appear a perfect family even though one evening in the drawing room at Riverton would prove that a lie?"

"When did you and Miranda decide to twist everything I've taught you into some derisive idea?"

"When it suited our purposes, of course." Trent reached forward and grabbed his mother's hand. "Mother, we know you only want us to be better. Better than we were the day before, better than what is merely socially acceptable, better than we could be if we didn't actually try."

A suspicious burn crept along Caroline's eyes. She wouldn't cry, but what mother couldn't help but be moved to hear this was what she'd instilled in her children?

"And now it's your turn."

"To be better? I'm trying."

He shook his head. "Not to be better than everyone else, but to be better than what you could be if you took the easy road."

"I am hardly taking the easy road." No, this path was painful and sad.

"I think you and Lord Blackstone could be better together than either of you are on your own."

"And if I disagree?"

He shrugged. "Then you make your own choice regardless. You taught us that, too."

Caroline fell silent. She could hardly keep glaring at him after the things he'd said. Her family was well intentioned but misguided. When she got home tonight, she would sit her two middle children down and inform them how their assumptions were erroneous.

But first she had to prove it to herself.

Chapter Eleven

Why had he come tonight? Why had he even stayed in London? As of yesterday, Cressida was officially, happily engaged. Contracts had been signed, but the two had elected to wait and have the banns read and the ceremony performed near the beginning of the Season.

That didn't mean preparations were waiting, though. In fact, this morning Cressida had bundled into a carriage to travel to her sister's country house to begin planning.

The only thing keeping William in London was his new resolve to be the man Caroline needed him to be. Cressida had assured him all the arrangements had been made for him to gain an audience tonight, but she didn't know how determined Caroline could be when she had made up her mind about something.

He wandered through the ballroom. What should he do until Caroline made an appearance? He didn't want to dance with anyone else, which meant he needed to be careful where he stood. There weren't so many people in the ballroom that he could easily hide. Fortunately that meant neither could Caroline.

Pausing near a pillar, he let his gaze roam the room. There were other widows in society, other women who would make decent companions and care for him and his home. Women whose children were all settled or at least out on their own. Women who had little to do with their grown offspring and would therefore bring no complications with them.

He couldn't imagine even walking through the park with a single one of them.

He didn't want *a* woman. He wanted *the* woman. He would rather hire out his spare rooms to younger sons in order to bring the life he was suddenly craving into his house than have any woman other than Caroline at his side.

The moment she entered the ballroom, he knew. The hairs on his arms danced as the very air he breathed seemed to change. His gaze went straight to her, as if an invisible string pulled every part of him in her direction.

Her deep, rich blue gown set off her blond hair and fair skin. From this distance, he could hardly see the blue of her eyes, but he could imagine how the gown would encourage them to shine. Her daughter was not with her. Instead, she entered the room on the arm of her younger son.

William blinked.

Lord Trent was in town? And Caroline had willingly left Miranda at home?

Her son's gaze moved about the room much as William's had done earlier, quickly passing over people. He was obviously searching for something—or someone—in particular. As soon as his gaze landed on William, it stopped. The blond head tilted, and his eyebrows rose in obvious question. What was the question, though? Was he telling William that protection had arrived?

Or was he asking if William wanted another chance?

Was it possible Caroline's children wanted to help him win her over?

William's heart pounded at the idea of expanding his family to include such strong men and women. It was obvious to him now that he'd craved a quiet country life because there, he could become complacent and numb while calling it peace.

Simply looking at Caroline sent an electric pulse through him, and he no longer wanted to find a way to be numb. He didn't want complacent, didn't want to simply wait for God or his children to call his name. He wanted to live. He had years left in him, and he wanted them to be as richly full of purpose as the lives he'd wanted for his daughters.

When his wife had died, he'd done what he had to do because life had handed him less than ideal conditions. Why couldn't the same determination apply to a fabulous condition? He loved Caroline. He believed she loved him. If he could convince her to marry him, then he could do whatever he had to in order to make the best of that turn of events.

And this time it wouldn't be a hardship, because the emotion pushing the need forward would be joy instead of grief. There was nothing that came with Caroline that was worse than living without Caroline.

He crossed the room and with a deep bow offered Caroline his hand. "Might I have the next dance?"

Caroline's spine stiffened. "I'm afraid this one is promised to my son."

Lord Trent gave a comically dramatic wince, stuck his leg out and gave his ankle a spin. "I'm afraid I can't, Mother. Twinged my ankle."

One pale eyebrow rose in her son's direction.

He gave a loud groan and shook his leg in the air.

One side of Caroline's lips tilted up. "And when, pray tell, did you injure yourself?"

He grinned. "Just now."

"I did not see you stumble."

Lord Trent bent one knee and let his head loll to the side before taking two quick steps from his mother's side. He straightened, continuing to grin. "There you are. Visual proof."

"A gentleman does not lie to his mother."

"But he does try ever so hard to make her happy." Trent turned to William, who was struggling not to laugh at the display before him. "My mother unhappily accepts your invitation. With my temporary blessing."

William nodded, understanding that for the moment, he had the support of her children, but that could be rescinded if he wasted this opportunity. "I shall keep her on the dance floor until she smiles."

With Caroline's hand tucked in his elbow, William turned toward the dance floor. Lord Trent strode off, no sign of a limp in his spry, energetic step.

Fortunately the dances were in sets tonight, and unless Caroline wanted to make a scene, he had her attention for at least the next two dances. Walking off the floor would be talked about for weeks. Before, her social concerns had worked against him. Now he would use them to his advantage.

There weren't many moments for conversation as they moved through the first dance, but William tried. Every attempt he made to discuss his new understandings was met by a clever turn to some inane topic such as the weather, the dresses, or the possibility that the lemonade was actually palatable tonight.

When the music started for the second dance of the set, there were a few moments of chaos on the floor as couples scrambled to adjust. Instead of the expected cotillion, waltz music was drifting through the air.

Caroline pressed her mouth into a disapproving frown. William followed her gaze to find Lord Trent standing beside the musicians, grinning. William smiled as well while he pulled Caroline into his arms.

They were right back where they'd started, but this time William wouldn't miss a chance to speak. "I've missed you."

She fixed her gaze on his shoulder. "You saw me two days ago."

So he had. He'd received a polite smile from across the room and nothing more. "I didn't say I missed your physical presence." He pulled her a little closer. "I said I missed you."

She sighed, "William."

"I heard you, I did. Now I need you to hear me. I don't care."

She frowned. "I beg your pardon."

"Whatever happens after we get married. I don't care. Move your daughters in. Move Trent in. For that matter, we can make up a room for the duke. I can purchase a house in Kent or take up residence at Riverton. We'll host balls and have three at-home days a week and purchase every vase from here to Cornwall to hold all the flowers from gentleman callers. I don't care."

Caroline's eyes widened. "What are you saying?"

"I'm saying that you and I both know how to make things work when we encounter an unexpected bad turn. Why can't we make things work for an unexpected good turn? I wasn't looking for you, Caroline, wasn't on the hunt for a wife, but suddenly you were there. Right where you'd always been, perhaps, but suddenly I could see you. Now I can't see anything else. I love you. We can make this work."

She blinked up at him.

William rushed on, "If you don't believe me yet, then I'll wait. Just don't shut me out. I'll court you until Lady Georgina signs the church registry if that's what it takes, but I don't want to be without you."

She stumbled and he pulled her closer, all but carrying her through the last steps of the dance. As the music came to a stop, she still hadn't said anything, had done little more than stare at him with wide eyes.

When the couples around them turned to leave the floor, Caroline made to follow, but William kept her hand in his. He guided her into place for the next dance.

Pink rushed up her neck and covered her cheeks. "William, we can't. The set is over. People will talk."

"I promised your son not to let you leave this dance floor until you smiled. I'm prepared to stay out here all night until you either believe me when I say I love you and we can make this work, or you tell me you don't love me in return."

The lines of dancers stretched out beside them. They joined the pattern, moving down the line until they were at the end. William nodded at the couple beside them, and the younger people smirked in acknowledgment before making their way back up the line, essentially leaving William and Caroline standing alone at the end of the dance floor.

Her voice was little more than a whisper and he had to lean in to hear it. "Why do you think we can do this?"

"Because we've both done what we had to before, taken on roles we weren't prepared for, hadn't contemplated, and didn't want. We've proved ourselves capable alone. How much more could we be together?"

William raised his gaze to where Lord Trent leaned against the wall, making no attempt to hide the fact that he was watching everything.

It was time to make good on his promise. William reached out and cupped Caroline's cheek. "We could do this even if it was only you and me against the world, but I think our families have been beside us without our even knowing it."

"People will talk," she said, though with far less conviction that she'd ever said it before. One side of her lips twitched as if she was giving a smile some consideration.

"There are worse things in life than for people to talk about how much we love each other."

The twitch turned into a lopsided tilt.

William pressed on. "There are worse things than having our children see two people who haven't let death rob them of their ability to love."

The other side pressed in and started to curve.

William's smile grew. "We don't have to marry tomorrow. I meant it when I said I would wait. As long as I know you are ready to walk with me, we can go at whatever pace you wish."

A smile bloomed across her face, wide and happy, even as a tear escaped her eye and trailed down her cheek.

It was completely ridiculous for William to keep them out on the dance floor until she agreed to this, but she had to admit it was also adorable. This man, whose daughter was not yet married despite her firmly attached situation, was willing to thwart social opinion to win her heart.

To even gain a chance at winning her heart.

Caroline blinked at him through the glaze of unshed tears gathered in her eyes. She loved him. How had she not seen it? Just because it was so different from what she'd felt for John?

Of course love would be different when found later in life. She would hardly be drawn to the wild burn that had appealed to her as a clueless young lady fresh from the schoolroom. Instead, with William, she found the glow of being her own person again. He needed nothing – wanted nothing – from her other than, well, her.

As she searched his smiling, relieved face, a sensation of comfort like that of a thick blanket on a winter's night wrapped around her. "I agree."

He tilted his head and considered her. "What exactly are you agreeing to?"

Caroline took a deep breath and committed herself. "A courtship. A public one. With the intent of marriage, of course. I won't be strung along."

"My dear, I would visit the archbishop for a special license in the morning if that was your wish. The only one delaying our union is you, and if I haven't made it clear yet, I'm happy to wait."

A flush worked up Caroline's cheeks. Before she went to bed tonight, she would be thanking God for all His blessings. The love and life she'd had with John had been so special, so unique. She didn't deserve such blessing twice in her life when so many women never even experienced it once.

"We've a lot to consider and much to discuss," Caroline said.

"That we do."

She glanced around. Half the dancers were stumbling as they tried to keep moving and watch what was happening at the same time. "Might we do that somewhere other than the dance floor?"

William's grin turned boyish. "You would leave the dance floor in the middle of the set? What will people say?"

"Far less than they will if I have to box your ears while we're standing here."

He was laughing as he escorted her to her son's side.

Trent and Miranda had made their positions obvious tonight. Didn't they realize how this would impact them? The idea that her beloved children were as ready to sacrifice for her as she was for them brought tears to her eyes. She'd always considered self-sacrifice a quality of motherhood, but perhaps it was more an aspect of family.

Trent accepted his mother's arm from William. "All sorted?"

Caroline laughed. "Hardly."

William sighed.

"But I do believe we're well on our way." Caroline nodded at Trent. "I've other children to discuss this matter with, after all."

Trent scoffed. "As if the messengers haven't been wearing down the road between London and Kent for the past month."

Caroline frowned. "You've been discussing me?"

"Of course." Trent shrugged. "It's not as if Miranda had anything else interesting to write in her letters."

"Well." Caroline swallowed. A lady did not reveal significant emotions in public, if ever, but she'd been throwing that rule to the wind so far tonight.

Trent squeezed her hand. "Even Georgina isn't selfish enough to want you to give up this opportunity."

Caroline frowned. "Georgina is becoming a lovely young lady."

"Yes, yes, she's an absolute angel. The point is, we all talked about it already. Griffith and Georgina will be arriving in two days. The lovely young lady required an extra day to pack and refused to rush the travel."

"A lady never forgets that her appearance is the foundation for a good reputation."

"That's all well and good, but—"

"And a gentleman," Caroline continued with force, "does not begrudge her the time required to maintain that foundation."

"Yes, mother."

Caroline nodded.

William lifted her free hand and placed a kiss upon her knuckles. "I shall call upon you tomorrow, then. And perhaps plan to have your family over for dinner a few days after?"

Trent leaned in and gave the loudest conspiratorial whisper known to man. "Griffith is friendly with the archbishop."

Caroline gracefully stomped on his toe.

"What? We were discussing family. It seemed an interesting fact to drop into the conversation."

When had her little boy grown into a man? One who managed life and responsibilities and cared for those around him? Somewhere along the way, Caroline had to admit she'd taken in his easy laughter and jovial attitude and mentally forgotten he was no longer the young lad she'd taken to Eton all those years ago.

Time had moved on. She smiled up at William. It was time she did the same.

Epilogue

Eleven Months Later

"Are you certain you don't want me to come with you?"

Caroline looked up from her partially packed trunks to where her husband of nine months was standing in the door. A pair of spectacles rested upon his nose, and a novel was tucked under his arm. He was dressed in shirtsleeves and trousers, looking head to toe like a country gentleman of ease.

"I'm certain. Besides, you've put off this meeting with the solicitor twice already." She crossed the room and wrapped her arms around him. It still seemed strange at times, having a man she could touch and be touched by again, but there was such quiet comfort in the strength of their union that any strange feelings were but momentary considerations in her mind.

She placed a quick kiss on his lips before returning to her packing. "How is your book?"

He settled onto a sofa near her window, telling her about the book he'd been reading and the fish he'd caught that morning before he'd met with his estate manager. All the while, she moved about the room, instructing the maids on what to pack in between making her own observations or asking questions.

Soon the trunks were closed and ready to be loaded into the carriage the next morning and the servants had departed, and Caroline settled onto the sofa beside her husband, who lifted an arm so she could snuggle into his side.

"What will you do while I'm away?" she asked.

"Besides miss you?"

She scoffed out a laugh. "You are craving the silence and you know it."

He shrugged one shoulder. "I'll still miss you."

It had taken Caroline a month to agree to marry William.

A month in which their families had dined together frequently and Caroline's children had demonstrated how well they could do on their own with only minimal input from her. It was both comforting and disconcerting to know that her family had grown so self-sufficient. She was still concerned for Georgina, but in many ways the young girl had always been more mature than her years.

Every week, as the banns had been read, Caroline had watched her youngest for any sign of strife. There was none. And when Caroline and William had wed, Georgina's smile had been as wide as anyone else's.

The true test had, of course, come with the Season. The last thing Caroline had expected was for Griffith to be the one who laid down the plan for managing Miranda's social movements. Caroline and William had lived—alone—in his house while all four of her children occupied Hawthorne House.

Whenever Miranda was receiving visitors or going out, Caroline would travel from her house to join her daughter. Sometimes William came as well, but often he stayed home.

"I shall miss you as well," Caroline said, "But Georgina needs me. I can't send her off to her first adult gathering on her own."

"'Tis wise to have her attend a few assemblies in the country before her London season."

"Yes." Caroline sighed. "It has been quite the year, hasn't it?"

Near the end of the Season, there'd been a scandal that overshadowed anything Caroline and William could have possibly caused, and the family had come through it stronger than ever. Perhaps Trent was right, and it really was just about being better than they'd been before. After three full seasons, Miranda still wasn't married, and Caroline was starting to realize that maybe that wasn't as horrible as she'd once presumed.

There was something to be said for living as an independent woman. Caroline hadn't known until they started making serious plans that part of her trepidation was a fear of losing that independence. Yet here she was, traveling on her own to care for her children and then coming back to the arms of her husband.

She couldn't have asked for life to take a better turn.

Caroline laid her head on William's shoulder, determined to take in every moment of this evening before she went away. As the sun set and the house settled, a quiet peace wrapped around her heart, and she sighed.

"Hmmm?" William set aside his book. "What's wrong?"

She looked at him and smiled before giving him a quick kiss and settling her head back on his shoulder. "Not a single thing," she said happily. She just might venture to say that everything was perfect.

A LADY OF ESTEEM

A Hawthorne House Novella

Originally published by Bethany House Publishers. EBook available from Bethany House Publishers.

Bethany House Publishers is a division of Baker Publishing Group, Grand Rapids, Michigan.

Prologue

Suffolk, England, 1803

Amelia Stalwood winced as the tower of fabric-wrapped wooden blocks crashed to the floor. She looked to the housekeeper, tears welling in her young eyes. "I'm sorry, Mrs. Bummel."

"Don't worry, love." The woman put her quill on the desk before leaning over to kiss Amelia's head. "That's why I put the rug in here."

"Amelia!"

The man's voice echoed up the stairs into the room Amelia and the housekeeper had turned into a combination office and playroom.

When Amelia had come to live with Lord Stanford a year ago on the very distant connection that Amelia's grandmother's sister's niece had been married to the viscount's deceased brother, he'd turned her over to the housekeeper and had very little to do with her since. He passed all his requests for her to be quieter through the butler.

That he actually wanted to speak to her was somewhat thrilling.

Amelia jumped up with a grin and ran to the stairs as fast as her spindly eleven-year-old legs could go. He was at the bottom of the stairs, looking confused as he turned circles in the hall, unsure of where she would appear.

She scampered down the stairs, with Mrs. Bummel following at a more sedate pace.

"Yes, my lord?" Amelia struggled to keep the breathlessness from her voice. The viscount looked the same as when she had met him a year ago, with a too-large coat, unkempt hair, and large spectacles taking up half of his face.

"Ah, Amelia, yes. Good news! I've hired you a governess."

"A governess?" Mrs. Bummel placed a hand on Amelia's shoulder. "I must say it's about time, my lord."

"Indeed, indeed. She's taking care of packing and whatnot. Should be in London by the time you get there. How long will you need to pack? Two days?" Lord Stanford's eyes glazed over as he stared into the distance. "I wonder how long it takes to get to London. Haven't been myself since I was a boy. Where's my map?"

He started to turn toward his study until Mrs. Bummel cleared her throat. "London, my lord?"

Amelia shrank into Mrs. Bummel's skirts, while the housekeeper's arm tightened around her small shoulders.

"Yes, yes, London. Perfect place for a child—don't you think? I've got an empty house in town, you know. Lots of noise, and people, and noise. Nothing like here. It's nearly barbaric to keep the girl here." His face screwed up in thought again. For the first time his unkempt appearance frightened rather than amused. "What did barbarians do with their children? I mean, they were barbarians. Do I have a book on barbarians?"

He wandered off muttering about what kind of person would be able to write a book about barbarians.

This time, Mrs. Bummel let him go, even as she pulled Amelia closer, whispering a prayer into the little girl's hair.

Amelia wrapped Mrs. Bummel's apron strings around her fingers, mourning the plans they'd made to walk through the woods this weekend in search of wild berries. As Mrs. Bummel's rough woolen skirts scraped the tears from Amelia's cheeks, she vowed to never make plans again.

Chapter One

London, England, 1812

The Lord had picked a horrible time to remind Miss Amelia Stalwood that she should have been a bit more grateful that everyone overlooked her very existence. She would have given anything for a bit of that invisibility now. But no, she had this man's complete and total attention.

Tumbling off a rolling library ladder into a man's arms was a difficult thing to ignore, after all.

Amelia tilted her head back, easing open one eye to look at her rescuer. His face looked strange upside down. The lips were the wrong shape. And entirely too close.

Her other eye snapped open as she met his curious gaze. She'd never seen eyes so blue, didn't even know the shade existed.

"Oh my." Had she spoken the words or had her lips simply shaped a puff of air?

A single dark brown eyebrow lifted along with the right corner of his lips. "Oh my, indeed."

Her face pressed against a hard shoulder covered in dark green wool, limiting her view beyond the snow white cravat. High cheekbones set off the brilliant blue eyes and impeccable hair.

"Thank you for your assistance." She looked up at the dark paneled ceiling. "I believe you can put me down now."

"Actually, I can't."

Amelia's gaze darted back to his face, then followed to where his eyes were pointing. Her feet and skirts were tangled in the rungs of the library ladder, exposing her boots and ankles—proof that impulsiveness led to folly.

She couldn't even do someone a good turn without it ending in catastrophe. Visiting her friend Emma had seemed like such a good idea this morning. So did volunteering to help the ill maid with her chores, despite the fact that Amelia didn't know the first thing about being a servant.

"Not that I mind," the man continued.

She grasped the edge of the ladder and, with the man's assistance, heaved herself back into a standing position. After regaining her footing and straightening her skirt, she braved another look at her unexpected companion.

He was tall. She could have run her fingers through his thick waves of chestnut brown hair without having to stretch. Not that she would. But she could think about it.

The dark coat topped a pair of tan breeches and well-used but expensive riding boots. A patch of white on his shoulder drew her attention. Was that her cleaning rag? Horror filled her as she saw the small streaks of grey on his shoulder made from the dust she'd been clearing from the massive amount of bookshelves.

"May I assist you down?"

"No, I rather think I can manage. Thank you." Given the flock of magpies making a home in her midsection, the words came out surprisingly steady.

She descended the ladder, plucking the cleaning cloth from his shoulder as she went. A puff of dust drifted into the air.

Her backward momentum continued until she'd crossed the room and put her back to the bookcase she'd recently been cleaning. That put two tufted leather chairs and a tea table between her and the man.

And the man between her and the door. Not the smartest maneuvering she could have done.

He exuded casual confidence, with one shoulder leaned against the bookshelf and one booted foot propped on the bottom rung of the now vacant ladder.

How had he gotten in? A swarm of servants covered the house, preparing for the owner to return in three days, ending his two-year hiatus from London. A man would have to be very skilled to avoid them all.

Or know the house very well.

Panic unfurled in her toes and worked its way to her throat as the man's identity became obvious.

She was in a room alone with the notorious Raebourne Rake. Reputations had been ruined for less. Amelia needed her reputation, or rather her utter lack of one. Her lack of scandal was the only asset she could truly claim if she found herself searching for work after her next birthday.

She wove the dust rag through her fingers, twisting until the rough fabric cut into her skin. "Lord Raebourne, I presume."

He inclined his head in a mock bow. "You seem to have the advantage."

Good manners opened her mouth to answer his unspoken question. Good sense snapped her teeth shut. He did not need to know who she was.

Pushing away from the bookcase, he ran a finger along one still dusty edge. "Thank you for cleaning my bookcase. I apologize for interrupting your endeavors."

"If you require this room, I can finish the job at a more convenient time." The lie burned her throat, but what else could she do? Besides it was only a partial lie. Someone would return to finish the room. Someone actually employed here.

"Can you? How interesting." He paced forward to lean on one of the tufted leather chairs. "When do you intend to do that?"

Never. "At your convenience, my lord. It is your house after all."

He nodded. "And you spend a great deal of time in it?"

"I'm usually in the kitchens, my lord." Amelia restrained a wince at yet another partial lie. Despite her many visits to the house, this was the first time she'd ever ventured farther in than the kitchen. She doubted he'd be interested that the reason she'd done so this time was because her friend Emma was sick. The man's housekeeper was a dreadful viper who threatened to fire Emma for neglecting her chores, unconcerned about the maid's inability to move five feet from the chamber pot.

"I'm curious," he said, once more inspecting the bookcases. "I know I've been away a while, but I don't recall the servants of this house dressing in well-crafted muslin gowns before."

Amelia's free hand clutched at the front of her gown, crushing the fine muslin between her fingers. It was simply cut and the drabbest of browns, but he was correct about the craftsmanship.

"You are known as a rather generous employer." Amelia pinched herself. He was known as a cad. A cad who'd left town two years prior to avoid a duel with a young lady's angry brother.

His eyebrows lifted even as his mouth turned down. For a moment the look of playful curiosity succumbed to a dark cloud of resignation. "I think we both know my reputation points in another direction."

Amelia blinked, and the sophisticated man of rumor returned, wielding his social power as casually as a riding crop. His face relaxed until it was poised on the edge of a smug grin. "Why don't we start with you telling me who you are, since I don't believe for a moment that you work for me."

Why, oh why, did the first nobleman she'd encountered in a decade have to be the devastatingly good-looking and debonair Marquis of Raebourne? Life would have been ever so much easier if she could have started with a nice baronet.

A homely viscount would have worked as well. Preferably one who was easily distracted, like her absent-minded guardian. He walked around his Sussex estate with unkempt hair, a too-large coat, and three pairs of spectacles tucked in various places on his person because he kept forgetting where he put them. It all testified to the somewhat endearing absent-mindedness and total harmlessness of her guardian.

The marquis did not strike her as absent-minded and he certainly wasn't harmless.

He rounded the furniture and advanced toward her. "I believe, under the circumstances, we can introduce ourselves. As you have surmised I am Anthony Pendleton, Marquis of Raebourne."

He bowed and looked at her expectantly. "And you are . . . ?"

"Not supposed to be here." The words spilled from Amelia's mouth before she could catch them.

The dark eyebrows climbed toward his hairline. His lips twitched as if they wanted to curve but he wouldn't let them. "Do tell."

She had to tell him something, and it had to be true. As a liar, she was abysmal. Most days she was happy to claim such a failure. "I don't work for you. Not really. I was . . . visiting. And Mrs. Banks required that this room be cleaned today."

Dear Lord, please don't let Mrs. Banks find out I've done any of Emma's cleaning. If the housekeeper found out . . . "Please don't tell her I was here."

His eyes locked with hers. His steady gaze became too much, and she looked down, stunned to discover she'd moved forward during her plea. "I won't."

Amelia's shoulders slumped in relief. As long as Mrs. Banks never knew Amelia had been here, Emma's job should be safe.

"I can't," the marquis continued. "You haven't told me who you are."

She intended to keep it that way. "God, help me," she whispered.

Hurried footsteps sounded down the hall, breaking Amelia's trance. Both she and the marquis turned toward the door. *No, not like that!* She couldn't gain her escape at someone else's expense.

Amelia ran along the edge of the room, her shoulder grazing the bookcase.

She collided with the tall, breathless maid running into the room.

Jane grabbed Amelia by the shoulders to keep both of them from falling. "Cook told me about Emma! She'll be in the suds if Mrs. Banks finds out you've gone past the kitchens to do her cleaning."

All efforts to shove the woman out the door failed. The maid was lost in her emotional rant. "You shouldn't be working. You're Quality, Miss Amelia!"

Amelia darted a look at the marquis, who wasn't missing a moment of the exchange. Jane turned as well. Her mouth dropped open.

Shivers skittered up Amelia's back and her stomach, twisted like Cook's kneaded bread dough. What if the marquis blamed Jane for Amelia's trespass?

She had to get Jane out of there. She needed a distraction or the marquis could stop them before they reached the back stairs.

More out of alarm than inspiration, she flung the cloth she'd been using on the bookcases toward his head.

The marquis snatched the fabric as it connected with his nose. A puff of dust settled in his hair as one corner of the cloth slapped against his forehead. The stunned look on his face was the last thing Amelia saw before she shoved Jane down the corridor.

They half slid, half ran down the back stairs. The hollow echo of their feet on the bare wooden treads mirrored the pounding in Amelia's chest. A swift glance over her shoulder revealed they were not being followed. A relief to be certain, but not enough of one to calm her frantic flight.

They stumbled into the kitchen, clutching each other to keep from falling. Momentum from their mad dash down the stairs sent them careening across the floor with little balance and even less grace. Cook shrieked and dropped a bowl of flour.

"Oh, I'm sorry!" Amelia searched for a rag to help clean up the mess.

"Miss Amelia!" Jane pulled on her companion's arm. "*He* could be on his way down here!"

"But I—"

Words failed as the sound of footfalls reverberated in the servant stairwell. They sounded too light to belong to the marquis, but Amelia wasn't going to wait around to find out.

Chapter Two

Anthony rested his head against the back of the seat in his carriage. Arriving three days early had thrown his house into turmoil, but if he'd stayed at his country estate any longer, he'd have talked himself out of coming at all. The friends who had convinced him it was time to reestablish his place in London society had returned to Town almost two weeks ago, leaving him brooding back in Hertfordshire.

To spare the sanity of his cook, he was dining with those same friends this evening.

Maybe they could help him forget the enigma he'd found cleaning his study. He'd become entranced the moment he saw her perched on the ladder, humming as she ran the cloth over the books and shelves. Her giggle of happiness as she kicked off the bookshelf and sent the ladder careening down the wall had fascinated him to the point that he forgot to move out of the way before the ladder connected with his boot.

Then she'd landed in his arms.

Two years ago the situation would have delighted him. He'd have flirted instead of remaining a good distance away from her after she was back on her feet. Those old instincts had been difficult to fight during the encounter.

Difficult enough to keep him from pursuing her.

Difficult enough he should avoid her. He was attempting to prove to himself and God that he was indeed the new creation the Bible said he was. Obsessing about a woman he'd met only hours before seemed too much like the old creation for his peace of mind.

Not that she fit his old ideal. With dark hair pulled back into a serviceable bun—devoid of a single face-framing ringlet—an unadorned mud-colored dress, and well-worn boots, she'd been a head-to-toe column of nondescript brown. Pretty but not classically beautiful, and without a hint of anything fashionable about her appearance.

He'd never seen someone so happy to be where they were, though. Her joy in the midst of the degrading act of cleaning was like nothing he'd ever seen.

Being attracted to goodness and joy was a sign he was changing for the better, wasn't it? It didn't hurt that goodness and joy was wrapped in the body of a woodland fairy.

The carriage stopped in front of the London home of his good friend, Griffith, Duke of Riverton. More proof that he wasn't the same man.

Up until two years ago, Griffith had been nothing but an aristocratic neighbor. He'd never set foot in the man's home for a gathering of anything less than one hundred people, even though their country estates sat within five miles of each other. Now Griffith and his siblings were the closest thing Anthony had to family.

The butler showed him to the drawing room, and Anthony grinned as he spotted Miranda, the elder of Griffith's younger sisters. "You provide a splendid welcome to Town."

Miranda returned Anthony's grin as she crossed the drawing room, her green eyes brimming with humor. "I shall accept the compliment, despite the lack of competition. Tell me again after the masses have a chance to greet you. I give it two days at most until they all come 'round for one reason or another."

"I haven't officially told anyone I'm back in London."

Anthony would have sworn it was impossible to snort in a ladylike manner, but Miranda managed to accomplish it. "That won't matter."

He couldn't stop a groan of discomfiture, though it lacked Miranda's refinement. He reached past the decanter of brandy to grab the lemonade. "I only want a chance to settle in without being pestered. It sounds unbearably egotistical, but I do believe my arrival in town is going to make me the prey instead of the hunter."

The very thought was enough to make Anthony long for his country estate once more. As he poured the lemonade he noted Trent, Griffith's younger brother, sitting in a chair by the fire. "Are Griffith and Georgina joining us this evening?"

"Griffith departed Town earlier this morning. He wants to get through some pressing ducal business at a few of his estates before the heart of the season." Miranda cut her eyes toward her brother. "Trent is irritated. Griffith promised to help escort me this year, and Trent claims big brother is shirking his duties. I adore being a burden."

Anthony counted himself grateful that he wasn't on the receiving end of Miranda's glare.

Trent coughed as he stood and tugged at his cravat. "Yes, well, Georgina should be along at any moment. Next to her I look positively cheerful. She is irked at us for not allowing her to participate in society yet."

"She was soothed considerably when I informed her she could join us for dinner this evening." Miranda turned her pinning gaze from her brother to her guest. "I believe she has a *tendre* for you, Anthony."

"All the smart women do." Anthony favored Miranda with his most charming grin. "I have been biding my time until you come to your senses and fall at my feet as well." He raised his glass in her direction.

Miranda grimaced. "That would be like marrying my brother."

Trent tried to hide his wide grin. "I doubt there'll be room for her once you make your first social appearance, Anthony."

Miranda cast a sideways glance at her brother. "Honestly, Trent, he hasn't set foot in the city for two years. You have to take into account that many of his acquaintances might have forgotten him."

Anthony coughed, trying to remind the siblings that he was in the room.

Trent gripped Miranda's shoulder and looked at the floor, slowly shaking his head. "My dear, dear sister, this man is a legend." He raised his head and pointed his glass in Anthony's direction, a crooked smile on his lips. "He told me himself."

Anthony's neck got hot. If he was going to blush for the first time in years, shouldn't it be about something much more risqué than that offhand comment?

"Yes, yes." Miranda waved her hand through the air. "The enormously popular bachelor possessing both title and fortune, notorious for racing, women, and various other pleasurable pursuits. While rare, men of that ilk are not impossible to find."

"What do you know of his 'pleasurable pursuits'?" Trent's gaze jerked to Miranda, his face bearing the stern cast of big brother instead of charming gentleman. Their green eyes, so similar to each other in shade and shape, locked across the room. His narrowed as an impish smile formed on his sister's face.

Anthony shifted, trying to avoid a deeper blush. He didn't like Miranda knowing anything about his former pleasurable pursuits either.

"Only whispers, I assure you. Women love to gossip when they visit, but no one tells unmarried ladies any details. They only share enough to scare all the decent young ladies away."

As the dreaded heat crawled farther up Anthony's neck and onto his ears, Trent's deep laughter filled the room. He laughed so hard he had to bend over and take huge gulping breaths of air in order to catch his breath back.

"Miranda, Tony is a marquis, and a rich one at that. He could have a string of debauched virgins—"

"Trent!"

"—and a passel of illegitimate children trailing behind him and still have his pick of any unattached woman in town."

"I suppose." Miranda hid her smile behind her glass. "Imagine if they knew he had the ability to climb apple trees while completely foxed."

Trent toasted him once more. "Not to mention his skill at remaining in said tree after passing out."

Anthony could have done without the reminder of his final drunken stupor, despite its fascinating and embarrassing conclusion in an apple orchard. It was, however, the event that brought Griffith into his life, changing it forever, so he couldn't completely detest the experience. At least the memory was sobering enough to cool the flush from his skin.

Miranda looked Anthony in the eye. "As long as you steer clear of any scandal, we should be able to find you that rare jewel who will overlook your past and see the changed man you have become."

What was he supposed to say to that? "Um, thank you?"

"Don't forget to watch for a jewel of your own, dear sister. I don't relish carting you around again next season."

Trent was saved becoming the victim of fratricide by the entrance of a vibrant young woman with masses of blond curls and laughing green eyes. Georgina danced into the drawing room, an engaging smile decorating her face. "At last, I have arrived. So good of you to wait for me."

Anthony stood as the spritely female dipped low in a curtsy of greeting.

She then twirled to Anthony's side. "If only you would consent to wait for me, my lord. My overbearing family will let me out of the schoolroom next season, and we can dance away in wedded bliss."

Anthony laughed and kissed the outstretched fingers, thankful for a less serious conversation. "Alas, fair maiden, I fear I am not worthy of your dancing slippers. I shall have to comfort myself with someone within the reach of these lowly arms."

"Oh pish!" Georgina, swatted Anthony on the shoulder. "You shall be the catch of the season. I wish I could watch all of London fall at your feet when they discover you are seeking a bride." Her sigh threatened to extinguish the candles across the room.

Picturing the beauties of London at his feet brought the morning's mishap to mind. "Miranda, do you know of a rather short brunette miss named Amelia?"

The footman entered to announce dinner.

"I am afraid you will have to be more specific, Anthony," Miranda murmured dryly as she rose to take Anthony's arm.

"I found a young woman dressed considerably better than your average maid dusting my study when I arrived today."

Trent laughed. "Was it a marriage-minded miss trying to get your attention?"

"If it was she did a terrible job of it." Georgina placed her hand on Trent's arm. "He can't call on her if he doesn't know her full name."

"I am sorry, but I cannot think of any women who would be dusting your study, Anthony," Miranda said as they passed the wide-eyed footman.

Anthony sighed. "Be a diamond and keep an ear out for me, would you? I would like to know who she is."

Chapter Three

She had to be vacant in the attic to even consider the request. Amelia choked down her bite of toast as she tried to come to terms with Mrs. Harris's request. "You want me to *what*?"

The loving housekeeper was the closest thing to a mother Amelia had experienced. Amelia would have done anything for the woman who'd done her best to show Amelia around London when the viscount had sent her here almost ten years ago.

Anything, that is, except return to the marquis' house.

Mrs. Harris plunked a bottle on the scarred worktable. "Take this tonic to Emma. You said she was still feeling poorly yesterday."

The bottle tilted as one side settled into a thick groove on the table.

Amelia had never thought much about the many dings and dents of the old table. She'd sat here for breakfast every morning and had eaten dinner at the table as well until Miss Ryan, her governess and companion, had declared it unfit for her station. Then they'd all moved to the dining room for the evening meal.

All it did was create more work in Amelia's eyes, but it made the servants feel as if they were doing something right so she never complained.

"Do you really think she needs it?" Amelia asked.

"Do you think that dragon of a housekeeper will keep her around if she misses any more work?"

Amelia ran her fingers over the rough surface until they wrapped around the smooth glass bottle. "Perhaps Lydia could take it," she asked hopefully, referring to the parlor maid with a mop of blond corkscrews popping out around the edges of her mob cap. "Or perhaps Fenton?"

Even before Mrs. Harris could spear her with a quizzical stare, Amelia knew her suggestions were nonsensical. As the lady of the house, such as it was, she was the one who should visit their friends and see to their care when needed. Sending the maid or the butler, who each had a full day's work to do, would be impersonal and strange.

If only she could claim other lady-of-the-house duties such as dinner parties and afternoon social calls. But when one only knew the servants of London's elite and not the lords and ladies themselves, a social presence was hard to come by.

"Is there something you aren't telling me?" Mrs. Harris placed a fist on one skinny hip and looked at Amelia with the same glare that had gotten her to confess to eating all the gingerbread cookies her first Christmas in London.

The housekeeper's eyes narrowed. "You look guilty. Like the time you snuck young Celia Scott into the dressmaker's shop every night for two weeks as if she was the shoemaker's elf."

"She got the job, didn't she?"

"At the expense of every candle in this house. I thought I was going mad when I couldn't find any." Mrs. Harris crossed her arms but didn't relax her accusatory glare. "What have you gotten yourself into now?"

If Amelia's choices were to deliver the tonic or tell the tale of the marquis, there was no need for debate. She clutched the bottle to her chest. "Not a thing. It's probably the busyness of the season getting to me. All the extra noise and traffic." Amelia popped up from her stool. "I'll take it now. As you said, she can't afford to miss another day." But even as she buttoned her spencer jacket and slapped a bonnet on her head, Amelia tried to come up with a reason to avoid going.

As she walked down the street, her mind swirled with all the reasons returning to the scene of her humiliation was a bad idea.

Once she'd cut through a back alley, the top of the marquis' house could be seen over the roof of his mews. The unfamiliar stench of horses and leather tickled her nose, reminding her how different his life was than hers. It was surprisingly encouraging.

He would likely still be abed. If he had risen early, he'd be off at his club or one of those other places men of leisure spent their time. He wouldn't be home, and he certainly wouldn't be in the kitchens. She'd be in and out without any additional embarrassing encounters.

By the time she was creeping through the enormous hedges toward the kitchen entrance of the marquis' Grosvenor Street home, her mental assurances had almost convinced her heart to resume its normal beat. A masculine chuckle caused it to stop altogether.

Amelia's feet grew roots. It couldn't be *him*.

She squatted low to see beneath the hedge. He lay on a blanket, a tray with a half-full pitcher of lemonade a few feet away and a large pile of cards on the ground next to him. He picked up a card. His low groan reached her ears before he tossed the card over his head and into the grass beyond. What could he be doing?

He sighed. "Lady Charles is hosting a soiree, hmm?" The white card hit the grass behind him. "I wonder if she stopped serving raw meat to her guests yet." He shuddered and moved on to the next card.

"A ball given by the Countess of Brigston. A crowd of that size would allow me to greet people quickly." A card went into the stack nearest his hip.

"Perhaps it's better to start small, though. I liked Harry Wittcomb well enough at school. A dinner party at his home could be enjoyable." The card went toward the pile at his knee.

She should move. This was the man's private garden. He had every right to expect that his verbal musings were falling on no ears but his own.

But what kind of man had a picnic in his own garden and threw invitations willy-nilly about the yard?

For goodness' sake, Amelia. It doesn't matter if the man is a paragon of virtue; he deserves his privacy.

But this behavior was too intriguing for her to leave.

Anthony picked up the next in the seemingly endless stack of invitations. Were all of these events occurring in the next few days?

He sighed and opened another invitation.

"A garden party. Dreadful bore those are, unless you know the other guests well. Who is Lady Galvine? I assume she is married to Lord Galvine but I've never heard of him either."

Snickering at his own wit, Anthony tossed the parchment over his head.

He picked up the next one.

"What are you doing?" The irate voice of his valet, Harper, sounded from his right.

A quick glance around the clearing confirmed that Anthony was not the target of Harper's verbal attack. Which begged the question of who was. Anthony rose and started running around the line of greenery.

Was Harper hurt? Was someone attacking him? Harper was a wiry little fellow, an odd choice for a valet, but the man could tie an impeccable cravat.

"Harper!" Anthony called out as he rounded the edge of the hedges. His foot slipped in the dirt, but he quickly steadied himself.

The last thing he expected to find was a woman snared in his valet's glare. And not just any woman.

The familiar brown dress, the alarmed chocolate-colored eyes, the severe bun. His mystery woman had returned.

She squealed as recognition dawned in her eyes. Both of her hands flew up to her face, leaving only her big brown eyes showing. Her gaze connected with Anthony's, and her eyes widened even more until a full rim of white surrounded the deep brown.

Harper's hand wrapped around the woman's upper arm. Her eyes cut to the valet. She whirled with such force that Harper was knocked sideways and required several steps to regain his balance.

Then she ran.

"Wait!" Anthony ran after her.

The woman darted a look over her shoulder. His call seemed to spur her to run harder. Anthony, however—in possession of much longer legs and not encumbered by skirts—was faster. He skidded to a halt, grabbing her shoulder and spinning her around.

Her gaze connected with his. Breath backed up in his lungs at the sadness mingled with fear he could read on her face. For the space of several heartbeats he stared into her big brown eyes, watching an emotion he couldn't quite name build within them.

"Go to Lady Galvine's," she whispered in a rush. "She treats her servants well and has spent an entire year planning the party. Her only daughter is in love with the Earl of Lyndley's eldest son and he with her, but they don't think that the earl will let his son marry her. Lord Galvine is only a baron. If you announced your arrival in London at her party it would increase her consequence enough that Miss Kaitlyn might be allowed to marry the earl's son."

She pulled away and ran behind the mews.

He gave chase, but by the time he reached the alley, she was nowhere to be found. His mystery woman had escaped again.

"Why are we here?" Amelia frowned at the row of glinting shop windows marching down Bond Street. After her encounter with the marquis and his valet she'd wanted nothing more than to hide in her room and wallow in useless grumbles and futile daydreams.

Daydreams in which her encounter with the marquis had taken place in a respectable place, she'd known exactly what to say, and her dress had been something other than serviceable brown.

"You've been moping about the house for over a week, grumbling about hedges and cleaning cloths. You needed to get out. Besides, you need a new dress." Miss Ryan, her governess turned companion, nodded to punctuate her statement, causing her black ringlets to bob against the sides of her bonnet.

Amelia blinked out of her reverie and looked down at her skirts. "There is nothing wrong with this dress."

As long as one didn't compare it to anything else walking down the street.

"Aside from the two layers of trim we've put on the bottom to hide the ragged edges, the pull in the back from where you mended a hole under the arm, and the fact that the waistline is three years out of date—no, there's not a thing wrong with it," agreed Miss Ryan.

Amelia didn't want to accustom herself to upper-class finery only to have it ripped away from her when she reached one and twenty in a few short months. Who knew if the viscount would continue to support her? Or if he even remembered she existed?

"My dress is suitable for what I do. None of my friends care that I've had to repair a tattered hem or two." Over the years she'd made lots of friends and she'd even invited them over to the house for tea occasionally.

But they weren't the type of friends to help a girl socially.

Miss Ryan shook her head. "You can't marry if you limit your socializing to the servants. You're a gentleman's daughter."

"I like the servants," Amelia mumbled. They'd been the only ones willing to talk to her when she'd been dumped in London at the age of eleven.

"Servants don't marry, dear." Miss Ryan ran a comforting hand along Amelia's arm.

"Neither do unknown wards of forgotten viscounts." Amelia crossed her arms and dared the companion to contradict her statement.

"This is London. You never know what the good Lord will make happen. Perhaps with the right dress." Miss Ryan smiled but didn't meet Amelia's gaze. "It changed Cinderella's life, didn't it?"

Before Amelia could ask where Miss Ryan was stashing a fairy godmother, she found herself grasped by the elbow and hauled into the shop.

Two elegant women sat in chairs near the window, sipping tea. Another cluster of three ladies looked at a book of fashion plates while two more perused a selection of fabric.

Amelia sputtered. "But this is Madame Bellieme's. It probably costs money to simply breathe her air."

"We've been stashing money away for ten years." Miss Ryan shrugged. "We aren't here to see her, anyway."

"We're not?" Amelia clapped a hand to her bonnet to keep it from flying off as Miss Ryan pulled her behind the golden silk curtain.

The sun coming through the back windows of the store was considerably brighter than the shadowed front room. Amelia blinked rapidly to adjust her vision.

"Miss Amelia!"

Amelia shook her head to focus on the speaker, a middle-aged woman in a light blue dress with her light brown hair pulled into a low bun. It took a moment for Amelia to recognize the impoverished gentry woman she'd met in the free pews at St. George's nearly five years prior. "Oh! Good morning, Sally. I haven't seen you in an age."

"Not since you helped me get that job in Hampstead Heath. I can't thank you enough for putting in a good word with the housekeeper there. I was privileged to act as companion to Lady Margaret until she passed on. I'm a lady's maid, now." Sally peeked at a folding screen partitioning part of the back room off from the rest of the work area.

Amelia looked at the screen as well. Sally's mistress must be behind there being fitted for a dress. "Are you not needed back there? I would have thought the lady's maid would be part of the fittings."

"I usually wait out here. Sometimes I visit with Celia. Her brother, Finch, is a footman for the family I work for now."

Miss Ryan turned from the folding screen that she'd been staring at since they passed the curtain. "Celia was very excited to know we were coming today. She said that sometimes she still slips in here at night to work by candlelight so that she can remember how badly she wanted the position."

A tall, blond young woman bustled out from behind the screen, smoothing her skirt over her hip. "Have those delivered to the house when they're finished, Madame Bellieme. I won't need the second ball gown until next week."

"Of course, my lady." The modiste was older than Amelia remembered, although it had been at least three years since she'd seen the woman.

"Sally, let's be going."

Amelia couldn't begin to guess what the elegant lady was thinking as her brilliant green eyes took in Amelia and the two servants, none of whom belonged in the inner sanctum of London's finest dressmaker—but at least the woman knew why Sally was there.

"Yes." Sally stepped away from their little gathering with a small wave. A green reticule, likely belonging to Sally's mistress, dangled from her wrist. "Have a good day, Miss Amelia."

Amelia nodded, not wanting to say anything to get Sally in trouble. Her mistress kept glancing back and forth between her servant and Amelia.

As the two pushed past the curtain Celia came out from behind the screen. "Miss Amelia!" She bounced across the back room and wrapped Amelia in her skinny arms.

Madame Bellieme gave Amelia a smile and a pat on the shoulder as she made her way back to the front of the store.

Amelia extricated herself from Celia, whose smile remained as strong as the hug.

"I'm happy to see you!" The younger girl reached out to give Amelia one more squeeze.

The enthusiasm inspired Amelia's own smile. "How have you been, Celia?"

"Better than I ever dreamed. Come, come, I've got your dress ready." Celia pulled her toward the screen, Miss Ryan pushing from the back.

Amelia's slight weight was no match for the two of them, and she found herself propelled across the floor even as the rest of her froze in shock. They already had a dress made for her? How? When?

"Madame Bellieme's fingers aren't working as well as they used to, and she's made me her secret apprentice. She says my eye for fashion and hand with a needle is almost as good as hers." Celia bounced in excitement, her dark bun bobbing about atop her head.

She hauled out a dress of beautiful green-sprigged muslin. "And there's a matching redingote as well. Come, come. Let's get you fitted."

The women pulled at Amelia's dress, eager to get her into the new gown. Amelia began to feel a bit of excitement herself as the soft fabric draped over her body.

Celia had used one of Amelia's old dresses for size, so it didn't require much altering to fit her perfectly. A few quick stitches along the seam of the coat and

Amelia was ready to go in the most gorgeous afternoon ensemble she'd ever laid eyes on.

After folding Amelia's old dress into a bandbox, Celia gave her another hug and told Miss Ryan to let her know when they wanted more dresses.

"This one is too beautiful." Amelia swayed back and forth, enjoying the swish of her new skirt. "I may never find another dress acceptable again." They all laughed as they left the partitioned area.

"Oh dear." Miss Ryan's voice was stilted, almost toneless.

"Oh my," Celia added.

Amelia looked around, but didn't see anything to cause their wooden surprise. "What?"

Celia stooped to scoop up a green reticule from the floor.

Chapter Four

"That can't be good," Miss Ryan said. "How could Sally have left it behind?"

"Can't you have it delivered?" Amelia looked around the little group. Why was this causing such concern? The solution was simple. The tall lady couldn't have been the first to leave her belongings behind.

Celia shook her head. "The footman is out already."

"I hope Sally doesn't get fired." Mrs. Ryan bit her lip.

Why the sudden concern for everyone's position? First Mrs. Harris feared for Emma, and now Miss Ryan mentioned Sally? Did they think everyone in eminent danger of unemployment?

"Lady Miranda is kind, but as a child she could be very emotional and unpredictable." Celia looked up at Amelia from the corner of her lashes.

Something strange was afoot, but Amelia couldn't begin to think what. "Lady Miranda?"

Celia nodded. "Lady Miranda Hawthorne. Sister of the Duke of Riverton."

Amelia hadn't realized what a prestigious position Sally had managed to get.

Resigned to another aristocratic encounter, Amelia took the bag. "Hawthorne House isn't far out of our way."

It was miles away socially but a mere two streets over physically. Amelia never visited Hawthorne House, despite knowing the butler and a few servants. It was too intimidating.

With the gorgeous green bag clutched in her hand, Amelia led Miss Ryan back out onto Bond Street.

They left the shopping district behind, chatting about the pretty wares in the various windows. Then, without warning, Miss Ryan fell into Amelia, nearly sending her to the pavement.

"Oh! Oh my, Miss Ryan. Are you all right?"

The older woman made her way to the side of the pavement to lean on the building. Her limp was drastic.

Amelia bit her lip. "Should we call a hack?"

Miss Ryan waved toward Grosvenor Square, within sight but in the opposite direction of their home. "I can make it back home. You go ahead without me."

"You . . . but . . . I can't go alone!"

"I'm sure Finch or Gibson will see that you get home safely." Mrs. Ryan squared her shoulders and limped down the side street that would take her toward Mount Street. "Remember Sally is depending on you."

Amelia looked back and forth from the companion to the distant square. Had Miss Ryan lost her mind? The reticule felt heavy in her hand. She couldn't take it home with her. It was either continue on to Hawthorne House or return the bag to Bond Street.

Since walking alone down Bond Street was an even worse idea than walking in Grosvenor Square, she continued on.

Hawthorne House loomed as Amelia crossed Grosvenor's Square. The grand columns were daunting even if one didn't know who lived there. Few homes in London were larger, but then few men were more powerful than its owner.

Amelia smoothed her skirts. The ensemble was still the most beautiful thing she'd ever worn or even seen in person, but it felt unequal to the task of socializing with the sister of a duke.

"Lord, be with me," she whispered before taking a deep breath and climbing the stairs. Her knock was so timid she didn't think anyone would hear it, but it was immediately followed by the scrape of the latch.

"Miss Amelia?" The butler's surprise was evident as he opened the door.

Amelia bit her lip. Should she have gone to the servant entrance? "Good day, Gibson. I'm making a delivery." She extended her arm, the green bag swinging from her fingertips like a clock pendulum, counting down the minutes to her next humiliation.

"Bless you! Come in. My lady discovered the loss of it moments ago." Gibson ushered her into a beautiful drawing room decorated in white and gold. "Please have a seat."

"There is no need for that, Gibson. I can leave the bag in the hall." The pleading edge to her voice made Amelia wince. Cowardly or not, facing and conversing with Lady Miranda seemed like a bad idea. Amelia's encounters with the marquis had proven how inept she was at interacting with aristocracy.

"She will insist on thanking you in person. Wait here, Miss Amelia, if you please." Gibson hurried from the room.

Throwing the reticule on a chair and leaving seemed like an inspired idea, but Gibson knew where she lived. The last thing she needed was Lady Miranda on her doorstep.

The blond woman from the modiste entered the drawing room, a warm smile on her face and open curiosity in her eyes. "Gibson tells me that you have my reticule?"

"Er, yes, my lady." Amelia stabbed her arm forward, the reticule once again dangling before her. Lady Miranda accepted it.

"We found it as we were leaving. Everything is in there. Celia knew it was yours so we didn't need to open it."

Small creases formed at the corners of glittering green eyes and the edges of slightly curved lips. Was she amused by Amelia's assurances? Perhaps she found Amelia's lack of composure entertaining. Amelia's fingers began to play with the drawstring of her own reticule.

"Thank you." The lady set the bag on a nearby table. "I am Lady Miranda Hawthorne."

"I know. That is, Celia told me who you were." Amelia clamped her teeth shut. She would not prattle on and reveal her discomfort. She was going to limit herself to three-word sentences. That allowed her to say little more than "Yes, my lady" and "No, my lady."

Lady Miranda dipped her head and raised her eyebrows.

"Oh!" Amelia cried. "I am Miss Amelia Stalwood." That was five words, but perhaps her name could really be counted as one. "Pleasure to make your acquaintance." Five words again. Very well, she would limit herself to five-word sentences so long as they were intelligent five-word sentences.

Lady Miranda smiled as if every visitor lost her wits. Maybe they did. It was a duke's house, after all. "That is a lovely dress. Were you picking it up?"

Gibson appeared in the doorway before Amelia could answer. "Would you care for tea, my lady?"

"Oh no, Gibson, I don't—" Amelia froze. That was her voice answering the butler. Heat rushed to her cheeks and her ears. Her nose felt like ice. She cut her eyes to Lady Miranda and found the other woman just as still, with her mouth slightly agape, as if she, too, had been about to answer the butler.

"Miss Stalwood, Amelia Stalwood, was it?" Lady Miranda recovered her composure first. "Do please stay. Gibson, tea would be lovely."

The butler bowed and spun on his heel to leave room.

Lady Miranda waved an arm in the direction of a white brocade chair. Amelia perched on the edge, ready to flee if the opportunity arose.

Celia's brother, Finch, strode in with a laden tea service before Lady Miranda could finish adjusting her skirts on the adjacent sofa. Had he been standing in the hall, filled tray in hand, when Gibson came in to inquire if they wanted tea?

Amelia blinked in surprise. Lady Miranda hesitated before indicating Finch should leave the tray on a low table.

"Thank you, Finch." Amelia closed her eyes. That had been her voice, again, acknowledging someone else's servant, by name no less. Lady Miranda was sure to boot her out through the kitchens at this familiarity.

Silence filled the room. Not even a clock ticked to fill the quiet. Amelia hadn't felt this exposed since she was ten years old standing on the viscount's doorstep with nothing but a trunk, a valise, and a letter from her grandmother claiming the most distant relational ties imaginable.

What was the woman sitting before her looking for? Was she finding it?

Finally, Lady Miranda concluded her inspection. She nodded her head and began fixing tea. "You know my servants?"

"Er, yes, my lady." Amelia tried to mirror the graceful restraint of the woman across the table.

Lady Miranda paused in silent inquiry after pouring a cup of tea. Her hand hovered over the pitcher of cream.

"Sugar, no milk, please." A thrill of confidence twirled down Amelia's spine. That had sounded almost cultured and sophisticated. Granted it was merely a request for tea, but—

"Are you on good terms with many servants?"

They were back to the awkward inquisition.

"I suppose." This was not going at all the way Amelia had anticipated. She wasn't ashamed of her acquaintance with lower London, but she never imagined a highborn lady asking her about it.

"I myself have always tried to be on good terms with those I hire, but I have never been able to refer to those in other homes by name." Lady Miranda held out a cup of tea.

Willing her fingers not to tremble, Amelia accepted the cup. Her definition of "good terms" was likely different than Lady Miranda's.

"You know my maid as well?" Another cup filled with tea. A splash of milk and the slightest bit of sugar joined it.

Amelia hastily swallowed her sip of tea. "Yes, my lady."

Lady Miranda added a selection of biscuits to a small plate and offered it to Amelia. "It isn't everyone who would make an effort to return someone's belongings."

"It was no trouble." What else should she say? Amelia nibbled at a biscuit to buy herself some time.

Another young woman entered the room, her astounding beauty making Amelia blink. Blond curls piled atop her head, with ringlets framing features that would make a porcelain-doll maker swoon. "Gibson mentioned tea." Her green eyes assessed Amelia. "Good afternoon."

Lady Miranda fixed another cup of tea. "This is my new friend, Miss Amelia Stalwood. Miss Stalwood, my sister, Lady Georgina."

Amelia slid her cup onto the table. Was she supposed to rise and curtsy? This was a duke's sister, after all. There had to be some form of proper address in this situation. In the end she performed an awkward head nod, which drew a smirk from the younger woman.

Amelia directed her eyes back to the floor, wishing she could sink through the floorboards into the servant domain below. She'd be ever so much more comfortable.

The sisters talked and sipped tea, occasionally asking Amelia a question. After the first few times, Amelia stopped stumbling over her responses and managed something resembling a normal conversation.

"You've been so gracious, bringing my bag here that I hate to ask you this." Lady Miranda poured a bit more tea into her cup. "But would you do another favor for me?"

Amelia swallowed. Could she say anything other than yes?

"Would you come to dinner tonight?"

Amelia bobbled her tea cup. Lady Miranda tried to hide a smile with a sip of tea.

When Amelia didn't answer, Lady Miranda spoke again. "It will be very informal. Family and one or two close friends."

Amelia felt skewered by Lady Miranda's green eyes, like one of the animals she had read about scientists studying.

"You would be a great help. Georgina isn't able to join us tonight, so our numbers will be off if you do not come."

Lady Georgina shot her sister a scathing glare. "Actually, I—"

Lady Miranda gracefully kicked Lady Georgina in the shin. Amelia's eyes widened. How long would it take to learn how to do such an uncouth thing with ladylike grace? Who would take the time to develop such a strange talent?

"I understand. I was sixteen once." Lady Miranda patted her sister's hand.

"I'm seventeen."

"Miss Stalwood, please say you will."

Amelia plucked at her skirts. It was impossible. How could she come?

"I need you." Lady Miranda clasped her hands in her lap, her eyes filled with pleading.

Amelia heard herself agreeing before she could think it through. Excitement tingled along her fingers, making her bury them in her skirts to hide their shaking. She couldn't back out now. All she could do was pray she wouldn't regret it before the night was over.

Chapter Five

"*En garde.*" Sunlight glinted off the thin metal as Anthony slashed his sword in Trent's direction. Sweat rolled down his back, making his white lawn shirt stick to his skin. Finding such a well-matched fencing partner had been an unexpected benefit of befriending the Hawthorne family. Spending time with the younger man was surprisingly enjoyable.

"How goes the bridal hunt?" Trent grunted.

Even if he was an insolent pup.

Anthony blocked Trent's sword, not about to let his opponent distract him with mere words—even though the hunt had thus far been an utter failure. "Dismal."

Trent laughed as he danced forward, jabbing his sword toward Anthony's belly. "No one you find appealing? What about the Laramy girl? I haven't met her yet, but all accounts are that she is incomparably beautiful."

"She is." Anthony knocked Trent's sword upward to force him backward a step. "Beauty is not the problem, but I'm beginning to think intellect is."

Anthony's foot slipped sideways, and he felt the blunted tip of Trent's sword strike against his ribs. Acknowledging the hit, Anthony pulled off his mask. "If all the aristocracy is as lacking in wit as this year's crop of marital hopefuls, our country is doomed."

"Lady Miranda and Lady Georgina," the butler intoned from the terrace doorway.

"Present company excluded, of course," Trent murmured, grinning.

Miranda's nose wrinkled as she stepped onto the terrace. "The two of you are . . . disgusting." She gestured vaguely in the direction of their sweat-matted hair.

Anthony ran a hand through his disheveled locks, feeling awkward in only his shirtsleeves. Had he brought his coat out onto the terrace with him?

Georgina's expression was more admiring than disgusted. "They have been exerting themselves, Miranda. It is a most gentlemanly pursuit. Did you know Trent was going to be here?"

"You see?" Trent said. "Intelligent."

"Of course I did." Miranda speared her sister with a look that called the young woman's intelligence into question. "I would hardly have come here if Anthony were home alone."

Anthony turned to put his fencing equipment away. It was best if the ladies didn't notice him snicker at their spat. After composing his features, he turned back to them and gave a slight bow. "Ladies, please excuse me if I don't greet you properly. I am, as you noticed, a bit disheveled."

Trent gave a dismissive wave. "Bother that, it's just Miranda and Georgina." He turned to his sisters. "What are you doing here?"

Miranda turned her back on Trent, while Georgina stared daggers in his direction.

Anthony became unnerved by Miranda's blank expression. Normally the most confident of women, she seemed a little unsure of herself.

"Whatever you were planning tonight, I am afraid you will have to send your regrets. I need you at dinner."

Dinner? She wanted his presence at dinner? He'd expected something considerably more painful and difficult. In truth, a respite from the social whirl would be more than welcome. After enduring more tedious introductions, boring conversations, and lackluster dance partners than he would have thought possible in a short two weeks, he was inclined to disappear for another two years, with or without the wife he sought. A quiet dinner with intelligent friends sounded like Miranda was doing him a favor instead of the other way around.

"You're inviting him to dinner?" Georgina's despair added to Anthony's confusion. Since when did Georgina not want him at dinner?

"Unless Griffith returned this morning, Anthony's presence is required." Miranda turned from her sister back to Anthony. "It is of utmost importance."

This was obviously about more than a mere meal, but he could handle whatever it was. Miranda was as near to a sister as he had. If it was important to her, he could suffer through it. "I am, of course, at your service, my lady."

Georgina gave a little sigh. "I wish I could be there."

Trent left off his experimental sword swinging to join the conversation. "May I be excused as well?" Miranda glared.

Anthony laughed, grateful God had brought this close-knit family into his life and suddenly looking forward to his evening.

Amelia stood in front of the same house, wearing the same dress, for the second time that day. Would she repeat the same blunders? Dinner was considerably more involved than tea.

A breeze rustled the leaves in the park behind her, luring her to turn and run. She could be back at her own home within fifteen minutes.

It wasn't really a viable option. If she wanted to eat tonight she was going to have to march through that front door and dine with Lady Miranda. Mrs. Harris would refuse to feed her.

Gibson's face appeared from behind a curtain, sealing her fate. If she ran now, every servant in London would know by morning.

She walked resolutely to the door and knocked.

Gibson answered the door, a wide smile stretched across his lean face. "Good evening, Miss. May I take your coat?"

His happiness bolstered Amelia's spirits, and she grinned back. She handed him her redingote and bonnet, but couldn't make her feet follow him toward the drawing room.

She was terrified.

"Hullo, there," called a voice from the stairs.

Amelia jumped and covered her skipping heart with her hand. A man was crossing the hall. Was this the duke? She knew the duke was young and handsome, but wasn't this man a bit too young?

Blond hair formed a neat cap against his head, skimming his ears and collar and almost brushing his eyebrows. His green eyes seemed friendly, though curious as he looked at Amelia standing three feet inside his front hall. There was little doubt that he was related to Lady Miranda.

"May I be incredibly bold and present myself? Lord Trent Hawthorne, at your service." He picked up her limp fingers and kissed the air directly above her knuckles.

Amelia watched her hand as if it belonged to someone else. She should say something. Her brain was forming the appropriate words to introduce herself as well, but more than her hand felt disconnected. Her mouth had forgotten the motions. Her lungs felt devoid of air.

This inability to express herself around these people was becoming tiresome. If she couldn't bring her tongue and brain into communication within the next ten seconds, she was leaving.

Ten . . . Nine . . .

"Not to worry." Lord Trent placed her hand on his arm. "I often have the effect of speechlessness on the lovelier half of the population. Mothers, of course, live in quiet fear of me attending a social gathering and rendering their daughters mute. The men, on the other hand, beg me to come so that they can enjoy some sensible conversation."

Eight . . . Seven . . .

A giggle sputtered through Amelia's lips. Was that enough noise to count?

Six . . . Five . . .

Finch stood at the door to the drawing room, his eyes wide. As they approached, he cut his eyes to the interior of the room and back to Amelia. Was he trying to communicate with her?

Four . . . Three . . .

"Alas, our other dinner guest has already arrived so I shall have to share your charms this evening. My sister will be down shortly. A small wardrobe issue. You know how that goes, I'm sure."

Two . . .

Amelia's cheeks turned bright pink. The man next to her was certainly aware that her wardrobe was inappropriate for the occasion. His blatant ignoring of that fact was both embarrassing and endearing.

One . . .

Her time was up. Amelia took a deep breath as she stepped across the threshold of the drawing room, but nothing came out as her eyes landed on an all-too-familiar sight.

Her feet comprehended what she saw first and came to a complete stop, causing Lord Trent to stumble. Then her blood understood and drained from her face, leaving her chilled and likely pale as death. The blood must have told her heart, because it began increasing in speed until a dull roar filled Amelia's ears. Finally her voice joined the party. "Oh my," she whispered. "You."

It was not the stellar conversational gambit she'd intended.

"My sentiments exactly," the marquis said.

Lord Trent looked back and forth between the two dinner guests. "You have already met?"

"Not formally. I do believe she likes to trespass on my property, though." Lord Raebourne smiled.

"Ah," Lord Trent gave the woman on his arm an assessing look. "Your devious duster."

"So it would seem." Lord Raebourne relieved Lord Trent of Amelia's arm. "Please have a seat, my dear. You're looking a trifle pale. I believe I introduced myself at our first meeting, but I quite understand if you have forgotten. Anthony Pendleton, Marquis of Raebourne."

All the blood that had previously left Amelia's face returned with reinforcements. She could feel the heat in her neck and cheeks and prayed that it was not as bright red as it felt. "Mishamtalwood."

Lord Trent and Lord Raebourne both leaned forward. "I beg your pardon?" Lord Trent asked.

Amelia cleared her throat and straightened her spine. She focused on a delicate green vase on a table behind and between the two gentlemen. "Miss Amelia Stalwood."

"I am *very* pleased to meet you, Miss Stalwood." A smile accompanied the statement, making Lord Raebourne's face engaging as well as handsome.

"And I you, my lord." Amelia thought her blush was a deep as possible, but when Lord Raebourne kissed her hand in a repeat of Lord Trent's earlier gesture, she positively flamed.

"I had a most splendid time at Lady Galvine's party. Her daughter is a jewel. I am sure that she and Lord Owen will do famously together." The corners of his mouth twitched.

Amelia's eyes grew larger with every word he spoke. Could eyes fall out of one's head?

"I . . . " Amelia struggled to find her tongue.

Lady Miranda burst into the drawing room, her breath coming short and fast. Had she *run* down the stairs? "Miss Stalwood, you have arrived!"

Both men in the room quirked a brow at her. Lord Trent looked decidedly amused while Lord Raebourne seemed almost accusatory.

The arrival of Lady Miranda helped Amelia feel like herself again. Still dismayed by the unexpected connection, but herself. Taking a deep breath, she stood, determined to make their last impression better than their first.

"Lady Miranda, I must apologize." She swallowed. "I am afraid I have to bid you farewell. You see, I was . . . That is to say, I have met your other guest, after a fashion, and I fear my behavior at the time would not reflect well on anyone claiming an acquaintance with me."

Amelia turned from Lady Miranda's wide-eyed amazement to the marquis. "My lord, please do not hold this against Lady Miranda. I have done her a small good turn, and she sought to repay it. For what it's worth, I do apologize for intruding upon your privacy. It shall not happen again."

Amelia looked at the occupants of the room. They all appeared to have eaten something disagreeable. She was slipping past Lord Trent when all three aristocrats burst out in laughter.

"I know, Miss Stalwood." Lady Miranda gasped for air. "Or I should say I suspected. Please, stay for dinner. No one is mad at you for dusting a library for a sick maid. Confused perhaps, but hardly angry."

Amelia's eyes flickered from one person to the next. They were smiling. Not polite we-don't-want-to-be-rude type of smiles, but broad smiles, the kind born of genuine amusement.

Lord Raebourne's grin was accompanied by conspiratorial gleam in his eyes. Was he recalling their second encounter?

It seemed her humiliation had to be complete. Amelia sighed. "It is not the dusting of which I am ashamed, my lady." Her voice was barely audible, even to her own ears. "I returned the next day, and—there is no polite way to say it—I spied upon his lordship in a private moment and was caught by his valet. It is all dreadfully embarrassing and—"

Amelia had to stop again as Lord Trent and Lady Miranda looked at Lord Raebourne and collapsed into a new round of laughter.

The marquis kept his bemused gaze on Amelia. "It is not quite the way it sounds. I was in my garden sorting through invitations."

Wasn't that what she said? Maybe not in so much detail, but . . .

Amelia closed her eyes in mortification as she realized that her phrasing implied she had spied upon him in much more intimate quarters. She needed to leave.

Head down, she made for the door, keeping her eyes locked on the veining of the marble floor. Polished shoes stepped into her view, forcing her to stop or collide into Lord Raebourne's chest.

Again.

She stopped.

"Please," he said softly. "Do not leave."

A single finger caught under her chin, forcing her gaze up to his.

"Stay and dine with us this evening. It will give us a chance to start afresh."

Amelia searched his beautiful blue eyes and found nothing but kindness and sincerity. "Very well." The unspoken forgiveness lightened her, allowing the corners of her lips to edge upward. "I shall stay."

He offered her his arm. With some hesitance, she gave him her hand, hoping there wasn't a right and wrong way to do so. Heat emanated through his coat, sending a thrill spiraling up her arm and into her lungs.

As they passed through the main hall to the dining room, Amelia spied Finch, Gibson, two housemaids, and Miranda's lady's maid huddled behind a large plant in the corner of the front hall, enormous smiles on their faces. One of the housemaids saluted her.

The support of her friends calmed her. Surely she could get through this dinner with what remained of her dignity intact.

Chapter Six

Anthony watched Amelia throughout dinner, noting the tremble in her fingers, and her wide, bright eyes. Even though he knew her full name now, he couldn't think of her as anything other than Amelia. It was all his imagination had to go on for days.

The knuckles on her hand were white as she gripped her serviette. Likely she was measuring every word and action to ensure there were no more embarrassing moments like the one in the drawing room.

He wanted to help her relax, free the engaging woman he'd caught glimpses of. How had Miranda found this woman?

As the fish course was cleared, he heard a low murmur from Amelia's direction. Had she thanked the servant for clearing her dish? His father had been a stickler for gentlemanly manners, but even the most polite in his acquaintance didn't make a habit of thanking the servants.

Which was rather inconsiderate when he thought about it.

His ears strained as the next course was set in front of him. Would she thank him again? Surprise made Anthony fumble the fork he reached for. Not only had she thanked the footman, but she'd used his name. His mysterious trespasser was on friendly terms with more than just *his* household staff.

The man answered with a quiet "You are most welcome, Miss Amelia."

A desire to learn everything about this woman rose within him. Did she like the food? What was her favorite color? Did flowers make her sneeze?

"Tony!"

Anthony jerked from his reverie to find Trent and Miranda looking at him with expressions of amusement. He cleared his throat. "Yes, Trent?"

"I asked if you'd been to Tattersalls since your return. They had some prime horses there last week."

Horses. Tattersalls. Had he been? "No, not yet."

Miranda smiled. "Too busy settling back into the glittering ridiculousness that is London, are you?"

The only response Anthony could generate was a grunt. His weeks back among the social whirl of the elite had convinced him more than ever that he had to marry this year. The temptation to drift back to his old life was so much stronger in Town.

Was that what drew him to Amelia? She embodied the simplicity he missed from the country, where he had learned who he was beyond cards and drink and women. She might not be the one he should spend the rest of his life with, but he couldn't think of any woman he'd rather get to know.

A smile tugged at the corners of his mouth as Amelia twirled a spoon through her turtle soup. It was obvious she didn't care for it, but she kept trying to choke down bite after bite. The footmen cleared the bowls before she'd managed to eat half of it.

"Anthony?"

Miranda didn't bother to hide her amusement as she tried to catch his attention.

He dabbed the corner of his mouth with his serviette and raised his eyebrows in inquiry.

"Miss Stalwood mentioned attending St. George's at Hanover Square. I asked if you intended to take up a pew there."

She had spoken? And he'd missed it?

Anthony cleared his throat. "Griffith has invited me to join your family pew at Grosvenor Chapel for now. I see no reason to rent a pew myself without family to share it with."

Miranda's eyes cut to Amelia and then swiftly on to Trent, her throat convulsing in her obvious attempt to choke down a laugh. His own gaze flew back to Amelia—its favorite place this evening. Was Miranda implying that Amelia should share his pew or . . . Oh. Anthony bit back a chuckle himself.

The poor woman was trying to slip bites of spicy bread pudding into her serviette. The footman behind already had a clean one at the ready, waiting until the appropriate time to exchange the cloths. Anthony pinched himself to prevent the encroaching laughter.

He forced himself to pay more attention to the conversation around him. Staring at Amelia all evening wasn't going to help her relax or allow him to know more about her.

"Trent, what are your plans now that you've finished school?" Perhaps discussing the young man's future would lead to discussing Amelia's. Anthony couldn't bring himself to direct personal questions to Amelia when she looked so uncomfortable.

Trent gave a vague, noncommittal answer, then proved he did not share Anthony's aversion to interviewing Miranda's new friend. "Did you grow up in London?"

"No. I lived in Suffolk until I was eleven." Amelia fell quiet for a moment, her fingers wrapped in the folds of the clean serviette.

Miranda's eyes narrowed. "Why haven't we met? Didn't you say your guardian is a viscount? Surely he didn't give you a season before my first one. You'd have been a child."

A brilliant pink washed over Amelia's cheeks, deepening to red as she looked around the table. "I-I'm not positive the viscount remembers he sent me to London. It was almost ten years ago."

Anthony choked on the very idea. How could a grown man of title and responsibility essentially turn out a young child?

His fingernails bit into his palms, and he glanced down, surprised to find his hands curled into fists underneath the table. It had been two years since he felt the desire to hit anyone. The unpleasant sensation was not welcome now. He barely knew this woman and he wanted to physically avenge her childhood wrongs?

Silence fell over the room. Miranda shifted her spoon to the other side of her empty bowl. Trent cleared his throat and decided his fingernails were utterly fascinating.

Amelia's eyes darted from one dinner companion to another. The poor girl must be panicking, thinking that once again she had said something to put her entirely beyond the pale. He couldn't go back and save her from abandonment as a child, but he could rescue her from her current awkward discomfort.

"Trent, did you hear about the new tailor that set up shop behind White's? Superb workman. Made Struthers look almost fit."

The small smile of relief on Amelia's face was all the reward he needed.

Amelia kept a mantra of proper behavior running through her mind. *Think before you speak. Sit straight and tall like a lady. Don't talk to the servants. Don't talk about the servants. Stop staring at the marquis.* Nervous laughter threatened to bubble up from her chest.

As she collected her redingote and bonnet from Gibson, she realized she was smiling. She had enjoyed herself despite the agonizing attention paid to every word and movement. Even if this taste of refinement made it difficult to return to simplicity, she was glad she'd come.

Anthony collected his own belongings from Gibson. After such an intimate dinner she found it difficult to continue to think of him as Lord Raebourne. "May I see you home, Miss Stalwood?"

"Oh!" A ride with Anthony would be considerably nicer than braving the walk home. She looked to Gibson, delighted when he gave a slight, almost imperceptible nod. "That would be lovely, thank you."

"Excellent." Anthony led her to his waiting carriage, a small smile gracing his handsome features. The kind of smile people wear without even knowing it.

The highborn ladies he socialized with probably thought nothing of being handed into a carriage by a charming, handsome man. For the orphaned daughter of a landed gentleman, it was all a bit overwhelming.

Amelia's nervousness grew as Anthony sat in the carriage seat across from her. She fiddled with the strap of her reticule as they rolled forward.

"Thank you." The words burst from her mouth in a rush. She hadn't intended to say them, but it was all she could think of, and the words of gratitude spilled from her lips before she could stop them.

Several moments passed before Anthony spoke. "You are most welcome, I'm sure, but I generally like to know what a lady is thanking me for."

Amelia swallowed her groan. She sounded like a complete ninny. The reticule strings twisted around her fingers as she gripped them together. "I am sure I was the last person you expected to dine with tonight. You could have made it a humiliating experience, but you were most gracious. Thank you."

Anthony's gaze fell to her fingers. Could he see her nervous habit in the low lantern light? A downward glance revealed a sliver of moonlight cutting right across her hands, highlighting the red-and-white splotches on her skin caused by the tightly wrapped strings.

She'd forgotten to replace her gloves after dinner. Her last hope of obtaining a modicum of sophistication drifted away on her sigh.

With a quiet clearing of his throat, he crossed the open expanse between the seats and settled next to her, sliding the gloves from his hands. Amelia's heartbeat sped up. What could he be thinking?

"Here now." Anthony gently took her hands in his. "You're going to hurt yourself."

His skin was warm and rough against her own. With utmost care, he untangled the strings, tsking quietly as he revealed the deep red marks on her fingers. He massaged the feeling back into her hands. "Bizarre meetings can make the best of friends. I have no wish to embarrass you. I confess to curiosity about your relationship with my staff, though."

The grin he gave her brought to mind a little boy trying to convince the cook to slip him an extra biscuit. At the same time, though, his hands held hers in a shockingly intimate gesture that she had never experienced in her life. Her brain couldn't decide where to settle.

His eyebrows drifted up in a questioning look. He still wanted to know about her connection to his staff.

"One of your maids is the niece of the cook next door. We played together as children. Through her I met others of your staff, and we have been friends since, though it is rare that many of us are able to meet together." Mortification shot through her. "Not that I think you don't give your staff adequate time off."

Anthony coughed and rubbed his hand over the bottom of his face. Amelia slid her freed hand into the folds of her skirt. He must disapprove of her association with his staff. Did he fear she would disrupt his household? "I would never ask you to adjust your household's schedule for my convenience."

His cough modified into a sputter.

"It would be dreadfully rude." She slumped back into the seat, her voice little more than a mumble.

The carriage rang with the sudden release of his laughter. "Miss Stalwood, you are without a doubt one of the oddest women in London."

Was that a good thing?

His laugh subsided to a wide smile. What was he thinking? Amelia started to reach for the strings on her reticule again. Anthony captured her hands in his once more.

"We must do something about this nervous penchant you have for creating tourniquets for your fingers." His thumb rubbed across her knuckles while Amelia ducked her head. His hands were large and warm, wrapping around her fingers in a way that made her feel cared for. She would gladly sit in this carriage all night if he would keep holding her hands in his.

He bent low, bringing his face into her downturned vision. "I have never met my servants' friends. Probably because they themselves are most often servants. I've never known anyone, gentry or peerage, who knows the names of someone else's footmen."

"I am merely a gentleman's daughter," Amelia whispered.

"You live in a home in London. You must be attached to someone of consequence." They stared at each other for several moments.

Why was he acting like a man fascinated with what he saw? She glanced down at their joined hands.

There were tales that among the *ton* a closed carriage was often used to steal a kiss or two during a courtship. This wasn't a courtship by any definition of the word, but this breathless anticipation and excitement must be what those other women felt. The sway of the carriage and the warmth of his hands lulled her into a fantasy where he would whisper to her and beg her for a kiss, like in *Much Ado About Nothing*, the only Shakespeare play Miss Ryan had been able to get Amelia to read.

"There was a time, not too long ago, when I would have taken this moment and kissed you."

Amelia crashed back into reality at his harsh whisper. She was always careful to keep her musings contained in her head, but had it slipped out this time?

"Trust me," Anthony continued, "you are safe now. I am a changed man." With a final squeeze, he released her hands and returned to his side of the carriage.

A burning sensation covered her eyes. She couldn't cry. Not here. Especially when there was no reason for tears. This man had promised her nothing, hadn't even implied anything. He'd been nothing but kind to her all evening. Yes, the idea that he would consider her as a potential wife had crossed her mind at dinner, but not with any thought of that becoming a reality.

Perhaps the notion that he might have found her a pleasant dalliance before his decision to pursue matrimony had spawned the threatening tears. One more indication that she didn't really belong anywhere.

The coach came to a stop. The soft scuff of the footman jumping to the ground to open the door sounded like a shot through the silent confines of the carriage.

Anthony sat back with a small frown. "I never asked where you lived."

Amelia lunged for the door as soon as it swung open. She stepped to the ground before turning back to face him. "I am also friends with your coachman. And your cook. She makes wonderful ginger biscuits." She dredged up a smile. "Good night, my lord." With a glance at the coachman, she waved and turned to the stairs. "Good night, James."

"Good night, Miss Amelia."

The steps to her front door had never felt so steep. She wanted to turn and get one last look at the marquis, to store up one more memory for her fantasies, but the tears slipping down her cheeks chased her into the house.

Chapter Seven

Spending the evening comparing the calculated flirting of London's eligible ladies to Amelia's honest innocence was unappealing to say the least, so Anthony welcomed Miranda's suggestion of an outing to the opera.

He welcomed it even more when he learned she intended to invite Amelia.

Miranda shook her head and laughed as Trent and then Anthony followed her out of the carriage to collect Amelia. "You've left Aunt Elizabeth alone in the carriage."

Trent pointed at Anthony. "He's the one who left her alone."

Anthony crossed his arms over his chest. "She's your aunt."

The discussion was interrupted by the opening of the door. Miranda halted one step into the front hall, blinking in surprise before continuing across the floor. "Miss Stalwood, don't you know you are supposed to make a gentleman wait so that you can make a grand entrance as you enter the room?"

"You are not a gentleman." Amelia's brows drew together in confusion.

"How very true, but they are." Lady Miranda stepped aside and indicated Anthony and Trent.

The blush he was coming to adore spread across her cheeks. She was beautiful. He recognized the dress as one Miranda had worn to several country assemblies last year, but the style suited Amelia as if she'd picked it out herself.

Her hair was adorably off center. Proof her maid was unused to such elaborate coiffures. Anthony considered suggesting Amelia find someone to teach her maid about hair. It was becoming apparent that many more outings such as this one were going to be in her future.

Anthony intended to see to it.

Miranda jabbed him in the ribs with her elbow. He shook himself out of his contemplation and glared at her. She tilted her head toward her brother, who was fawning over Amelia. The pup had already told the girl how beautiful she looked. Repeating it would make Anthony look like a simpleton.

He cleared his throat before stepping forward. "Might I escort you to the carriage?"

"Of course." Amelia accepted her cloak and reticule from the butler before waving in the direction of the drawing room. Three servants clustered in the drawing room doorway, waving back and grinning.

The carriage was a tight fit, with the three ladies on one side of the carriage and the men on the other, but all agreed it was better than taking a second carriage. It didn't take long to reach the opera house, and most of that time was taken up with introducing Amelia to Trent and Miranda's aunt, Lady Elizabeth Breckton.

Anthony marveled at the wonder on Amelia's face. The opera had yet to begin—they were, in fact, still taking their seats—and already she appeared rapturous.

Miranda linked arms with Amelia as they entered the private box. "Miss Stalwood, you must sit up front. You shouldn't miss a moment of your first opera."

As Amelia settled into a seat at the railing, Trent wedged himself past Anthony, aiming himself for the seat next to her. He was brought up short by a heavy hand on his shoulder. Anthony was surprised to realize it was his own. He didn't remember moving it.

Trent turned to face him with a huge grin.

"Yes, Anthony?" His face was the picture of innocence. Anthony knew better.

Trent was teasing him, the obnoxious pup. Anthony tried to regain his dignity. "I believe, since it is my box, that I will take the prerogative of the other front seat."

"If we wanted to be proper, Miranda should get the other front seat." Lady Elizabeth tapped Anthony on the shoulder with her fan before settling into the backmost seat, an indulgent smile on her face. "I've seen the show already, so

I'm perfectly happy to sit back here where I can make sure all of you behave yourselves."

Anthony sighed, looking from the empty chair to Miranda's grinning face. Being a gentleman could be irritating at times. He bowed and gestured toward the front of the box. "If you please, my lady, your chair awaits."

"Thank you, my lord." Miranda took the seat next to Amelia, grinning like a fool.

Once Miranda was seated, Amelia began talking about all the elegantly dressed people in the boxes around them and the extravagant sets on the stage.

Anthony moved to his seat in the row behind the young women. Hooking his foot around the back leg he angled the chair before sitting down, anticipating it being more pleasurable to watch Amelia watch the opera than to enjoy the show itself.

The show began, and all of the box's occupants fell into silence as the story played out on stage.

Just enough candles had been left flickering for Anthony to watch the emotions cross Amelia's face. It was the best show in town.

At intermission Miranda announced herself positively parched and dragged Trent and Lady Breckton off in search of refreshment. Anthony slid into Miranda's vacated chair.

"It's so beautiful," Amelia whispered. "What language is it?"

Anthony's eyebrows shot upward. "French."

It was hard to remember sometimes that Amelia's upbringing was unconventional. Every woman he knew had at least a passable knowledge of French.

"I don't know French, but it doesn't seem to matter. The story is very sad."

He considered her profile, pondering the best course of action. Assuring her that the story took a turn for the better might ruin the experience for her. She turned and he found himself drowning in her glistening brown eyes. Was she about to cry? "She is not going to die is she?"

When was the last time a woman of his acquaintance had shown this much emotion over anything, much less simple entertainment?

"There is a happy ending." He couldn't resist the urge to smooth an escaped curl of hair back behind her ear.

Her eyes widened. He could feel his heart beat, his chest expand with each passing breath. What was she thinking? He searched her eyes, looking for any spark of interest. Something in her expression that told him maybe, just maybe, she wondered about him as he wondered about her.

"Miss Stalwood, I—"

"We have returned. I forgot to see if you were as parched as I, Amelia, so I procured you a glass of lemonade." Miranda's voice and manner were overly bright as she reentered the box.

Anthony sighed and looked out over the opera house. What had he been about to say? Words had been forming in his mouth but not in his head. He should probably thank Miranda for interrupting him, but he mourned the moment as he relinquished the front seat back to her.

Amelia had never seen anything like the crush of people outside the opera house after the show. Even more amazing was how everyone strolled about talking to each other as if it were a party, calling to each other and carrying on as if rows of carriages weren't waiting to be filled.

Even as Amelia climbed into the carriage, she heard people calling for Anthony and another woman grabbed Lady Miranda by the arm.

Lord Trent clambered in behind her, settling back to wait as if it were the most natural thing in the world. Amelia tried to copy his nonchalance.

"There is a bit of a chill in the air this evening. Is your cloak warm enough?" Lord Trent asked.

"Oh yes." Amelia was so light-headed from the evening she wouldn't have noticed if her toes had turned blue. "I hope this doesn't cause a setback on your head cold. Are you fully recovered?"

"Yes, quite, I—" Lord Trent frowned. "How did you know I'd been ill? That was weeks ago, when I first arrived in London."

"Oh, well, I think Fi . . . someone might have mentioned it to my maid Lydia. I didn't think a thing of it until now." Amelia gripped the edges of her cloak and tried to smile. The effort felt wooden at best. How did one tell someone they'd been the subject of gossip without making it sound like a horrible breach of privacy?

Lord Trent looked thoughtful. "This *someone* was a servant, I assume?"

Amelia swallowed. "Yes, my lord."

He laughed. "Does that happen often? Servants sharing about our health and the like?"

"Servants gossip worse than any member of the *ton* ever could." Amelia winced at how awful that sounded, but it was the truth.

Lord Trent looked skeptical.

"It's true!" Amelia defended. "*Ton* gossip is strictly speculation, from what I understand. What someone might have seen or overheard filled in with conjecture and suspicion. Do they ever know for a fact?"

"Rarely," Lord Trent conceded.

"Servants *know*, my lord. They see and hear everything, and they like to talk about it."

His gaze grew thoughtful again as the rest of their party finally climbed into the carriage and the conveyance made its way back across London.

"That was splendid, Lady Miranda. Thank you for inviting me," Amelia said.

"I cannot remember the last time I had as much fun. It is most refreshing to see things through a new pair of eyes." Lady Miranda reached over and clasped one of Amelia's hands. "You must call me Miranda. I believe we're going to be great friends."

"Then I am Amelia." Under the cover of her cloak Amelia pinched herself.

"I intend to drag you to the Hofferham ball with us next week, Amelia. Are you available Thursday?"

Amelia bit her lip. The true question was whether or not she would be able to procure the appropriate clothing between now and then. The dress Miranda had sent her was lovely, but it was not a ball gown.

"I have no other engagements." Amelia wound her fingers together and held them tight to keep from shouting her happiness out the window. No doubt Miss Ryan would have her on the doorstep of the modiste at the crack of dawn.

"Does this mean that I have to go to the Hofferham ball Thursday?" Lord Trent grumbled.

"Of course." Miranda huffed and crossed her arms over her chest. "Who else would escort me?"

"Anthony will be there. Can he be your escort?"

Miranda frowned. "Anthony is not a relation, you ninny. Besides, how do you know Anthony is attending?"

Lord Trent grinned. "If he wasn't before, he is now."

Anthony opened his mouth but closed it again a moment later with a bit of sheepish shrug.

"Nevertheless, Trent, you are accompanying me and Amelia." Miranda gave a decisive nod. "Resign yourself now."

Amelia looked at London passing by outside the window and smiled.

Chapter Eight

Memories of the opera outing filled Anthony's head the next day, finally sending him from his house in a desperate attempt to find distraction. He let his head loll back against the coach cushions, allowing it to rock back and forth with the swaying conveyance. If God felt charitable today, there would be someone interesting at his club. Waiting five more days to see Amelia was driving him to Bedlam.

Perhaps he should have James change the direction of the coach and head over to Mount Street instead. There was no reason why he couldn't pay her a call, other than a lack of proper chaperonage and a great deal of potential embarrassment on her part. Considering her clothing situation, he was afraid that her housing might be less than amenable as well, despite its fashionable location.

The last thing he wanted to do was cause her shame, but he'd be lying if he said her situation wasn't part of her appeal. What he could give her would far outweigh the scandal of his past.

The rocking stopped, and moments later the footman opened the door. Anthony poked his head out and found a scene vastly different than the white-blocked edifice he expected. Instead of seeing Beau Brummel in White's prestigious bay window, he saw women. Lots of women.

What were all of these women doing on St. James Street? They weren't supposed to even walk down St. James Street, much less patronize the establishments lining the gentlemen's road.

A closer look at the shops revealed the glittering windows and wares of stores catering to decidedly female customers. "James! Where the blazes are we?"

"Bond Street, sir."

Anthony looked up to find the insolent coach driver staring straight ahead. A look to the footman proved that he, too, found the passing traffic of immense interest. "I know we're on Bond Street," Anthony growled. "The question is why?"

James looked down at Anthony, eyes wide. "You said you wanted a hat, sir."

"I wanted a . . . ? I don't want a hat." He turned to scowl at the frippery in the nearby windows. "Even if I did want a hat, I wouldn't come here. I'd go over to— Miss Stalwood!"

Amelia was exiting the milliner, a pink hatbox swinging from her fingertips. A tall woman with a tight black bun showing beneath her plain bonnet stood behind his captivating brunette angel. What amazing luck.

He looked over his shoulder at James, only to find the man once more enthralled with the traffic. Luck had nothing to do with this little encounter. His coachman appeared due for a small bonus.

"My lord, I didn't expect to see you here." Amelia stepped forward, shock lining her face, her fingers twisted in the twine holding the lid on her hatbox.

"I must admit I didn't expect to be here." He bowed and sent a look in the other woman's direction.

Amelia's arm jerked as if she had intended to gesture to the woman beside her, but couldn't. Probably because her hands were so twisted in string. The woman's fingers were going to fall off if she kept doing that. "Lord Raebourne, this is Miss Ryan, my companion."

The woman smiled at Anthony and then emitted the worst fake gasp he had ever had the misfortune to witness. "Oh dear," she muttered. "I believe I left . . . something in the shop."

He liked the companion, fake gasps and all. His attention reverted to Amelia and her tangled parcel twine. A single step brought him close enough to reach down and untangle her fingers. The worn gloves bore creases from the string's loops. "The pleasure is mine, Miss Stalwood. A new bonnet?"

"Oh . . . well, yes. I recently purchased a few new dresses and none of my bonnets match my new pelisse . . . But you don't really want to hear about that, do you?"

No, not particularly. "Of course. I find it beyond interesting. Do you have any more shopping to do?"

"Not really. Although one can always look around even when they aren't shopping for anything in particular." She looked into his eyes. Her shoulders began to pull in a bit and he feared uncertainty was setting in. This woman was just now getting comfortable enough to look him in the eye without blushing. He couldn't let her retreat back into herself.

"Have you been to Gunter's?" The popular tea shop was just the thing. The afternoon was warm and no one would think it odd for them to partake of one of the establishment's famous ices without a chaperone.

"I adore Gunter's! I'm particularly fond of the chocolate ice. Not very original of me, I know, but it seems to be what I always end up with." Her smile broadened a bit more.

"I insist you let me get you one, then. I'll have my men fold down the top of my—" Amelia's restrained giggle stopped him midsentence. A glance over his shoulder revealed that his servants had already taken care of converting the carriage into an open-air conveyance. Yes, a bonus was definitely in order.

"Shall we remove to Gunter's, then?"

"Oh yes." She looked down at her hatbox and then back at the shop behind her. Miss Ryan exited, nothing new in her hands, which surprised him not at all.

"I'll take that home for you," she said, pulling the hatbox string from Amelia's fingers with a deft twist. "Going to Gunter's?"

Anthony tried to be stern as he caught his coachman's eye, but he was afraid his frown looked more like a smirk. He was being manipulated, but he couldn't bring himself to care. Maybe he'd enlist this creative band of servants to aid him further. If this was what they could manage on their own, things could only improve with his cooperation.

"Yes." Amelia looked stunned as she watched Miss Ryan give a small wave and trot over to a tall man with a skewed wig, hatbox securely in her arms. A puzzled look crossed her face. "Fenton?"

Anthony offered a hand to help her up into the carriage. "My lady?"

Amelia drew her gaze from the retreating maid and gave him a wry smile. "I'm not a lady."

No. But she could be. He grinned. "I know."

He clapped his coachman on the back as he climbed into the seat across from Amelia. "To Gunter's, James. Unless you have another surprise for me."

"I hear he has added a new flavor, my lord. It is a berry Miss Amelia is rather fond of." The coachman guided the carriage into the flow of traffic.

Anthony couldn't get the wide smile off his face. Definitely giving that man a raise.

Anthony stared at the Bible lying open on his desk. Since returning to the city, he'd had a difficult time maintaining his morning Bible reading. The different hours and increased distractions reminded him of the way his life used to be, making him feel unworthy of the sacred words.

Restless energy pulsed through him, making it impossible to remain in his seat. He stood in a rush, reaching for the darts he used when he needed to think.

He thumbed the tip of a dart. What did London mean to him? He flipped the dart in his hand and flung it at the board.

"Drinking." *Thunk.*

"Revelry." *Thunk.*

"Women." *Dink. Clank. Clatter.* Anthony watched as the third dart spun a wide circle across the floor. That was the crux of the problem.

Drinking had been easier to avoid than he anticipated, though he was finding many of his former friends were much less entertaining than he previously thought them.

The revelry of London was still alive and well. A good card game or conversation at his club, the crush of social gatherings, all things he had enjoyed before and found pleasure in again.

The women were the problem. Or rather a single woman. His infatuation with someone as sweet and pure as Amelia was at odds with the memory of his previous peccadilloes. No amount of praying and Bible reading would change his past. Even if God didn't hold him accountable for it anymore, Anthony couldn't see how she wouldn't.

Amelia was a ray of sunshine whenever he saw her. She scattered his thoughts even as she brightened his day.

While they'd enjoyed ices at Gunter's she'd confessed that she hadn't read much, but she enjoyed fictional tales of other lands and historical travels. They let her imagine she was somewhere else, far from England. Anthony smiled as he recalled her blushing and ducking her head until her nose nearly touched her shoulder.

The gold lettering on the spine of a copy of *Gulliver's Travels* caught his eye. He'd liked the book as a child, imagined little people living under his bed for a year after his governess read it to him. He stooped and slid the book off the shelf. It was as good an excuse as anything else.

His free hand reached out and scooped up the wayward dart. Straightening, he weighed the book in his hand. With barely a glance, he launched the dart at the board. The ends quivered as it struck the target.

He rolled his shoulders, a satisfied smile creeping across his face. It wasn't easy to force his new life in where his old life had flourished, and he looked forward to finding a wife and retreating back to the country where things were simpler. If loaning a book brought him a little closer to that goal, then he'd willingly pack up the whole library.

Amelia and Miss Ryan tripped over their feet. Again. Amelia stifled a giggle as Miss Ryan frowned. They'd cleared the drawing room of most of the furniture and were attempting to dance. Miss Ryan's efforts to remember the dance steps her friend had taught her were admirable, but Amelia knew she would never feel confident enough to step onto the floor of a London ballroom.

Still, she loved Miss Ryan for trying.

"Now I believe that you and the gentleman place your hands on each other's shoulders." Amelia and Miss Ryan awkwardly tried to hold each other's shoulder with a low degree of success.

"This cannot be right," Miss Ryan muttered.

Amelia laughed. "I don't think it will matter if I know how to waltz or not. I doubt I'll even dance. The experience of a London ball will be enough."

"Pish posh!" cried Miss Ryan. "You listen to me, young lady. I've seen you in that new gown, and I know that some young buck is going to ask you to dance. Why, those two young lords who have been escorting you around town will ask for certain. Let's try again."

Since it made Miss Ryan happy, Amelia returned to the middle of the floor.

"May I be of assistance?" a deep male voice inquired from the doorway.

Amelia whirled to find Anthony handing over his hat to a grinning Fenton, a book tucked under his arm. Her neck began to flush, and she prayed that it would not spread over her cheeks. She forever found herself blushing in front of this man.

"We are learning to waltz." Amelia's voice was so soft she wasn't sure he heard her.

"It is quite difficult when neither of us is aware of the proper forms." Miss Ryan relinquished her spot on the impromptu dance floor.

"How fortunate that I came along, then." Anthony's eyes never left Amelia's. The anticipation of being held in his arms made her skin prickle. Even when she dared to dream that he'd ask her to dance, it hadn't been for a waltz.

He held the book out. "Have you read *Gulliver's Travels*?"

She shook her head and reached out a hand to accept the volume. "I'm sure it will be delightful."

Miss Ryan swept by, snatching the book as she crossed to the settee by the fireplace. Fenton stood in the doorway with a twinkle in his eye.

Anthony took Amelia's hands in his own. "Your hand does go on my shoulder." His voice was low, causing Amelia to lean in to hear him. "Mine rests at your back. I hold your right hand in mine."

Amelia stared at their joined hands. How long since she'd been in the arms of a male? Fenton had never been much for hugging, but he had stopped entirely when she turned fifteen. She had forgotten the sensation of being protected and cared for that a man's arms could project.

"Now we twirl about the room." Anthony began to hum a tune.

He guided Amelia in the steps of the waltz, occasionally correcting the placement of her feet. "No, when I step in this direction, you will step to the other side and our arms will meet here, above our heads."

Amelia tried to follow and ended up stepping on her own foot. As she strove to catch herself, her toe caught and shifted her slipper off of her heel. The following step sent the slipper skittering across the floor to bump against the wall.

She froze, staring at the offending shoe, unsure what the correct etiquette was for returning a slipper to one's foot when in the presence of a man. "I believe, my lord, that I am destined to embarrass myself at every one of our meetings."

Sighing, she maneuvered herself into the corner of the wall, holding her skirts to retain her modesty while she wiggled her foot back into her slipper. When she turned to face him, Anthony was grinning.

And alone. When had Miss Ryan and Fenton left the room?

"Perhaps we should try a quadrille. As you stated, you are unlikely to dance the waltz at your first ball."

For the next hour, Anthony instructed Amelia on the basic steps of London's more popular dances. While she would hardly shine as the most graceful woman in the ballroom, if she were asked to dance Thursday, she felt that she would indeed be able to execute the basic steps without crashing into too many people.

"Thank you, for a delightful afternoon." Anthony accepted his hat and coat from Fenton, whose immediate appearance proved her servants hadn't left her quite as alone as she'd thought.

"It is I who should thank you," Amelia said. "If you had not come by, anyone seeing me dance Thursday would have immediately labeled me a provincial."

"Anyone seeing you dance Thursday will be too busy being jealous of the gentleman you partner to worry about you missing a step or two." He lifted her hand in his and brushed a light kiss over her fingers.

Amelia blushed once more, amazed she hadn't caught fire in the past hour and a half, with the many compliments the marquis gave her. He must think her complexion was permanently flushed. With one last look into her eyes, Anthony donned his hat and hopped lightly down the stairs to the sidewalk.

Chapter Nine

Despite the bleakness of the next morning, Amelia's spirits remained high. How could they not after the most amazing week of her life?

She rushed through her breakfast, anxious to put together a tray for Miss Ryan. Sometime in the night, the older woman had become quite ill. She would probably be in bed for days, but even that didn't faze Amelia.

It was doubtful that Miss Ryan would be able to partake of anything more than tea, but Amelia loaded the tray with toast and a warmed mug of broth as well.

A loud knock echoed through the house as she crossed the hall to the main staircase. Fenton rushed by her to answer it. Though she was curious to see who would be calling this early in the morning in dismal weather, the tray was getting heavy and she still had to climb the stairs with it. She didn't wait.

"May I help you, sir?" Fenton asked.

Amelia shook her head at the mix of condescension and graciousness in his voice. He was getting much better at answering the door of late. After seeing Anthony out the day before he'd claimed to be fitting in with the rest of the upper-crust butlers.

The rasp of hacking coughs greeted her as she shouldered her way into Miss Ryan's room.

"Tea. Bless you!" Miss Ryan flopped back against her pillows, fever making her look pale and flushed at the same time.

"I brought some broth and toast as well. Perhaps you can stop coughing long enough to partake." Amelia set the tray on the small writing desk and set about preparing Miss Ryan's tea. She was handing Miss Ryan the cup when Fenton appeared in the doorway.

"Miss Amelia? There is a solicitor downstairs to see you."

A solicitor? Here? What on earth for? She glanced to the window, now streaked with rain. "Oh my, he must be soaked. I'll grab a blanket as I go down. Miss Ryan, I shall return as soon as possible. Fenton, please ask Mrs. Harris to come help Miss Ryan finish her soup."

"Right away, ma'am."

Amelia grabbed a blanket from the chest at the foot of the bed before scurrying down the stairs. A solicitor. Had he been sent by the viscount? Was he there to give her instructions on vacating the property by her birthday?

She bustled into the drawing room with part of her mind still abovestairs with Miss Ryan. The companion's discomfort was a more immediate, though significantly less permanent, problem than the viscount's cessation of support.

Awaiting her in the drawing room was a very short, very round man wearing round spectacles. Round water droplets ran slowly down his round top hat to splash in small round dots on the worn rug at his feet.

She extended the blanket. He didn't take it.

"My name is Mr. Alexander Bates of the offices of Chandler, Bates, and Holmes. I need to speak with the personage in charge on a very important legal matter." The man pulled himself up to his greatest height—which put him at the same height as Amelia's nose—and made every attempt to appear as important as possible.

"I am in charge." Amelia clutched the blanket to her chest. Dear Lord, help them. He was going to kick them all out immediately.

"Ah, the governess."

"I beg your pardon?" She had thought of becoming a governess but as of yet hadn't even applied for any such position. Had one of her friends taken it upon themselves to find her a position?

"The governess," he repeated.

"The governess?"

The man harrumphed loudly. "For the child."

"The child?" What was he talking about?

Mr. Bates looked very grim. Amelia thought about offering him the blanket again, but it didn't appear as if he realized he was wet. Perhaps he had the wrong house.

"While it is no nevermind to me if a person hires those who are lacking in wits, you can be sure I will relay this exchange to the heir." He snapped a packet of papers from his greatcoat pocket and held them in front of his eyes.

Heir? Oh no. A sinking feeling hit Amelia in the stomach. If there were an heir, then that had to mean—

"On behalf of Chandler, Bates, and Holmes, I would like to extend heartfelt condolences for your recent loss." The little man's voice held no emotion as he read from the papers.

Amelia felt her jaw slacken. He was going to call her a lackwit and then carry on delivering his message without any explanation or apology?

The truth of her changed circumstances began to sink in. Amelia dropped into the closest chair. A soft *whoosh* hit her ears as the blanket fell to the floor. What was going to happen to them all now?

"As I am sure you are aware, there was no direct heir. An extensive tracing of the family tree has located the next male relation and he has been notified of his inheritance. He has agreed to take up the wardship of one Miss Amelia Stalwood, age eleven . . ." Here Mr. Bates paused and glanced up. "Though I suppose she might be twelve now." He looked back down at his papers. "Regardless, the care of Miss Amelia Stalwood has been taken up by the new holder of the title.

"The heir has arranged for the child to live with his mother and stepfather at their estate in Essex until further arrangements are made. He wishes to place her with his family as soon as possible to help her deal with her grief. You and the child are to depart at nine o'clock tomorrow morning."

Amelia felt cold and pale. She never knew someone could actually feel pale. She couldn't leave tomorrow. The ball was tomorrow. She didn't want to leave London at all! There must be a way to delay their departure. "There is an engagement tomorrow—"

"Your comfort matters not." The little man frowned, the first emotion he shown since he arrived. "He wishes the child stabilized immediately. It is your job to see that she is prepared."

Were Amelia actually a child, she would likely appreciate the sentiment.

But she wasn't a child. "I am not eleven."

The man frowned. "I should hope not."

"Amelia Stalwood is not eleven. Nor is she twelve. I'm afraid your information is outdated."

He looked at his papers, as if he couldn't fathom being wrong. "She is still here, isn't she? The papers indicate she is to remain under the guardianship of Lord Stanford until she reaches the age of one and twenty."

She could lie. Add a few months to her age and be free. But honesty was a trait that God praised, wasn't it? Mrs. Bummel had always thought so. Would He honor her honesty? "Yes, I still live here, and—"

Mr. Bates continued as soon as he heard an affirmative answer. "The quarterly allowance will be adjusted accordingly for the departure of the ward and the governess. Further arrangements for the house will be made at a later date."

Mr. Bates tipped his hat in Amelia's direction, placed his stack of papers back into his coat, and exited the room, stepping on the blanket that had fallen from her cold fingers. He had never even taken a seat.

Amelia ran after him. "But, I—"

"Nine o'clock tomorrow. Good day."

And then he was gone, leaving the drawing room before Amelia could draw in a breath.

"Sir, I insist you stop." She chased the solicitor into the hall. "There's been a misunderstanding and it must be corrected."

He paused with his hand on the door latch, condescension and exasperation in every line on his round face. "We have established that Amelia Stalwood is not yet of age. Therefore she is bound by her guardian's wishes. I have done my job by delivering the message despite this dreadful weather. If you have further problems, I suggest you take them up with the new guardian. Good day."

He opened the door enough to slip from the house and slammed it behind him, as if he were afraid she'd chase him out into the street.

Rain continued to pelt the window, seeming to echo the words of the departed solicitor. *"Amelia Stalwood, age eleven . . ."*

She knew that the viscount never loved her, did not even think much of her. But to have meant so little to him that once she was out of his sight neither he nor his solicitors remembered that she would continue to age?

Tears were inevitable. Once the shock wore off, the hurt and fear would remain. She would curl into a little ball and feel the pain. But she welcomed her current numbness more than she would have ever imagined.

Placing one foot in front of the other, she trudged up the stairs and into Miss Ryan's room, where she found the entirety of her little servant family. Lydia, the parlor maid, was changing Miss Ryan's sweat-soaked sheets. Mrs. Harris was trying to convince Miss Ryan to take one of her homemade remedies. Fenton was replacing the chamber pot. Miss Ryan must have cast up the soup Amelia had coaxed her into eating.

All activity stopped as Amelia stood in the doorway. How awful did she look? She felt small and thin, a piece of parchment poised to blow away in the wind. All three able-bodied servants began to rush toward her until Amelia held up her hand.

She looked into the face of everyone in the room before speaking again. "Lord Stanford has passed away. A carriage will arrive to carry me to my new guardian in the morning. Miss Ryan can follow once she is well." If she needed to come at all. Perhaps Amelia could secure a position and Miss Ryan could seek work in London, where their connections could work in her favor. "Now, if you will excuse me, I need to pack."

Amelia did not meet anyone's eyes as she turned and walked down the corridor to her own room.

It would not take her long to pack all that she considered her own. She had little left from her parents and had no reason to acquire many personal objects to remember life in London.

The new pink ball gown hung on the outside of the closet, reminding her of how close she'd come to a different life. There was nothing to do now but pack it up and let it remind her of the joyful moments.

More than anything, Amelia wished for the courage to stay, but there was little doubt she would be supporting herself soon. As soon as her true age was revealed to the new viscount, she'd be looking for work.

It would be better to find work in Essex. London held too many reminders of what almost was. Once away from those remembrances, she could be happy. She would make herself be happy.

A deep, steadying breath filled her lungs. As it whooshed out again, she wiped her hands firmly down the front of her skirt. Clothing wasn't going to pack itself. There was much to do before the carriage arrived in the morning, and she still had to help take care of Miss Ryan.

Lydia appeared and began folding and packing Amelia's few dresses in a trunk. "Why do you have to go?" Lydia whispered.

"I have no way of supporting myself if I don't go. I confess I thought that I had months before facing the day I would be on my own. We were so ignored here, away from Lord Stanford's books and studies, I thought I would be able to ease into making my own way in the world. I'm afraid I'm at the mercy of the new viscount."

Lydia's grin was as shaky as it was cheeky. "Maybe he'll be young and single. The marquis seemed to like you well enough. A viscount's not as good, but he'd be able to support you right and proper."

Amelia threw a pillow at her friend. The beginnings of a smile reached the edges of her lips. With a shake of her head she turned back to the trunk.

Silence remained as they finished packing, but the air felt a little lighter.

Chapter Ten

The scene was too reminiscent of the one that took place when she left the viscount's for London ten years ago. Amelia sat on a trunk in the front hall, clutching a valise, waiting for the promised carriage. A basket of Mrs. Harris's best cooking efforts sat on the floor at her feet. She, Miss Ryan, and Lydia had said their good-byes an hour ago. Only Fenton remained, pacing from window to window.

A strong knock on the front door made Amelia jump. The second had her clutching the valise to her chest. The third sounded like a death knell.

Fenton wrenched open the door to reveal a liveried footman standing tall and straight like the guards in front of the palace. "The carriage for Miss Stalwood and Miss Ryan has arrived."

Amelia placed one foot in front of the other with deliberate precision. There was no room for hesitation today. God had promised her nothing but this moment, and she would make the best of it. "Good day. I am Miss Stalwood, but please call me Miss Amelia. And you are?"

The footman shifted his weight. "M'name is Gordon, miss. Jeremy Gordon. I thought there was to be a child?"

"I am pleased to make your acquaintance, Gordon. I'm afraid there's no child today. Only me. Miss Ryan is unfit to travel, unfortunately. If you would be so good as to assist me with my trunk, I will not delay our departure any longer. I have a basket of scones and biscuits and other good things prepared by my housekeeper that I will be more than willing to share on our journey. Shall we be off?" Her tension uncurled as she discovered her voice could remain steady. She even managed a smile.

Gordon gave her basket a strange look but said nothing about it as he hefted her trunk. "Will this be it, miss?"

"Yes, that is everything." Everything she had to mark twenty years of life fit in a single trunk. "Thank you, Gordon."

The driver helped Gordon secure the trunk. He started to yawn and ducked behind the carriage out of sight.

Amelia followed him. "Are you well?"

The man flushed. "I beg your pardon, miss. We didn't arrive from Essex until late last night."

And now the man had to make the drive back. Amelia couldn't help but wish they'd taken a day to rest. Then she could have attended the ball tonight. She felt a bit guilty over that. The driver and his employer thought they were rushing to the aid of a distraught young girl. She held up the basket. "Would you like a raspberry scone?"

The driver and footman exchanged glances again but then graciously accepted her offer of pastries.

Gordon handed her into the carriage and toasted her with his last bite of scone. "These are quite good, milady."

"My— That is Mrs. Harris is an extraordinary cook." Amelia fought back the tears at the thought that Mrs. Harris was no longer her cook. She had no claim to the woman anymore. "Please, call me Miss Amelia. Everyone does."

"Very well, Miss Amelia." His smile looked a bit more genuine as he shut the door and climbed atop the carriage. "You get comfortable. It shouldn't take us long. The roads seemed fairly empty this morning."

The steady clop of the horses' hooves gave Amelia something to cling to. All she had to do was maintain her composure until the next hoof fell. If she could manage that, by the time they reached Essex she would be in complete control of her faculties.

She watched the buildings roll by, expecting to take the same road out of London that she'd arrived on so many years ago.

The sudden turn took her by surprise. This road took them deeper into the heart of Mayfair. Were they lost? Perhaps they'd gotten turned around, unfamiliar with the tight streets of London.

After a bit of struggle, she managed to open the window and lean her head out. A fat raindrop fell on her forehead before she could ask if they needed assistance. Another soon joined it and within moments the sky was full of pelting rain.

Amelia jerked her head back inside. They must be staying in London somewhere overnight instead of risking the country roads in the rain.

A trickle of hope wormed into her mind, even as she tried to squash it. If they were staying in London for the night, could she make it to the ball?

A few more turns took them clear to the other side of Mayfair. Amelia had never visited this area, so she wasn't likely to find anyone willing to help her get to the ball. The warm glow of hope faded away.

They stopped in front of a simple but stately terrace house, at least six windows across.

Gordon flung open the door and lowered the step, water dripping from his nose.

"We're stopping here?" Amelia hated making him stand in the rain, but she couldn't just walk into someone's house without knowing who they were or what they expected.

"Of course, Miss Amelia. Lady Blackstone is expecting you." Gordon reached out a hand to help her alight. "She thought a trip to Essex might be a bit much for a grieving child, so she came to London to meet you."

A scraping noise preceded the driver carrying her trunk down to the servant entrance.

Gordon rubbed a hand along the back of his neck. "'Course, you're not really a child."

"I'm afraid that's going to take a bit of explanation." Amelia took a deep breath and stomped out of the carriage. Her determination caused her to slip on the stair, nearly sending her bottom first into a puddle.

Gordon righted her before resuming his formal stance.

"Thank you." She stared at the steps to the front door, all determination replaced by fear.

"You're getting wet, miss."

"Yes. Right. I should go in, then." She flew up the stairs as if another moment's hesitation would make everything disappear. The front door swung open as she approached, and her momentum sent her careening into the front hall. Her slippers slid across the slick marble, and Amelia managed her second narrow escape in as many minutes. It wouldn't do to meet her hostess by sliding across the hall on her backside.

The butler closed the door slowly. He didn't have a smile on his face, but his eyes crinkled a bit at the corner. "Would you care for a towel?"

Amelia gratefully accepted the length of linen he extended toward her.

"There is a fire laid in the drawing room. I'll have Lady Blackstone summoned. You're a bit earlier than she anticipated."

The butler took her wet pelisse, but the dress underneath was still damp. Amelia retreated to the room the butler indicated, but she refused to place her sodden clothing on any of the beautiful upholstered furniture. Instead she stood by the fire, enjoying the warmth on her skin as cold trepidation seeped through her blood. Who was Lady Blackstone? What had she been told? She had a vague recollection of a Lady Cressida Blackstone getting married last year. Had that been her name before or after she'd gotten married?

Another carriage clattered to a stop outside the house. Had Lady Blackstone been away?

Curiosity propelled Amelia to the window, but she couldn't tell anything about the people who alighted from the carriage. Two women wearing deep-hooded cloaks and a man with his greatcoat pulled up close to his top hat rushed up the stairs.

Amelia heard footfalls in the hall as she crossed the drawing room. She recognized the butler's quiet gait from earlier, but the heavy tread of boots and the swish of slippers were new.

Wanting to know the situation before bumbling into it, Amelia peeked around the partially closed drawing room door. She couldn't see the people entering from the street, but she saw the elegant woman coming down the stairs from the upper floors and the mountain of a man approaching from the back of the house.

The woman had touches of grey threaded through her dark blond hair. She reached a hand toward the large blond man in riding clothes. "I'm glad you managed to be here this morning. I must have misunderstood— they told me a woman had arrived."

The man gestured toward the front door, where presumably the newly arrived party had shed their coats and cloaks.

"Mother!" a young, slightly familiar female voice called.

Amelia tried to see the front of the hall without opening the drawing room door any wider, but it was impossible.

The girl continued. "I'm begging you to convince Miranda to stop this mission."

Amelia jerked away from the door. *Miranda?* It couldn't be the same Miranda. That was impossible.

"She's not a mission. Besides, she sent me a note this morning canceling our plans for the evening and then had her butler tell me she wasn't home when I went by. I think she's scared and means to drop our friendship entirely. Mother, you have to help me make her see reason."

It *was* the same Miranda. Amelia had wanted to tell her good-bye since she had little intention of returning from Essex, but she put off writing the letter until all she had time to do was scribble a note that she wouldn't be able to go to the ball. But how could she . . . ? Why would she . . . ? Had they called the woman *Mother*?

"Of whom are we speaking?" The older woman's smile was indulgent. Definitely that of a mother.

"Some poor girl Miranda has decided to yank into society as a sacrificial lamb," Georgina muttered.

Amelia paused in the act of reaching for the door latch. Were they talking about her?

"That is not true," Miranda grumbled.

"Trent has decided to court her," Georgina continued.

"That's not true." Trent walked into view. "Good morning, Griffith. What brings you to town? By the by, I think she was lying in that note she sent this morning. It was rather vague."

Miranda huffed. "Why would she lie to me?"

Amelia crossed her arms and frowned. She hadn't lied. Unforeseen circumstances was a perfectly acceptable explanation for why she wouldn't be attending the ball.

"Beg pardon," a voice she assumed was Griffith's said, "but of what are we talking? Aren't you all here to meet my new ward?"

"I met a lovely young *disadvantaged* gentlewoman and have befriended her." Miranda paused. "Trent does appear to have decided to court her though. What do you mean you have a new ward? Who died? No one close or I'd have heard about it."

Amelia's head was spinning. She looked for a second door out of the drawing room. She couldn't possibly face them now, not after hearing that conversation. How could she face Trent when her heart was already Anthony's?

"Nonsense, Miranda. I have merely befriended her as well. I value my head, you know. Anthony would kill me if I courted her when he's already claimed her for himself."

There wasn't another door. She was going to have to face them. With the towel pulled tight around her shoulders, she eased the drawing room door the rest of the way open, but no one noticed her.

The man she assumed was Griffith was looking from one family member to another.

His mother looked delighted. "Anthony is courting her?"

"Of course not," Georgina said. "He has a marquisate to think about."

"I do so love it when you're wrong," Trent said, smugness oozing from his smile. "He's been to call on her already. Even took her to Gunter's for ices."

"That was her?" Georgina pouted.

Miranda clapped with glee. "Everyone's talking about that. No one could see the lady for the tree. Rebecca Laramy claimed he'd taken her, but I knew it couldn't be true."

"This is all fascinating," Griffith said, "but a young girl is going to be arriving here soon—"

"How young?" Georgina's eyes narrowed.

"You never said who died," Miranda said.

The import of Griffith's statement penetrated Amelia's spinning brain. *He* was her new guardian. But how was that possible? How could God do that? The one friendship she'd formed where the other person had nothing to gain but her company was about to be tainted with obligation. "Oh my."

Five heads twisted in her direction.

"Amelia!" Miranda danced across the hall and wrapped her arms around Amelia.

"Who are you?" Miranda's mother walked forward with a frown. "Are you the governess? What did you do with the child?"

Georgina coughed. "She's a servant?"

Miranda frowned. "But I thought you were the ward of the Viscount of Stanford."

Amelia swallowed. "I am, but—"

"No," Griffith said, "the viscount's ward is an eleven-year-old girl, I'm expecting her here any minute."

"But the maid told me the girl had already arrived." His mother, who was presumably the Lady Blackstone who lived here, looked very confused. "So you must be Miss Ryan."

"Miss Ryan is sick. She couldn't accompany me. I'm—"

Trent grinned. "I like Amelia better than an eleven-year-old girl. Can we keep her instead?"

"Mind your tongue." Lady Blackstone poked Trent in the chest. "We take care of the less fortunate in this family, and a young girl who's been uprooted twice is most unfortunate."

"Her name's not Ryan—it's Stalwood." Miranda crossed her arms over her chest.

"But the ward's name is Stalwood," Griffith said. "Amelia Stalwood."

Everyone stared at Amelia in silence. The sudden quiet was heavy. She gave a tiny wave. "Hello."

"You," Lady Blackstone finally said, "are not eleven years old."

Chapter Eleven

It took only five minutes for them to explain that Lady Blackstone was Miranda's mother, who had remarried the year before.

It took almost an hour for Amelia to relate her story to the curious family. She didn't know who was more surprised—them at finding out who the ward truly was or her at discovering she was now connected to a duke. It was a step up in society she couldn't have even dreamt of.

"How did you manage to inherit a viscountcy?" Trent asked.

Griffith shrugged. "The first Duke of Riverton was the second son of the fourth Viscount of Stanford."

"That must have made family gatherings fun." Trent grinned.

"They weren't a very prolific bunch. The viscounts that followed each had one son who married and produced one son of his own." Griffith shook his head. "A couple of them also had daughters, but they had to trace back nine generations to find another male heir."

"The Hofferham ball!" Miranda cried.

"What?" Lady Blackstone set her cup of tea aside gracefully, despite her obvious confusion.

"You can't still be thinking of going," Georgina said.

"Of course I am!" Miranda wrapped an arm around Amelia, who sat next to her on the settee. "It is the perfect time to announce Amelia's new status."

"But we haven't unpacked her trunk yet," Lady Blackstone said.

"Perfect. Don't. I insist that she come live at Hawthorne House anyway. The rain has stopped, so we can lug her trunk over there now." Miranda smiled at everyone in the circle, excitement bursting from her.

"I don't have a maid," Amelia said. Not that Miss Ryan had proven to be of much help when it came to dressing Amelia in finery. The hairstyle she'd worn to the opera had taken hours and even then it'd been a bit lopsided.

"Sally can help you. Or Iris. Iris is the upstairs maid. She's fabulous. If I didn't have Sally I'd hire Iris in a moment."

No one could come up with a sufficient objection, so Amelia bundled herself and her trunk into a carriage once more, though with a considerably lighter heart than that morning.

In the whirlwind that only a competent household can accomplish, a room was prepared, her trunk was unpacked, and clothes for the evening pressed. Amelia had barely caught her breath before she found herself in the hall of Hawthorne House, Gibson smiling like a proud papa.

"Now, my dear, do not worry about a thing. You will be marvelous tonight." Lady Blackstone, who had insisted on being called Caroline, because there was no place for formality among family, smoothed a piece of Amelia's hair back. "Doesn't Amelia look lovely this evening, William?"

Lord Blackstone, who had married Caroline the year before, smiled at Amelia and then his wife. His daughter was the one whose marriage Amelia had heard about. "That she does, my love, but I think your encouragement is causing more flustering than bolstering."

Amelia snapped her fan out, moving the air toward her face in an attempt to ward off the impending blush.

Trent, Miranda, Amelia, and Griffith rode in one carriage with Lord Blackstone and Caroline in a carriage directly behind them.

Miranda talked incessantly about how much fun it was going to be having Amelia around the house. Amelia didn't say a word. Breathing was about all she was able to manage. After all the ups and downs, the gaining and losing of hope, she was on her way to the ball.

The horses slowed to a stop, jolting her against Miranda. The footman, Gordon, swung the door open and stood stiffly, waiting to assist. He broke form for a moment, glancing sideways into the carriage to wink at Amelia. The wink gave Amelia more confidence than anything Miranda or Caroline or even Griffith could have said.

Amelia stared up at the house, unable to believe she was here. She remembered over the years seeing the glow of houses lit up with so many candles they were visible from the next street. Now she would see what was going on inside with her own eyes. Her heart filled with bubbly happiness. God was good. Even if He'd taken a bizarre route to get her to this place.

Trent gave Miranda his arm and grinned like a mischievous little boy. "I can't wait to see Anthony's face."

The brother and sister trotted off, leaving Amelia to revel in her dream world as she and Griffith waited for Lord and Lady Blackstone. People streamed by her in a beautiful rainbow of silks and satins. A sudden urge to see if the interior was as awe-inspiring as the exterior released her feet from their invisible prison. She glanced around to find her companions and discovered them a few steps away with small smiles and damp eyes.

"How long have I been standing here?" She hated how her voice trembled, but there was nothing she could do to stop it.

"However long you needed." Griffith offered her his arm and led her into the building.

The noise of the ballroom reached her first, an indistinct swell of voices and music. Amelia's heart sped up, and her palms began to sweat. Thankful for the gloves, she gripped Griffith's arm tighter.

The ballroom was like a painting come to life. Beautiful people, beautiful music, and beautiful decorations swirled together in a mass of splendid color.

A small flight of six stairs led down into the ballroom, giving Amelia enough height to see two blond heads cutting a swath through the crowd. Miranda and Trent were making good on their intention to rush to Anthony's side. Her gaze followed their intended path until she found him dancing. Her overactive imagination made her think she could see the vibrant blue of his eyes.

Seeing him again when she'd thought she never would made her feel funny inside. Her rapidly beating heart rose from her stomach to her throat. She couldn't breathe anymore but at least she was no longer queasy.

When he'd come by the house, she'd begun to hope his apparent interest was genuine. Surely that would only continue now that her circumstances had changed.

Wouldn't it?

Anthony wasn't sure why he had arrived so ridiculously early to Lady Hofferham's ball. Griffith's vague note ensuring his attendance had intrigued him, but he doubted the mystery would provide enough distraction from his disappointment over Miranda's early-morning note telling him Amelia wouldn't be coming.

He murmured the appropriate pleasantries to his dance partner as he handed her to her mother. She was nice enough, but so were many of the other dozens of women he's danced with of late.

Perhaps he should return to the country and try again next year. His obsession with the absent Amelia kept him from considering any other candidates. It was insupportable. He had been in her company a scant number of times. Surely it had not been enough to warrant this incessant comparison of every other woman to her.

Miranda and Trent accosted him as he walked away from the young woman whose name he had already forgotten. The beauty of Miranda's wide smile took him by surprise. Wasn't she supposed to be nearly as disappointed as he was?

Lady Helena Bell was working her way across the ballroom toward him. There was another problem he could do without. She'd been following him since his first public appearance in London. Miranda told him she was bribing people to tell her where he went each evening so that she could show up as well. Her intentions were embarrassingly obvious, but he wanted no part of them. Why wouldn't the lady simply go away?

"Hullo!" Miranda called cheerfully, snagging his arm and pulling him back around to face her. Trent stood behind her rocking back and forth on his feet, grinning like an idiot.

"Good evening," Anthony said cautiously. "Where is Griff? He said he was going to be here."

"Oh, he is here." Miranda giggled.

Anthony braced himself. Miranda never giggled.

Trent cleared his throat. "We convinced him to delay his entrance until we found you."

Anthony began to worry.

Trent's grin got even wider.

"He has a solution for your doldrums caused by the impossible infatuation you have with Amelia," Miranda chirped.

"His Grace, the Duke of Riverton, Lord and Lady Blackstone, and Miss Amelia Stalwood!" the bailiff cried from the doorway.

Anthony's head snapped to the front of the ballroom. Had he heard correctly? Was Amelia actually here?

A vision in pale rose stood beside Griffith. It was her. Even from this distance, he could see the banked excitement on her face. He could almost feel her pulse race under his fingers, see the blush behind her ears, threatening to spread charmingly to her cheeks if she became the center of attention.

He pushed past Lady Helena as he crossed to the entrance, ignoring her huff of indignation. Miranda and Trent could deal with his pursuer's hurt feelings.

His mouth dried as he took in every detail. Her dress was elegant, a ball gown any woman in the room would be proud to wear, yet still quintessentially Amelia in its simplicity. Her brown hair had been piled on her head with a single large ringlet draped over her right shoulder. His fingers itched to bury themselves in that ringlet. It was wide enough to wrap around his wrist. How had she gotten it to do that?

She wasn't looking at him, was enthralled with everything around her, swiveling her head from side to side in an effort to take everything in as she walked down the stairs. When she finally saw him, her eyes lit from within and pink tinged her cheeks. He had never seen anything lovelier in his life.

"Miss Stalwood." He bowed over her hand and kissed the knuckles. He'd never despised a glove more in his life. "It is a delight to see you again."

Two people come up behind him. The rustle of her gown as she bounced in excitement gave Miranda away.

Anthony spared her and Trent a scathing glance before directing his attention back to Amelia. "I thought you weren't coming."

"Neither did I. So much has happened since yesterday, I can't even begin to understand it all," Amelia said.

Anthony offered Amelia his arm. Her smile was small and sweet as she laid her hand in the crook of his elbow. Over her head, Anthony caught a glance of Lady Helena glowering in their direction. He shrugged. He had never given her a reason to believe he was interested. It shouldn't take long for her to move on to some other unsuspecting nobleman.

The evening whirled by in a swirl of colors and sensations. Anthony escorted her straight from the stairs to the dance floor. Terrified that she would forget the steps, she barely managed two words to him. He didn't seem to mind, giving her an understanding smile as he escorted her back to Caroline.

While she'd been dancing, the news that she was the duke's new ward had circulated through the ballroom, and a queue of gentlemen awaited her arrival. Introductions and requests to dance arrived with such regularity Amelia began to feel light-headed. Her frequent pleas of breathlessness were not always because she didn't know the dance being done. Her dancing lesson with Anthony hadn't been extensive enough for this level of popularity.

After two hours, Caroline allowed Anthony to dance with her again.

"How are you enjoying your first ball?" Anthony led her onto the floor.

Amelia's hand tingled as she felt the warmth of his arm through her glove. Dancing with Anthony was more exciting than any of her other partners. "I know a lot of the attention is curiosity over the duke's new ward, but it has still been a wonderful experience."

The dance pulled them away from each other for a time, but when they came together again, he asked, "Did I hear Sir Hollis reciting poetry earlier?"

Amelia tried not to giggle at the memory. The man's hastily constructed ode to her pink gown had been sweet, but horrible. "Yes. He was quite enthusiastic about it."

They parted again, and she could only smile at him as the dance moved along. Eventually they stood in the middle once more.

"I never understood before what drove all the young fops to spout flowery bits of terrible poetry." Anthony took her hand to walk her around the end of the line of dancers. "I think I do now." Amelia couldn't hold back a small smile.

The dance drew to a close. Griffith was waiting by Caroline and Miranda when they returned. "My drawing room is sure to resemble a hothouse by tomorrow afternoon."

"Gibson will have to station himself permanently by your door," Anthony added.

Miranda looped an arm through Amelia's. "I've no doubt the man is looking forward to it. Didn't you notice the maids clearing the flower arrangements from the hall tables as we were leaving? I think the servants are anticipating your success as much as I am."

Caroline cocked her head to the side. "Gibson *did* seem more exuberant this evening. Why is that?"

"Because everyone loves our dear Amelia."

Miranda could not have said anything that would please Amelia more. As long as her old friends knew she hadn't forgotten them, she could enjoy everything this new life had to offer.

A tall woman with icy blond hair walked by, eyes narrowed as she looked at Amelia and Anthony.

Perhaps everyone wasn't as happy with her new good fortune as Miranda seemed to think.

Chapter Twelve

Trent, Amelia, and Miranda strolled slowly down the path beside Rotten Row. The place bustled with society's upper crust, but Amelia was content to focus on her strolling partners. Over the past three weeks the sheen of the promenade had worn off a bit as she realized others were looking around in judgment instead of fascination.

"It feels odd having Trent out of the house," Miranda said.

Amelia thought of all the school stories Trent had shared. "Hasn't he been out of the house for years?"

"But his home was still with us. Now he has lodgings of his own."

"Imagine how strange it is for me. He's living in my old home." Amelia grinned at Miranda, hoping to disguise how strange it truly made her feel. She'd been visiting several times a week with Mrs. Harris, Lydia, and Fenton. Those visits would have to stop since Trent had officially taken possession of the house yesterday.

"You realize I'm here, don't you?" Trent asked.

Miranda continued the conversation without acknowledging his interruption. "I suppose it would be difficult for you. I mean, he's eating at your old dining table." A wide grin split Miranda's face. "Do you think he kept all the curtains? I believe I remember seeing lace in a window or two."

"Mrs. Harris planned to remove the more feminine frippery from around the house."

Trent coughed. "I am walking between the two of you, even."

Miranda frowned. "That is no fun at all. I shall continue thinking of him drowning in ruffles. It makes me laugh."

Amelia rolled her eyes. The image was certainly a funny one, but it was also disturbing. Trent was eating off dishes she used every day in her former life. He was sitting on the sofas that she'd had re-covered. At least Mrs. Harris had set him up in one of the other bedrooms so she didn't have to picture that awkward scenario.

"How was your first evening in your new home, Trent?" Amelia hoped hearing Trent's stories would make the house more his than hers.

"Oh, so we've decided I can be part of the conversation now?" Trent straightened his cuffs. "You neglected to mention that you lived in the strangest house in London."

Amelia frowned in confusion.

Miranda laughed. "I've been in the house, brother. There's nothing strange about it."

Trent grunted. "They ate dinner with me."

Amelia giggled.

"Who ate dinner with you?" Miranda's brows drew down over her eyes.

Amelia's giggles grew into a laugh. She could visualize what must have happened.

"Who do you *think* ate dinner with me?" Trent stopped and crossed his arms over his chest.

"You couldn't have invited guests over. Half of your things are still at Hawthorne House."

Amelia gave in. The idea of Mrs. Harris and Fenton sitting down to dinner and treating Trent the way they had treated her was too comedic to resist. The brown ringlets Iris had so carefully fashioned that morning bobbed happily against her head. It certainly wasn't fashionable to laugh this loud or this long, but Amelia didn't care.

That realization distracted her brain enough to allow the laughter to begin to ebb. She didn't care! From the first moment Amelia had met Miranda, she had been constantly worried about her dress, her manners, and her speech. The desire to impress engulfed her, even after securing a place in the family.

Her gaze flew around the circle, touching on the now familiar faces. Miranda smiled though confusion filled her eyes. Trent's disgruntled frown was exaggerated in an obvious attempt to make her laugh harder. She loved these people, and they loved her back.

A blessed freedom she hadn't realized she'd missed the past few months filled her heart. It was a new confidence that would probably falter at the next ballroom door, but for that moment she was nothing but herself. It felt glorious.

"Wasn't it better than eating alone, Trent?" Amelia's giggles settled into a wide grin.

"I wouldn't know. I didn't have the chance to find out."

"Find out what? If it's as delightful as Amelia's smile indicates, I want to be included in the revelation."

Amelia turned, a smile still stretched across her face, to see Anthony dismounting from his horse. Tossing the reins to his groom he approached the group. Amelia felt some of her peaceful confidence sliding away. She clung to it with ruthless determination.

"What are we talking about?" Anthony looked back and forth from Amelia to Trent.

"Trent bought the lease to my house," Amelia said.

"What?" Anthony all but yelled the question and sent an accusatory look at Trent.

"Well, she wasn't living in it any longer. And to be fair, it wasn't actually her house. It was Griffith's."

Miranda crossed her arms and huffed. "Would someone please tell me what happened last night that is so funny? Trent, did you or did you not enjoy a quiet dinner at home?"

"Oh, I was at home. No guests over at all."

"Then what could have possibly happened?"

Trent gestured at Amelia. "Why don't you tell them what you neglected to warn me about?"

Amelia blushed as she smiled. "I would have to wager a guess that Mrs. Harris and Fenton ate dinner with you."

"No!" Miranda shook her head in shock.

Trent nodded. "Lydia too. Afterward, Fenton and I even sat down to a glass of port."

Amelia's giggles started all over again.

"Isn't that the butler?" Anthony asked.

"Yes. Yes, he is." Trent's voice was flat as he closed his eyes and hung his head.

Miranda and Anthony joined in Amelia's renewed laughter.

"Would you like me to speak to them?" Amelia offered.

"No, I don't need you to speak to my servants. How awful would that be if every time I wanted to get something done I had to go across town to collect my brother's ward."

A horrible thought crossed Amelia's mind. "You're not going to dismiss them, are you?"

Trent smiled at her. "No. I think, given time, I'll enjoy having the most unconventional house in the neighborhood. Truth be told, I was wondering how I would handle living alone. It was going to be quite a transition, having no one to question my comings and goings, no one to talk to in the evenings. I'm sure it will be tricky finding the right people to fill in the rest of the staff, but I think it might work for me."

"I'm glad. I'd be happy to help you find suitable employees. I know several people who might fit in well."

"I'll manage." Trent shook his head, but his smile was bright. "Well, Anthony, care to help me see these ladies home? Then I believe I shall go spend a few hours at the club and make Mrs. Harris wonder what happened to me."

Anthony offered Amelia his arm. "I would love to, Trent."

The walk back to Hawthorne House was uneventful, filled with meaningless chatter about the weather and the upcoming parties. As Amelia climbed the stairs, she realized she had gotten through an entire conversation with two attractive, titled gentlemen, and she hadn't once twisted her ribbons around her fingers.

She smiled and danced the rest of the way to her room. Life was good, indeed.

Anthony slapped his gloves against his palm as he climbed the stairs to Hawthorne House. The betting book at the club had convinced him that his behavior now was nearly as bad as it had been two years before. If he allowed it to continue, someone was going to be hurt.

There was an entry for a bet that he'd be married to Amelia by summer.

Underneath that was a bet that Lady Helena would manage to drag him to the altar.

Two pages over, a line stated that Lord Howard had bet twenty-five pounds that Griffith would call Anthony out for his dealings with Amelia.

It didn't seem to matter that Anthony had never declared himself, at least not in so many words. All of London saw his infatuation.

But they also knew his reputation.

He couldn't let Amelia get caught up in the tentacles of his past, not when she had so many opportunities now. Being Griffith's ward meant the men were lining up to dance with her. The drawing room saw a neverending stream of gentlemen on days when the ladies were at home.

How could he ask her to choose him over one of those more respectable men?

The door opened before he could lift the brass knocker.

"I'm afraid no one is receiving visitors today, my lord," Gibson said.

Anthony thought through all the plausible reasons why he should be allowed entry when it was obvious that no one else in London was making it past the portal.

Before Anthony could speak, Gibson continued, "It would be a shame to waste your walk here, my lord. Perhaps you'd like to borrow a book from His Grace's library before you return home?"

A book? The butler was offering him a book? Anthony narrowed his gaze as he saw the glint in the eyes of the otherwise stoic servant. "A book, you say?"

"Yes, my lord. I would feel obliged to grant you, as a friend of the family, access to the library." Gibson raised a brow.

"A book is the very reason I'm here, Gibson. How very astute of you."

Anthony thought Gibson might have rolled his eyes as he gestured Anthony into the hall, but the crafty butler turned his head so Anthony couldn't be sure.

After shedding his coat and hat, Anthony jogged up the stairs to the library, hoping he'd interpreted the hidden message correctly. Knowing Amelia's close relationship with the servants, he wasn't sure what he would find. Amelia, anxious to see him, or Griffith, demanding he declare himself.

His heart beat faster as he approached the library, anticipating seeing Amelia curled up with a book or lazily browsing the shelves. The fact that he'd come here with the purpose of breaking their unofficial courtship fled his mind and a grin broke across his face. Maybe she would be on a ladder cleaning. There would be a much different outcome were she to tumble into his arms now.

He slammed a mental door on the path his mind tried to take.

The object of his musings was not lounging, but furtively searching the library. "Looking for something in particular?"

She whirled around, eyes wide. "Anthony!" She slapped a hand over her mouth. "Er, I mean, Lord Raebourne."

"I think I like Anthony." He knew he liked *Anthony*. Hearing his name on her lips sent a shiver from his heart to his toes. Maybe it was selfish, but he couldn't find the will to walk away from this woman.

"I hear you referred to in that way—I mean, here in the house. I did not mean to presume—"

"Stop." Anthony crossed the room and took her by the shoulders, relishing the precious, fragile feeling of her small bones under his hands.

A blush stained her cheeks as her gaze darted to the floor. Feeling pained at the loss of her deep brown eyes, he hooked a finger under her chin to regain her attention. His voice was hoarse and quiet when he spoke. "I like hearing you call me Anthony. I like it very much."

Her smile was small and shy but reached all the way to her eyes. "Truly?"

Pleasure at her smile drowned his guilt. Maybe he could be enough for her. He was willing to spend his whole life trying.

"Truly." Anthony slid his hands down her arms until he clasped her hands in his own. "May I call you Amelia?" She nodded.

He wanted to kiss her. To take her in his arms and mark her as his own. But he'd just promised to give her the best he had to offer. With great reluctance he released her hands and forced himself to take a few steps to the bookcase, putting a globe between them. "What were you looking for?"

"Oh! Nothing, well, not nothing. It would be silly to look for nothing. I thought that with the number of books here there might be a family Bible, but I suppose it is at the country house."

Of all the answers Anthony had expected, the family Bible wasn't among them. "Are you wanting to check up on the births and deaths of various Hawthornes?"

"I was more interested in the Bible part than the family part." Amelia twisted her fingers into her ribbons.

He'd told himself he wouldn't touch her again, didn't trust himself to do so, but he couldn't bear to see her tie her fingers up in knots. "As adorably charming as I find this little habit of yours, I would rather you not be nervous around me."

"I can't help it, my lord."

"Anthony." He gave her freed hands a squeeze and trailed his fingers along her wrists, feeling like the cad everyone assumed he still was.

"Anthony," she whispered.

"As it happens, I can solve your dilemma. What you seek is in Griffith's study. Come along." With a clear objective in mind, Anthony gave himself permission to take her hand. It helped him overcome her obvious reluctance at invading Griffith's private space.

The door was ajar, and Anthony poked his head in to determine if they would be disturbing Griffith. The room was empty, so he pulled her in behind him. He directed her to a pair of wingback chairs angled in front of the fireplace with a small table in between. "He keeps it here. His habit is to read first thing in the morning."

Amelia picked up the black leather-bound book. She sank into one of the wingback chairs and placed the book in her lap. She opened the heavy tome and lovingly riffled the pages.

"I've never held one," she whispered. Her smile of reverent anticipation punched Anthony in the stomach, sending him into the other chair. Sheer joy covered her face.

"It's wonderful to hear the parts the bishop reads in church, but I have often wondered what the rest of it says." She ran her hand along the goldembossed spine. "The housekeeper at Lord Stanford's house used to tell me Bible stories."

Amelia smiled at the memory. "She always told me to remember that someone even more powerful than King George loved me."

Anthony dredged up skills left dormant since his days of high-stakes card games and forced himself to relax and reveal nothing. Amelia had never talked about her childhood, so he didn't want to risk distracting her from revealing this glimpse into her young life.

Amelia took a deep breath and adjusted her position in the chair. Anthony was waiting patiently for her to tell him more. Maybe he needed to know more of her background before declaring serious intentions.

"My parents didn't want me." Amelia winced at the abruptness of her statement, questioning her intent to share her past. It might be more than he'd come for, might even convince him to cease his attentions.

She forged on regardless. Better to know now if her past would scare him away. "They wanted a son. Father despised my uncle and he needed a son to inherit the entailed estate."

Pride had kept them from ostracizing their daughter. She was educated, dressed according to her station, and paraded about in front of their friends as an attractive young girl who might someday make a wonderful match and become a credit to the area. But she was never loved, never coddled or hugged or even taken for a walk.

"They weren't bad parents," Amelia said with a shrug. "They just didn't love me. All their attention went to trying to conceive a boy."

In the end, that desire had killed them. "The doctors said the benefits of sea bathing might help my mother conceive, so they planned a trip immediately, even though I'd come down with a dreadful fever. They stopped at a posting inn on the way to Brighton. There was an argument in the tavern below and a fire broke out.

"Uncle Edward arrived within days." He'd offer to let her stay, but he had no intention of raising her as his own. Amelia'd had no desire to follow in

Cinderella's footsteps as companion and maid to his daughters. "Grandmother took me in, but it was too much of a strain on her limited finances."

Amelia glued her gaze to her toes. How hard it was to admit that no one wanted you, particularly when sitting next to the man you hoped would want you more than anything else in the world. "The viscount took me in but left me in the care of his housekeeper."

Memories of Mrs. Bummel had always made Amelia smile, and now was no exception. The woman had taken one look at the lost little girl and deposited her at the kitchen worktable with a plate piled high with biscuits and a large mug of hot chocolate.

"Mrs. Bummel did the best she could, but she had work to do and I was only ten," Amelia said. "I followed her around a lot. She was nice. Even when the maids burnt food or broke something.

"The other servants talked a lot about the viscount and what a disservice he was to the title. She never did. I thought it was just because she was a higher servant, but she said Jesus wanted her to treat the viscount with respect, so she would." The only time she'd complained about the viscount was when he decided to send Amelia to London.

"When I left for London, she said I didn't have to go alone. That Jesus would go with me everywhere if I committed my life to Him." Amelia shrugged. "It's been good, knowing I wasn't completely alone, but I know there's more." She ran a hand over the worn cover once more. "I never had a chance to look for myself."

The book covered her entire lap, but the awkwardness of handling it didn't bother her. As she flipped the pages, the words began to swim in front of her eyes and she realized tears had formed. "Where do I even begin?"

"Griffith told me to start in John," Anthony whispered before rising and kissing the top of Amelia's head.

And then he was gone. Amelia felt him leave. She had poured her heart out to him, telling him things she'd never told anyone. And he was leaving. She couldn't blame him. Who would want someone of her background?

"He's right—John is an excellent place to start."

Amelia turned in the direction of Griffith's voice.

He crossed the room and knelt in front of her. "Keep this one. I can get another."

Amelia looked down at the book. She had known for years that Jesus was with her and that He had promised to take care of her, but this was a gift she had never expected. She may have lost Anthony, but gaining a family who cared for her would mean so much more. "Thank you."

"You're welcome." Griffith grinned. "And if Mrs. Bummel still works at Harmony Hall, she is going to get a large bonus."

Chapter Thirteen

Over the next two weeks, Anthony gave up any pretense of avoiding Amelia in public. He kept as much distance as he could, wanting to give her the chance to enjoy society she'd never had, but he was never far away.

His reward was that her smiles came more frequently, her blushes lessened. Confidence grew until she had no problem meeting his eyes. The ribbons she'd added to her dresses to accommodate her nervous habit had swung freely as she danced.

Until tonight. Anthony frowned as he watched her wind her fingers tightly in the ribbons. Her normal wide-eyed fascination had become subdued and withdrawn.

Something was definitely wrong. People had been talking all evening, their stares becoming more open with every passing minute. Old gossip couldn't be that interesting. He racked his brain for anything he could have done recently to inspire such avid talk.

Whatever the news, if his name was part of it, his past was surely part of it as well. Amelia would hear of it.

And then she'd have nothing to do with him.

Anthony hid himself in an alcove behind the refreshment table, unfit company for anyone but unwilling to leave. Despite the covering of potted plants, Griffith found him.

"We have a problem."

If Griffith thought there was a problem, it was already very bad. And personal. Nothing set up Griffith's bristles except problems directed at his family. Anthony took the offered glass of lemonade and leaned a shoulder against the wall, trying to appear casual.

"It would seem some people are questioning whether or not Amelia is truly my ward."

Anthony took another sip, focusing his eyes on the whirling couples as the blood rushed through his head. Possibilities swam through his head, but he took a deep breath to clear them. There was no use in jumping to conclusions. "Nonsense. Who else would she be?"

"Lord Howard implied she could be my father's by-blow."

Anthony froze with the glass an inch from his lips. That scenario had never run through his mind. "No one of any intelligence would believe your father had an affair, much less an illegitimate child from it. Your parents were quite famously devoted to each other. Even I have heard the stories."

"Nevertheless . . . " Griffith said. He looked as if he didn't know quite what to say next. He didn't have a chance to figure it out before Lord Geoffrey Chester stumbled into the alcove, nearly ripping a tied-back curtain away from the wall.

If the fumes emanating from his laughing mouth were anything to go by, Lord Geoffrey was already deep in his cups. Anthony turned his head in search of cleaner air.

"I commend you, my man." Lord Geoffrey waved a finger in Anthony's direction. "I thought you'd gone soft in the country, but this is masterful. A mistress in the London ballrooms!"

Anthony saw Griffith's eyes dart in his direction. He didn't dare meet them. If he saw censure or belief in his friend's gaze . . . No, it was better to remain directed at the pompous windbag threatening Anthony's attempt to rebuild his reputation.

He'd been so careful. How could anyone think he harbored a mistress?

Anthony considered punching Lord Geoffrey, but it would likely leave him passed out on the floor and that wouldn't get Anthony more information. Instead he raised his glass and took a small sip of lemonade. "Of what are you speaking?"

Lord Geoffrey turned toward Griffith and laughed. "Must say I never figured you for playing into one of his rakish schemes, though."

Anthony could almost taste the whiskey on the other man's breath as he leaned closer.

"Tell me, man, did your skirt really cry at the opera? Got you a softhearted one?" Lord Geoffrey reached out and took a swig of Anthony's lemonade.

He coughed loudly and frowned before slamming the glass back into Anthony's hands. "Are you buffle-headed, Raebourne? Don't you know the good brandy is in the card room?"

Anthony set his cup on a nearby ledge, trying to find the right words. He'd been to the opera but once since returning to London. Yes, Amelia had cried, but that had been weeks ago, before anyone in this room knew of her existence.

Lord Geoffrey clapped a hand on Anthony's shoulder before stumbling away, talking over his shoulder. "Not sure what you mean to accomplish but it's right entertaining for the rest of us."

Anthony turned his back to the crowded room. "Who could have started such a rumor? It certainly did not originate from a man who cannot tell the difference between brandy and lemonade."

"We need to get out of this alcove." Griffith straightened the sleeves of his coat and ran a finger beneath his cravat. "Hiding behind these plants won't gain us any information."

Amelia went through the dance by rote, her mind occupied, as it often was, with Anthony. He seemed out of spirits this evening. Her partner mentioned something about the weather. Why was it always the weather? Did other ladies find the temperature and amount of cloud cover fascinating? She certainly didn't.

The whole evening had been strange. Most people had accepted her warmly or been indifferent to her presence the past few weeks, but tonight most of their greetings were cold. The unmarried ladies had given her the cut direct.

Even her hostess, Lady Mulberry, had looked unsure when Amelia arrived. Had she not been on Griffith's arm, Amelia might have found herself escorted from the house.

After the final curtsy of the dance, she pled the beginnings of a headache and took herself off to the retiring room, hoping to find Miranda along the way.

It took her an hour to cross the ballroom, with the number of people who refused to step out of her way or scowled at her until she decided to change directions.

How fickle the world she'd thought she wanted was. In a single evening Amelia became all but ostracized. She considered spending the rest of the ball in the kitchens. At least the servants still liked her.

Amelia held her head high even as she trembled. Behaving as if everyone weren't dragging her name through the mud was harder than she'd imagined it would be.

Whispers followed her everywhere. Even from people she hadn't met. Some were shocked that she dared to show her face. Others questioned their hostess's taste in letting her in the door.

Just as she found Miranda, a bold slur to Amelia's honor was hissed from within a passing group. Miranda's fingers curled into a fist. "The next so-called lady who dares to open her mouth against you will feel my wrath."

Amelia appreciated the desire to defend her, but what could Miranda do? "Do you intend to engage her in fisticuffs?"

Miranda shrugged. "I could pull her hair out. That would send a message."

When the next derogatory whisper came their way, Amelia pulled Miranda from the ballroom before her vow could be tested.

"Where are we going? That vile woman deserved a good dressing down. You are the ward of a duke. You don't malign someone under the protection of a duke." Miranda stumbled after Amelia as they walked down the hall.

"I need somewhere to breathe." Amelia pulled Miranda into the ladies' retiring room, where two young women were working to clean a pale pink slipper.

"Champagne! All over my shoes. They are completely ruined."

The other girl looked up from the soiled shoe. "How did this happen? It's soaked through."

"I was taking a glass from the tray and suddenly it tipped. The footman caught all of the glasses, but the contents of half a tray of champagne spilled down my front." The girl pouted as she held her skirts away from her body.

"It's quite fortunate you can't see it on your skirt. You would have had to go home."

The two girls looked up at Amelia and Miranda standing in the doorway. The girl in pink, who had earlier told Amelia that she had seen through her disguise of innocent niceness from the beginning, grabbed her sodden shoe and stomped out of the room. The other girl hastened after her.

With the retiring room empty, Amelia and Miranda took some time to pray and breathe. The Lord answered by keeping the room empty a full twenty minutes and calming their spirits.

"We could leave," Miranda said.

Amelia shook her head. "No. I didn't need them before, and I don't need them now, but I refuse to hide. I finally feel I know who I am and won't let them take that from me."

Miranda nodded, and they returned to the ballroom arm in arm.

The dance floor was far less crowded than normal. With such a luscious piece of gossip to chew on, everyone gathered in groups around the edge of the dancing area.

Amelia didn't know what to do now, so she stood near the doorway, clinging to the notion that she hadn't let them chase her away.

One bitter spinster who'd called Amelia a bit o' muslin passed by them wailing about huge globs of melted candle wax in her hair. No one in her party could figure out how it happened.

Amelia looked around. Had anyone thought to ask the little maid smiling in the corner as she affixed fresh candles in the sconces? She probably knew.

"We could still leave," Miranda whispered.

Amelia swallowed hard. "Perhaps that would be best."

"Did you really teach her to dance?" Griffith leaned a shoulder against the wall as he and Anthony reconvened in the alcove.

Anthony grunted. "It was a brilliant idea at the time. I spent nearly two uninterrupted hours in her company."

"Two inappropriate hours you mean." Griffith grinned. "I should call for pistols."

"You'd make Lord Howard a good bit of money."

Anthony looked around the ballroom. An entire evening of questions and they'd come no closer to fixing the problem. Around the ballroom, groups of London's elite bent their heads close to each other, no doubt discussing him or Amelia.

He took a few steps to the refreshment table and snagged an éclair before stepping back to the wall. It gave him a reason to stand around. Griffith selected a glass of lemonade.

Trent approached them with both eyebrows raised. His hands were clasped behind his back as he strolled, seemingly without purpose but managing to cover the distance in mere moments. "What are we contemplating as we scowl across the ballroom?"

Anthony knew him well enough to feel the tension behind the joviality. "I am trying to figure out who despises me enough to have me watched."

Griffith started visibly. "What makes you say that?"

"People are mentioning things they shouldn't know about. One pup had the audacity to ask me if I often had my mistresses clean my house. How could anyone know that?"

"I've had no luck determining where the rumors started." Griffith raised his glass to his lips only to realize it was empty.

Anthony hid a grin as Griffith tried to pass off the blunder by placing the glass on a passing servant's tray. "Nobody will say, but an inordinate number of people heard things from Lady Helena."

"It's not her," Trent said confidently. "At least, not the initial information source. If she had known the day Anthony arrived back in town, she would have come up with some reason to see him."

Griffith nodded. "She's made no secret of her desire to marry you. It's why she turned down Lord Henry last year. She might have known about the opera, but she wasn't watching your house when you arrived."

The three men continued to hold up the ballroom wall, glaring with varying degrees of efficiency at anyone who approached them. Their vantage point from behind the refreshment table gave them an unobstructed view of a large grouping of people, Lady Helena among them.

A nearby servant held a tray of champagne. As Lady Helena passed, the servant tread upon the hem of her ball gown, effectively tripping her. She reached for the arm of a nearby admirer only to find he had turned away to answer another servant's offer of a puffed pastry. With nothing to stop her forward momentum, Lady Helena fell face-first into the punch bowl. Trent slowly stood up from the wall. "It would appear I was wrong." "About what?" Griffith and Anthony asked in unison.

Trent shook his head as if to bring himself out of a trance. "Amelia once told me that servant gossip is worse than *ton* gossip because they *know*. They know everything."

"And the servants love our Amelia," Anthony said quietly. He watched as Lady Helena accepted condolences amongst an assortment of poorly hidden laughter.

Then he cursed.

Griffith blinked.

Anthony grimaced. "Apologies. Old habits and all that."

"What do we do now?" Trent asked.

Anthony rubbed a gloved hand over his face. He could think of multiple ways to find vengeance, but none he'd be willing to stand before God and admit. What did they do now? That was a good question.

Chapter Fourteen

"You should have made her stay home," Anthony grumbled. He, Trent, and Griffith were once more holding up a ballroom wall, trying to decide what to do about the constant tongue wagging. The rumors had moved from truth to ridiculous with no end in sight.

Griffith groaned. "I would hate to see the state of my house if I had a displeased Amelia under my roof. The servants would revolt. No doubt I'd have gruel for dinner, holes in my shirts, and the most foul-smelling tallow candles they could find."

"The footmen rearranged the chairs in the front drawing rooms so that she could sit and watch the people walk by." Trent snickered.

The mental imagery made Anthony smile, but it didn't lighten his mood. "You should have told her not to dance, then."

Griffith and Trent followed Anthony's gaze to the dance floor. "There are worse chaps than Mr. Bentley," Trent said.

"Yes, but other chaps didn't corner me earlier to see if I was finished dallying with Amelia yet."

Griffith winced. "Perhaps I should cut in."

Anthony shook his head. "I'll go. You keep an eye on Lady Helena. I'm likely to hurt her if I stay here."

"It is a dreadful mess, all this gossip."

Amelia was already regretting accepting the dance with Mr. Oliver Bentley. It had seemed like a fine way to pass the time but now she wasn't sure.

"Despite my low rank, I am quite plump in the pocket."

The bizarre conversation had her longing for a discussion about the possibility of rain. Should she congratulate him on his financial prowess?

"With the scheme uncovered, they'll soon have to let you go. I own a home on the edge of Piccadilly, very circumspect."

The couples around them gasped.

She looked around and was stunned to see Anthony at the edge of the dance floor, fists clenched at his sides. What was he doing? He had been avoiding her all evening.

"Sir," Amelia strained to appear calm even as her heart threatened to break her ribs, "I believe we're delaying the dance." She hated deliberately sounding empty-headed, but the alternative was to spit in this man's face. Amelia wanted to still like herself tomorrow.

But the man continued, "He's flaunted you too publicly to keep you if he wants to take a wife."

The couples to either side of them stopped and stared, mouths agape. The hypocrisy sickened her. They themselves had likely been trashing her reputation earlier in the evening. Since they'd stopped moving, though, the whole dance had stumbled to a halt, leaving Amelia with nowhere to go.

"Well," she said, looking at her dancing companions, "the dance appears to be over. Good-bye."

Desperate to move, she started walking but had no idea where to go. Anthony appeared at her side and took her arm to escort her, not just off the dance floor, but clear out onto the terrace.

As soon as they were free of the ballroom, Amelia released Anthony's arm to lean against the balustrade. "What an insufferable man."

"I am sorry, Amelia," Anthony whispered.

He looked so tortured. Had this gossip brought him such anguish, then? How was that possible? The man had single-handedly fed the gossip mill for years. "Anthony?"

"I should take you back in. All I wanted was to get you away, but out here—"

Amelia cut him off with a shake of her head. "In a moment. I think I need the air. And the space."

He reached out to rest his hands on her shoulders.

Amelia looked down, a slight blush of pleasure on her cheeks.

Anthony gently forced her face up with a knuckle. "You are a wonderful woman. Pure and innocent and gentle and kind. Right now inside that ballroom people are saying hideous things and yet you smile. That man—" Anthony stopped for a moment to gather his composure.

"You would have been well within your rights to give him the cut direct, but you would have finished the dance. I can't understand it. I want to destroy him and everyone else thinking poorly of you.

"But you . . . I've never seen a greater display of God's love in action. I admire you more than I can say, and you deserve the very best man that the world has to offer."

Amelia held her breath. She'd truly never expected to be a part of London society or have a family. Society could go jump in the Thames now that she'd found a family. Perfection would be if the man before her felt the same way about her.

His passionate speech gave her hope. This was it. He was going to reassure her that he loved her despite the hard times ahead.

"I am not the best man that the world has to offer."

Amelia gasped and tears sprang to her eyes. He was supposed to want to protect her, to marry her and spirit her off to his country home. where the rumors couldn't touch them.

"If I were a man like Griffith, well known for being upright and moral and all the things a gentleman should be, this tale would not carry the believability it does. It has brought to light for me that I am not the kind of man you deserve."

Amelia's breath rubbed her throat raw as it jerked in and out of her chest. She shook her head. Anthony's grip tightened on her shoulders until she finally looked up into his face. The pain in his eyes cut her to the bone.

"If I leave you alone," he whispered, "eventually the gossip will die down. With Griffith continuing to support you, you'll find a man that deserves you."

The first tear slid down her cheek. Amelia could do nothing to stop it. His eyes followed it as it fell to the stone. She struggled for words, for composure.

"I am not proud of who I've been, Amelia. I cannot bring that past into a life with you. I am sorry."

"Your past means nothing to me!" The words felt ripped from her chest as he turned to walk away.

Anthony slowly faced her. "It is because of the person they knew me to be"—he jerked his arm, pointing back at the ballroom—"that they have come up with this story! It is my fault that you were so severely insulted just now."

"You are no more responsible for what that man said than I am. You cannot take the blame for another's actions."

Anthony stared at her, unmoving, all the love she could ever want shining behind the hurt in his eyes. She had to make him understand. Then a shutter fell over his gaze. He was blocking her out.

Her hands reached for him, desperate to make him understand. "You have given your life to Jesus. There is no condemnation left for you to claim. I read that, in Romans. You are as pure as I am!"

She gripped his arms with all her strength. "I don't care what you did before. Don't you know that I have heard everything about you? It is not only my name being tossed about in there. That man they talk of is not the man I see in front of me."

Anthony cupped her face in his hands, caressing her cheeks with his thumbs. The shuttered look began to clear. Was he seeing the truth? Was she reaching him?

Without warning, he slid his hand to her neck and leaned in to kiss her. The kiss was fleeting, but she clung to the warm connection. She could taste her own tears on his lips.

Anthony ripped himself away, anguish stamped across his features once more. "I had no decent right to do that. Amelia, I'm so sorry."

He took a step back. "You may not see that man, Amelia, but he still lurks somewhere inside of me. I shall see him in the mirror when I remember this moment." He turned and fled down the stairs into the garden.

How could he walk away? Amelia stood on the terrace, arms wrapped around her body. She stood there while the tears dried, while the shock faded and anger took its place. If he didn't feel anything for her, she could have accepted his rejection, would have welcomed it even. But using his past as an excuse was unacceptable.

Music drifted on the night air, reminding her of the swirl of people, ambitions, and lies. Why had she wanted that world?

"There you are!" Miranda rushed across the terrace and wrapped Amelia in a hug. She hauled her into a swath of light that shone from an upstairs window.

Her frown was dark, but not enough to make Amelia care how much the tears had ravaged her complexion.

"Come along." Miranda hauled her through a side door and into the retiring room. "What happened?"

"He's gone." Amelia resisted the urge to cry again. "The details are of little consequence. Would it be possible for us to go home?"

"Everyone saw Anthony escort you from the floor. He has not made another appearance so you must."

Miranda handed her a dampened cloth. "Wash your face before we return."

Amelia wiped the crusty tear tracks from her cheeks. "Thank you."

Miranda's silent support wrapped around her. If it came down to it, Amelia knew the other woman would risk her own reputation to stand by Amelia.

She deserved better. Griffith and Trent and Caroline deserved better. Even Mrs. Harris and Fenton deserved better, because who knew what the servants were making of the entire mess.

They didn't try to hide as they entered the ballroom. The more people who saw Miranda and Amelia together, the better. Neither of them counted on one of those people being Lady Helena.

"Embracing your spinsterhood, Lady Miranda?"

Miranda tensed, her grip pinching the bones in Amelia's hand. "I beg your pardon?"

Lady Helena turned her cold glower to Amelia. "Consider it a friendly suggestion from someone who spends a bit more time on the dance floor than you do. The company you keep is important."

"Then I should leave before someone notices this exchange."

Air hissed between Lady Helena's teeth as she stared at Miranda. "Tread lightly, Lady Miranda, for I have the ear of many esteemed young ladies. Your brothers are still unwed? I've warned everyone I could about associating with this . . . well, her." She wrinkled her nose in Amelia's direction. "Perhaps I should warn them of the whole family's character."

Amelia couldn't take it anymore. Anthony was lost to her. She would not lose her family as well.

Visions of the grim looks on Griffith's and Trent's faces when she'd crossed paths with them earlier prodded her onward. She stepped forward, giving Miranda's hand a final squeeze before letting go.

"I do not think we have been properly introduced. Allow me to rectify that. I am Miss Amelia Stalwood, ward to the Duke of Riverton."

Lady Helena scoffed. "I know who you are."

Amelia's eyebrows rose. "My apologies. I assumed you were under the impression that I was a woman of loose morals and wicked character."

"As I said, I know who you are."

By this point someone had noticed the confrontation, and a crowd began to gather around them. The opportunity to share the truth would not come again. *Lord, help me protect my family.*

A calm settled over Amelia. She prayed God would give her the right words. "You have my sympathies."

Amelia blinked, surprised to discover the words were true. She did feel sorry for Lady Helena, who must feel desperate to go to these measures.

Lady Helena's eyes narrowed. "It is not I who will never be able to show my face in London again. I have better sense than to flit about with such a man."

"And yet you wanted to marry him."

A ripple of laughter rolled through the otherwise silent crowd.

"I wanted to be a marchioness."

Those closest to the women gasped.

"Lady Helena." Amelia's voice was quiet, causing everyone in the immediate vicinity to lean forward. "I pity you."

One would think Amelia had just spit on the other woman, the way the crowd drew back in shock.

"What did you say?" Lady Helena's head tilted slightly to the side as she glared at her opponent.

"If this is all you have, I pity you. Your ploys may have hurt the man I love, but that is not all that I have. Even if you succeed in placing these ballrooms beyond my reach, you will never ruin my life. I do not give you that power."

Amelia wasn't sure what her goal had been in this confrontation, certainly not to enter a full-fledged battle of wills. But now that such a volatile cannon had been fired, Amelia could do nothing but wait and see if it would strike true or if a counterattack would be coming her way.

And then she didn't care. She was done with Lady Helena, done kowtowing to the opinions of the *ton.*

Turning her back on Lady Helena, she addressed the avid listeners. "I shall say this once for the benefit of you all. I have never behaved with anyone—man, woman, child, aristocrat, gentry, or servant—in a way that would reflect poorly on my new family."

Amelia stepped toward Lady Helena and lowered her voice, with little hope that what she said would not travel farther than its intended ears. The surrounding listeners were too attuned to the conversation. "Lady Helena, you are as unmarried as I am. For all your schemes and lies, you have yet to obtain your goal. Perhaps it is time to change tactics."

Amelia turned on her heel. "Good evening to you all."

With head held high, Amelia plowed into the crowd, hoping they would give way. They did. All the way to ballroom's exit.

Once she left the room, noise erupted, nearly deafening even out in the hall. How could anyone hear what anyone else was saying? But then again, maybe they didn't care. It seemed more important to be talking than to be heard.

As she put the ballroom behind her, Amelia felt as if she left her courage there as well. She was shaking by the time she made it to the front door.

Then they were there, all of them. Miranda, Griffith, and Trent, even Caroline and Lord Blackstone wrapped their arms around her, whispering words of encouragement, acceptance, and even love.

They piled into their carriages, and even through the darkness caused by Anthony's loss, Amelia saw a faint glimmer of hope about her future.

Chapter Fifteen

By the next afternoon, Amelia was convinced that everyone in London had lost their mind. From the moment the first matron arrived under the guise of checking after Amelia's health—she had looked quite pale when she left the ball the night before—the drawing room at Hawthorne House saw a constant stream of visitors.

While Amelia had braced herself for a bit of sympathy and a handful of supporters, she never imagined the venomous slander against Lady Helena Bell.

"I have always said that girl would come to no good."

"She set her cap for my son last year, and he made a narrow escape of it, he did."

"Rest assured, she shall not be receiving an invitation to any of my gatherings. I have put it about to my friends that they should strike her off as well."

"I blame her parents, I do. That is what comes of doting so on a child. They become spiteful and hateful." It was enough to make a girl ill.

The men, who began arriving at a more conventional time, were not any better.

"Lady Helena is all that is bland and lifeless next to your splendid coloring."

"I've written an ode to your spirit and honesty. Would you like to go for a ride and hear it?"

"Will you marry me?"

Griffith had put a cease to the proposal by ushering Mr. Craymore to the door with a friendly but firm hand. "I do not believe that now is the appropriate time for that discussion. I shall let you know when it is an acceptable time to renew your suit."

"Much obliged to you, Your Grace. I am sure you will be anxious to settle her off during her current peak of popularity."

"Pompous man," Caroline said when they heard the front door shut. "Gibson, we will have no more visitors today."

Miranda pointed at Gibson. "Unless it is Anthony." She flopped over the side arm of the sofa. The break in ladylike decorum testifying to the exhausting drama that had played out among the tea cups in the drawing room.

"Anthony will not be visiting today, I can assure you," Amelia whispered. Her vision blurred as tears filled her eyes. "This isn't what I wanted."

Caroline and Miranda both turned to her with looks of inquiry.

"I never sought to hurt her. I wanted . . . I wanted to set things right. This is wrong."

Caroline picked up Amelia's hand and rubbed it between her own. "My dear, in situations with the *ton* there must always be a villain. In every story someone must be the profligate. If you are innocent, then she must be guilty."

"And she is." Miranda shrugged at her mother's exasperated look. "You earned everyone's admiration last night. That forces Lady Helena to be the scoundrel for daring to hurt you."

"How do I stop it?" Amelia smoothed her ribbons across her lap.

Caroline sighed. "Perhaps if Anthony were to return—"

"She declared her love in front of half of London." Miranda punched a needlepoint pillow. "If he doesn't return to her, he's a fool."

Griffith reentered the drawing room and sprawled himself in a wing chair, rubbing his forehead and temples. Amelia knew how he felt. She was trying to hold off a threatening headache herself.

"I wish to go away," Amelia announced.

Griffith dropped his hands and opened his eyes but made no movement otherwise.

"If it is not possible for me to actually leave London, can we tell everyone that I did? I will remain in the house, and no one will be any wiser."

Caroline began to protest, but Griffith held his hand up to stop her. "I have a house outside of London. We have been known to retire there for a breather in the midst of the season. With any luck Lady Helena will go into hiding as well. If neither of you is in Town, the *ton* will find something else to talk about."

Anthony stared at the ceiling, not ready to get out of bed yet. His servants were probably still scrambling from his surprise arrival at his country estate the night before. They hadn't expected him until well after the end of the season.

He rolled over and punched a pillow. "Why, God?" he groaned. Why would God bring Him so far and taunt him with something so precious? How could a loving God bring him to the brink of happiness and then snatch it all away?

The answer materialized, as if the Lord himself had spoken in Anthony's ear. *I didn't take it away. You did.*

Anthony jerked upright in bed, instinctively pulling the covers over his bare chest. Knowing God was always present was different than feeling like He was standing at the foot of the bed.

Then the import of the words sank in. God hadn't taken Amelia away from him. Anthony's own guilt and selfishness had tossed her aside. How could he be so foolish?

"Good morning, my lord." The butler entered with fresh water, preparing to act as Anthony's valet. Harper was probably twisted in knots because Anthony had left him behind.

"Have you ever done something so nonsensical that you were convinced you had mutton for brains?"

The butler froze, casting a look around to see if anyone else was in the room. Anthony laughed at how much Amelia had affected him. He hadn't thought twice about conversing with the butler. The butler was apparently having second, third, and fourth thoughts about answering.

"I beg your pardon, my lord."

Anthony swung his legs over the side of the bed and rubbed his hands over his face. "I did something nonsensical. Did I really think I could save her by abandoning her?"

Chalmers cleared his throat. "Her, my lord?"

Anthony nodded. "I left her standing on that terrace like a coward. Planting Bentley a facer was a bit honorable, but I should have done it at the ball instead of outside his house."

"Er, of course, my lord."

"Why would I do something so cork-brained?" Anthony stabbed his arms into his dressing gown and began to pace as he tied the robe around his middle.

Moments passed. Chalmers looked as if he wanted to bolt, and Anthony couldn't blame him. The butler must think his master had gone mad.

"If I may be so bold, sir, I think you might be looking at this the wrong way."

Anthony gestured for the man to continue.

Chalmers cleared his throat. "It isn't a mental question. There is no logical *why*. I don't know what you've done, my lord, but it sounds as if it's a matter of the heart, not the mind."

Anthony nodded.

"Then focus on truth, not logic. Stop trying to figure out why and look for what is."

Anthony stood in stunned silence. He had a very profound butler. When things settled down he was going to make it a point to have more discussions with the man.

"Logically," Anthony began, pacing the room once more, "I would fall back into my old habits and ways, being the person they thought I was. The truth is that I'm changed."

Chalmers yanked the bellpull and began selecting clothes from the dressing room, nodding that he was still listening to Anthony's ramblings.

"There isn't any sense to it, because it was the work of God, not myself." Anthony strode to the window and looked across his land.

A jacket joined Chalmers clothing selections as he spoke quietly with the footman who'd answered the bell call.

"If God can accept me, then why can't she?"

The voice hammered his ear once more. *She did.*

"She did." Anthony's voice dropped as the truth became clear. He'd been too distraught at the ball to hear it when she voiced it, but his mind had stored it away until he was ready.

"There is no condemnation left for you to claim."

"I am forgiven," he whispered.

He crossed the room and grabbed Chalmers by the shoulders. "I have been given a new life, and she is willing to join me in it. Only a fool leaves a woman like that alone, Chalmers."

"Quite right, my lord."

"I'll need a fresh horse. The one I rode in on can't return to London today. And clothes. I'll need—" Anthony broke off as he noticed the riding breeches and jacket Chalmers had set out.

"The horse is being readied now, my lord." Chalmers pulled out the razor. "Might I suggest a good breakfast before you leave?"

"Yes. Breakfast." Anthony stood dumbfounded. Never had he realized how right Amelia was. People were people, no matter their class. Some were kind, some were smart, and some were mean and petty.

He dressed quickly and when he left the dressing room found a breakfast tray laid out in his room.

Chalmers gathered the dirtied linens and prepared to leave.

"Chalmers," Anthony called. "I have a project for you while I'm away."

"Does she have a favorite color, my lord?"

"Color?"

"Yes, my lord. Does she have a favorite color? If you wish me to see to freshening the mistress's chambers, it would be helpful to know her favorite colors."

Amazing. How had Anthony managed to hire the smartest butler in the country? "Pink," he said, remembering her delight over her first ball gown. "She likes pink."

Chapter Sixteen

The house outside London was peaceful and cozy, though still large by Amelia's standards. Most of the family seemed relieved to leave London behind. Even Trent had joined them on their exodus. Only Georgina seemed bitter about the move.

Where her attitude had been sullen before, she was positively churlish now. Even angry. Amelia had tried to talk to her, determined to do everything she could for this family that had taken her in, but the other girl would only glare and make snide comments.

In an effort to avoid Georgina's anger and Miranda's pity, Amelia tried to take a nap. An hour of staring at the ceiling left her restless. Despite the threat of rain she considered a walk in the garden. Maybe she could interest Trent in a game of piquet.

She strolled down the corridor, taking as much time as possible to get where she was going.

"Amelia! Amelia!"

Her head snapped up. That voice . . . Could it be? She ran for the stairs, heart tripping through her chest, trying to go faster than her feet could carry her. Was she dreaming?

She hit the top of the stairs and saw a figure striding across the front hall.

It was him.

He was more disheveled than she'd ever seen him, breathing hard, running his hands through his hair. Never had he looked more handsome.

She floated down the stairs with no recollection of her feet on the treads.

"Amelia," he breathed as they met at the bottom of the stairs.

He took her in his arms, crushing her and freeing her at the same time. His lips skimmed her cheek as he whispered.

She couldn't make out the words over the roar in her ears, but she knew what they meant. He loved her. He wanted her. He would risk everything for her.

His lips found hers and the warmth shot straight to her heart. She tasted salt. He was crying.

He pulled back, resting his forehead against hers. "I missed you."

She smiled, tears of her own threatening to fall. "I missed you too."

His laughter rang through the hall as he wrapped his arms around her and twirled her through the room. "What a fool I was to think I could walk away from you."

Anthony set her back on the ground but didn't let go. "I came from Hertfordshire. I rode all the way there the morning after I left you on the terrace and I had not been there a day when I realized what a cork-brained idiot I was. I went back to London and Gibson told me you were here. Amelia, I love you. And if a man is blessed enough to find a good woman to love, he does not turn his back on it. I suppose in all propriety I should ask Griffith but I am going to ask you first. Will you marry me?"

"No!"

Amelia turned toward the scream, stunned to find Georgina in the doorway to the parlor, shaking. "You cannot marry *her!* It was supposed to be me. Me!"

"Georgina?" Amelia asked softly. Her gaze swung back and forth between Georgina and Anthony, confusion muddling what few thoughts Anthony's confession had left intact.

Anthony stood there, his mouth slightly open, clearly too shocked to say anything.

Georgina's face contorted with anger. "For two years you have been coming to Riverside Manor, and every time you were there I did everything I could to show you I would make a wonderful marchioness. It was going perfectly until you told Griffith you were ready to take a wife. I begged Mother to let me come out. I begged her because I knew if you could just see me as a woman you would pick me."

"Georgina, I . . ." Anthony stepped away from Amelia but still held her hand in his. His free hand began to reach for Georgina before falling back to his side.

"But they wouldn't let me come out. So I tried to stop you. I told Lady Helena everything. She deserved to know what a mistake you were making, choosing *this* woman. Don't you see how poor a marchioness she would be?" Georgina pointed an accusing finger at Amelia. The visual daggers caused Amelia to wince.

"I knew you would never marry Lady Helena. But you were supposed to abandon your plans to marry Griffith's ward and wait until next year and then I would be there and you would choose me."

"Georgina," he said quietly. "I love Amelia." He dropped Amelia's hand to take another step toward Georgina.

But the young girl must have realized what she'd done, the secrets she'd revealed. She began to shake. Amelia felt pity welling up inside of her.

"Stay away from me! All of you!"

Amelia turned to find that Miranda, Caroline, Trent, and Griffith, and even Lord Blackstone had all been drawn to the front hall by the commotion. Everyone looked uncomfortable with the confession.

Georgina spun on her heel and fled through the parlor and out into the gardens.

Anthony made to go after her but Caroline stopped him. "Let her go. Her pride has been hurt, and a young girl's pride can be massive indeed. You can talk about it when she calms down."

They retired to the parlor to await Georgina's return. Unofficially engaged—Amelia had, after all, not gotten the chance to respond to the proposal—Anthony sat next to Amelia on the settee, holding her hand in his.

He shook his head. "I never knew. I thought she was just your scamp of a little sister. I never saw . . ."

"None of us did," Griffith said.

Anthony gave him a wry smile. "Unfortunately, I have a bit more experience than you do. Looking back I can see several signs that I missed. I am truly sorry."

Amelia leaned forward and took Anthony's face in her hands. "You are very good at taking blame, thinking your past qualifies you to be at fault in every situation. Well, I will have you know that I short-sheeted my governess's bed, placed beetles in the raisin pudding, and lied about anything and everything if I thought it would get my parents' attention. That, sir, is as much of a sin as whatever you did. I sit here forgiven. It is about time you realized that you do too."

Anthony looked into her eyes. Amelia didn't know what he saw there, but it was enough to lift the dark gloom from his face.

"You're right, my love. It is time to forgive myself."

He reached out and smoothed the hair back from her face, leaned forward, and brushed his lips softly against hers.

Miranda sighed.

Griffith cleared his throat.

Caroline sputtered as she swallowed a laugh.

Trent cheered.

Amelia pulled back fanning ineffectively at her flaming cheeks.

Anthony dropped a kiss on her forehead and grinned rakishly.

"Well, I suppose you will have to marry her now," Griffith muttered.

Eventually Caroline went after Georgina. The girl looked young as she joined them in the drawing room. Amelia's offer to make her a bridesmaid caused her eyes to widen. "Why on earth would you do that?"

"Everyone deserves a second chance." Amelia couldn't fault Georgina for trying to create the best future possible for herself, even if her methods were more than a little questionable. A lifetime of watching people get things she thought she wanted made Amelia sympathetic to the young girl. Maybe it could be the start of a new relationship for them.

Amelia would ban her from the proceedings at the first hint of sabotage, though.

Anthony smoothed his thumb across Amelia's knuckles. "I cannot wait until I can call you my wife."

"You'll have to wait until we return to London," Georgina said. "Despite my lapse in judgment, I know how the beau monde works. If you don't want this gossip following you forever, they need to see a happy courtship."

Anthony groaned as Miranda and Caroline agreed with Georgina's claim.

"You'll forget the delay soon enough. We have forever, after all." Amelia smoothed his hair back from his face, marveling at the realization that she now had the right to do that.

"Forever. If the way I feel right now is any indication, we shall live happily ever after."

"At the very least, it will be blessedly ever after," Amelia added. "For if God never grants me anything else in this life, He has given me you, and that is more than I ever dreamed of."

Anthony kissed her gently, ignoring the groans from the rest of the room. "Blessedly ever after has a very nice ring to it."

THE LADY'S MAID

A Hawthorne House Novella

Prologue

London, England 1812

Meeting a new employer for the first time was an anxious experience for most any servant, but Lydia Smith was certain that having such an encounter around the main dining table made the apprehension at least five times worse.

She glanced at the clock as it chimed seven and leaned toward the housekeeper, whispering, "Are you certain we should be doing this?"

Mrs. Harris straightened her mob cap and lifted her thin, pointy chin. "Of course it is. We must start as we mean to go on. Eating with the servants in the dining room was good enough for Miss Amelia, after all."

Miss Amelia had also been eleven when she'd first moved into the house, all but cast out by her guardian and left to be raised by the servants. That had been nearly ten years ago, and a similar-aged Lydia had been hired as the maid of all work, but also as something of a companion and playmate.

The former mistress of the townhome was all grown up now and living with her new guardian on the other side of Mayfair. She was attending balls, walking in the park, and catching the eye of a powerful marquis. Lydia rather thought her dining experiences no longer included the company of servants in any capacity other than, well, serving.

Now the house in Mount Street belonged to that guardian's brother. The younger brother of the duke would be arriving any moment now for his first meal in his new home.

And Mrs. Harris intended for the entire household to join him.

Not that the household was very large at the moment. The only other servant aside from Lydia and Mrs. Harris was Fenton, the aged butler currently waiting in the front hall to escort Lord Trent to the dining room.

It would be something of a miracle if they didn't find themselves turned out on their ear before the soup grew cold.

The scrape of the front door opening was followed by the low buzz of voices. Slowly the rumble grew louder and more distinct as Fenton led the man to the dining room.

"Mrs. Harris has prepared her specialty tonight, my lord." Fenton's voice was rough with age and rare usage, but carried a hint of pride as well.

"I look forward to trying it." At least the new lord sounded somewhat amused and not already irritated.

The pair filled the dining room doorway and Lord Trent's gaze slowly slid about the room, taking in the worn and shabby condition, the array of prepared food dishes, the two women situated beside the table.

And the four place settings laid out upon the surface.

A low laugh joined his wide smile and the shake of his head. "Amelia did warn me."

One small thread of tension unwound from Lydia's spine. If Miss Amelia had prepared him for this likelihood, perhaps she wouldn't lose her position after all.

Lord Trent stepped fully into the room and turned to Fenton. "I'm afraid I didn't fully appreciate Amelia's instructions tonight. My valet has gone round to the servant's entrance."

Fenton didn't even pretend to maintain a proper London butler's stoicism as he returned the younger man's smile. "I shall see that he is greeted and bring an additional plate up for him."

After a slight bow, the butler left the room. Lord Trent clasped his hands together and took in his surroundings once more. "Mrs. Harris and Lydia, I presume?"

"At your service." Mrs. Harris accompanied the words with a small curtsy, nudging Lydia with her elbow to indicate she should do the same. Lydia hastily bent her knees and stopped herself from rolling her eyes. How was she to know the proper amount of deference to show when one planned on joining their employer for dinner?

Lord Trent walked to the plate at the head of the table. "This is where I am to sit, yes?" His grin grew more crooked and boyish as he looked at Mrs. Harris. "Or is this where you eat, as you are so obviously the woman who is actually in charge here?"

Lydia covered her mouth to prevent the snort of laughter. The man might be willing to accept a few idiosyncrasies on Miss Amelia's recommendation, but obviously he wasn't intending to let a misfit band of servants run his life as they'd done the previous tenant's.

A flush crawled up Mrs. Harris's neck, but she only nodded and lowered herself into her own seat. Lydia followed suit because what else was she to do?

Footsteps rang up the stairs from the kitchen at a rather faster pace than Fenton was normally known to travel. Lydia frowned at the door. Was something wrong?

Moments later Fenton walked in, eyes wide and chest pumping fast as he tried to catch his breath. His pale blue eyes turned immediately toward Lydia, widening even more as if attempting to send her a message.

She hadn't the faintest idea how to interpret such a look.

Then another man, presumably the valet Fenton went to fetch, entered the room. His hesitancy indicated he was far less comfortable with the idea of joining this dinner party than his lordship was, but still his shoulders remained straight and sturdy as he stepped around Fenton.

Lydia slid her gaze to the newcomer, lips already turned into an encouraging smile.

But then everything in her froze.

This was not some poor, unknown man thrown into a situation of unusual circumstances.

No, this was Finch Scott. The boy next door. The man she'd fancied for years.

And the reason dining with her new employer was now the least of Lydia's concerns.

Chapter One

Avoiding a person who lived in the same house was a difficult task, but Lydia was determined to excel at it. Every method she could conceive of fell under one of two concepts: other people could be used as a distraction or additional work could provide an excuse to be somewhere – anywhere – else. Lydia's work duties were triple what they'd been before Lord Trent's arrival, but she hoped the arrival of the newly hired additional maids and footmen today would add to her protection.

So far, all her attempts to avoid Finch had done nothing but put her directly in his path. How was she always in the laundry when he brought Lord Trent's clothing in? Why did he constantly go up or down the stairs while she was dusting, no matter when she chose to perform the task? Mrs. Harris's refusal to let Lydia dine at a separate time didn't help matters either.

That, at least, would be solved with the additional staff. No matter how familial Mrs. Harris wanted to make the house, she couldn't put everyone from Lord Trent to the new scullery maid at the same table at the same time. That would have to become a privilege of the upper servants and Lydia could flee to the safety of the scarred wooden table in the kitchen.

"How many maids are starting today?" Lydia prayed Mrs. Harris had been able to find the number of maids they'd discussed. Aside from the dining excuse and the safeguard of their presence, she desperately needed help with the work. She gathered her dust cloths and dropped them into an empty bucket she held in one hand before collecting the broom to take upstairs. "I don't know how I was managing to do it all even a month ago."

Mrs. Harris snorted. "We shut up nearly three-quarters of the house, washed our own dishes, and had no guests aside from a neighboring servant or two."

Lydia blew out a long breath at the reminder of just how much life had changed. And so quickly as well. "I can't imagine Lord Trent even walking through the kitchens, much less seeing to his own plate and fork."

"Nor should you. That is why the new staff is coming." She ran a finger down the page of the notebook that had become an ever-present companion since they'd learned of Lord Trent's impending occupation. Despite being the housekeeper of the townhouse for nearly fifteen years, this was the first time she'd actually had to do so with the titled owner in residence.

It was enough to make Lydia thank God she only had to deal with the strain of taking on the role of head housemaid. Despite having seniority over the maids who would be arriving any moment, Lydia was only nineteen. Hardly an age that inspired a great deal of authoritative respect.

If all those years of seniority had been true, usable experience, she might feel differently. Instead, she'd simply been a member of a strange little family living in a house that was too large and too fine for all of them. Well, perhaps not all of them. Miss Amelia was soon to be the Marchioness of Raebourne, after all.

Despite that, she had tried to take her duties seriously, to care for the cleaning and upkeep of the house. Still, she'd known that any shortcomings on her part would be overlooked and no one would truly scold her for leaving a portion of the job undone for a day or two. Such leniency no longer existed.

Now every room, with the possible exception of the nursery, was to be ready for occupation at any time. That was the normal expectation of an aristocratic household. Lydia didn't have much knowledge of bachelor lodgings, and Lord Trent's older brother's far larger and nicer home was only a few streets away in Grosvenor Square, but it still seemed reasonable for every guest room in the house to be ready at any time.

Even if people did not stay the night, drawing rooms would soon be occupied by guests of the highest rank and importance. While Lord Trent didn't seem to be exceptionally high in the instep – he was still dining with the servants on occasion after all – Lydia had seen enough of the aristocracy to know all of them weren't like that.

She moved to the stairs, bucket clanging and broom dragging. While help was to be here by midday, she couldn't depend upon anyone else to assist with today's chores. With one foot propped on the bottom step, she turned back to Mrs. Harris. "Have you set the half day schedule yet?"

When the staff had been tiny, it had been a simple matter for Lydia to take her free half day whenever she wished. Now there would need to be a schedule, and it would have to be adjusted according to the needs of their employer.

Mrs. Harris sighed. "I haven't even given it a thought." She took her pencil and scribbled something in her notebook, then gave Lydia a small grin. "I'm not in control of Finch's schedule, of course, but I can try to have your day match his."

Embarrassment burned through Lydia's body, making her grateful for the dark shadows of the stairwell. There'd been a time, not that long ago, when she'd deliberately tried to match her time away from work to that of Finch. His family lived in the flat beside her family's, above the shops in Oxford Street. She had timed her visits home to give herself a chance to see the man who had once been the boy she played jacks with and was now the one she pictured at her side whenever she indulged in fantasies about having a different life.

On occasion when she was lying in bed at night or cleaning the dust from a carpet or polishing a table, Lydia liked to daydream. She would imagine she was a shopkeeper or a country home caretaker or some other job that was far beyond her reach but would have allowed her to build a life and a family of her own. They were impossible dreams that filled the boring hours of her day but never received serious consideration.

Yet Finch Scott had been in every single one of them.

And now he was living in the same house, sitting at the same table, and far too entrenched in her everyday world for comfort. Her safe, unattainable fantasy was now a real-life temptation. How was she meant to handle that?

Probably not by attempting to see him during her free hours away from work.

She cleared her throat and tried to give Mrs. Harris a smile. "That won't be necessary. The novelty and the challenge have worn off now that I could encounter him around every corner."

And if God could change her thoughts and feeling to make that statement truth instead of lie, Lydia would be ever so thankful.

Mrs. Harris gave a sharp nod. "Glad to hear it. I was concerned when I heard Lord Trent intended to hire a new valet when he moved out of Hawthorne House. Finch has worked there for years as one of their head footmen and was a logical option."

Lydia blinked at the housekeeper. "You knew he'd be moving in? And you didn't warn me?"

"Well, I didn't know for certain. There was no reason to cause a fuss if he didn't get hired." She snapped the notebook closed and walked toward her small office at the other end of the kitchen. "Since nearness has snipped the bloom from that particular rose, it seems I had nothing to worry about."

Lydia said nothing and Mrs. Harris paused to look over her shoulder. "I don't have anything to worry about, do I?"

"Of course not." Another lie. Or perhaps not. It wasn't as if Lydia could actually do anything about it. She was a maid. He was a valet. They worked in a home in London. The reasons domestic servants remained unmarried were vast and valid. Not the least of which was the question of where they could possibly live.

Still, Lydia paused while dusting the dressing table in one of the bedrooms to ensure her corkscrew blonde curls weren't too frazzled.

She jumped at every creak and groan and scrape of wood, afraid it would be Finch entering the room.

And, worst of all, while smoothing already pristine bed linens, she couldn't quite stop the flash of an image in which she and Finch weren't caretakers or shop owners, but the master and mistress of their own little townhome.

She stabbed her hand into the mattress, creating a large wrinkle in the coverlet, hoping the marred perfection would break the mental imagery that could bring nothing but agony and heartbreak. Surely the influx of maids and footmen today would be the solution.

Yes. Once the house was fully staffed, it would be impossible to forget that she was counted among those staff. Her responsibilities would increase, and she would remember why she'd taken such a job in the first place. A roof over her head and food in her belly, with the ability to save her earnings or use them to help her family, were real things to value.

When the new faces that were destined to be the answer to her problem arrived, Lydia ran down the stairs to meet them.

A young girl named Marie was assigned to the scullery, so Lydia would no longer run the risk of being caught up to the elbows in wash water when Finch brought a tray down from Lord Trent's rooms or assisted in the clearing of the dinner dishes.

Diane and Frances were to assist Lydia in the upkeep of the rest of the house. Diane was a year younger than Lydia. Frances was three years older but seemed to have no disputes with Lydia's authority as she showed them the house and divided up the tasks.

While being in a position of authority, even this small one, was daunting, Lydia did her best to embrace the benefits it brought. Since she was assigning the areas, it was a simple matter to have Diane see to the cleaning of the master's chambers while Frances saw to the ground floor public rooms and the study. Lydia took the cleaning of the top floors no one currently used.

It was a strange division of tasks, but neither maid questioned her about it.

Either Lydia was relaying her instructions with perfect confidence or servants who'd worked in other, normal home situations simply did not question those higher in the hierarchy than themselves. That was something Lydia would have to learn if she finally lost her mind from working in the same house as Finch and was forced to seek employment elsewhere.

But that wasn't going to happen.

As Lydia lay in bed, staring at the ceiling and muttering her prayers, rest came easily for the first time since Finch had walked through the dining room door. This new plan would work. She had removed every reason for her to wander into Finch's path. It would be as if they still worked in different homes.

Everything was going to be fine.

The plan worked perfectly for three entire days.

Then it all blew up in Lydia's face.

Actually, it blew up on Diane's feet. And skirt. And arms. And hair. Her face was one of the few dry places on her body, since she'd raised her arms to shield herself from the torrent of water, soap, and sopping wet linen as the old laundry bucket gave way to the massive load of fabric that was bigger than any this house had seen in a decade.

Lydia stood in the door to the scullery, mouth agape as she took in the scene. "Are you injured?"

Diane shook her head and her wet mob cap slid off the side of her head. "The lye had cooled. I was starting to pull everything out to rinse it."

At least no bodily harm had been done. The room and the maid, however, were a mess that was going to take an age to clean. With a shortage of hands, laundry had been neglected these past weeks, and nearly every clean set of linen had been used to prepare for the new people moving in.

Lydia blinked. "Did you freshen Lord Trent's bedding yet?"

Diane looked up from her seat in the massive puddle, eyes round in panic. "No, I didn't. I'd brought the last of the dirty ones down and thought I'd move these over to rinse before putting the last ones in to soak."

A reasonable choice, but one that meant they had a more pressing need than this disaster of a scullery to see to. Lydia nodded. "Marie will help you in here. I'll see to the bedchamber."

Fortunately, they had added new, finer linens to the household when Lord Trent arrived, and one solitary set remained folded in the cabinet. Lydia scooped it up and started for the stairs. Just because she was walking directly to the place where most of Finch's duties were located did not mean she was going to see him for the first time in days. Breakfast had long since passed. Surely Lord Trent had dressed for the day and gone out by now. Finch had plenty of tasks that did not require him to be in the bedroom itself.

Despite her many self-assurances that the room would be empty, she gave a soft knock on the door and held her breath.

"Enter."

A chill swept over Lydia's skin. Lord Trent was still here and in his rooms.

Which likely meant Finch was in the room as well.

This was going to require a little audible encouragement. "I'm a normal servant in a normal house in normal London. There are maids moving about every day and no one is giving them a lick of attention. I can do this."

Lydia squared her shoulders, took a deep breath, and eased the door open just enough to slip inside with her clutched bundle of sheeting.

She kept her face down, eyes glued to the edge of the carpet, as she gave a shallow curtsy and moved toward the bed. That was how one kept a normal distance between those who lived in the house and those who worked in it. At least Lydia assumed that was how it worked.

Still, it felt too strange not to acknowledge the fact that she was in his room, so she said, "I beg your pardon, my lord. I thought you'd gone already." She set the bundle of linen on the nearest corner of the foot of the bed. "I'll return later to see to the righting of your rooms."

"Nonsense." Lord Trent crossed from the dressing room to the bed and flipped the top of the blankets back. "Lydia, isn't it?"

Her gaze darted up to meet his kind, green eyes. "Yes."

"Well, Lydia, as you can see, I'm not using the bed right now, so there's no reason for you to see to it later."

"I...um, that is, if you're certain." She tried to maintain her visual connection with Lord Trent, truly she did, but she couldn't keep her gaze from slipping to Finch, visible beyond his lordship's left shoulder. He held a jacket in each hand and his face was clear of any emotion. It was impossible to know if he was irritated, amused, or delighted by Lydia's appearance.

"Of course I am certain," Lord Trent continued. "Did you wait until Amelia had departed the room to change the sheets for her?"

"Miss Amelia frequently helped, my lord."

Lord Trent's eyebrows lifted and he coughed before laughing. "I'm afraid I'm not ready to go that far down the road of unconventional living." He turned and took one of the jackets from Finch. "Perhaps Mr. Scott can be of assistance, though." Those green eyes appeared amused now as they flitted back and forth between Lydia and Finch. "I'm certain he'd be happy to help."

"Of course." Finch's voice was soft, but he didn't look at Lydia. Instead he gave his attention to the jacket remaining in his hand.

Lord Trent considered the room for another few moments while Lydia stood frozen. Should she proceed with the bedding? Formulate some form of decisive end to this conversation? Run from the room and not stop until she reached Hampstead Heath?

Finally, the nobleman nodded. "I do believe Amelia was correct."

"About what?" Lydia asked before she could stop herself.

"Hmm?" Lord Trent straightened his cuff as he gave Lydia an absent grin. "Oh, nothing of import. She mentioned that when the servants behave as family, living alone is far less boring."

If there was an appropriate response to such a statement, Lydia couldn't think of it.

Lord Trent didn't seem to need one, though, as he turned and strode from the room, leaving her in the exact position she'd been hoping to avoid.

Alone in a room with Finch.

"Do you need my assistance?"

"The task is always simpler with another set of hands, but no, I don't require help. I've plenty of experience doing it on my own." Even though the large master chamber had hardly been entered, much less used, until the past few weeks, one bed was much the same as any other, wasn't it? Mrs. Harris had helped when they'd been preparing the room for Lord Trent's arrival, but Lydia was confident she could see to the task on her own.

Eventually.

She didn't particularly relish having Finch watch her try, though. What if it took her several attempts? The last thing she wanted to do was show weakness in front of him.

"There's no reason to make things more difficult than they need to be." He draped the jacket over the back of a chair. "I'll help you."

Her hands held only the slightest of trembles as they set about fitting the bedding. Hopefully Finch was distracted by the task at hand since she couldn't very well stuff her fingers beneath the fabric she was attempting to smooth.

The silence that fell between them was as comfortable as it was awkward, so Lydia broke it. "Are you enjoying your new position?"

Finch nodded. "I enjoy having more to do than stand around and open doors. Are you pleased with the change of duties?"

Was she? She certainly missed the atmosphere they'd had when Miss Amelia lived here, but those times had held a certain air of doom as well. They'd all known the situation couldn't continue forever. All the years of experience wouldn't have meant much when it came time to find another position. "The work feels more important, which is nice."

She glanced about the room, seeing signs of Lord Trent's occupancy everywhere. "It is strange, though," she continued, "not working alone."

Finch laughed as he changed the covering on a pillow. "You can hardly expect to be able to take care of everything yourself."

"There's still only one person living here, though." Lydia sighed. "How did everything change so much?"

As he set the pillow back into place, Finch appeared to give the question serious consideration. "I don't think the situation is that simple."

Lydia reached for the other pillow. "Why do you think that is?"

"Because God works in the nuances and details as much as in the circumstances. Just think of how many households and situations could be stated in the same simple way. Take my family, for example. My youngest brother shows promise and talent so he needs an apprenticeship."

"That is a common enough situation." There were many families were only one child showed aptitude for a specific set of skills.

Finch nodded. "But not all of those families require everyone to contribute to making that happen." He smoothed the top coverlet. "Michael would never be able to get there with only my parents' assistance. But Celia and I looked at our potential future career options and decided to be part of the solution."

"Is it going to be enough?" After years of watching Mrs. Harris fret over Miss Amelia's future, Lydia knew the best of intentions weren't always enough to change circumstances.

Finch nodded. "With my additional wages as a valet, there should be enough to purchase his apprenticeship by this time next year."

What would it be like to have everyone working together to make one life better? It was true she hadn't had much choice but to go into service either, but her situation had been more about filling in her injured father's lost wages than anything else. "How does Michael feel about that?"

"We're family." Finch shrugged as he collected the jacket from the chair. "We help each other."

Lydia's fingertips trailed over the now smooth bed coverings. "Do you resent it? Being the one to do the helping? Giving up opportunities in your life to make his better?"

"Not really." He laughed as he stepped into the dressing room, lifting his voice so she could still hear him. "What did I actually give up? I think I would have taken this path, even if Michael hadn't needed the money."

"Oh." What could Lydia say to that? Obviously Finch wasn't imagining an entirely different life while he brushed coats and shined boots. "Of course."

"What about you?" Finch leaned against the door jamb and considered her. "Would you have made different choices if your father hadn't gotten hurt?"

Would she? Perhaps. "I suppose I'll never know what other options I might have had."

And didn't that seem to be the saddest part of all?

Chapter Two

"I beg your pardon, sir?" Finch maintained the stoic expression he'd been taught during his years of service in Hawthorne House, but his insides trembled in reaction. He'd been warned that being a valet would come with a collection of unorthodox requests, but he couldn't possibly have heard Lord Trent correctly.

"I want you to redecorate." Lord Trent squinted and looked about his bedchamber. "Not the entire house, of course. You only need address the rooms I primarily use. This one. My study. Maybe the private parlor out there." He gestured toward one of the doors leading from the room.

Finch would have gladly departed through any of the doors and maybe even the window if it meant this conversation had never happened. "Redecorate."

"Yes."

"And you want me to oversee it?"

Eyes widened under lifted brows before his employer said, "Well, I've certainly no idea how to do it."

And Finch did? He should take Lord Trent to the small valet room one floor up and ask if that was the look he wanted, because it was all Finch knew. A quilt he'd had since childhood lay on the bed, a collection of wooden animals carved by his younger brother sat atop the dresser, and a few items of clothing hung on the wall hooks. It was hardly fit to be the room of a duke's second son.

He swallowed and tried once more to find a way to have heard the assignment wrong. "My lord, I..."

The words trailed off and Finch let his mouth slowly close around the silence. He could not give the impression he was not capable of accomplishing this task. He'd been Lord Trent's valet for less than a month. If he failed in his duties now, he could lose the job entirely. Returning to his position at Hawthorne House wasn't an option, so there'd be nothing to do but start over somewhere else, assuming he could even get a job after being let go by one of the Hawthornes.

There was nothing for it but to find a way. "Of course, my lord. Whatever you wish."

Lord Trent grinned. "Excellent." He waved his hand about the room. "We'll close this room off while the work is being done, of course. You'll give the workmen their instructions for wall coverings, window treatments, and the like."

Finch swallowed. *The like* was the part he was most afraid of. He felt a modicum of confidence in his ability to choose furniture, but what about everything else? Even the idea of selecting a curtain was baffling.

"I've spoken to Mrs. Harris." Lord Trent picked up an orange vase from table by the window and turned it about in his hands. "You're free to pull one of the other staff to assist you." He frowned at the vase before gazing at the ceiling, face scrunched in concentration. "What was the head maid's name? She was in here two days ago."

"Lydia, sir." Finch choked the words out through a suddenly tight throat. Surely his lordship wasn't going to suggest Finch work with Lydia to decorate these spaces. That was far too... personal.

The confusion cleared from Lord Trent's face as he smiled and nodded. "Right. See if she can help you. She knows this house well. There might be pieces you can use from other rooms or some such." He frowned at the vase before setting it back on the table. "Perhaps not that piece, though."

"I'll see that it is removed, my lord." As to the rest of it, well, Finch simply wouldn't comment on it. That way he wouldn't have to feel the guilt over lying or the trepidation of contradicting his employer. He enjoyed spending time with Lydia, had even indulged in the occasional flirtation with her when they'd encountered each other outside their families' homes. Something such as this, though? Decorating a home together could put ideas into his head.

Dangerous ideas he was better off never entertaining if he was going to be happy.

There had to be someone else who could assist him with this project. Maybe Mrs. Harris? Or the butler Fenton? They both knew the house as well as Lydia did.

"Excellent." Lord Trent waved an arm about the room. "You'll also see to having my things moved to another room for the duration?"

Finch began gathering the discarded clothing items, as much for something to do as a need for efficiency. "Do you wish to use the chamber on the other side of the private sitting room?"

Lord Trent shuddered. "The mistress' chamber? Goodness no. Isn't it full of frippery?"

"I haven't a clue, my lord." In truth, Finch had been in very few areas of the house. As a footman, he'd gone everywhere. He had carried items, delivered messages, and escorted guests, among other duties that could take him to any corner of the home. Now, though, he need only concern himself with the places his lordship went.

"Any room is sufficient, as long as I don't drown in lace when I go to bed," Lord Trent said with a careless wave of his hand.

"I'll see to it, sir." That, at least, should be simple enough. One of the rooms had to have a more masculine air than the others. If not, he could have all the trimmings and bedding removed and replaced with the items currently in the master chamber.

If only the remainder of the task was so easy.

Lord Trent gave himself a final inspection in the mirror, then turned to the door. "I'll be out for the day. I haven't decided yet if I'm staying at my club this evening or attending that party."

"I shall have your evening kit and another change of clothing ready for whatever you require."

His employer gave him a thoughtful look. "Excellent thought. The starch might well have fallen out of this cravat by this evening. I may need a refresh even if I decide not to rub shoulders with the fancier of my set. Well done, Finch."

At least he wasn't falling short in that area of the job, then. The area at which valets were intended to excel. Whoever heard of a valet needing to know about... Finch glanced about the room at the four-poster bed, the landscape paintings, and the mismatched basin and water pitcher. Despite its apparent age, the room still held an air of elegance and opulence. Though Finch had been surrounded by such for half his life, he hadn't the first idea how to go about creating it.

With a grin and a nod, Lord Trent departed. He seemed to have not one hesitation in leaving Finch alone with this new project.

Finch crossed the room and grasped the edge of the curtain in his hand. He rubbed his fingers together and felt the threadbare condition of fabric that had seen too much sun. His fist closed over the cloth as his eyes slid closed in a long, solemn prayer. He was going to need every bit of assistance God could give him in order to accomplish this task.

As he set the dressing room to rights, more questions came to mind. Ones he should have asked his employer. Was he meant to start working on this project today? When did Lord Trent anticipate moving out of this chamber? This week? This month? This afternoon?

That didn't even begin to take into consideration what his intended timing might be for moving back into his refurbished rooms.

Perhaps the housekeeper would have those details. Lord Trent had mentioned speaking to Mrs. Harris about the project. Surely she would have known what questions to ask. Seeking her out for that information would also give him the chance to convince her to help him so he didn't have to request Lydia's assistance.

Not that Lydia wasn't capable, or at least as capable as any of the rest of the staff. Despite her age and the fact that her experience in this house had been far from the usual aristocratic atmosphere, she seemed to be doing an admirable job. It was obvious this room hadn't been used for years, but there'd been no issues with dust or signs of infestation when Finch had arranged Lord Trent's personal belongings.

Of course, cleaning skills didn't mean she was any more adept at selecting furnishings than he was.

Finch shook his head as he made his way belowstairs to seek out the housekeeper. The reason didn't matter. It simply felt inappropriate to discuss preferences of decor with the girl he'd grown up next door to, and selecting furniture felt far too intimate.

In such an abnormal situation, he had nothing to depend upon but his instincts, and his gut knew he didn't want to do this with Lydia.

He found Mrs. Harris in the housekeeper's office, a brand new ledger book spread out on the desk before her. After he knocked softly, she bid him enter without looking up from the numbers she was writing in a neat column.

Finch waited until she finished and gave him her attention. There wasn't a smile on her face, but her expression was open. If only Finch knew more specifically what he needed to ask this woman. Only Lord Trent could terminate his position, but if he upset the housekeeper, she could make it impossible for him to do his job.

He cleared his throat. "Lord Trent informed me I am to oversee the refurbishing of his private rooms. He mentioned he had already spoken to you about his needs for this project?"

"Yes, yes, he did." She waved a hand about in the air. "Feel free to move anything about from elsewhere in the house. Though we're doing our best to be prepared for it, he hasn't mentioned an intention to do any entertaining, so even the drawing room and hall items are available."

That wasn't really what Finch wanted to know. "This seems a potentially time-consuming task."

"More than you know." Mrs. Harris shook her head. "You'll have to visit the furniture showrooms and fabric warehouses. Then there's meeting with the workmen and explaining your choices."

He couldn't have asked for a more perfect opening. "I am, of course, prepared to work such excursions and meetings into my duties, but I'm afraid I haven't much experience in this area. Might you be able to lend a voice to the decisions?" That was all he needed. If someone else told him what to choose and procure, he could go and place the orders.

She laughed, but it was tight with underlying tension. "Gracious, no." One hand smoothed a page of the ledger in front of her. "I've a great deal of learning to do myself while adjusting to how Lord Trent wants his household to run. Not to mention he isn't here enough to make hiring a cook necessary, but there are still more mouths to feed."

"Perhaps Fenton, then?" A coil of tension began to tighten in Finch's middle.

"I doubt he can spare the time, either. You must have noticed the new footmen we hired are rather green." She shook her head and clucked her tongue. "The maids like the unorthodox reputation of this house well enough, but experienced footmen tend to shy away."

Finch understood that sentiment. He certainly would have fled such a house were he not attached to the owner. Working his way from house boy to first footman had been difficult and required a great deal of attention and work. From early on, he'd had the goal of one day becoming a valet. To have the clear hierarchy of progress removed would have been devastating.

Almost as devastating as the fact that he was fast running out of options. Perhaps if Mrs. Harris were to agree to a change in the environment, he could put off the redecorating?

Finch cleared his throat. "The dining situation is rather unorthodox."

Mrs. Harris pointed her pencil at him. "I've already agreed that the lower servants will need to adhere to a more traditional schedule and location, but I'm not budging further. Lord Trent is a family man, despite his bachelor status, and I'll not have him bumping around this house so disconnected that he abandons it and we're lost in the middle of London like we were when the viscount decided to move to the country."

Finch could only stare. The woman did realize that bachelors around London, likely around the world, managed just fine without making connections with their servants, didn't she? And in Lord Trent's particular case, his family was so loving, doted on each other so much, that mere walls were not going to change anything?

Then again, Finch had never worked in an all-but-abandoned house. Nor did it matter if he thought her reasoning valid. He was hardly in a position to force her to change. Mrs. Harris might be willing to abandon certain elements of servant hierarchy, but Finch couldn't abandon years of training and start arguing with the housekeeper.

"Why don't you ask Lydia?" Mrs. Harris turned her attention back to the ledger as she pointed toward the ceiling. "She's cleaning the second-floor bedchambers today. We've maids enough to see to the essential daily cleaning. It won't hurt for a day or two of dust to accumulate in the unused rooms if she adjusts her routine to assist you."

Two people of authority had now sent Finch to Lydia. He had no more room for argument.

Unless, of course, he didn't actually need assistance. Was there any chance he could do this on his own?

Instead of seeking Lydia out, he took himself off to the drapers. A single conversation with the shop assistant there, who could barely contain his disdain and amusement, told Finch that no, he was not ready to make these decisions on his own. It should have been the same as selecting a coat and pairing it with trousers and a vest, but it wasn't. All of these different pieces had to be chosen separately, but were dependent upon each other and had to be appealing for far more than a few hours in a single day.

His head pounded from all the questions he hadn't been able to answer.

Still, he didn't seek Lydia out upon his return to the house. Instead he went about his other duties, insuring every possible set of clothing was prepared for Lord Trent's evening. When word came around that his lordship would not be returning home at all until late, Finch busied himself putting everything away again.

Dinner came and went.

Evening duties were seen to.

Through it all Finch avoided Lydia. She'd been at the end of the corridor when he'd come out of the master chamber once, and he'd all but dived back into the room to keep from having to speak to her. If he spoke to her, he'd have to broach the subject of working together, and he just couldn't shake the feeling that it was going to be a bad idea.

The next morning, though, when he'd had to hem and haw through Lord Trent's questions about which bedchamber he would be moving to and what the timing looked like, Finch knew he could put it off no longer. The discomfort he couldn't quite identify wasn't enough to keep him from doing his job.

With a deep breath and a prayer for strength, he went in search of a head of springy blonde curls.

Chapter Three

Lydia ran the dust cloth along the edge of the table but didn't bother to move the empty vase or flick the rag into the corners. The surface had been thoroughly cleaned just last week, and the only person who'd been in here since was her.

It felt strange, not knowing what the master of the house was thinking or planning or even considering. At any moment the house could be called upon to host a party, house overnight company, close up for the season, or prepare to welcome a family of renters. It was the way of the aristocracy.

Since she very much wanted to be worthy of the role she'd been given, Lydia was determined to keep the house in a perpetual state of readiness. Lord Trent could – and should –expect his staff to keep all areas of the house ready for anything at any time.

That didn't make the constant cleaning of never used rooms any more enjoyable.

The one benefit worth clinging to was how many valid excuses it gave Lydia to spend her days wherever Finch wasn't. A tactic of avoidance wouldn't work forever, but all she needed was another week or two, maybe a month, and she'd be able to get her thoughts straight.

Already, she was finding other things to keep her mind occupied when faced with the monotony of certain tasks. Just yesterday she'd spent the entirety of her time sweeping out the fireplaces imagining how often the maids working roadside inns had to complete such a chore.

Of course, then she'd moved on to sweeping the dust and cobwebs from the corners and considered whether or not the innkeeper's wife ever had to step in to clean the rooms and what it would be like if she and Finch ran an out of the way inn somewhere.

Still. It was progress.

She flicked her cloth over the bedpost before smoothing the teeniest of creases from the dark blue bed coverlet she'd aired out three days ago.

"Oh, good."

The relieved male voice had Lydia near to jumping out of her skin. She whirled around, hand dragging across the coverlet and creating a wave of wrinkles along the bed surface. Finch stood in the doorway, looking about the room with a relieved expression.

Lydia took a deep breath to steady her pounding heart, then gave her attention to smoothing the coverlet once more as she said, "Are you looking for something?"

"Lord Trent's new bedchamber."

Lydia couldn't possibly have heard him correctly. This room hadn't even been used when Miss Amelia lived here. She and her companion had used the other two rooms on this floor. "He doesn't intend to continue using the master's rooms?"

Finch stepped into the bedchamber and gave it one more satisfied perusal. "He wishes to have the room refurbished and needs somewhere to stay while the work is done." He shook his head. "I'd begun to worry because the other two rooms on this floor were not going to be acceptable options."

No, they wouldn't be. It made sense that Lord Trent would want to redecorate. While nothing in the house was falling apart or in gross disrepair, there also wasn't anything modern or fresh about it. Aside from a piece or two of furniture they'd been forced to have recovered, the furnishings of the house hadn't been updated in at least twenty years.

Lydia looked around the room as well, a small thrill of pride momentarily distracting her from the fact that she was alone with Finch. It would seem that keeping every room in the house ready for occupancy was already to her credit. Finch could move Lord Trent's belongings this very minute.

Well, she might dust all those corners she'd just skipped first.

Finch let out a sigh and rubbed a hand over the back of his neck before moving his gaze from the room's simple decoration to Lydia. "You have to help me."

"Of course." That was her job, wasn't it? "I'll have the room ready in less than an hour. I do think the footmen would be better assistance at moving his actual belongings and such, though."

He shook his head. "No, not that. With the redecorating."

"Why would you—"

"He's tasked me with overseeing it."

While Lydia was doing her best to hide the holes in her knowledge about seeing to the upkeep of an aristocratic home, she was more than willing to confess she hadn't any idea what details the role of a valet entailed. From her basic understanding, though, this didn't seem a usual request. "Are you to watch over the workmen? What could he be worried about them finding? Lord Trent has hardly lived here long enough to have secrets tucked within the walls."

Finch shook his head. "I'm not watching the workmen. I'm telling them what to do."

Lydia fell silent, unable to comprehend the sentence correctly or quickly. "You are to select the furnishings?"

"From the wall coverings to the rug." Finch pinched the bridge of his nose. "Would it be bad form for a man to ask his mother to assist him in his work?"

Lydia had, of course, met Finch's mother. She was a delightful woman, but... "Do you think she knows more about fine accouterments than you do?"

"No." Finch moved to the small dressing room and opened the door to inspect the space. "Aren't there magazines for this? Or a shop I can walk into and order a prepared collection of matching fabrics and furniture?"

"Not that I'm aware of. Perhaps Mrs. Harris knows? Or Fenton?" Lydia's heart went out to Finch. He was as new to his new role as she was, but he had far more different tasks to learn. How horrible to have the responsibilities flipped on end while still coming to understand them in the first place.

Finch shook his head. "Their days are already lacking enough hours. You know the house. Lord Trent said I should get you to help me."

She knew the man was aware of her name, since he had used it when she'd come to put linens on his bed, but beyond that, she couldn't imagine why he'd give her a single thought. Now he had all but assigned her to spend time with his valet. "I suppose I could rearrange my cleaning schedule, but I don't know any more than you do."

This was a death knell for her plan. She couldn't avoid Finch if she was working closely with him every day for several weeks. She needed time to something else to occupy her mind as she performed her mundane daily tasks.

Apparently she wasn't going to get it. Instead, she was being given a trial by fire.

This would be the perfect evaluation opportunity. If she could survive with her head on straight, then she could rest assured that working under the same roof as Finch would not leave her in utter devastation.

And if she couldn't, it would be a sign that she should seek out other employment.

She took a deep breath and pasted a wide, fake smile onto her face. "Where do we start?"

Finch said nothing, but his terrified expression indicated he didn't have a single idea.

Lydia tried not to smile, tried to keep her heart from sliding about in a silly puddle, but his lost look was endearing. "Did he give you any ideas?" she asked. "Perhaps an example or suggestion?"

"I think I'm to do whatever I like best."

"That at least makes it difficult to go wrong."

Finch gripped the back of his neck with both hands, eyes closed in agony. "Are you daft? That means everything could go wrong."

"How so?"

"What if this is a test? What if he believes my ability to dress his room indicates my ability to dress his person?"

Then he was a clueless man who had fooled the entirety of London into thinking he was playing with a full deck of cards. Unfortunately, fear wasn't always rational. Neither was any other emotion, come to think of it. "We won't let that happen."

Just because Lydia didn't want to work in the same house as Finch didn't mean she wanted him to lose his position. She continued, "This may not be the typical domain for servants, but we've plenty of friends who've seen the process."

"That's true." Finch rolled his shoulders and let out a sigh. "They should at least be able to tell us where to start."

Lydia's smile relaxed into one that was entirely real as the perfect idea came to her. "We should go ask them. Separately. We should go in two different directions and ask different people what they think."

Why had Lydia been worried? Her plan for avoidance was still in effect. She could help Finch without going about London with him.

"That's a good place to start." Finch nodded. "Then we can discuss what we each learned." He nodded his head in the direction of the other empty rooms. "We can turn one of the extra rooms into an office of sorts to work together in."

Lydia's smile tightened once more. So much for perfect plans. Meeting alone with Finch was going to be much worse than walking about London would have been. She could hardly take it back now, though. Through a tight, gritted smile she said, "I can't wait."

A great deal of progress was made over the next week. All of Lord Trent's personal effects were moved to the new chamber. The dressing room was organized. A team of reputable workmen were found and hired and would begin the transformation of the rooms in three weeks' time.

That last had been arranged by Mrs. Harris, who'd been very apologetic about her inability to help him more. Finch hadn't the heart to tell her that finding workmen was probably the only part of the assignment he could have comfortably done on his own. What he wanted her to do was tell him what he needed to have those men do when they arrived.

He'd seen Lydia very little in the days since they'd struck their agreement. It shouldn't have been anything of note, as he hadn't given her a great deal of thought when he'd first moved into the house, but now the lack was as noticeable as a scratchy seam on his shirt collar.

When he'd worked as a footman, he would go weeks between visits with her. Ever since she'd agreed to assist him, since arrangements had been made that could put him in her company more than ever before, he'd frequently recalled those previous encounters and how enjoyable they'd been.

It wasn't unusual for her to be visiting her family at the same time he was visiting his. They would meet up as they were leaving and have a pleasant conversation while seated on the steps to the alley behind the shops. After a while, they would continue their journeys home, and he would go that extra little bit out of his way to see her back to Mount Street. Those brief engagements always left him with the vaguely painful pleasure one got when bothering an almost healed scrape.

Now, knowing she was in the house and mere floors away, knowing they would soon be spending more time together, knowing those enjoyable conversations could be happening on a more regular basis was making him restless. This was what his intuition must have feared. On some level, he must have known that seeking her out would open the possibility to seek out those momentary pleasures that had once been out of his reach.

He wanted to enjoy the way excitement seemed to radiate around her like the curls that wouldn't ever stay in her cap. He wanted to feel the warmth of her smile and hear her laugh or contemplate the questions that challenged him to think.

Those were dangerous things to want.

As he slid a pair of polished boots into place in the dressing room, it occurred to him that this project might actually be a gift.

How often did people want things that turned out far less delightful than they'd anticipated?

What was the harm in taking the few weeks of work needed to plan the refurbishment to enjoy spending time with Lydia? The newness would surely wear off and they could settle into a simple, companionable friendship.

It wasn't as if there was any other option. They were set on paths that would help their families and provide housing and provisions for themselves for many years, possibly their whole lives. Some maids eventually married and left domestic service, but if Lydia had such inclinations, she'd never mentioned them.

Finch frowned as he departed the dressing room and made one last check of the bedchamber beyond. If someone had asked him if they were friends before he'd moved into this house, he'd have said yes. And yet, since moving in he'd seen her very little. Somehow, even though he was living under the same roof as she was, he knew as little about her everyday life as he ever had.

He didn't even know where she'd likely be right now.

With no more time to delay on making decisions – or at least making decisions about what decisions needed to be made – he set off to find her. She wasn't in any of the other bedrooms on the second floor, nor was she in the kitchens. The scullery, with its brand new, larger laundry tub, was occupied only by the new, young scullery maid, but she was able to direct him to the small work yard behind the house.

There he found Lydia, putting all of her small might into beating a rug nearly twice her size with a carpet rod.

Considering her diminutive stature, the light haze of dust and fine pile of dirt below the hanging carpet was impressive. His gaze trailed over the large floor covering. It seemed in far better condition than the other rugs in the house. There was no wear along the edges and the colors were still even throughout the design. Once she paused to catch her breath, he stepped forward. "Where's that rug from?"

She took a deep breath and braced her hands on her hips. "The nursery."

Finch blinked at it. "I didn't even know there was a nursery."

"I'm not certain the last time it was used as such, but it was certainly built to be one." She shrugged. "I thought this might work in the parlor."

Despite Mrs. Harris and even Lord Trent telling him to use anything from the house, he'd yet to look about with such intentions. It seemed strange, to walk through the house with the mind of pilfering items from one room to fill another. Perhaps he'd spent too much time trying to be part of a room's scenery to consider picking it apart.

Whatever the reason, he'd not been doing the work, whereas Lydia apparently had.

A slight flush crossed his neck. "Er, yes. It should be perfect in there."

"Other than this, I'm afraid I haven't much to help you." She picked up the rod, ready to beat at the carpet again. "I collected some catalogs and the maids a few houses over said their mistress continually fretted over how the drapery and the furniture fabric looked together."

"Isn't that the entire consideration? How things look together?" Finch frowned.

"As I said, I'm not much assistance."

It was still more than Finch had done. "We should look at the catalogs and start with the furniture." He'd accepted enough deliveries to know that some pieces took a while to procure. "Perhaps it would be more expedient to have existing pieces recovered?"

"It would cost less as well." Lydia nodded toward the house. "While he may be the son of a duke, he is a younger son." She frowned. "Aren't they always having to be more aware of money than their brother?"

"I wouldn't know. I'm always aware of money."

Lydia laughed and beat the carpet a few more times. A few puffs of dust emerged, but nothing like she'd been managing when he came out.

She set the carpet rod aside with a satisfied nod. "That should do it." Her gaze then lifted to the sky. "Does it look like rain or can I leave it out for the night?"

"For now the sky is clear." Was he truly so desperate to appear helpful and alleviate the guilt of having done nothing that he was inanely analyzing the weather? "We can check again this evening."

She nodded and moved toward the house. "Have you learned anything?"

He should admit he hadn't, but he didn't want to look like a failure. "There's a team of workmen scheduled to start in a few weeks. They'll begin by moving out all the old furnishings, but we'll need something ready for them to do to the walls after that."

"What we need," Lydia said, "is something that tells us what Lord Trent likes. Are his clothes of a particular style? What about books?"

"His clothing is simple. Well made, of course, and in the latest fashion, but he's not garbing himself like a peacock."

"What about his old rooms?"

"In Hawthorne House?"

Lydia nodded.

Finch searched his memory, trying to remember the last time he'd had reason to be in Lord Trent's rooms at Hawthorne House. The man had still resided there the first four days of Finch's employment as his valet, but the color and style of the curtains had been the last thing on Finch's mind. "I haven't the faintest idea."

"Do you think they would let us take a look?"

It was a better idea than any he had. "It wouldn't hurt to ask."

They set off across Mayfair. It should have felt similar to the many other times they'd walked through the city, but it didn't. Finch was very much aware that this time Lydia would be returning with him. They were setting out with a common goal, would be moving toward the same destinations for the entire afternoon. Shoulder to shoulder, they would be leaving and returning together.

A sense of rightness and belonging made him twitch as they crossed into Grosvenor Square. It felt far too good to be on a mission with Lydia. They'd left the house in silence, but after he pointed out a particularly adorable cat in the window, the conversation had flowed freely from topic to topic.

They passed a food stand and Lydia stopped to look over the contents.

"Look at those hazelnuts. Aren't they beautiful? Mrs. Harris uses them to make a root vegetable gratin that is absolutely delicious."

"We should take some home with us then." As soon as the words were out, Finch's stomach twisted. This entire business was far too appealing. Working alongside Lydia, planning future meals with Lydia, considering home to be the same place Lydia laid her head every night.

She procured the hazelnuts and shoved them in her bag before they continued walking. As Hawthorne House came into view, he knew he could tell Mrs. Harris why her casual, familial atmosphere was dangerous.

He couldn't afford to think of his employer as a friend, to think of his house as a home, to think of his own wants and opinions if he wanted to continue working for families who lived in homes such as the large white stone mansion in front of him.

If he wanted to have a future, he could not afford to think about Lydia.

Chapter Four

Lydia clenched her teeth to keep from gaping at her surroundings. She'd been in several fine homes over the years, but generally no further than the kitchens. She'd even been in Hawthorne House's kitchen before and had gaped at its modernity and size.

As Finch led her up the back stairs, she marveled at how it felt finer than anything she cleaned in the house in Mount Street. The family wasn't in residence, which was why the butler had let them in at all. That and the fact that he knew Finch and the staff here loved Miss Amelia – now Lady Raebourne – almost as much as Lydia, Mrs. Harris, and Fenton did.

They'd had to promise not to go into any room other than Lord Trent's former chamber, but Lydia wished she had the gumption to ask for a tour of the other servant areas. What were the maid rooms like in a house such as this one?

Probably better if she didn't know.

Some of the doors were open, so Lydia peered into them as they walked down the corridor. Plush carpets, gilded frames, and vibrantly colored fabrics that showed not a single thread of wear filled the spaces. How could Lord Trent leave lodgings such as this for the aged, humble abode he resided in now?

They came to a closed door and Finch knocked lightly before lifting the latch and swinging the portal open. The room beyond was exquisitely decorated in shades of blue and gold.

The embroidered coverings were aligned perfectly in the center of the bed, with sharp tucks at every corner. The various surfaces of tables and chairs gleamed as if they'd been polished mere minutes before. The drapery was pulled to a precise position that allowed a sliver of sunlight to slash across the floor while missing the geometrically patterned carpet and the elegant paintings on the walls.

"This was his room?" Lydia couldn't deny the space was exceptionally beautiful, but it didn't seem to align with the man who joked about with his housekeeper and drank port with his butler after dinner. The owner of this room would have set Mrs. Harris straight that first night, not sent Fenton to collect his valet.

Finch frowned as he, too, looked about the room. "Yes, this is it. I remember it, now that we're here. It doesn't quite... fit him, does it?"

"My thoughts exactly, though you spend far more time in his presence than I do." Her hand extended and she curled the fingers into a fist just before touching the pillow on a chair to discover how soft it was.

Finch sighed. "He would have given ideas for look of this room, though, wouldn't he?"

Lydia shrugged. "Unless he cared as little then as he appears to now."

She stepped further into the room, looking into one corner that seemed empty, unbalanced, as if whatever had been sitting there recently had been moved. The yawning space eased some of her discomfort. Even in a house such as this one, they snitched from the unused rooms to improve the others.

Finch sighed. "Lady Blackstone is a very particular woman. Even more so when she was living here than she is since her marriage. It is possible she determined the look of this room herself."

"For a room that once held a man's most personal belongings, it feels rather cold and impersonal, doesn't it?" Lydia stepped over to the dressing table to examine it more closely. The wood wasn't scratched or discolored. If anything had set upon this surface, the furniture didn't carry the memory.

"As I have recently moved them all not just once, but twice, I can assure you the man has a large collection of personal effects." Finch gave a light laugh.

There were certainly enough drawers and cabinets in the room's furniture to hold a variety of knick-knacks. "I imagine they were all neatly stored away when he was here. I doubt we'd have been able to learn much about him by standing here even when he was in residence."

"Isn't that how we all live, though?" Finch crossed to the window and flipped the drape back to examine the window facing side. "Would your room tell anyone about you?"

Would it? Until recently, Lydia's attic room had been more of a place to store her clothing than anything else. She'd lived all about the house. Each threadbare sofa and sun-faded wall had felt like home. The bed had only been used in the summer, as she'd often chosen to spend winter nights in the room off the kitchen where Marie was sleeping now.

Lydia ran a hand along the back of an elegant wooden chair. "If one walked into my attic room, like we did here, I suppose they wouldn't find anything of note. It is the house that feels like home to me. There is so much of it that feels personal and comforting, but I suppose I've made little impact on it."

"I wouldn't say that." Finch walked back to her side. "Not all impacts are about leaving a visual mark." He grinned. "Sometimes it's about removing something. Just imagine how much dust would coat those surfaces without you there."

Lydia smiled in return, but she didn't quite feel it.

Finch sighed. "I don't think this room is going to provide the inspiration we'd hoped for."

She shook her head in agreement, suddenly wanting out of these cold, beautiful surroundings, out of the unknown splendor that made her feel her truly insignificant place in the world.

It made her desperate to do a good job on Lord Trent's spaces. While the bedroom hadn't been personal, it was the environment he'd grown up in. There wasn't an inch that didn't declare elegance, refinement, and poise.

"What was it like, working here?" Lydia asked as they descended the stairs back to the kitchens.

"More comfortable than it would appear. It's a good family. They expected a full day's work, but they gave fair pay in return. They always made their expectations clear."

Lydia frowned. "It would seem Lord Trent has decided not to carry on that tradition."

Finch shook his head, lips tilted into a slight smile, but lines of concern edged the corners of his eyes. "He asks about my progress every few days, but he never wants to know particulars about what I've chosen."

A snorting scoff of laughter escaped Lydia. "That's fortunate, since we've chosen nothing aside from a rug."

"He doesn't seem concerned about that either."

They exited the kitchen and Lydia squinted in the full sunlight. "What does he want to know?"

"If I'm working with you, how much time we're spending on it. The process seems more interesting to him than the outcome."

Concern welled up as they walked along the edge of Grosvenor Square's elegant green space. "You don't think he intends to dock our pay or anything, do you?"

"He's not that sort of man. I mean, we're doing what he asked us to."

Lydia looked back at Hawthorne House, its large, white brick face taking up most of the street on that side of the square. She wanted them to get this right. Not simply because she wanted Finch to do well or wanted their employer to be happy, but because by doing this, by having a say in these changes, she was making her mark on the house.

That blue and gold room hadn't reflected Lord Trent, but it had been distinctive in its own way. Whoever had chosen the furnishings had left an impression on anyone who would later view it.

She could do the same. From this project on, there would be a piece of her to see in that house.

At least, until someone else came along and took it away, because none of it was actually hers to begin with.

Lydia lay awake half the night. From the time they'd left Hawthorne House behind, an idea had been niggling at her mind, just out of reach, and she couldn't help but believe that idea was the answer they were seeking. Somewhere between the final settling of the house and first creaking steps of pre-dawn work, the idea crystallized in her mind.

She rushed through her morning duties, then set off to find Finch. Every other time they'd worked together, she'd waited for him to come to her.

As if that would keep her heart safer. All it had managed to do was make her wish he would come after her for another reason some day.

That was over.

Her idea was the perfect answer to their problems, but it was also the key to her demise. If she wanted to go through with it, she had to tell Finch before the other voice in her head convinced her not to.

Knowing he would be cleaning up the dressing room and preparing for the rest of the day, she went to Lord Trent's temporary chambers and gave the door two light taps.

Lord Trent's cheerful "Enter" nearly had her fleeing down the stairs once more. Why was he still here? Normally, he would have departed the house half an hour ago.

Before she could give in to the urge to run away, the door opened to reveal Finch. Beyond the valet's shoulder, Lord Trent was looking in a mirror and adjusting his waistcoat. He glanced toward the door and smiled. "Ah, Lydia, isn't it? Come in, come in. Mrs. Harris and Finch tell me you're lending a feminine hand to the redecorating of my rooms."

Finch pushed the door open wide so Lydia could take a single step over the threshold. She couldn't entirely disobey a direct request, after all.

As Finch moved back across the room to assist Lord Trent into a dark green jacket, his lordship grinned at Lydia and tossed her a wink over his shoulder.

Once the jacket was settled in place, Lord Trent gave his reflection a nod and turned his attention back to Lydia. "He hasn't been too much trouble, has he?"

Why was he talking to her? How was she meant to answer? Lydia might not have experience working with many—or really any—aristocrats, but she'd heard enough tales to know that direct conversation aside from instructions was rare. Teasing, such as Lord Trent seemed to be doing, was unheard of.

"Uh, yes, my lord." That was always the right answer, wasn't it?

Finch's eyes widened and Lydia played the brief conversation over in her mind. Oh, no, that had been the absolute wrong thing to say. "I meant, no, my lord. No trouble at all. You've nothing to concern yourself with."

"I haven't?" Lord Trent's eyebrows rose as he looked from her to Finch. "That's not what I hear."

Lydia swallowed.

Finch said, "It's not?"

"No. Amelia tells me Fenton likes to sing carols around the house as Christmas comes and he's not very good at it. I'm very concerned for our ears."

Finch seemed to deflate as he leaned back into the dressing table, and Lydia couldn't help but laugh as she met his gaze. In that moment she felt connected to him. In the space of a few heartbeats, they'd shared a gamut of emotions and thoughts. Coming out on the other side felt like something of an accomplishment.

Lord Trent looked at each of them once more before nodding and leaving the room. Despite his jovial attitude, he was as crisp and elegant in appearance as the house he'd once lived in. He also seemed as comfortable as could be in the far shabbier conditions he was now surrounded by.

She was more convinced than ever that her idea was the right one.

Once even the echo of Lord Trent's footsteps had faded from the air, she turned to Finch. "I know what we should do."

"About the room or about my heart, because it may never beat the same after that scare you gave me." He shook his head.

Lydia grinned. "The rooms."

"That's far more useful." Finch straightened and began gathering up the items that needed to be returned to the small dressing room. "What should we do?"

"Whatever we want."

He frowned, half bent over the dressing table. "That doesn't seem wise."

"Neither does giving the task to your valet, which is why I believe this is the answer. I don't think he knows what he wants, but he wants something different than his mother's home. Everything about Hawthorne House is the epitome of aristocratic elegance."

"And now he wants servant shambles? I don't think so."

Lydia laughed, even as her heart quaked with the implications of what she was about to say. "Not a shamble, no, but perhaps what we as servants view as elegance? What would someone from our walk of life consider beautiful?"

He rubbed a hand over his face and looked around the room. "It would at least be better than this, I suppose."

"We've no other ideas, so what have we got to lose?"

He gave her a wide grin. "Aside from our jobs?"

As he grabbed Lydia's hand and pulled her from the room, she couldn't help but think that maybe that wouldn't be the worst thing that could happen.

Chapter Five

Finch would never claim to have a great extent of knowledge about marriage, romance, or love, but he'd never heard of anyone getting snared into such emotions by looking at fabric.

And yet a mere two weeks after they'd resolved to choose as if for themselves, here in this warehouse with a clerk who was clearly doubtful of their authority to be making such selections, Finch couldn't stop imagining what it would be like if they were doing this for their own home instead of someone else's. Given the way they were selecting things they personally liked and wanted, the comparison was inevitable.

Of course, they wouldn't be choosing such fine fabrics for their own home.

They wouldn't even have a home, because neither of them would have a job.

"I like that one." Finch pointed to the green fabric Lydia was continually running a hand over despite letting her eyes travel to the other racks and bolts of blues and purples.

She looked down at the fabric, a small smile touching her lips as she pinched a section and rubbed it between her fingers. "Does he like green? Nothing in his Hawthorne House space was green."

"What happened to choosing what we wanted?" Finch placed his hand on her shoulder and squeezed. "It worked well enough for the study selections."

"This is for his bedchamber, though," she whispered, as if afraid to let anyone know why they were shopping for fabric. "It seems more...important to get it right."

"The only way we will be able to make any decisions is to choose what we like." He might as well have said the only way to make the decision was to pretend it was for their own room.

The way her gaze met his and then skittered away, he had to assume a similar thought had crossed her mind. Was that thought causing her a similar anguish as well?

"I like this one," she said.

"Me too."

This time when she looked up, she didn't immediately look away. It was obvious something pained her, but he had no way of knowing if it was concern over getting this project right or something more. What if she wasn't forming the same attachment to him that he was to her?

What if she was?

Warmth from their connected gaze joined with the heat emanating from where his hand was still on her shoulder and all but melted every resolve he'd ever had. He stepped away and turned toward another section of fabric. "We'll need a coordinating upholstery for the chair."

And so it went. The more comfortable they became with simply choosing what they liked, the more quickly the details fell into place. Some of the pieces were chosen from furniture maker showrooms, others were pulled from the house and sent off to be recovered or refinished. Fabrics were chosen, curtain designs were selected, wallpapers were considered.

Every night, Finch took time to remember the benefits of his job and the opportunities it would bring his younger brother.

Every morning he was reminded of how much he truly enjoyed what he was doing.

And each afternoon, as he and Lydia saw to one more item, had one more conversation while walking about town, shared one more laugh, and made one more memory, he wondered if all those resolves were wrong.

When the final piece was chosen and sent off to have the garish red cushion covering replaced with a green brocade, Finch felt equal parts relief and melancholy.

There were suddenly chunks of free time in his day, as he'd learned how to do all his other duties more efficiently to have time to shop and plan with Lydia. After all, Lord Trent could hardly have gone about with an unbrushed jacket or an unstarched cravat simply because his valet was musing over wall coverings.

Finch wasn't certain what to do with himself, and he had to fight the urge to continue to seek out Lydia.

Unlike him, she'd needed to put off some of her duties. Now she had time to see to the deeper cleaning needed to reclaim rooms neglected for over a decade. The amount of sand scrubbing required to renew the wooden floors made Finch's knees hurt just thinking about it. Not to mention how all of that sand scrubbing only added to the daily battle with dust.

He'd been friendly with the maids at Hawthorne House, but he'd never considered their daily work before. Now he knew everything one did in a day. Or at least, what Lydia did in a day. The other two maids likely had similar jobs, but he didn't silently track them through the house like he did Lydia.

While he could always find a reason to seek her out in the house – Lord Trent needed fresh towels, there was a smudge on the window – all those excuses only added more work to her plate and didn't get him what he truly wanted.

He wanted to talk to her. He wanted to share a laugh with her. He wanted to stroll about London and comment on how it changed with the seasons.

It had been three days since he'd had a reason to talk to Lydia and he was feeling the loss. Because she ate belowstairs with the maids and he ate in the dining room with the upper servants, he couldn't even share a conversation with her at mealtimes. That was possibly the only piece of this sad situation he could change.

"Don't you think this is strange?" Finch set aside the spoon he'd used to eat the beef stew and considered his dining companions.

"What is strange?" Mrs. Harris dabbed at her mouth with the serviette.

"This." Finch lifted a hand to indicate the dining room. "Eating up here."

"I thought we'd been over this." Mrs. Harris frowned at him like the mother she seemed to want to be. "We're a family here. Family eats abovestairs." She turned to glare at the door down to the kitchens. "If only the rest of them would eat up here as well. I don't know why Lydia insisted on moving back down there."

"You know why," Fenton said. "You just don't like it."

Finch knew why, too. It was one of the many things they'd discussed on their walks.

While part of Mrs. Harris was thrilled at having a full household to run again, she seemed far too determined to cling to some of the aspects of life she'd had with Miss Amelia. One of those aspects being the idea that the occupant of the house wasn't actually the one in charge of how it ran.

"Do you think of Lord Trent as a son then?" Was this a form of maternal need born of never marrying or having children of her own? Would this happen to Lydia one day?

Possibly.

Unless she married someone along the way.

Such an idea didn't sit well with Finch.

"Of course not." Mrs. Harris straightened her serviette and looked at the ceiling thoughtfully. "Perhaps a nephew."

Fenton nearly choked on his stew.

While Mrs. Harris might not want the restrictions of social propriety, Finch was well aware they still existed. Even as an upper servant, he was not in a position to berate the housekeeper. Not unless he was delivering a message directly from Lord Trent.

And that man actually seemed to enjoy the occasional unorthodox meal he ate at home.

Finch would enjoy eating with Lydia.

He pointed to the empty chair at the head of the table. "Perhaps we should only eat up here when his lordship dines? It feels wrong to be using the dining room without him."

"I'll not have the other servants put out by our moving up and down." Mrs. Harris shook her head. "As much as I don't like it, I suppose Lydia has the right idea about who eats where. This household might grow in the future and this room only seats ten."

Because the lack of adequate seating was what would make the entire staff dining with the master awkward.

In one last attempt at seeing Lydia, Finch took his own dishes down to the scullery.

She wasn't there.

After Lord Trent left the house the next morning, Finch gave up finding an excuse and simply sought her out. She was dusting the dressing table in the unused chamber intended for the mistress of the house. The workmen could be heard beyond the wall the room shared with the other bedroom.

"How are you?" Finch asked.

She looked up from the table and smiled, but quickly gave her attention back to her work. "I'm sleeping better now that I've a full day to do my work."

Finch shifted his weight. As glad as he was that she was no longer working into the evening and was getting adequate rest, he didn't want her entirely happy. Didn't she miss spending time with him as much as he missed spending time with her?

Not that he could ask such.

Instead he said, "Enough hours certainly makes the work easier. I even find time to take a short break or two during the day."

She nodded and her mob cap shifted, letting two ringlets out to bounce against her neck. "It is nice to take a breath every once and a while."

"We should do it together."

Her grin was wide, but her glance upward didn't quite connect her gaze to his. "Breathe? I think that is something everyone tends to do on their own."

Finch shook his head. "No, take our break."

She froze for several long moments, then began jabbing her cloth into the crevices of the scrollwork lining the top of the table. "And do what?"

"Sit. Go for a walk." He leaned against the wall. "I miss talking to you."

"We're talking now."

"You know what I mean."

Lydia sighed. "I miss talking to you too."

"That's settled then. When you finish your morning cleaning, and before you go to the storeroom or the laundry, we'll visit." Finch couldn't stop his grin. He could have saved himself days of discomfort by making this arrangement earlier.

This time when she looked up, her blue eyes stayed connected with his. "I'd like that."

Thus began Finch's favorite new tradition.

Lydia arranged her schedule to finish her morning rounds in the room beside Lord Trent's temporary quarters, the one where they'd previously spread out catalogs and stored the items they'd pulled from around the house. As soon as Finch set the dressing room to rights and prepared an extra change of clothes in case Lord Trent stopped home unexpectedly needing to change, he would join her.

He would sit in the wooden chair by the fireplace and she sat in the small window seat nearby. They'd found a small game table when they'd been seeking out furniture and Finch moved it into the room so they could spend their respites playing backgammon while they talked.

Though neither of them had ever expressly declared their time together to be a secret, there was a large chance the rest of the house was unaware, and Finch was happy to keep it that way. None of the other servants had reason to climb to this secluded upper floor unless called, and it made their time together private, cozy, and precious.

Having no one else know had the added benefit of preventing anyone from asking him about it. He didn't have to explain that he didn't care whether or not he won the game. Didn't have to admit that this had become his most valued time of day. Didn't have to justify how long a break he took.

And, perhaps most importantly, he didn't have to face the fact that these moments were being stolen from time and couldn't last forever. As long as he never had to say it out loud, he could pretend everything was just the way it had always been.

There was a time not too long ago when Lydia would have declared herself entirely ambivalent on the matter of backgammon. Now she wasn't certain if she loved or loathed the game, but she'd never be able to look at the board the same way again.

What was Finch thinking to have proposed they spend this time together?

What had she been thinking to agree?

She'd been so strong for the weeks they'd worked on the room and made their selections, constantly reminding herself their time together was limited, tied to a task with a defined end date. She'd told herself it wouldn't cause her any additional pain to have a few more treasured moments to savor in her memory.

Finch's need for assistance was long gone, and with it her excuse for allowing herself to toy with such emotional danger. And yet here she was, nurturing their connection. Every time they shared a joke or discussed an insight or considered the different merits of each answer to a question, her feelings grew a little stronger.

This was no longer a pretty little daydream about what it would be like to be married with a family. Now she suffered a deep longing for a partner in life. She knew what it was to work not just alongside Finch, but actively with him. She knew what it was to argue and compromise and be won over.

She'd had a taste of what could never be and letting go was going to be devastating. Was there a way to limit the pain? Was this game they were playing, in both the literal and figurative senses of the word, going to make it better or worse when the hurt finally came? Was there any way to make the coming heartache just a little bit smaller?

It was only a matter of time until she found out. These clandestine meetings could not continue forever, could not stay a secret forever. One day they would end, and she would have her answer. Until that day came, she could lie to herself and pretend it wasn't going to be that bad. If pain was inevitable, why rob herself of precious memories?

The lie held and her enjoyment continued until the morning she sat facing a backgammon board and the empty chair beyond it. Finch had been required to take his half day in the morning instead of the afternoon because of Lord Trent's schedule. She'd known it, and yet, out of habit, she had come to this room.

And she'd been forced to face the truth.

It was only a matter of time until her heart shattered under the weight of practicality. She'd been clasping on to the thinnest thread of hope even as she knew it wouldn't last.

The next day, when Frances asked to switch half days with Lydia, she readily agreed. If she weren't in the house, she couldn't take a short rest with Finch. Let him stare at an empty chair for a morning and realize the futility of what they were doing. If they both chose to walk away, it would be easier.

It had to be.

The time was going to come when they had to make a choice. When it came time to sacrifice her heart or his job, she knew which one Finch would choose.

And when he did, a part of her was going to wither and crumble away.

Chapter Six

Things were no better a week later.

Lydia closed the door to her family's home and stared at the rain falling beyond the walkway overhang. Even with the steady drizzle, there were people going about their business. The rumbles of horses and wagons and various conversations drifted around her, dampened by the rainy atmosphere until it felt like she was momentarily a step outside of the real world.

Here, with her childhood behind her and the rest of her life waiting for her return, she felt a moment of peace. Not the sort that came when everything was right in the world, but the kind of peace that settled when a person knew it was time to make a decision.

Instead of walking out into the rain and making her way back to Mount Street, Lydia lowered herself to sit on the stairs leading to the alley behind the shops. Normally there would be too much stench to sit here for long, but the rain created a sort of blanket, keeping the smells, the sounds, and the future at a distance.

How long could she allow things to continue as they were? Nothing would come of it. She was as trapped in the middle of two possibilities as surely as she sat between two worlds. The question was, did she have the courage to force herself to choose?

Light, steady footsteps approached on the walkway behind her and she pressed herself closer to the building to allow the person room to pass. The feet stopped at the top of the steps anyway and Lydia looked up.

Finch looked back at her, his face as pensive as her own likely was, if it reflected her current inner turmoil. "May I join you?"

"Of course." Lydia waved a hand at the step, welcoming him to sit with her because she was too weak not to grasp whatever part of him she could get.

He sat but said nothing, and they both stared out, contemplating the rain.

The peace she'd felt earlier solidified into a sort of resolve, compelling her to ask the question she'd never dared give voice to. "Have you ever considered doing something else with your life?"

He was silent for a moment as he flicked a thread from the knee of his trousers. "Something other than service?"

She gave a nod and a shrug, her resolve pushing her forward, but not necessarily onto a clear path. "Yes. Or perhaps leaving London."

He gave a soft laugh. "You know I want to leave London. Not forever, of course, but I would like to see more of the world."

She did know. It was one of the things he talked about often as they slid their black and white chips around on the backgammon table. "That's why you wanted to be a valet."

He nodded. "I could never afford to travel on my own, but with someone else..."

"Are you traveling any time soon?" Lydia held her breath. Perhaps this was the perfect answer. If Lord Trent was going away for a while, then she could get some space from Finch, get her head in a better place, maybe even get over this infatuation entirely.

He gave her a small grin. "Trying to get rid of me?"

Yes. No. Lydia would never truly desire a life free of Finch, but she knew she desperately needed some space. "I wouldn't say that. I simply...."

She simply what? Wished he had different aspirations? Wished he worked a different job? Wished life wasn't quite so complicated?

How was one supposed to share that what had begun as a friendly flirtation had grown into something stronger? How was one meant to know if the other person even considered their interactions a flirtation? She certainly knew strong emotions could change how she looked at a situation.

"You simply what?" Finch asked.

"I'll simply miss you," she blurted out. How could she tell him she wished everything was different while not wishing he was a different man? If Finch weren't who he was, then she wouldn't love him.

Wait. Love? She couldn't love him. That led only to madness.

Then again, where did she think all these smiles and secrets and stolen moments were heading, if not for love? She truly was a fool.

"I will miss you, too." Finch's voice was quiet, almost difficult to hear over the rumble of the world around them.

She could see it, a torturous pattern of him leaving, traveling the country or even the world with Lord Trent, her adjusting to life without him and convincing herself all would be well, him returning and throwing everything into a whirl once more.

It was a cycle that would one day drive her mad or drive her to hate him. She couldn't live with either of those outcomes. If she couldn't learn to stay away from him in the house, to see him and not crave more, then she would have to leave. There were no other options.

"I already miss what we could have been."

Oh, she hadn't meant to say that aloud. If they weren't returning to the same house, she'd run down these steps, out into the rain, and never look back. What good would it do, though? Tonight. Tomorrow morning. He'd be right there, still giving her the intense, quizzical look he was giving her now.

"What are you saying, Lydia?" Finch's voice was serious, and Lydia could not refuse him a genuine answer.

"Haven't you ever considered it? If life was different, if we were different people. Well, I suppose this would be a moot conversation if we were different people, but if we had different futures." She sighed. "If our situations weren't made of paths all but set in stone, I can't help but think we might have had a future."

"You miss the family we could have made."

"Yes," she said before realizing that her agreement would reveal as much as his quick understanding had. He too had thought about it. He too had considered it.

And he too had realized it was impossible.

Something within her cracked. Later, she could take the time to determine if it was her heart, her pride, or her dreams. For now, she just had to get away. She jerked to her feet and, face averted, all but ran down the steps and into the rain. There was no reason to pretend to Finch that she wasn't an emotional mess. She'd all but spilled her feelings at his feet. He wouldn't expect her not to be shattered.

"Lydia, wait!" Finch pounded down the steps after her and put a hand on her shoulder.

She could have pulled away, could have continued walking or even running down the alley to the street, but they were going to the same place. Avoiding him wasn't really an option, so she looked up at him instead. At least, if she started to cry, the tears would mingle with the rain and no one would be able to tell the difference.

"Are you saying you love me?" Finch asked.

Was she? She hadn't said those words, hadn't even meant to imply them, but what else could it mean, that she wanted to change everything about their lives just so she could be with him. "Yes."

He swallowed hard and lifted one hand to push his dampening hair away from his face. "I don't know how I should respond to that."

"That is an answer in itself, is it not?" He wasn't telling her he loved her. He wasn't declaring that he woke with a smile on his face each morning because he would be spending a little time with her that day. He wasn't telling her she wasn't alone.

"I'm a valet, Lydia. I can't…" He blew out a deep breath. "I can't allow myself to consider such things."

"And I can?" Lydia stomped her foot. "Do you think I did this intentionally?" Perhaps she had when he'd been entirely unattainable, but since he'd up and moved into her home, she'd tried so hard to fight it. "I couldn't help myself."

She waited, wanting to run, but knowing she needed to hear what he would say.

He looked into her eyes for a long time before whispering, "I couldn't help myself either."

Hope flared bright in her chest, uncaring of the multitude of practical answers they'd yet to find. He was saying that he, too, cared. He was all but admitting he loved her, too.

But then he kept talking. "A servant can't afford to dream of things such as love and family. It will only doom them to dissatisfaction."

"I know." Oh, how she knew. The flare of hope shuddered into a pile of ash.

"I want to find happiness."

She gave a short, flat laugh. "That would be nice, wouldn't it."

His answering smile was sad. "I have to keep my dreams realistic. At least the ones I entertain during the day."

She nodded. "That's very wise of you. I shall take it under advisement."

"Lydia—"

She shook her head and held up a hand to silence him. He was right, after all. She'd known it all along.

"I would like to still be friends." The catch in his voice had her looking up at him, when moments before she'd thought she would never be able to look him in the face again. Were there tears on his face, too, or was the rain coming harder now?

"That would be nice." She licked her lips and plowed on. If they were going to be honest about the future, they might as well include their present in the damage. "But we need to be realistic."

"Maybe..." His words choked out and he swallowed and tried again. "Maybe in a few years. When Johnny is settled in his apprenticeship and—"

Lydia shook her head, her rain-soaked curls sliding down and sticking to her face. She left them there like a layer of armor as she peered at him through the wet strands. "You know we can't keep going like this." If they did, what was currently the most delightful torture would become nothing but pain and resentment.

"I know."

Strength she didn't know she had came from somewhere in her heart. She loved this man. Maybe, just maybe, he loved her in return. It was time they loved each other enough to stop the pain from growing. "I hope you get to travel to all the places you've ever dreamed of."

"Lydia..." His protest faded and his eyes grew sad. He, too, must know it was time.

"Goodbye, Finch."

She turned and walked away. Her original plan of avoiding him by whatever means necessary would have to be renewed. She could act as if he wasn't there, had never been there, had never been more than a man she'd grown up near.

As she slogged back to the house, she prayed one day that would all be true, because if it wasn't, she would have to love them both enough to leave.

Finch had worked in London's finer homes since he was ten years old. He'd started as a hallboy and worked his way up. As a first footman for a duke, he'd served many a fine, high-ranking aristocrat of peculiar tastes and requirements.

Never had he walked around a home as carefully as he did the day after Lydia tore his heart out. Or perhaps she'd torn her own heart out and his had leapt out of his chest in sympathy.

It was simple enough to go about his morning duties, but once Lord Trent had departed for Hawthorne House and work on the papers he'd left there until his new study was ready, the true difficulty of Finch's situation became apparent.

Was she planning on meeting him in the room next door as she normally did? If so, he didn't want her hurt by his lack of appearance. After their talk, they both knew it wasn't wise to continue on as they had been, yet he wanted to see her.

How twisted was it that the only person he wanted to talk to about their mess of a situation was her? She was whom he wanted to go to for advice and she was the one person he couldn't bare his heart and mind to. No matter what they felt, there was no choice but for them each to continue on alone. To pretend anything else was a lie.

He would avoid her and the room where they'd played backgammon. It was the only sane choice to make.

With his arms full of linen shirts to take downstairs, he pressed his ear to the door to make sure no one was bustling about in the corridor beyond before he opened it. He hastily stepped past all open doors so he wouldn't be tempted to look in and see if she was working inside.

Belowstairs was even more difficult, as he couldn't blame his sneaking about on an attempt to disappear as servants at work were meant to do.

He was exhausted before he even made it to breakfast.

Was this what his life would be now, until Lord Trent decided to take a trip somewhere? It wasn't sustainable.

Compared to Hawthorne House, with its ballroom, multiple drawing rooms, and significant presence along one side of Grosvenor Square, the terrace house in Mount Street was small. Even with both of them dedicated to staying out of each other's way – and he was certain Lydia was being equally careful today – it was only a matter of time until they crossed paths.

To make things worse, he missed his friend already.

Was all this sneaking about, constantly worrying they might run into each other, really any better than the situation they'd been in before? He certainly wasn't thinking about her any less.

Instead of returning to Lord Trent's room via the back stairs, Finch took the main stairs to the first floor. Lydia cleaned toward the servant stairs each morning, so he had less chance of encountering her if he went up the main stairs instead.

Unless, of course, she was changing her patterns as well in an attempt to avoid him. What if, in trying to avoid each other, they actually placed themselves in the other's path?

Finch's head began to pound.

Rubbing his temple, he looked back down the stairs to the large clock in the front hall. He had hours before Lord Trent would possibly be returning home, since he'd mentioned going to an auction at Tattersall's, then on to his club.

Finch retraced his steps back to the front hall, departed out the front door, and jogged down the steps to the street. Hopefully no one had seen him exit the front door instead of the servant's entrance, but if they had, it was hardly the first time a member of the lower class had gone up or down the steps of this particular house.

As he took in a large lungful of air, he realized just how shallowly he'd been filling his lungs inside the house. The further he walked, the easier it was to breathe.

Part of his job was to make sure he knew all the latest fashions and have Lord Trent's dressing room stocked with all the necessary personal products. They hadn't been low on tooth powder, soap, candles, or even razor blades when he'd helped Lord Trent get dressed that morning, but it wouldn't hurt to have a spare of anything, just in case.

He could also stop by the haberdashers or take in the gentlemen walking along St. James to make sure the cut of his master's coat and the press of his cravat were the height of fashion. He hadn't been working with Lord Trent long enough to know exactly how early into changing fashions he liked to be, but for now, he'd assume the man liked to be at the front of the charge if it meant getting out of the house to do a little studying.

In the end he procured only a new stropping strap for the razor blade. If he were going to keep doing his job well, he couldn't stay away from the house for too long.

And if all he was going to have in life was this job, he truly did need to do it well.

Finch stumbled to a halt. What an uncomfortable thought, to have nothing in life but a job. When he'd gotten old enough to see domestic service as more than simply a way to help his family, he'd begun to see it almost as a gift from God, a way in which he could use the stature and appearance God had blessed him with to make other people's lives better.

That was the other reason he'd aspired to be a valet. The idea of having one person to focus on, one life to improve, had been appealing.

When had he lost that? How could he now think of it as nothing but a job? Had God's purpose for his life changed, or had Finch been the one to change? If it had been him, was that a good thing or a bad one?

Lost in thought, he entered the house through the servant entrance and walked straight into Lydia. She squealed and jumped back, holding the partially filled bucket of water away from her. Some of it still sloshed out, getting drops of water on both of their shoes.

"I'm so sorry," she said before hastily turning and walking – no, running – in the other direction, back toward the kitchen where she'd likely gotten the water in the first place.

As he watched her go, his heart cracked open and the truth he'd been avoiding since the day before became clear.

What had changed was everything.

Chapter Seven

Staying was impossible.

It didn't matter how well Lydia planned or how careful she was, avoidance didn't work like it had when Finch first moved into the house. Physically she hadn't seen him in over a week. In her mind, however…

Every room, every task, every thought made her think of him. They'd walked through each of those rooms, inspecting art and furniture while talking and laughing about any topic under the sun. The ghosts of those memories refused to be removed like so much dust.

It would pass one day, she was certain. Eventually she would smile again. Eventually she would be able to think of him without crying. Eventually she would be able to visit her family without staring mournfully through the wall.

If her current anguish was anything to go by, though, that *eventually* would likely come much faster if she recovered somewhere other than here.

Lydia stared at the ceiling of her little attic room. Beyond the thin walls, the other housemaids shuffled about, preparing for the day.

It was strange to consider this room, which she'd previously used only during the warmer months, was now her only space. For years, the entire house had been her domain and every inch had felt like home.

Now none of it did. Now it was a stabbing reminder of how she had gotten far too relaxed and allowed impossibilities to enter her mind. Finch had been right about that. She shouldn't have ever allowed herself to pretend another future could be hers.

For her own sake, she needed to become a normal servant with normal ambitions and a normal perspective. The fastest way to do that was to work in a normal house, where everyone knew their place. This house, with its blurred rankings and unsteady positions, was not normal.

It was time to go.

Her resolve lasted until she left the attic behind. There was one of the rugs she'd repeatedly beat free of dust. The worn but shiny banister was warm under her hand, as if it was wishing her good morning. A brief detour through the front hall and the drawing room, the rooms she'd been the most dedicated to keeping clean when Miss Amelia resided here, tugged at her heart.

Perhaps she was being too hasty about deciding to leave. There was still a chance things could settle into an acceptable routine. The Season was over and most of London's elite – including the rest of Lord Trent's family – had fled for the country. Surely Lord Trent would follow and he would take Finch with him. Maybe then she could recover, reclaim her peace and stay in this house.

After all, she'd practically grown up here. Mrs. Harris had comforted and advised her as much as her own mother.

She would give it a few more days. Another week, perhaps. Surely she could at least hold out until next Monday.

In the end, she couldn't make it to noon.

Making Frances clean the upstairs bedrooms had kept Lydia from seeing the backgammon board, but the drapes in the drawing room were a similar shade of green to the ones they'd chosen for the private parlor.

Then Fenton asked her to take the post to the study. That had been the first room they had completed their choices for, but Lydia hadn't realized the work had already been completed. She stood in the midst of the room, turning a slow circle and admiring the final product, remembering how she and Finch had debated over the darkness of the furniture.

Perhaps she should reassign this room to Diane as well.

Lydia fled to the uppermost rooms, the ones where no one aside from the occasional maid ever went, and batted ineffectually at the thin collection of dust that had accumulated there. When she got to the nearly barren nursery, she crumbled into a sobbing heap. She would never hold a child of her own, with Finch's dark hair and her blue eyes.

Recovery wasn't happening here.

It was time to leave.

She made her way to the kitchens where Mrs. Harris was preparing to make bread. Her smile was the same efficient, brief but authentic curve it had always been, but the sympathy in her eyes revealed she knew everything had gone wrong. Just as she had warned Lydia it would.

With a shake of her head, the housekeeper muttered, "I warned him about this."

Lydia frowned. "I beg your pardon?"

Mrs. Harris clasped her hands together. "You look like you could use a cup of tea."

"What I could use is a reference."

The housekeeper's eyebrows rose as she measured a pile of flour into the wide wooden bowl atop the worktable. "You intend to leave us then?"

The tone of her words, both understanding and disappointed, made Lydia wince. "I must. It will be far easier for me to find another position than Finch." She took a deep breath and plunged on, saying the words aloud for the first time. "I'm the one having a problem. I'm the one who can't make it through the day without becoming overwrought."

Mrs. Harris sniffed. "How would you know? You haven't seen the boy in days."

That was true, but it didn't change anything. "I'm still the one who should leave."

"That will be a great disappointment to his lordship," Mrs. Harried answered with a sigh and a shake of her head.

Lydia frowned. "I highly doubt he cares who cleans out the fireplaces. He's not even in the room when they're swept."

"True. But he was uncommonly excited about the novelty of being the first aristocrat he knew with a married valet."

For a week, Finch sought a possible solution. The one he finally landed on wasn't great. If he were honest, it wasn't even good. The most that could be said for it was that it was feasible, but that was more than he'd had on the steps outside his family's flat, so he would take it.

The only question remaining was whether or not he could actually make it happen. Could he turn his back on his current opportunities? How would Lydia feel about it if he did? He certainly wouldn't agree to her making such a sacrifice.

Then there was his family to consider. If he changed his future to save for a family of his own, would there be enough to maintain his brother's apprenticeship? How long would it take for him to be stable enough to ask Lydia to join him?

Unfortunately, the letter before him didn't hold any of those answers. The only question it answered was whether or not he could work on his uncle's friend's fishing vessel.

Nowhere in the crookedly scrawled lines was an indication of how his family would react or even if Finch would be good at fishing. There was no promise Lydia would be willing to wait, or how it would torture him to spend that time apart from her.

Not speaking to her now was scraping against his soul, but at least he could hear about her from other servants, could lurk about corners and catch a glimpse of her, could develop a reason to talk to her when his desperation grew truly great.

If he took the chance, would he spend the rest of his life wondering what would have happened if he'd stayed with Lord Trent?

If he didn't, would he always regret not choosing Lydia?

That was the only question he could answer with any sort of confidence. Yes. He would always regret not choosing Lydia.

He had to try. It would hurt to walk away from the opportunity he'd spent half his life working toward, but he would forever mourn the loss of a life with Lydia if he didn't at least try to make it happen.

He folded the letter and stuck it in his pocket before turning back to the clothing he'd been readying for the move back to the master chambers. Tonight he would talk to Lydia, then he would use his next free day to talk to his family.

After that, he would resign his post, make his way to the coast, and work as hard as he could to become proficient enough to have Lydia join him.

Hopefully it would be a matter of months, not years.

Finch swallowed as he stacked the handkerchiefs. Would their love survive that long? Without conversations in the rain or late-night confessions? Without frequent sightings and secret smiles? Even if they decided to spend precious funds on postage, how often could they write each other? Any more than twice a month would only extend their time apart.

Cracks of practical fear pierced his plan. Finch had worked hard all his life. Some of his tasks had been physically laborious, but he wouldn't pretend it was anything on the level of being a fisherman. Could he even do the job? Would he end up trapped on the coast, seeking a footman position at nearby country estates just to earn a living?

What moments ago had seemed like a crack of light around a closing door now looked like nothing more than another set of locks.

Lord Trent stepped into the dressing room door and clapped his hands before rubbing them together. "It's finished."

It took Finch a moment to realize there was no way his employer could have read his mind and been referring to either Finch's career or his possible relationship with Lydia. "My lord?"

"My rooms. The workmen said they've finished." His lordship grinned widely. "Shall we go see them?"

He looked rather like a child on the morning of his birthday, but Finch couldn't begin to guess why he was being included in the other man's glee. His lordship's family maintained a close relationship and he had dozens of friends. Why celebrate something that obviously meant a great deal to him with his valet? If it meant that much, why not have more say to begin with?

Not wanting to disappoint his employer – particularly if there was even a slight chance he would one day require a reference – Finch set the clothing aside and joined Lord Trent.

Moments later they stood in the private parlor before the door to Lord Trent's bedchamber. This room certainly looked fresher, though Finch couldn't help but focus on the remnants of the previous arrangement Lydia had been too emotional about removing.

"I've been waiting for this moment for years."

Finch turned back to Lord Trent. What was the man talking about?

His lordship reached out and laid a hand on the door latch. "I've been collecting the pieces, but it didn't seem right to redecorate my mother's or brother's houses."

What was the man talking about? Finch frowned. Lord Trent hadn't given the slightest bit of input in the room. They'd been forced to make choices as if the space was their own.

When the door swung open and they stepped inside, Finch's confusion only grew. He recognized nothing. The enormous half tester bed was intricately carved and immediately drew the eye, and the other furniture in the room was equally as unique. An old drum was being used as a table, beside a chair that could only be sentimental, given its worn condition.

"But..." Finch stood in the center of the room, turning in a slow circle. "Where is the green carpet and the four-poster bed?"

He couldn't remain stoic, couldn't hold back the question. This was the room he and Lydia had spent the most time on. They'd struggled over these choices, desperately wanting to make this most personal of spaces as nice as possible for him.

Lord Trent clapped Finch on the shoulder. "It's out in the stable. Would you like to see?"

The stable? Had the unusual living conditions of the house started to meddle with this man's mind? "My lord?" Finch managed to ask.

"Come along." Lord Trent turned and left the room. Finch scurried to trail behind him. There hadn't been time for Finch and Lydia's choices to have been seen and rejected. Besides, it seemed Lord Trent had known what he wanted from the very beginning. Nothing about this situation made sense.

He had to rush to keep up with Lord Trent's quick strides. His lordship was nearly running in anticipation.

No one occupied the work yard as they cut across it, and the stable was just as empty. As close as they were to Hawthorne House, Lord Trent had elected to keep his phaeton and horses there and send a footman for them when needed.

Inside, the stable was far cleaner than Finch had expected. Who was maintaining this unused space?

Lord Trent bounded up the stairs and Finch followed, noting a few of the steps had new boards for treads.

At the top of the stairs, Lord Trent threw open the door to the room that would normally have housed a coachman or the head groom.

Everything Finch and Lydia had chosen lay beyond that door, or at least some variation of their choices. The posters on the bed were somewhat shorter, the elegant writer table a simpler version of the one they had selected with the son of a duke in mind. The fabric draped along the smaller window bore two fewer flounces than the pattern they'd chosen.

"I'm afraid I don't understand, my lord."

"Do you remember when we moved in, Finch?"

"That was barely three months ago, my lord. I should hope my mind has not abandoned me to that extent yet."

"It is rather recent, isn't it?" He sighed. "Yet it seems so long when one considers all the changes." Lord Trent laughed and waved a hand toward Finch. "Mostly for you, I suppose. No one's questioned my daily comings and goings much for a while now, though my mother did write last week to ask what sort of social schedule I am maintaining."

Finch swallowed. He'd thought himself discreet, not that he'd done anything wrong, but Lord Trent must have seen what was happening. "You are, I assume, referring to my relationship with Lydia?"

"Yes."

"I can assure you, my lord, we've done nothing untoward."

"Didn't say you had." Lord Trent frowned. "You aren't going to tell me you don't love the woman, are you? I'd hate to think I'm that poor of an observer."

How had he known? Finch had only admitted it to himself two weeks ago. "I… well, yes, I love her, but my current position—"

"Yes, yes." Lord Trent slashed a hand through the air, then crossed his arms over his chest as he contemplated the ceiling. "Do you know the problem with being the product of one of London's most notorious love matches?"

"I... no, sir."

"I can't bear to see them go to waste."

"My lord?" Finch tried to follow his lordship's logic, truly he did, but it wasn't making any sense.

Lord Trent nodded. "I had it on good authority you and Lydia would be the loveliest of love birds if not for the restrictions of your respective stations."

Good authority? Who could that have been?

"In fact, I was warned about it before I hired you." Lord Trent pointed at Finch. "I did my own research, though. Watched you both, discussed the idea with Mrs. Harris. Everything pointed to my informant being correct."

"But, who?"

"Amelia, of course. The woman who grew up in this house." Lord Trent shrugged. "I can only assume she'd heard Lydia talk about you for years and was able to surmise you were equally intrigued during her short stay at Hawthorne House."

Finch had always liked Miss Amelia, ever since she had helped his sister find a job as a seamstress for one of the best modistes in London. He'd talked to her several times while she'd lived with the Hawthorne family, but he couldn't recall ever mentioning Lydia.

Was he so transparent to everyone but himself?

"Now." Lord Trent rubbed his hands together. "You should know that when I do something, I like to do it well. Mrs. Harris has convinced me an unconventional household will add greatly to my happiness, so I've decided to embrace the idea. I'm offering you the unique opportunity to be a married valet."

"A married valet?" Finch's heart sped up and his fingers began to itch as his body understood the implications before his mind did.

"Married. I won't have you dillydallying under my roof. I'm not that unconventional."

"Of course not, my lord."

Finch's mouth went dry as Lord Trent laid out the details of how he envisioned everything working together. There would be times, of course, sometimes long stretches of it, when Lydia and Finch would be apart. Lord Trent was far too accustomed to having his valet to consider traveling without one.

He'd already considered the changes they could make if and when a family came along as well.

Staying in London was always an option, but there was also the possibility of managing a country home – "there are certainly enough options amongst my property-loving family" – or joining a business - "my money's invested in more than one of those and they'd love to do me a favor" – or even stepping into a trade – "I've always fancied being a sponsor, but that's not really something men tend to do for one another."

Through it all, Finch said nothing. What could he say? Lord Trent was standing there, offering Finch everything he could possibly want. Slowly, the idea that the offer was real, that this room was real, sank into his brain. "I don't know what to say, my lord."

"Say you'll get those banns read sooner rather than later. I would like any gossip caused by this to settle before everyone starts trotting back into Town." Lord Trent patted Finch on the shoulder. "Feel free to stay a while. If my cohort is doing her job, a certain blonde maid will be finding her way out here very shortly."

"Thank you, my lord." Finch all but shouted the words as his future blossomed before him, brighter than he could ever have imagined.

"You are most welcome, Finch." Lord Trent rolled his neck back and forth, then adjusted his coat over his shoulders. "You should also know I'll be home more now this is settled. I didn't know how else to give you time to court or whatever one would call it, so I've been finding reasons to stay out of the house." He grinned. "I think my club believes I've made up my new address and am secretly living within their walls."

For the rest of his life, Finch would work for this man and ensure every speck of his job was done to perfection. Never had a servant been granted more humanity than he was getting in that moment. "I'll be ready, sir."

Lord Trent took a deep breath and looked around the room himself, as if he couldn't quite believe he had done it either. "I find the closer I am to couples in love, the more I want it for myself. Perhaps it's time I seek out a proper wife of my own." He grinned at Finch. "If I let you make all the mistakes first, I'll be the most educated bachelor in London."

"I'll do my best, sir."

Then Lord Trent was gone and Finch was alone.

But only for a moment.

Lydia would be here soon and he had to be ready. He couldn't show her an ounce of hesitation when he asked her to be his wife. They would be doing what no other couple of their acquaintance had ever done. They would be forging a new, and by many unaccepted, path.

Onlookers would have enough concerns. There couldn't be a single implication he felt the same.

Chapter Eight

Lydia gaped at Mrs. Harris. "You can't be serious."

"Why not? This household hasn't functioned normally for well over a decade, and I see no reason for it to start now." Mrs. Harris sniffed and cracked an egg into the pile of flour in the bowl.

"But… the guests… and appearances… and…" Lydia dropped onto a stool as a hundred possible scenarios shot through her head. Each one induced more heart pounding than the last. "What if we have children? What if he gets married and has children?"

"You think his lordship is so clueless he doesn't realize the likely results of allowing his head parlor maid and his valet to get married?" Mrs. Harris scoffed. "You've not spent a lick of time around the man if you think that."

"Of course I haven't spent time around him." Lydia threw a towel at the housekeeper. "I'm a maid."

"Yes, yes, but it was your choice to move back to the kitchen for meals."

Lydia hugged her arms to her middle. "That was a choice of propriety."

"It was a choice of self-protection. Needless, may I point out."

How could she possibly have known? Never would she – or anyone else of sane bearing – have guessed Lord Trent might want her and Finch to be together. Could he really mean for them to keep their jobs and have a family? Lydia shook her head. It was impossible. It wasn't done, not even here. "Mrs. Harris—"

The housekeeper silenced Lydia with a pointed glare. If her hands hadn't been knuckle deep in dough, an accusing finger would likely have joined the expression. "Lydia Smith, if you can look me in the eye right now and tell me you don't love that man, don't dream of marrying him, and would be happy to move on without him, I'll personally help you find a new position before the sun goes down tonight."

Lydia remained silent, because she couldn't say any of those things. She did love Finch. She had dreamed of having a family with him. Mrs. Harris knew this because they'd all teased her – Miss Amelia and Fenton included – about adjusting her schedule so she could see Finch. It had been something of a game, until it became far too real.

"You know I can't say that."

"Yes, I do, and that's precisely what I told Lord Trent when he asked me."

Lydia nearly toppled from her stool. "He asked you? You didn't tell him?"

"I'm not that bold, my dear. I'd already upended that man's life by sitting down at his dinner table. There is a limit to my audacity, you know."

"Actually, I didn't know."

For a moment, Lydia thought she was in actual danger of having raw dough thrown at her, but instead the housekeeper just gave her a pointed look as she threw the lump into a wooden bowl. "Besides, Miss Amelia beat me to it."

Lydia dropped her head to the table.

Mrs. Harris chuckled. "You honestly think that man would give a valet and a maid the authority to redecorate his house without a reason?"

"Well, no, but I'd assumed his reasons were eccentric aristocratic ones." In truth, she'd been so caught up in the mix of feelings stirred up by spending so much time around Finch, she had barely considered the ridiculousness of the situation after those first few days. "Why would he do that?"

Mrs. Harris draped a towel over the bowl before crossing to Lydia and cupping her face in hands still coated with flour. Hopefully it wouldn't get into her hair.

"Because, my dear Lydia, not every obstacle in life must be conquered on your own. Sometimes God puts people in our lives who have the abilities and resources needed to overcome the problem." She rubbed a thumb across Lydia's cheek and gave her a loving smile. "Do not reject a blessing simply because it was given instead of earned."

A tear slipped down Lydia's cheek to rest on Mrs. Harris's thumb. Was it possible? Could God truly have made the unthinkable happen? Was He granting her heart's desire without making her sacrifice something or achieve some drastic accomplishment? "Why me?"

"Why not you?" Mrs. Harris smoothed a cluster of curly tendrils from Lydia's forehead. The remnants of flour on the housekeeper's hand had now mixed with Lydia's tears and were going to cake into her hair. She couldn't bring herself to care. She would wash her hair every day if it meant she got to stay here with the servants who had become like family and marry the love of her life.

"You are as important to God as anyone else. Why wouldn't He answer your prayers? Why wouldn't He give you more than you dared to dream of?"

Lydia shook her head, the prick of pulling hairs the only thing convincing her the moment was real. "But why me and why not..." She waved her arms about in the air, trying to come up with examples of people she knew who hadn't received miracles, who had been forced to make the best of a bad situation, who were still pleading for God to intervene.

Mrs. Harris pulled her hands away, the softness of moments before replaced with the far more familiar sensible and practical demeanor. "You're going to ask me why the Creator of everything thinks your living an unconventional life fits better into His plan than you doing what so many other heartbroken young women do and throw themselves into more work?"

Lydia blinked. "Well, yes."

Mrs. Harris shrugged. "I couldn't begin to guess."

Then how was Lydia supposed to trust that this was a blessing she was meant to have? How could she accept this without constantly worrying it would disappear?

"But I know one thing," Mrs. Harris continued. "You can't live your life questioning God. You'll never come out the winner of that game."

Could she do that? Could she trust that God knew what was best? Lydia swallowed. If anyone had asked her two days, or even two hours ago, if she trusted God, she would have said absolutely yes. Even as she was staring down the idea of making a new life, of breaking her own heart, she'd have said she trusted Him. Why was it so much harder to trust Him through something good?

"Now." Mrs. Harris pushed a cloth covered basket into Lydia's arms. "Take this."

The basket was unexpectedly heavy and Lydia had to scramble to keep from dropping it. "What is this?"

"A picnic dinner." Mrs. Harris shook her head as if the answer should have been obvious. "You take that on out to the coach house."

"The coach house?" The tiny stable at the back of the property had gone unused for Lydia's entire employment. As far as she knew, it was musty and dirty and like as not the home of four-legged animals decidedly smaller than the horses it was designed for.

"Yes." Mrs. Harris grasped Lydia's shoulders and turned her to the door leading out to the small work yard that separated the house from the stable. "You're functioning on trust now, remember? Go."

Lydia went.

And with every step, her hope grew until it burst through her, forcing her lips into a wide smile and her feet into a near run. Whatever awaited her in the stable was going to be fabulous. She trusted Mrs. Harris, but more importantly, she trusted God. Even if He wanted to give her something good.

Finch strolled through the room, touching every piece of furniture, running a hand over every bit of cloth, opening every drawer and cabinet. Finally it all had become real and his mind managed to wrap itself around the truth that he wouldn't have to give up his old dream to attain his new one.

There would be difficult days in the future and choices would have to be made, but for today, for this moment, he could have it all. At the pace his vision of the perfect future was changing, there wouldn't be a scrap of loss to be felt when the time came to make those difficult changes.

He would do it now if that was the only way to have Lydia, but what a gift that he didn't have to.

The door behind him creaked open and he turned to see Lydia framed by the old timbers. Streaks of white marred her face and hair, but the wide smile and the bright, happy eyes he had feared were lost to him forever made her the most beautiful sight he'd ever seen.

He crossed the room, but a large basket kept him from being able to pull her into his arms. Since the room wasn't large, the tiny table was in arm's reach and he quickly took the basket and set it to the side.

Then he hugged her. He held her close and felt the pounding of her heart, the trembling of her happy breaths. "I love you, Lydia."

She froze against him and then her back shuddered as a laugh drifted up from where she was smashed against his coat. Her arms squeezed him tightly before she tilted her face to look up at him. "I love you, Finch."

"Will you marry me?" Despite being all but certain of her answer, he held his breath and every muscle in his body tightened in fear and anticipation.

"Yes." A sound somewhere between a sob and a laugh escaped her. "I told myself there wasn't a way, that I had to stop hoping if I wanted to be happy. I even stopped myself from praying for it." She took a shaky breath and gave him that wide smile once more. "But it would seem God wanted to answer me anyway."

"I couldn't have said it better myself." Finch smiled back at her before giving in to the temptation that had been nagging him for weeks. He lowered his head and briefly touched his lips to hers in a gentle kiss. It lasted but a moment, but its profound significance was life-changing.

This woman was going to be his wife. A life he had never even imagined now lay before him.

And he couldn't wait to start.

"We can have the banns read starting this Sunday. In less than a month, we'll be moving in here." Finch stepped away from her, but kept one arm around her shoulders as he indicated the rest of the small room with his free hand.

She looked around, eyes growing larger and larger as her mouth gaped open in surprise. It was much the same reaction he'd had, but she was certainly far more adorable than he'd been.

"We get to live here."

Finch nodded. "For now. We'll likely have to move eventually, but this will be our family's first home."

They walked the small room together, Lydia inspecting everything from the bed linens to the wall coverings to the knobs on the three-drawer chest. Finch trailed after her, unwilling to let her step more than a few inches from his side. As they went, he shared everything he and Lord Trent had discussed.

Finally, they sank into the two chairs flanking the small table in the corner and tucked into the contents of the basket. It was a celebration dinner to be sure, but nothing was as sweet as seeing the lightness return to Lydia's voice and face. Even her hair seemed springier.

She finished her cup of lemonade and sat back in her chair with a sigh. "What did we do to deserve this, Finch?"

Finch looked at her, then at the room, and finally down at the remains of the meal that had clearly been packed with love. "Not a single thing." He reached over and took her hand, giving it a squeeze as he looked into her eyes. "And that makes it the most meaningful gift of all."

Want more?

Continue the story of the Hawthornes by reading Miranda's story in *A Noble Masquerade.*

Lady Miranda Hawthorne acts every inch the lady, but inside she longs to be bold and carefree. She pours her innermost feelings out in letters to her brother's old school friend, a duke--with no intention of ever sending these private thoughts to a man she's never met. Meanwhile, she finds herself intrigued by Marlow, her brother's new valet, and although she may wish to break free of the strictures that bind her, falling in love with a servant is more of a rebellion than she planned.

When Marlow accidentally discovers and mails one of the letters to her unwitting confidant, Miranda is beyond mortified. And even more shocked when the duke returns her note with one of his own that initiates a courtship-by-mail. Insecurity shifts into confusion at her growing feelings for two men. When it becomes apparent state secrets are at risk and Marlow is right in the thick of the conflict, one thing is certain: Miranda's heart is far from all that's at risk for the Hawthornes and those they love.

Go to KristiAnnHunter.com to learn more, find links, and sign up for the monthly newsletter so you never miss out on important announcements!

Acknowledgments

This book has been one of the most terrifying but also satisfying of my career. There is a sense of knowing *I did this* when I hold it in my hand.

By no means did I do it alone, though. So many people came alongside me to help make this happen.

A million thank yous to the ones who told me I could do this in the first place. Jacob, my blessings, the Voxer girls, my friends, other writers, and even those who were disconnecting from my path as it made a turn. I wouldn't have had the courage to move on without you.

To my loyal readers, particularly Ashlee, who helped me dig through my early novels to make sure that I retained the facts I'd already established, thank you. Without your help I'd have been paralyzed in fear over getting it wrong.

Thank you to the many authors who sat with me, offering their expertise and the answers to a thousand and one questions. Melissa, Mimi, Rachel, and so many others, your knowledge made a world of difference.

My lifegroup who has become more like a family, thank you for your prayers, for buying copies to hand out to every one of your family and friends, and for checking in to make sure I was holding on to my sanity. Particular gratitude goes to Angie. Your talents are amazing, your support is genuine, and I'm so glad I can now expense it when we go out for coffee.

Finally, thank you to you, dear reader. Without you, this book would be nothing but a formalized daydream. You bring it full circle. You make this job worth doing. Thank you for honoring me and my stories with your time and attention.

About Author

Kristi is the RITA® award winning author of romance novels from a Christian worldview. Her books include the Regency era set Hawthorne House, Haven Manor, and Hearts on the Heath series. Look for her first contemporaries in early 2023.

She is also speaker, teaching classes in writing as well as Biblical and spiritual topics. She has spoken to writers' groups, schools, and young women's groups at churches.

When she is not writing or interacting with her readers, Kristi spends time with her family and her church. A graduate of Georgia Tech with a computer science degree, she knows that life rarely takes the turns we expect. While she still spends hours a day on a computer, now she's living out the dreams of her childhood and creating stories for others to enjoy and be inspired by.

Learn more at KristiAnnHunter.com or by finding Kristi on Instagram @kristiannhunter.

www.ingramcontent.com/pod-product-compliance
Lightning Source LLC
LaVergne TN
LVHW091336230325
806616LV00038B/939

* 9 7 8 1 9 5 9 5 8 9 0 1 3 *